Forever

Forever

Timmothy B. McCann

KENSINGTON PUBLISHING CORP.

KENSINGTON BOOKS are published by

Kensington Publishing Corp.
850 Third Avenue
New York, NY 10022

All Kensington titles, imprints and distributed lines are available at special quantity discounts for bulk purchases for sales promotion, premiums, fund raising, educational or institutional use.

Special book excerpts or customized printings can also be created to fit specific needs. For details, write or phone the office of the Kensington Special Sales Manager: Kensington Publishing Corp., 850 Third Avenue, New York, NY 10022, Attn. Special Sales Department. Phone: 1-800-221-2647.

Kensington and the K logo Reg. U.S. Pat. & TM Off.
Dafina Books and the Dafina logo are trademarks of the Kensington Publishing Corp.

ISBN 1-57566-757-6

Printed in the United States of America

Acknowledgments

I must start by acknowledging God for first giving me a level of talent and then allowing me to share it with you. I would also like to take the opportunity to thank three authors on whose shoulders I stand:

James Baldwin. You gave us stories that transcended the norm. You allowed us to look at ourselves in a different light in spite of what others thought. *From Another Country* to *The Fire Next Time* you told stories with passion and from the soul.

Ralph Ellison. You created a masterpiece that none other could compare. It was you who said, "If the Negro, or any other writer is going to do what is expected of him, he's lost the battle before he takes the field." May each writer in our quest for the perfect sentence keep that in mind.

Richard Wright. Your words were a success commercially to the astonishment of the masses. But they were a success long before reaching the stand. You had a moral compass that was evident in each novel. Your search for truth was unparalleled, therefore I thank you for giving millions the insight into what it feels like to be a native son.

Lastly, thank you Karen Thomas for taking my best and making it better. Thank you Tanya McKinnon for assisting me in shaping my future, and to all I mentioned in my previous work, I thank you for remaining in my corner.

Until . . .

Timmothy B. McCann
P.O. Box 357814
Gainesville, FL 32635-7814
www.TimmothyMcCann.com

Winter

Chapter 1

Some pray to marry the man they love.
My prayer will somewhat vary:
I humbly pray to heaven above
That I love the man I marry.

—Pastor Rosa Stokes
"My Prayer"

JANUARY

They were going on their honeymoon next week. The wedding was planned in minute detail. Everything was rehearsed, from which foot to lead with as the attendees would march down the aisle to the best man's toast. But Betty never counted on the rain. She never anticipated having to move the wedding inside the church. The thought that her day would feel like a nightmare had never crossed her mind. But most of all, she did not anticipate that she would feel alone.

As a child, Betty dreamed of the day she would marry. He would be the one man she loved and they would say, "I do," in a small chapel on a hill before God, family, and friends. Doves would fly above the church as she and her groom walked outside, to be greeted by well-wishers releasing butterflies into a Florida-blue sky. With the air sweetened with lilacs, they would pose for the perfect photograph, and she would squeeze his hand just to remind herself that this was the moment she'd waited her entire life to enjoy. But she never imagined as she stood before the window on the rainy afternoon, watching the Mercedes approach, that he'd be late, that her teeth would grind, and that she'd feel trapped between her head and her heart.

Her stomach constricted like a boa as she watched the approaching black automobile from the pastor's study. Although she could not walk away, she could not will herself to say, "I don't."

And then the vehicle pulled into the vacant lot, used for parking, beside the church. As a lady opened the door and released her purple umbrella to shelter herself from the rain, Betty felt a hot, awful joy, because it was not Drew, and there was still a chance he wouldn't show at all.

Pacing in her gown, she beckoned the voices in her head to be silent. Her foster mother's voice shrilled, "He's a good man, and how many good black men are there today?" Friends told her how lucky she was to find a man like Drew Staley and warned her not to let him slip away. She'd asked herself so many nights before, "How could you leave the best man to have ever come into your life?" and never had an answer.

She glanced out the window, and again there was no sign of her groom. Maybe he shared her apprehension, she thought as she removed her gloves by the fingertips and massaged the insides of her sweaty palms. Unable to sit, she walked the length of the study, refusing to look in the full-length mirror. Seeing herself was akin to committing a cardinal sin in God's house, so instead, she breathed in shallow gasps of air to calm herself, looked at the oak floors, and walked back and forth. Back and forth.

"Why do you love me?" she'd asked him, and his reply looped in her mind like a rusted chain of words. "You mean the world to me." Simple, unthought-out words that meant little or nothing to Betty. Staid words he'd heard on television or in a love song but not what she felt were from his heart.

A visceral fear washed over her the night before Drew proposed, as he held her and said, "You know it's the right thing to do." His retort burned in her memory because she didn't know how to say no. Although a part of her wanted to, she could not will the words past her lips.

Betty walked toward the arched window again as another vehicle approached the church, a tear trembling on her eyelash on what should have been the happiest day of her life. The catering truck sloshed around to the church's dining hall, and she closed her fatigued eyes, attempting to erase the image of a past love, and leaned against the wall.

Betty noticed the time on the clock as the door swung open with enough force to blow papers off the pastor's desk.

"What in the fuck . . . I mean, what in the world is this Negro's problem?"

"What do you mean?" Betty asked with a knee-jerk response as she wiped the corner of her eyelash with her knuckle.

"Please," Jacqui retorted, "you know exactly what I mean. What's his problem? Stefan called, and he's not home—paged him and everything. Did he tell you he was having second thoughts?"

"There you go, Ms. Overreacting. Have you thought of the possibility that he could have had car problems? Have you thought—"

"That's why God made cell phones, which you said he never leaves home without." Betty continued staring out the window. "I'm telling you, Drew's having second thoughts. I could tell last week."

"How could you tell?" Betty asked, mock laughter in her tone.

"It wasn't anything he said, just the way he acted. Like he was being forced into doing something he didn't want to do. He's trying to back out, and the punk couldn't think of a way to do it besides not showing up. I know that's hard to handle," she said, walking closer to her friend, "but think about it. Drew is Mr. Promptness. And all of a sudden, on the most important day of your lives, he's a no-show? He was supposed to be here thirty minutes before the wedding, and he's late?"

"Jacqui," Betty said almost to herself as her true sentiments showed on her brow. "Not now, okay? I can't go there with you." And then she gave the window her full attention as a gust of wind blew the rain against the glass.

Jacqui cleared her throat, straightened her back, adjusted the platinum band of her watch, and then said, "Okay, I'm sorry. I shouldn't be in here downing him on a day like today."

"You have a right to say what's on your mind. It's just that I can't talk about it now. All I know is this. The man loves me and . . . and I feel fortunate we're getting married. I mean," she continued as she could feel the weight churn deep inside her stomach, "Drew's good in so many ways." Jacqui paced in the path traveled by her friend as she rubbed the nape of her neck. "He's kind and passionate, and I know something happened. I know he wouldn't be late otherwise."

"Betty, how do you—Never mind."

"Say it."

"No, never mind. I'm out of order, and today I just want to be there for you. That's all."

"Say it, Jacqui. What were you going to say?"

After a pause, Jacqui walked across the floor toward Betty and said, "You know something? I've never heard you really say you loved this man. Not like you used to say it when you talked about you know who. You always tell me how much he loves you and how you all are going to do this and that after marriage, but—"

"I love him. Okay? Is that all you wanted to ask? I love him. Jacqui, you should know that if I didn't love him, I wouldn't be here today. You know me better than—"

"Betty, something ain't right," Jacqui interrupted, "and I can't put my finger on it. But more than that, I can't figure out why you're not telling me everything."

"Because," Betty said, her voice rising an octive, "everything is fine. We don't need to have this discussion again. I don't know what answer you want to hear, but everything is okay. This is a minor not a major."

"All right. If that's what—"

"Jacqui? It's a minor . . . not a major, okay?"

Betty's friend returned to the pastor's desk, sat on its edge, picked up his black stapler, and transferred it from hand to hand. As she looked toward the clergy's library, she said between clenched teeth, "Now I understand what Lauryn meant when she sang, 'And they wonder why women hate men.' "

With her hands on her waist, Betty snapped around toward Jacqui and said, "What do you want from me?"

"I want you to tell me the truth, Betty!" Jacqui replied as she stood and dropped the stapler to the floor. "Is that asking too much?"

"I tell you the truth, and you don't want to hear it!"

"You still didn't say you love him."

"I told you I loved Drew ten seconds ago!"

"I know what you told me, but you still didn't say it!"

After a silent beat, Betty walked over to her maid of honor and gazed into her eyes without blinking as she swallowed and uncurled her fist. "I love Andrew Patrick Staley!" Then a pause settled over the room as Betty cupped her hand over her mouth to block the pain and Jacqui eased off the table and followed her across the room. As she walked closer, Betty could feel sensations rising that she refused to acknowledge. And then Jacqui looked down at her friend and put her arms firmly around her. As they hugged, Betty looked over her shoulder and noticed that her groom was officially twenty minutes late.

"You're right, it's me," Jacqui muttered. "I've got more issues than a library. Sorry to put you through all of this on today of all days. I guess I'm just nervous."

Betty closed her eyes for strength before she backed away and then said, "We all have issues. I know you're there for me. That's not even a question." As another vehicle came up the muddy, winding road past the basketball court, they both peered out the window, but it wasn't his. "He'll show." Betty smiled as she shook her head. "Something happened, but he'll be here."

Ever since they were undergrads, the two ladies shared an unshakable bond. Betty, who was an honors student, admired Jacqui's tenacity. Many mornings she would hear her return to their studio apartment well past midnight, and when she awoke, Betty would find her roommate at their shared desk asleep, her head on top of textbooks. While Jacqui was as tall as the average man and several years older than most incoming freshmen, the two coeds quickly became friends.

Before they crossed over into Greekdom, Jacqui's line name was Li'l Sister Hades, due to her hair-trigger temper. Although she played basketball in her sophomore year, her hands remained soft, her dark skin unmarked, and even for special occasions she wore her straight black hair in a single ponytail.

Betty was seen as carrying herself in a dignified, precise manner. After the first sorority party they attended, Jacqui often kidded her because she always learned dances as they were going out of style. Li'l Sister Immaculate is the name she was dubbed when she pledged because she showered three times a day, wore her jeans with a pinch-tight crease, and even though she lived on a college budget, her hair was done each and every Saturday.

After Betty graduated from law school and Jacqui attained her MBA, their plan was to buy a duplex. The first one to marry would sell her interest in the property to the other, but that dream faded after Jacqui fell in love for the first time soon after tossing her tasseled orange-and-blue cap in the air. The love burned deep and strong but soon faded and took with it much of Jacqui's respect for herself and the opposite sex.

It was Jacqui who interceded when Betty could not sleep for weeks after her ex-boyfriend, Evander, took advantage of her heart. And Betty who picked up an intoxicated Jacqui on a rainy night after Yancy held a gun to her head in a drunken stupor and would not allow her back into her home. Now it was Jacqui who was there on the most important day of Betty's life to pick up whatever pieces would fall.

"Make my day," Jacqui said as she recalled a game they played in college.

"Please. Not now."

"Come on. It'll relax you."

Folding her arms with a smile, Betty sighed, rubbed her palms together, and said, "Okay. Make your day? I got it. I see you having a great time tonight dancing to your favorite song and—"

"Please. We don't even have a favorite song."

"Well, line dancing. But I see you going home tonight. Thinking about the wedding and not leaving the house until about noon tomorrow."

"Nice thought but unrealistic. You get a seven for that one. Okay, let me make your month. I see you and Drew getting married today. I see you sexing deep into the night. I see you waiting until he is about to reach his peak and then slapping him for being late."

"That's what *you* would do, Miss Jordan? You suppose to be saying what I will do!"

"Anywho. I see you going to Cancún and having a great time. I see you coming back to Florida and your business being a little rough, since you spent so much time away sexing all over Central America. But I see it picking up by the end of the month. Now," Jacqui added, "make my year."

"You get an eight for that. Well, let's see. I see Jacquetta's blowing up. Since you love to read so much, I see you finally writing that cookbook you've been threatening to write, and I see you expanding. Maybe another restaurant in another city. Let's see." Betty pondered, her fingertips to her lips. "I see you and Stefan together still. I don't know about marriage 'cause I don't know how well he knows you yet."

"Meaning?"

"Does he already know you're married?"

"Four. That's all you getting, because I'm not married to Jacquetta's. I don't see us as being married, either, but it's not because of my job."

"A four? Please. You're in denial."

"You know, there must be a hundred attorneys down there," Jacqui said as she poured herself a cup of coffee, added cream, and then changed her mind about drinking it. "I think I even saw Renfro with his racist a—with his racist butt."

"You know you really should come to church more often."

"Hey, I go to church. In fact, I—"

"Jacqui," Betty said with laughter in her voice, "I've told you weddings and funerals don't count."

"Oh, then I guess voting wouldn't qualify, either, huh?" As both of the women smiled, they gazed at the rain hitting the top of the pelican-gray canopy below. "So, other than this mess with Drew, did you ever imagine it would be like this?"

"Yes. I thought it would be just like this. I didn't imagine people having to breaststroke to the church, but I guess it's right, since rain sorta brought us closer."

"I met one of his cousins down there. You know that big fat one named Annie Doris, but I didn't see his mom. She riding with him?"

The hurried sound of footsteps coming up the stairs caught their attention as Betty answered, "Yeah, they're riding together. She's no longer driving."

"I hope she's feeling better. Did he tell you why she couldn't make the rehearsal dinner last night?"

"She hasn't been doing well since she moved into Parkside." She continued as the footsteps got closer to the door and then proceeded past it. "Drew tells me that when this man she married died a couple of months after their wedding, she just lost it. But I'd imagine it would be hard. After all, this is the second husband she's had to bury."

"Not to change the subject, but last weekend Stefan asked me to visit his mom again."

"Really?"

"Yeah, he's feeling all matrimonial, but I don't feel like getting strip-searched to see her."

"See, God don't like ugly." Then she looked at Jacqui and asked, "You are joking. Right?"

"Please, she ain't in jail, but I swear she's more than likely the only DeCoursey not in jail. Everybody he talks about in his family, from Little Pooky to Big Ced, serving time. If they have a family reunion, I told him they won't need names on their T-shirts. Just numbers. You know what they say about acorns and trees."

Betty smiled. "Does he like working for the new agency?"

"Yeah, he likes it. But I wish he would take acting lessons, since so much of the movie industry is moving south. For now, he's content with modeling every now and then and driving the delivery truck."

"I thought he was going to head back out to L.A. to try his hand at acting again."

"He's tired of the L.A. scene. Butlers, brothers, pimps, and punks. We talked about that last night. But those are the dues we must pay to get into Hollywon't."

"Well, I admire him for holding on to his principles. He's been in the business what, twenty years?"

"Next month will be twenty-one, actually."

"It takes courage to work toward a dream that long with little to show for it."

"I know. I mess with him about it sometimes, but he still thinks he can get runway work in Milan or Paris. I have to appreciate his drive if nothing else. I admire him for that, though, because it takes guts to follow your dreams."

"Drew tells me he's in the gym three hours a day now." As Jacqui shook her head in agreement, Betty asked, "So who else is downstairs beside family?"

"Everybody and then some. How many invitations did you all eventually send out?"

"One-fifty. I sent out about fifty, but he wanted to invite most of his best clients, and his family is here in town, so it grew from there. It's funny, though," Betty said as she looked out the window at yet another car that had pulled into the parking area, "when we started discussing this, it was going to be the two of us plus you and Stefan, and we were going to get married on a cliff in Trinidad. But then he wanted to fly in a few friends, and I thought of my foster parents and Carol and some people at the old firm, and before you know it, we're whittling down a list of five hundred."

"Were you all really going to do that corny island thing you always used to talk about?"

"Yeah. I mean, I wanted a traditional wedding at one time, but the more I thought about it, the more I thought getting married like this was something a little less personal. But it was just going to be the four of us standing barefoot in the sand and watching the sunset."

"Please," Jacqui said with a cluck of her tongue. "I don't do shoeless for nobody. Not with these hammer toes."

"You still wanna get married in your uncle's church?"

"Naw. Well, I guess so. I just don't think about it that much anymore. If it happens, it happens. I got too much going on with the restaurant. Besides, I still need to find someone to close on the weekends."

"There you go. And you gonna stand there and say you're not in denial?"

"Well, you might have a point. Jacquetta's been ver', ver' good to a sister. But me and Stefan are not hardly at that point. He's a nice guy and all, but forever and ever?" Jacqui said, and raised her voice at the end of each sentence. "Until death do us part and all that stuff? I don't think so."

"So what's wrong with this one?"

"First of all, have you noticed the amount of lotion the man uses on his hands? But wait. You talk like I'm trying to eliminate him for some reason. It's not like that. Shit, I'm . . . God forgive me. I mean to say, I'm thirty-seven years—"

"Thirty-eight, Jacqui. It's enough for you to be cursing in God's house; don't get us struck on top of everything else going on today."

"Whatever," Jacqui replied with a reflective smile. "I want to get married, but at this point in my life, I just got to be sure. I'm not going to say I do unless I'm absolutely, positively, unconditionally sure." And then she looked through her friend's eyes and said, "I'm not going to do it because of my age, and I'm not going to do it because he seems to be Mr. Right for right now." Like dust in the wind, Betty's smile blew away as Jacqui continued. "You know how you feel when you're sitting with, say, three friends and four guys come over and everyone pairs up? You know how you sorta feel obligated to talk to this fool because he's just staring at you in spite of his polyester pants, pocket protector, and jacked-up breath? Well, in my case, Stefan's that guy—minus the bad breath and clothes. I don't think I have a friend who is not married, getting married, or already divorced, but I'm simply not ready to dance."

The words gashed Betty's soul, but instead of defending her circumstance, she felt the hurt behind her friend's eyes and then looked at the clock, which showed that he was forty minutes overdue. As a heavy knock came at the door, she returned to the window to gaze at the petulant skies and await Drew.

"Who?" Jacqui asked the person twisting the doorknob.

"Me, girl. Why you locking the door?"

Jacqui rolled her eyes upward with a fake aggravated look as she opened the door and smiled at her companion. "So what's the latest on *your* friend?"

"Listen, he'll be here," six-foot-four Stefan said in his rich southwestern accent as Betty turned her head in his direction, wanting to know if he'd actually heard from Drew. "I ain't talked to him or anything," he continued, "but I know Drew, and I know what this day means to him. Something happened, I'm sure, but he'll be here." Betty looked away and rubbed the back of her forearms to occupy her hands.

"Have you called—"

"I've called everywhere, everything, and everybody," Stefan said. "I would go out looking for him, but I know as soon as I leave, the brother'll show, and then you'll be looking for me."

"I swear, if that sonova—"

"Jacqui!" Both Betty and Stefan said together.

Staring at her best friend and then the clock, Jacqui said as her eyes bulged and she waved her stiffly extended index finger, "I can't help it! If he don't show up, Betty, he's got me to deal with! I swear. Now, enough is enough. People down there getting restless, and we got to tell them something eventually. If you want me to go down there and do it, I will, but somebody has got to—"

"Why you all up in her business? Huh? Betty's a grown woman, and she knows how she wants to handle this. Like I said, there's probably a fender bender or something, and I know Drew will be here in a minute."

"Have you spoken to him?" she shouted, hands fisted at her waist. "Huh? No? Then no, you don't know jack, now, do you! Don't start with me, Stefan. Not today!"

"Listen," he said as he pointed his long finger downward. "I'm just saying you ought to let them handle their situation. How would you feel if everyone is headed home when bro drives up? You don't know what could have happened to him."

"And I don't want to know," Jacqui said with attitude. "And let me tell you something—"

"Hey!" Betty shouted, and then lowered her voice, "I don't need to deal with this." Jacqui and Stefan looked at Betty as she once again checked the clock and her body visibly shook. "I know he's late, but this is a call I have to make. All right?" Jacqui, slowly shaking her head, reclaimed her place on the pastor's desk as Stefan sat on the love seat on the opposite side of the room.

"Now, Stefan, I know you're concerned with Drew, and Jac, trust me, I'll do the right thing."

As Jacqui bowed her head, she gripped the edge of the desk so tight, crooked veins in her hand appeared in places they were not before. As she looked at her friend, The words Betty wanted to say crystalized into a tear that slid down her quivering cheek. "I'll do what's right . . . okay?" Hearing the emotion in her voice, Stefan and Jacqui looked up as Betty continued. "Stefan? Do me a favor? Would you go down and ask the pastor to come up here a minute?"

Stefan stood as if he wanted to say something to Jacqui or Betty but then turned and left the room.

"Thank God you got rid of him. See what I was talking about? I ain't hardly ready to marry that fool no matter how many times he ask me."

"Jac?"

"Yeah, honey?"

"Can you give me a few minutes?"

With reluctance, Jacqui leaned away from the desk and brushed the wrinkles from her black silk dress with a smile of supplication on her face. "You know whatever you do"—and then Jacqui's voiced lowered to a whisper to contain her sentiment—"I got your back."

Shaking her head, unable to speak or draw more than a shallow gasp of air, Betty looked out the window one last time as Jacqui left the room. The clock showed it to be ten 'til the next hour as Betty searched for the right words to say to friends and family below. How do you tell two hundred people that the man you thought would love you forever has not shown up? Then she lifted her head, steeled her will, turned, and headed for the door.

Chapter 2

He loves too much
who dies for love.

—Randle Cotgrave
Dictionary

As if his head were connected to a swivel, Drew looked both ways as he ran through the second light on his way to the church. Nervous energy pulsated throughout his body like a neon light in Vegas, and he gripped the steering wheel tightly, with a fleeting glance in the rearview mirror. Hearing an ambulance in the distance but seeing no blue lights in tow, he took a breath and punched the accelerator.

Just three more lights, he thought. *I hope they didn't cancel it. Just three more lights.* As his car swept through the rain, he wished he'd charged the battery in his cell phone on a day nothing went as planned. He wished everyone he knew in town, except his mother, were not in the church awaiting his arrival. Drew also wished it was a Sunday instead of a Saturday so that the church phone would not be off the hook. *Just three more lights, Betty. I've just got three more lights.*

As he got closer to the intersection, a Mack truck filled with rocks covered by a flapping mesh canopy pulled dangerously close in front of him, but he could see where they were both going to make the light. *Almost there. Betty, don't give up, love. Don't give up on me yet.*

Although the CD played the song from the night he proposed, silence blocked the sound like a shadow blocking the sun. Running through the next intersection, all he could think of was the day he'd first laid eyes on her and how he knew somehow, some way, they would never part.

"Betty, don't listen to Jac!" he said aloud, nervously bouncing his fist on his thigh. "Believe in me, love. Don't give up!"

Drew and Betty had a whirlwind romance culminating on a balmy summer night when they were caught in a downpour on Amelia Island. As the rain fell, they both ran for shelter until Drew suddenly stopped and said over a laugh, "Hey, wait a minute. We're already wet, so why are we running?"

It was on the secluded beach with the rain soaking their bodies that they revealed parts of themselves previously unexposed. As they walked with only their pinkies locked, Drew shared with Betty how she'd taught him to love again after his previous heartbreak, and she told him that the last few months had taught her to trust. And then she stopped swinging her arm, stood silent in the downpour, and pushed her fingertips into the pockets of her black jeans.

"What's wrong?"

"Nothing," she replied in earnest as her left eyebrow raised a fraction above the right. "And that's what scares me most about you. I mean, *nothing* is wrong."

"You almost say that like it's a bad thing," he said as he softly rubbed the raindrops from her face with the back of his forefinger.

"It's not. I know it's not. I try to think about all this with my head and . . . Well, I know something is going to happen. But my heart keeps telling me that with you all I get is worth all I may lose. I mean, I believe in you Drew more than I ever thought I would ever believe in a man again. But I can't lie," she said as reality veiled her face. "I'm just so afraid that one morning I'll wake up and you'll be gone. I know we agreed to check our baggage at the door, but this is one piece I just can't seem to get rid of. And I'm sorry about that."

"Time."

"What do you mean?"

After a reflective pause, he whispered, "I wish you could understand how much I care for you. But since you can't, time will answer your questions. I mean, Betty, since the moment I saw you in the restaurant, when I didn't even know your name, I knew I wanted to be with you. Before I said hello or actually before I even knew you existed, I just knew I wanted you. You're a beautiful lady, Betty. I love the way you walk with one foot directly in front of the other. Like you're

walking a tightrope. I like the way you fix your nails when you're working on a problem in your mind. I like the way you smile sometimes
when you sleep."

"I don't do that," she said with an adolescent pout.

"Of course you do. And you're also the smartest woman I've ever
known. But as smart as you are, there is one thing you could never
know. And that's the feeling I get whenever you say good-bye." As his
eyes traced the shape of her lips, he continued: "You're the calm I
need so badly in my life, and although I've had relationships, you're
the only one who moved me from the moment I saw you. The *only*
one," he said as he squeezed her hand with each word. "You can't
fathom how much I want you, and I can't find the words to express
it." Lightning variegated the darkened skies above as he continued.
"All I know is if one day I call your name . . . and you don't answer, I'll
never be the same." Seeing the tears clouding her eyes, mixed with
streaks of rain, he tilted her head up with his thumb and forefinger
and covered her trembling lips with his.

After they kissed, Drew could feel the tension decrease in her body
as she held her head over his heart, and he knew the words he'd
searched for before were found in a simple touch. When they separated, Drew stroked her arm with the back of his large hands and repeated from his heart, "Baby, something tells me deep inside you
know it's the right thing to do. But all I know is, I would never be the
same without you in my life. So if you need time, I'll give you time.
If . . . well, if it's something else you are looking for, just tell me what
it is and I'll do it. I just don't want to lose you."

"Damn!" Drew screamed, shoving his palm into the horn and his
foot on the brake, which made his car skid to an "S" stop behind the
rock truck. The light was yellow, and the driver at the front of the
line chose caution instead of driving through the intersection on
the wet road. Rolling down the window, Drew leaned his head out of
the automobile to see how many vehicles were ahead of his. Then,
although the light was red, he looked at the digital clock on his
dash, backed up a half-car length, and sped around the vehicles,
blowing his horn as he crossed the thick white lines of the intersection.

"One more light, baby. One more light!" he said aloud as he increased his speed on the slick pavement, leaving an arch of water behind him. With the sound of another emergency vehicle in the distance, his thoughts turned to the morning on the beach.

After they returned to the suite, they made love unlike ever before, and in the midst of the passion, Drew felt he knew what Betty wanted. Since her last relationship ended because her mate was untrustworthy, she needed assurance that for them, through thick and thin, things would never change, that the love they shared wouldn't be one of convenience.

The next day, Drew told Betty he had to run into town for business but would be back in time for a special dinner. At sunset, they both dressed in black linen and dined at The Cheesecake Factory, which was an exclusive restaurant on the revolving-roof top floor of a hotel overlooking the Atlantic.

"This is awfully sweet of you, honey," Betty said. "So what's the occasion? Its not our three-month anniversary. That's next week."

"No. It's the last night of our very first vacation, and I just wanted to do something special for you. Something you'd never forget."

After dinner and a comedy show, the two lovers walked barefoot in the sand as Betty told Drew several lawyer jokes that were not too funny to him, but he laughed at her effort more than at the punch line. And then Drew came to a certain spot on the beach and stood still. "You know what happened here, don't you?"

"Yeah, of course I do. It's where they fought the Battle of Gettysburg," she said with a giggle in her tone. And then her voice matured. "Seriously? It was in this spot last night where you made me feel more loved than I've ever felt before. And I mean that."

The response was more than Drew imagined he would hear from the woman who rarely even said the words "I love you." He leaned forward, lowered his voice, and whispered, "Thank you. I needed to hear that."

"You know, it's hard for me to say things sometimes. I just hope you can feel it," the demure litigator replied as she gazed at the bending stalks of sea wheat. "I want to say certain words, and I want to tell you what I need, but sometimes they get, I don't know. Stuck? When I'm alone at night, I find all the words I want to say to you," she said as Drew blanketed his arms around her. "But when I look at your smile, I lose them. I guess it's hard to give what you never really got."

"Meaning?"

"Love. I don't mean love in the traditional sense. I mean an unrelenting love, with no strings attached, that says no matter what, I'll be here for you. A love you get without having to earn it. I've never experienced that. I thought I did once, and I guess that's why I said last night that you scare me. You scare the hell out of me because you give so freely what I need so much, and sometimes I don't know if I can handle it."

As Drew looked upon the dark blue horizon, Betty's eyes rose toward the sky. "You see how bright the stars are? After my mom died, I remember being told she was in a better place. So I would often stare at the sky and look at the stars because they looked like little pinholes that allowed me to see Momma in heaven. I imagined her being in a place that was so bright that the light just burst through the sky. And whenever I would see a star disappear, I knew she was watching me. The stars were proof that there was a God, that there was a heaven, and that Momma was there. And after all I've been through with men in my life, Drew, you're proof that, that . . ."

Holding his breath for her to complete the thought, Drew asked, "What?" Then he felt her body relax as if she allowed the words to be swallowed.

Drew attempted to turn Betty toward him but could not, so he eased in front of her and whispered, "I love you, and I'll be here for you until the day that eight times eight times eight is four. Okay?" he said as she smiled at the reference to their favorite song. "I'll be here for you, girl, until the seas and trees get up and fly away. Okay?" Betty shook her head yes. "I'll be loving you, Ms. Betty Ann Robinson, soon to be Staley, forever." When Betty eased onto her tiptoes to kiss him, Drew backed away, his fingers softly on her shoulders. "Not now, love." And then he turned and walked toward a white Styrofoam cooler that was on the beach and brought it back to Betty, who shook her head slowly.

"What are you doing?"

"Well, I knew I wanted to bring you back to this spot. And I knew it would be a moment we would never forget. So, when I went out today, I picked this up," he said, holding the cooler toward her.

"Aww, sweetie. You bought me an Igloo? You didn't worry about it getting stolen," she asked as a man walked toward them. Then she shook her head and said, "Any man can pick up diamonds or pearls.

But it takes a special man to think of camping equipment for his lady."

"I swear, everybody's a comedian now'days."

As she took off the lid, she said, "Whoa. Drew, Clicquot? You bought Veuve Clicquot for us to drink here on the beach?"

"Well, after last night . . . I just wanted to do something special for you."

Betty took the cooler from him and placed it on the sand as she walked back into his embrace. "You're too much. You know that?" And then she eased once again onto her tiptoes, and once again Drew backed away. "What's wrong?"

"Nothing. Nothing at all, but I was thinking," he said as the large man wearing a black vest walked closer to them. "On such a beautiful night, with the moon full and the sound of the ocean rolling, it would be perfect if I'd brought my stereo. Then we could listen to our song."

"Hon-ney, that's okay," she said, holding him close. "It's already a per—"

"No. No, it's a good night," Drew said as he looked at the red-headed gentleman with flowers in his hand only yards away from them, "but it's not perfect. Ahh, excuse me, sir, could I persuade you in some way to sell me those flowers?"

"Drew!" Betty said, embarrassed.

"What? They're yellow, and I forgot to pick up flowers when I was in town today."

"Eh, sorry, dude, but they're not for sale," he said as he walked by the couple.

Looking wide-eyed at Drew, Betty said, "I cannot believe you asked that man that."

Ignoring Betty, Drew continued, "I didn't mean to offend. But it's for a special occasion. Next week," he said as Betty shoved her elbow into his ribs, "me and this lady will be together for three months, and every week I've given her flowers except this one."

"Drew," Betty said under her breath, "it's okay."

"No, it's not okay, honey. I want to say I gave you flowers every week we dated, and I don't want to screw it up now."

And then the man turned and walked back toward them. As he headed in their direction, he said, "You know something; I under-

stand how you feel, bro. I used to feel just like that, and well, it's a
long story. But, dude, I can't swap the buds."

"That's okay," Betty repeated. "He's just kidding, anyway."

Standing in front of them, the gentleman said, "You have a very
special man here, and what I'll do is this. I run a li'l bistro and flower
hut on the other side of the beach; it's nut'n special. But I'll, like, give
you these roses on the condition you two continue to love each other.
Cool?"

"Thanks," Drew said, accepting the token of love and then kissing
Betty on the cheek. As the man turned to walk away, Drew's open
smile closed. "Ah, excuse me, sir?" The man turned in a frustrated
motion without answering. "I'm sorry to bother you again, but did I
see a harmonica in your back pocket by chance?"

"Drew!"

With a silent chuckle, the man asked, "Why you ask? I don't have a
harmonica stand. You play?"

"Not even at gun point. But I was just going to ask if you could play
it. See, we don't have any music tonight and—"

"I can't play very well, dude. Sorry," he said, and headed on his way,
leaving deep work-boot imprints in the sand.

"Can you play at all?" Drew shouted.

"Okay, now that's enough. Sir," Betty interceded, "thanks for the
flowers. That was kind of you. Have a nice night."

Then the man walked toward them again with kinked eyebrows
and a half-smile. "Dude, I know just one song. That's all. I bought this
thing at a pawn shop, and I'm still learning how to—"

"I don't care what the song is. It could be 'Chopsticks,' 'The
Farmer in the Dell,' or 'Hickory Dickory Dock.' Would you play it?
Tonight we would dance to 'Pop Goes the Weasel.' "

"Where did you find this guy?" the man asked Betty with a smile,
looking thoroughly confused. Then he shook his large freckled face
as he cupped his alabaster hands around the tiny silver-and-gold instrument. Drew placed his arms around his lady and whispered in her
ear, the words this is how much I love you as the blues musician
played a perfect rendition of their favorite song by Stevie Wonder.
With the roll of the ocean providing the background music, Drew
kissed Betty on the crown of her head as she rested in his arms. The
scent of her hair, the touch of her skin, the glow from her body as-

sured him. The way she sighed gave him confidence. Although he previously had doubts, they perished in the ocean and he knew that he could never allow the moment to pass.

When the last note vanished in the damp breeze, Drew thanked the musician he would later introduce to Betty as John Popper and told him he'd be out to listen to his group the Blues Travelers the following weekend. Betty stood in awe.

"I hope you know that I'm going to get you good for this."

Drew turned her toward him and said, "I'm waiting with bated breath," and then they kissed as the edge of the waves giggled at their feet. Opening their eyes, they both stared at each other, and their polite, simultaneous smiles turned into childlike laughter.

"Just when I figure I've got you pegged, you go and do something spectacular. It's getting to the point where," Betty said as Drew dropped to his knee in the water, "I don't know if I should—Oh, my God, Drew. No," she said as her eyes swelled and he held her hand softly between his.

"Betty?"

"Drew, no," she repeated, shaking her head vehemently.

"I'm not perfect. Far from it, actually. But never have I wanted to prove myself to be perfect as I've wanted to do so for you. You make me smile when there's nothing funny. You make me want to cry when everything is going fine. And like I said before, I cannot imagine"— he pulled out an emerald-cut diamond that sparkled in the moonlight—"living without you in my life. I know we have not known each other for a long period of time, but all I know is that whenever I hang up the phone, my heart stops, and it doesn't start again until you say hello. We've both had our share of heartbreak, but if you're willing to try and if it's possible, I'd like our past to be a prologue to this moment, to this night.

"I know I don't deserve you in so many ways, Betty," he continued, "but I'll do everything I can to be the man you deserve." Betty swallowed yet another no and put her hand over her mouth as he slid the ring over her third finger. "I've said all that to say this. Miss Betty Anne Robinson, I'd be so honored if you would spend tonight, tomorrow, and most importantly, forever with me."

Betty froze. She looked into his almond eyes and shook her head no. Then she repeated the word, "Yes, yes, yes."

Watching her acceptance, chills climbed the ladder of Drew's spine, and then she kneeled in the water in front of him, and as they looked at the first ring of its kind to adorn her finger, she shed a tear.

Drew saw the church in the distance as a Mark IV filled with people dressed in white pulled out of the parking lot.

"Betty, please don't tell me you did it!" And then his car skidded on the wet pavement and ended up under the canopy. As he retrieved his jacket from the passenger seat and whipped open the door in one motion, he saw Jacqui headed his way. *Aw, man, I can't deal with her now.* Then he saw Betty. She was dressed from head to toe in the silk form-fitting V-neck wedding gown he'd never imagine would look as good on her as it did at that very moment. Betty grabbed the bend of Jacqui's arm and spoke sternly to her as Drew jogged toward them.

As he got closer, he could almost hear Jacqui's angered breathing, and then she turned away, refusing to look at him, and said to the people staring from inside the sanctuary, "Everything is all right. Show's over; everything is fine."

"Betty, I'm so sorry. Did you cancel the wedding? Are the people still here?"

"No," Betty said after a respite as her jaw muscles tightened and released. "I was headed down to do just that when Pastor asked me to give you a few more minutes. Drew, how could you?"

"I can never say how sorry I am. I can't tell you how bad I feel about what happened."

"How bad you feel?" she asked as her lips curled downward.

"I know. That was selfish, too. Its Momma. I went by to pick her up, and she was depressed about something. I waited for her to get dressed, and before anyone knew it, she'd walked out in the rain. So I just panicked. We called the police and—"

"Honey, I'm sorry," she said, reaching for and holding his hand. "Did they find her? Is everything all right?"

"Don't apologize. Yeah, we found her about a half mile from the home. Soaked to the bone and shaking but otherwise okay. I tried to call you. Even stopped along the road a couple of times. But I guess the phone was off the hook at the church, and I knew you would not have your cell. I just—"

"Drew," Betty said as she freed her silk-gloved hand and removed the veil that had fallen in her face. "Are you sure we should do this? I mean absolutely, positively, unconditionally sure?"

"This is no way to start a marriage. But Betty, you know how I feel. I know I want to grow old with you and only you." And then he kissed her on the forehead and said, "So, to answer your question, there is no way in this world I could be more sure. But under the circumstances, if you would like to wait, I understand. Regardless of what happened, I messed up our day, and I just want to earn your trust again."

"But do you really love me, Drew? I mean beyond the words," she asked as the pastor jogged toward them from the sanctuary.

"You ask me this all the time, and I know why. Because you're waiting for me to say certain words. But I don't know what those words are. The simplest way I can say it is, I need you. I care for you. I want you. But above all, I love you. That's all I know to say anymore." And then, with the shine of a tear in the rim of his eye, he breathed the words once again inaudibly. "I just love you."

"Betty. Drew?" the pastor said. "Under the circumstances, would you like to talk for a moment in my office?"

Drew looked back at Betty and whispered, "It's your call."

Betty cleared her throat and said, "I think we know what we should do."

Chapter 3

The peace of God came into my life when I wedded her.
—Alfred Lord Tennyson
(about his wife)

"Okay, it's me. Jacqui. Or should I say Jacquetta Jordan . . . from Duval Heights . . . in Florida. I know you more than likely don't even know my voice, but—Aww, what's the use?" Jacqui said as she stood alone in the pastor's forty-watt restroom. Then, looking toward the crucifix on the back of the door, she said, "Let me try this again. I hope I don't sound like my ole drunk uncle who only prays when he needs something. But if I didn't need something, I guess I wouldn't be doing this at all. But I'm not asking for personal reasons, either.

"It's just that . . . Well, it's Betty, and I know you know her. She always tells me I should pray, and so I guess it's only right that if I'm gonna do this, I should do it for her." Then Jacqui discerned her reflection in the mirror and clicked off the light. The bathroom was completely dark except for the L-shaped trace of light at the perimeter of the doorway. With a nervous squeeze and twist of her index finger, Jacqui turned her back to the mirror, leaned against the basin, and continued to speak in darkness.

"Actually, I don't know what to do or how to do it. This girl is making a big mistake, Lord. I know it, you know it, and she won't admit it. I don't know why the feeling is so strong, but I know it like I know my name, and I'm all-out. I don't know what to do or say. He seems nice enough most of the time, but I know something is wrong. I've tried to

say, to do, everything I could the past couple of months to get her to
see the light, but I even sound bitter to myself when I say it."

"Miss Jordan? Is you in dea'?"

In a whisper, she continued: "I can handle these situations. If something like this were to happen to me, I know I would survive. But not
her. This time last year she was head over heels in love with Evander,
and now she's in love with this guy? And getting—"

"Miss Jordan? They waitin' for you downstairs."

"Okay," Jacqui shouted from the darkened room with a smile in
her voice. "I'll be right down."

"Now, Lord . . . if that's what you like to be called. Lord, all I'm asking you to do is if this guy is not legit, and I don't think he is, but I
could be wrong . . . But if this guy isn't straight, just don't let her fall
too hard this time. And also if you would—"

"Miss Jordan?" the preteen voice shrieked. "They need you to come
down ra't now! The music is playing and every—"

"I'll be ra't there," Jacqui mocked, then turned toward the sink and
continued. "As I was going to say, Lord. If you would touch Stefan's
heart also. I don't know what it's going to take to make him see the
light, so if you could just let him know, if you do things like that, that
I love him and that one day I would like to—"

"Miss Jordan? It's time to—"

"Can you not hear, li'l bitc—" Catching herself, Jacqui released her
firm grasp of the basin, turned on the light, and said, "Sorry. I'm
coming out now." Jacqui glanced at the crucifix once again and said,
"Thank you for listening."

Then Jacqui unlocked the door as the child ran down the hallway
screaming, "Oww, yaw'll, she in dea cussin'!"

"I just hope you can kinda ignore that last part, Lord, but even *you*
know she tried me that time."

The first eyes Jacqui saw as she walked downstairs were those of her
friend. No longer were they glistening, and the fear previously shown
had abated and been replaced with anticipation. Betty smiled at
Jacqui as she stood at the end of the wedding-party line. The dress
that Jacqui had picked out was an original, made of ivory poult-de-
sole. It had a ten-foot train, a romantic bustle skirt, and the pearls
were imported to form the back of the bodice. The long hand-
embroidered ivory gloves and silk tulle veil gave the bride a look of a

fairy tale come to life. "If this is what you want," Jacqui whispered to herself as she walked toward Betty. "If this is what you gotta have, I got your back."

"Jacqui, tell me you were not doing what that child came down here and told everybody you were doing?" Betty whispered.

"What are you talking about?"

"My niece said you were up there making noises in the bathroom," Stefan chimed in. "We almost had to delay the wedding again 'cause you couldn't get out the bathroom?"

"Please. I was up there—" She looked at Stefan, dressed in a black English cutaway and smoke pinstriped slacks, and then back to the bride and said softly, "I was up there just saying a little prayer." As the words swung in the air like a pendulum, Betty looked at Stefan, and then they both started laughing together. "See? See how you all are? Thick as thieves. I try to do the right thing," she said as the wedding planner opened the doors to the large church, "and you all make fun of me."

"Okay, guys, gals. Just like we practiced at the rehearsal. Lead with your left. And one, two, three. One, two, three," the sandy-blond planner chanted.

"Well, it's not that, Boo," Stefan replied. "It's just that we've heard it called a lot of things before. But never praying."

"See, you just gonna make me act ugly up in here, aren't you."

As they got to the door, Jacqui glanced over her shoulder one last time at Betty, who stood rejuvenated beside her foster parent. With a raise of her eyebrow, she asked if she was okay, and the bride shook her head yes.

Stefan looked at Jacqui and asked, "So, are you nervous? Maybe just a little bit?" Jacqui noticed the calm in his eyes and the stillness of his voice.

"Not atall. This ain't nothing," she replied, a mixture of fear and doubt spinning in her throat.

Then she felt Stefan lace his strong fingers in hers and rub the back of her hand firmly against his thigh. "Well, hold tight 'cause I'm scared to death."

In a tom-tom drum cadence, the wedding planner clapped her hands up and down. "One, two, three. One, two, three," and Jacqui and Stefan marched into the building.

The cherry-wood walls arched high in the cathedral, and above them Jacqui noticed a string quintet and a boys' choir dressed in golden robes singing Puccini's "Nessum Dorma" in the mezzanine. There were thick pillars along the aisle wrapped for the occasion with twinkling eggshell lights. As she and Stefan walked lockstep in between the observers, Jacqui bit the soft flesh inside of her mouth.

The church was sprinkled with plum-colored lilacs, and a ray of reddish sunlight beamed through the once-darkened clouds as the rain subsided.

Nearing the front of the church, Jacqui noticed the look Stefan and Drew exchanged, and then the groom looked at her, and his smile dissipated.

"One of these days," Stefan whispered to Jacqui.

"What do you mean?" she replied, barely moving her lips.

"Just what I said, one of these days." And then he looked at her and finished his thought. "I can't wait."

As they separated at the front of the church, Drew and Stefan gave each other a masculine embrace with a fist pound to the center of each other's back. Jacqui took her place and looked to the entrance of the church for Betty, but the door remained still.

As the strings subsided, the lighting dimmed, and a hush fell over the audience. For an awkward moment, people looked at each other, and Jacqui watched for movement from the door and then gazed at Drew, who stood unwavering.

The door remained still.

The pastor audibly cleared his throat to get Jacqui's attention, but she refused to look his way. Then, from the corner of the church, the sound of fluttering wings were heard. Two turtle doves flew to the top of the high-ceiling sanctuary in a circular pattern and out an open stained-glass window, garnering awed tones from the congregation.

From the silence, the brooding sound of a lone baritone was heard high above the listeners. Heads turned from side to side before looking up to find an unaccompanied instrumentalist with a rolling emotional tone flowing from the brass instrument. From nowhere the feathery-soft timbre of brass was layered by the sound of a simple viola. The two mismatched instruments met and intertwined in the air as they played "Bach's Air on the G String," which encompassed the attendees.

A group of children, none of which could have been of school age, trickled through the entrance of the building. There were smiles from the audience as the little girls spread yellow and white rose petals while smiling for photos and boys walked in dressed in jonquil cutaways with eggshell-white vests and ascots, carrying clear balloons. Jacqui was totally against the balloon idea when the wedding planner suggested it, but as they approached the front of the church, she had to admit she was wrong.

When the children separated on both sides of the sanctuary, the music diminished, and then the large doors reopened. The eyes of the congregation rested on Betty as the organist struck up the bridal refrain.

Betty walked down the aisle with an assured smile as her elderly foster father, who tilted his body to walk, accompanied her. Each person on the end of the aisle was given starlight bells to ring as the bride passed his or her pew, which gave the moment an aura of enchantment.

Holding her bouquet of lilacs and daffodils securely in place, Betty smiled with grace at individuals she knew and even laughed with the rest of the church when a little boy's balloon slipped out of his grasp and he tried to wrestle one from another child. When he couldn't, he started to cry and ran to his father's arms, drawing sympathy from the assembly.

Betty stepped to the front of the church and smiled at her foster father and then Drew, but then, totally unexpected by Jacqui or the wedding planner, she walked over and warmly hugged her bridesmaid.

"I love you, girl. You know that?"

Jacqui was tongue-tied as she shook her head and swallowed a tear as memories burned through her mind. And then Betty backed away as an attendant adjusted the train of her gown, and she returned to her place before the cleric.

The ceremony proceeded uneventfully as the pastor, dressed in white with a crimson sash over his gaunt shoulders, spoke of the values of honesty, fidelity, and the sanctity of marriage.

"These are not just words." His voice bellowed as he was occasionally encouraged by an amen from the congregation. "No, these words are spoken by the one who commands even the angels above us and the wind that encompasses our mortal bodies. The King of Kings and Lord of Lords."

After he completed the ministerial portion of the ceremony, the pastor looked at Drew and asked him to repeat the vows. When Drew spoke, Jacqui wanted to believe he was sincere as she felt Stefan's gaze. At each word Drew spoke, she watched Stefan's lips form. *What are you doing?* she asked him in her thoughts. *Please don't do this if you don't mean it.* Jacqui avoided tearing by looking at Betty, whose face was beginning to show the weight of the moment. She was close enough to see her tremble as Drew repeated, "From this day forward." *Hang in there, girl,* Jacqui thought. *Hang in there.*

Then Betty cleared her throat, stood taller, and prepared to repeat the vows. Her restiveness, which was not initially seen in her smile or the way she stood, was shown in the quiver of her bouquet. As she spoke the words, Jacqui felt she had the strength to look at Stefan, who continued to watch her. There was so much in him she adored. He had a hard-core side, but he could also be soft and tender. He was from the streets of Oak Cliff, in Dallas, yet he had a heart that Jacqui felt at times could be cloned for so many of the men she'd dated who were heartless.

She once told him how she hated going to dances because, due to her height, she would always end up dancing alone. To which he melted her fears with a kiss and replied, "Jacquetta Marie Jordan, you'll never dance alone again." If there was a man for her, it had to be Stefan, but she didn't know when or if they would ever have a special day of their own.

"To have and to hold," Jacqui whispered with Betty as she looked into Stefan's eyes. "In sickness and in health. From this day forward." And then the final words slid down her throat like cold vanilla on a summer day as she said, "Until death do us part."

At the reception, Jacqui checked to make sure everyone was being served. Her events manager reassured her she had everything under control and to take the evening off. Walking through the crowd, she saw the bride, who had changed and was speaking to a couple of local politicians. People were in small clusters conversing when she felt a tap on her shoulder.

Without saying a word, she turned around, and Drew hugged her firmly. With her chin uncomfortably on his shoulder, Jacqui patted his back as if she were burping a baby and then pushed away from his hold.

"Listen. I just want to say thank you for all you did in the last couple of weeks. The reception is—I don't know what exactly to say," he said, looking for words with his gesturing hands. "But thanks. Thanks for everything."

"Betty's my girl," Jacqui said in a monotone. "What'd you expect?"

"I know that," Drew replied. Then he gathered himself and shouted over the jazz in the background, "I know how close you two are. I know this all went down fast, but let me just say that there is nothing in this world that I wouldn't do for Betty. She means the world to me, and I'll always be there for her. As long as she'll have me." Jacqui smiled as she slowly folded her arms over her waist. "So you're going to give me a chance? Hmm?"

"I was just smiling, Drew, because all the words you used sounded so nice."

"Because they're sincere," he said with his hand over his heart.

"They also sound just like the words Evander used to say to her. Strange, huh?" Then her smile vanished as she turned and walked away.

Weaving through the crowd like a strand of yarn in a crochet vest, Jacqui looked for Stefan and saw him standing on the stage, talking to the saxophone player. Walking toward him, she mumbled to herself, "Who the fuck he think he is? Come up in here over an hour late with that weak-ass lie and think I'm gonna fall for it? Please. He don't know who he messing with."

Stefan, seeing her headed toward him, walked her way. "Baby, everything is looking great, and the salmon tastes wonderful."

"Thanks," she said as Stefan kissed the back of her hand and then her cheek.

"What's wrong?"

"Nothing. So did any of your family make it?"

"Big Ced is up in here somewhere," Stefan said as he rubbed his thumb across the spot on the back of her hand he'd kissed, "but I haven't seen him yet."

"What he doing here? I thought he was on house arrest or something."

"See how you are? Ced's been out three months. Little Pooky on house arrest."

"Have you had a chance to talk to Betty?"

"Naw, I saw her a few minutes ago, but they've been mobbed so far," he shouted.

"Umm, well I spoke to Drew."

"Really? You and he actually spoke? As in exchanged words?"

"Don't be funny. We spoke and even hugged."

"Okay, now, see you had me going for a minute there," he said as Betty approached, "but then you just had to add that last part."

As Jacqui placed her hand on her hip, Betty came up and said, "You guys still going at it?"

"Please, that's him. So, how does it feel, girl? Do you feel the urge to run around the place, waving your arms like Oprah in *The Color Purple*, screaming, 'We'zz, married! We'zz married folks nah!' "

"You crazy. Naw, I don't think it's fully sunk in yet, but so far," she said, fidgeting with the diamond on her finger, "so good. Hey, I had some of the salmon, and it is slamming. Why don't you put it on the—"

"Cost too much to put on the menu and takes too long to prepare. But I'm glad you like it."

"Come here, girl," Stefan said as he wrapped his muscular arms around Betty and, as they released, held her hands. "You look beautiful. I'm happy for you. For both of you."

"Thanks, Step. We appreciate all you did this week also."

"All who did?" Jacqui asked with arched eyebrows.

"Don't start, Jacquetta Marie!" Betty said over a laugh.

"So where's Drew?" Stefan asked. "I haven't had a chance to talk to a brother since the toast."

"He just went back to the nursing home to make sure everything is okay," Betty replied.

"Dag, why didn't he tell me? I would've went with him."

"That's nice, but I think he needed to slip out and just spend some time with his mom. He called, and they said everything was okay, considering, but he just wanted to make sure."

"Heifer was probably just liquored up," Jacqui said, unheard by the others.

"Well, I'ma go grab me a little more fish before it's all gone. You all want anything?" Stefan said.

"Naw, shuga, go handle your biz," Jacqui replied as Stefan walked away. Then she looked back at Betty and said, "So, what's up with his mom? Does she have Alzheimer's or something? You really believe she went out on a day like today and started wandering around?"

"No, she doesn't have Alzheimer's. At least I don't think so. But she has been acting a little strange the last few days, actually. I don't know what happened, but she used to call, and she and I would talk for hours. But in the past few days she's been very abrupt."

"Hello, Betty," an elderly blue-haired lady said.

"Hello, Mrs. Grison. I had no idea you were here."

As the two women spoke, Jacqui watched a young lady she had not met who appeared to be flirting with Stefan, and then he looked her way as Jacqui returned her eyes to Betty and the older woman.

"Well, I just wanted to say, Praise God. I think you and he make a fine, fine couple. Always keep God first," Mrs. Grison said in her creaking voice as she walked away.

"Yes, ma'am." Betty looked again at her friend and said, "I haven't seen her in five years. They're coming out the woodwork now. So tell me, do you really think Drew would make this up?"

"No," Jacqui said, looking at Stefan. "I was just curious."

Jacqui looked at the clock and was surprised that people were still mingling in the grand ballroom of the hotel, although it was past midnight. The pastor, who'd changed into a light blue leisure suit, watched hawkishly as his daughter danced with a man twice her age. And the string musicians sat together in a group, drinking shots and laughing at the jazz combo. Jacqui watched a flower girl eating yellow chocolate-covered strawberries as if nothing else in the world mattered, and then the little girl looked around and stole her mother's.

Sitting down for the first time, Jacqui crossed her legs, removed her shoes, and stiffly massaged the ball of her foot with her thumb. As she watched the couples, she couldn't restrain the cynical inner thoughts cutting through her mind from wondering if her time had passed for such a day.

So many men had come through her revolving door in her early twenties, but she was too busy building Jacquetta's. In her late twenties, the door did not revolve as much, and she thought about artificial insemination until she met Yancy at a pool party, but he left her in her early thirties. It took years to even consider allowing another man to heal the wound in her heart, but she gave the opportunity to do so to Stefan, whom she met the week of her thirty-seventh birthday. So as she relaxed and watched the couples in pairs dance, the aroma of love still in the air, Jacqui leaned back in the chair and thought about the game she and Betty had played. She thought how close Betty was to being right when she asked her to "make her day," and then she rubbed her palm up and down her shin, closed her weary eyes, and soaked in the bliss of the jazz combo's rendition of "Winelight."

Sitting in the chair, Jacqui was awakened by full soft lips on the tip of her nose. For a moment, she felt like a flower being attracted by the mere scent of water. Opening her eyes, she first noticed his ripe lips, which at times were filled with so much love. Her eyes traveled to his neatly manicured goatee and high cheekbones covered by smooth, rich ebony skin. She looked at his freshly shaved head and then, lastly, into the Asiatic eyes, which looked sleepy even when he was awake, as he took a knee in front of her and held her hands over his heart.

"Baby, you must be tired." And then he whispered, "You were snoring."

"Really? I'm sorry," she said as she withdrew her hand from his and discreetly wiped her mouth. "I just decided to sit down a minute, and next thing I knew, you were here."

"Are you ready to go home?"

"No, I can't go yet. We're leaving with Betty and Drew. Did he make it back yet?"

"He rolled up about ten. So, this turned out pretty good. You guys outdid yourselves."

"Thanks. I just wanted it to be perfect, and in spite of that stunt your boy pulled, it worked out all right."

Stefan smiled. "Are you feeling matrimonial again?"

"What do you mean?"

"Just what I said. Everyone here's looking like they got Noah's Ark reservations and whatever, so you must be at least thinking about it," he asked, still on one knee.

Leaning toward him, Jacqui asked, "Why are you going there? Do you feel an 'I do' on your tongue?"

"Naw," Stefan replied. "It's not even like that." He leaned back. "I mean, don't get me wrong. I want to one day, and I can't imagine doing it with anyone but you, but I want our day to be just like this."

"Again I'll ask you. What are you talking about?"

"Let's face it, Jacqui. I'm a wannabe model at best. That's all I know. That's all I've ever known and all I want to do. And look at this," he said, gazing around the immense hall filled with numerous well-to-do attendees. "I can't give you this. You a big-time, MBA, chamber of commerce, hobnob with the big boys, whateva' whateva'. What I got besides a bagful of gonnas? I'm street. I'm a hustler. That's all I know. You deserve all of this." Jacqui sat up straight, smiled, and slowly ran the tip of her tongue across her lips as she searched for the right response.

"Let me understand. Is this one of those 'It's not you, it's me' kinda line you guys use? Besides, I thought we were over the money thing a long time ago. And besides that, who's asking you for anything? I mean, anything," she said, shaking her head, "besides you."

"It's not some line; it's a man thing. I can't go into a relationship at that level knowing we're not on equal footing. I know we discussed the money issue that time you proposed, but it was really never settled. Even the Bible say you must be equally yoked. I already live under your roof; you help me with my car insurance half the time; you buy the groceries, and you even bought yourself a gift for Christmas and told Betty I bought it for you." As Jacqui looked into his eyes with surprise, he said, "Don't worry, I never let on. But I'm getting crushed in the middle. It's like a part of me wants to go do something, anything, to feel like I'm contributing. But the other side of me would rather live on the streets and see this dream through than quit now. I'm forty years old, Jacqui, and you would think I would've given up on the game, but, well, I can't. At least not yet. Every time I hear the phone ring, I think it's the call from Artie saying, 'I hope you're sitting down.' "

Laughter was heard as both Stefan and Jacqui looked toward the dance floor and saw the polyester-clad minister dancing with Betty and Mrs. Grison. And then she looked at Stefan and said, "What I'm about to say, Stefan, has nothing to do with you per se. But I don't understand you at all, and if I live to be as old as Methuselah, I know I'll be just as much in the dark. How do you expect me to survive? Black women, I mean. And by you I mean black men. You don't sit me down in some fancy house. You save that for them, and that's okay, because I'm a survivor. But when I go out there and snatch and pull and grab mine, what do you say? You can't handle *my* success? And then if I cross over, you look at me like I'm wrong? And now *you* feel crushed in the middle? Talk about damned if you do or damned if you don't. Tell me, Stefan, what are we supposed to do?"

Stefan rested his forearms on her knees as he bowed his head in thought. Then he slowly raised it and looked at Jacqui, whose face was inches away from his. Holding her hands again, he said, "All I know is this. I love you, Jacquetta Marie. You see so much in me that even I don't see sometimes. After Glynis, I never thought I would be able to give myself to anyone totally. But I have with you, and it's because of one reason. You believe in me." Then, with a swallow, he said, "Jacqui, I want to marry you more than I can even find the words to tell you. I would be honored for you to be my wife. Hell, girl, I wanna have *your* baby." Jacqui could feel the blood leave her face. But then he let go of her hands and said, "But I can't. And I won't let you or anyone else make a decision for me that one day we may both regret." A stiff breeze blew through the marrow of Jacqui's bones as the last man on her dance card stood, looked down at her, and walked away.

"Testen' one, two, tree, fo'. Can you 'ear me?" the saxophone player said, tapping the microphone with his fingernail. "Good. Le'seen, I have a special request from a brotha named Stefan to him lovely lady Jacqui. Is Stefan 'ere?" he asked as Jacqui watched the man in her life walk through the double door of the kitchen. "Stefan? Sho ya face, brotha. Don't act like Stef'funny. Oh, well, I guess him couldn't wait and has left weet him lady. Jacqui by chance be 'ere?"

Holding her head down, she heard the applause as the warmth of the bright light shined on her. Then she held her head up and waved to the dreadhead on the stage. "Oh, tat Jacqui? Hey, we loved da' fish. Well, I'm gonna serve dis up right fo you sho'nuff. Hopefully your man will be back 'ere soon, no?"

Clearing his throat, he disconnected the saxophone from the black strap around his neck and placed it on the stand as he hummed to get the right pitch for the other musicians. And then he stepped to the microphone in the midst of the blue spotlight, looked toward Jacqui, and said, "Dis one for you, Jacqui."

As he sang, a few men looked at her sitting alone then took their date's hand and headed for the dance floor. Jacqui looked out the window and caught a glance of Stefan walking toward her car, opening her door and driving off.

During the song Jacqui held her chin up with dignity. This was Betty's day and she would not allow it to be spoiled by anyone. She embraced herself, swayed back and forth to "Just The Way You Look Tonight," and once again danced alone.

Spring

Chapter 4

Graze on my lips; and if these hills be dry,
Stray lower, where the pleasant fountains lie.
                                    —William Shakespeare
                                    Venus and Adonis

MARCH

*H*ello. This is Jay Anderson, Magic 101.3 News. The Gainesville Police Department has reported that they are not yet prepared to release the names of the two bodies found in the trunk of a car in the Kennedy Holmes Apartments area. The two ladies in their early twenties were in the stolen car of NFL football star and local resident Tobias Parker, who was reportedly on vacation. In a statement—

Betty clicked off the radio and leaned back in her chair, which squeaked for oil. Her brown-toned office was small, dank, and rectangular in shape. There was a wooden border waist-length from the floor and a ceiling fan that assisted in cooling the unit. As she sat surrounded by law journals and files, she slowly attempted to reduce the tension in her body.

"Inhale," she said softly to herself, filling her lungs and counting to twenty. "Exhale," she whispered as she methodically released the air through her lips. "Inhale," she repeated, and once again duplicated the anaerobic exercise. And then as she said, "Exhale," a little of the anxiety seemed to leave as she opened her eyes.

The home of Robinson-Staley, attorney at law, was previously a convenience store that was sublet into four offices. Before she moved in, unit C had been occupied by the Blue Chip Game Room, Parker Pest Control, and most recently, Madam Alexei Palm Reading. The fading terra-cotta wallpaper was peeling in places, and the often wet heat in her unit rarely worked, but it would have to do for the remaining months of her two-year lease.

Sitting erect in her chair, Betty refocused on her profit-and-loss statement as she attempted to block the sounds from the massage parlor next door. Between the occasional shouts of "What the . . ." and "For a hundred dollars, I know I better get . . . ," she would listen to the aria played on her portable stereo in the background.

Everyone told her not to expect to see a dime of profit in the first three to five years, so she expected the fledgling business to be struggling at this point. But after eight months, she did not expect to be covered in a sea of red ink.

Before leaving one of the most prestigious law firms in the South to fly solo, she had verbal agreements with several major clients that they would follow her. Now that she was a sole practitioner, few of the corporations had followed through, and she was feeling the effects.

As the phone rang, Betty shook her head and put the statement in a file marked Take Home. When she pulled out a pending lawsuit she was working on, she remembered that her one and only employee had not returned from lunch.

"Thank you for calling Robinson-Staley, attorney at law. May I help you?"

"Hey, honey? Carol still on lunch break?"

Hearing her husband's voice, Betty relaxed her tone and body. "Yeah. What time is it?" she asked, then searched her desk to uncover her watch.

"Half-past two. Did she leave at her usual—"

"She must have had errands to run or something," Betty replied, dismissing any additional drama. "Oh, yeah, before I forget, thanks for the flowers. That was sweet of you."

"So they arrived. Describe them for me?"

"Well," she said, trying to remember what they looked like, since she could not see them on her secretary's desk, "just a simple vase with what looks like cream-colored roses and baby's breath. I love it."

"So did you understand the card?"

"Not exactly," she said, sliding away from her desk and retrieving the peach-scented envelope from the drawer. "I was meaning to ask you about that. What does 'I fit like a glove, so come find me,' mean?"

"Well, Counselor, I guess you will have to use your Perry Mason powers of deductive reasoning to figure it out."

"I fit like a . . . ," Betty repeated in an attempt to decipher the meaning of the words. "What are you talking about?"

"Don't you like surprises? Besides, I felt bad about the last few weeks and wanted to make it up to you."

"Is your mom feeling better?"

"Last night was tough, but we'll see. I plan on meeting with her doctor tomorrow to find out if she can give her something for the anxiety."

"Umm. So," she said, shuffling the files loud enough for him to hear them on the phone, "what else is going on?"

"Not a lot. I'm in the car headed over to meet with a client. Have you eaten lunch yet? If not, I can swing by and drop something off."

"No, I'm fine. Unfortunately, I'll more than likely just eat a larger dinner tonight."

"That's the other reason I was calling you. Don't eat dinner."

Closing her eyes slowly and trying to figure out a way to be tactful, Betty replied, "Hon, I won't get in tonight until after eight, so I really don't feel like going out."

"And who said anything about going out? I told you I could burn?"

Carol, Betty's secretary, peeked into her office to let her know she'd returned. "So you're going to cook—cook?"

"You seem shocked."

"No, not shocked," she said, curling the telephone cord around her finger. "But when you consider that when I moved in you could have turned your kitchen into a guest bedroom, since you were never in there, I thought you were just running your mouth."

"Guest bedroom, huh. Well," he replied over a soft chuckle, then lowering his voice, "we'll see my love. I'll have to serve it up good tonight, and when I'm done, I promise to leave you begging for more."

With laughter she replied, "Talk, talk, talk, talk, talk. Don't let your mouth write a check your body can't cash. So what does this 'fit like a glove' stuff mean?"

"You'll find out in time. So, it's a date?"

"Yeah, if you don't mind me getting in so late. I've got to meet with this drug dea—I mean," she said clearing her throat and uncurling the telephone cord from her finger, "a gentleman charged with trafficking less than five grams of a controlled substance. But he should be gone no later than seven o'clock."

"So you decided to defend this guy, after all?"

"I don't want to, because once you get into criminal law, it's a slippery slope. But it's constant business, and it keeps the lights on until we get a few more corporate retainers."

"Betty?"

"Yes?"

"I've told you I don't mind giving you . . . investing in . . . floating your business for a while. We're ahead of projections, and I know you don't like talking about this, but—"

"New subject. Soooo"—she stalled in search of a topic—"you're not going to explain the glove thing, huh?"

After a reflective pause, Drew replied, "No." And then his voice brightened as he said, "Well, look at that. They're breaking ground about three blocks from the house for a Toys-"Я"-Us. Can you believe that? We can walk here with little Drew or Betty one day."

"Umm. So anything else going on?"

"Not a thing. But before I forget, I really want to apologize again for last night."

"I understand, baby."

"But it's the fourth or fifth night in the last two weeks. I mean, some nights she's fine, and then others she's—"

"I understand," Betty said as she leaned back in her chair and looked at the beige water circles in the cork tile above her desk. "I'm not some young bride, honey, who'll be up under you all the time. That's just not me. I've been single a long time . . . as in all my life. I know you have obligations, and I know you love me. We'll find time to be together." Drew was silent on the other end of the phone. "So . . . no more clues for tonight, huh?"

The pause stiffened, and then he replied, "Yeah. I mean, no. No other clues."

"Okay, well, I'm excited."

After a delay, Drew asked, "Why don't we ever talk about kids anymore? I guess I just need to know how you really feel about us sometime, and the direction—"

"About what? Children or us?" Betty asked.

"I mean, I know neither of us have been married before, but I get the sense that something is wrong. That maybe we're not connecting. Maybe we're not where we should be as a couple, which is why—"

"Honey, I don't think anything is wrong," she said calmly. "We've both had a lot of pressure on us lately from careers, family, et cetera, and when you add the craziness of the wedding day, let's just say things got off to an interesting start. But I understand, and I'm not going—One second, sweetie. I have a call coming through. Can I put you on hold?"

"No, I need to make a few calls before I get to my next appointment. If I don't hear from you, though, I'll see you tonight?"

"I really do love you, Andrew Patrick Staley. Okay?"

"I know."

"Seriously. I do. Sometimes it's hard to show it, and I thank you for being patient. But I do love you, Drew."

And then, above a whisper, he replied, "But I think I love you more."

As he said the words and hung up, Betty allowed the phone to slide from her ear to her cheekbone. The utterance of those words from him twisted like a knife, for she knew they were true.

"Hello, this is Betty Staley. May I help . . ." And then, leaning away from the phone and raising her voice, she shouted, "Carol, they must have hung up. Do you know who it was by chance?"

"Sorry, I was unable to catch the voice . . . and he would not leave a name. He . . . he said he couldn't hold for long."

Hearing the tone of her assistant's voice, Betty asked, "Are you okay out there?"

Silence. Betty walked the five steps into the indigo reception area, which was a hair larger than her office, and asked, "What's wrong? You not feeling well?"

Her secretary raised her head, and the reddish hue around her nose told Betty everything she needed to know.

Carol was a soft-spoken woman who always extended her pinky when eating or drinking. Often when she spoke she would use the word "livid," and whenever she would say it, her eyes would roll upward, and her tongue would touch the roof of her mouth. But as she looked at her boss, this was not one of those times.

"What happened this time?"

Carol shook her head and then buried her nose and mouth in a Kleenex as she said, "Sorry I was late. I can come in a little early on Monday to make it up if you like."

"No, that's fine," Betty said, leaning away from the wall and standing straight. "These things happen." She looked at the clock on her secretary's desk, exhaled, and then said, "Do me a favor? Call to confirm that interview and then meet me in my office?"

Betty sat behind her desk, her spruce fingernail arched in a tepee, lightly touching her lips. "Bet, I'm sorry I'm late again. It's just that—"

"Carol, I don't mean to cut you off, but that's the least of my worries. I knew if you were late, it was something dramatic. I just wanted to say that I'm concerned about you and your welfare. Is there anything, and I am not just saying the words . . . I mean it. Is there anything I can do to help you in this situation?" Carol sat frozen as her bottom lip started to quiver. "If this is something you would rather not talk about, trust me when I say I understand. I'm not calling you back here because it's affecting your work, because it's not. You always get the job done, but whatever it is, is affecting you and I can see that," and then the tears dripped one by one like water from a melting sickle of ice. "You're important to me. In a sense, we're all we got to depend on, so I just want you to know that—"

"Son'bitch, put me out . . . again! This time over some he-said-she-said nonsense, and it's getting old. It's really getting old. It's my fucking con—" And then, shaking her head, she regained her silence and composure.

Betty waited before speaking, surprised at the language her reserved secretary was using. She leaned on the cracked armrest of her chair and asked slowly, "How long has this been going on?"

"Too long. I mean we met twenty years ago, and since then it's just been one thing after another. First I hear this talk about us being a couple, and then it's I need my freedom. I don't know if I'm coming or going sometime. One day it's let's fly to Hawaii to get married, and the very next day I'm getting smacked about trivial BS in *my* condo! In the past three years alone, Bet, I counted," she said as her white face contorted with anger, "and we've broken up five times. And now things are getting even more . . ." Her words faded as Betty noticed the beginning of a bruise on her cheek.

Speaking deliberately in an attempt to choose her words with caution, Betty asked, "Have you thought about counseling? Not for both of you. But to get some of your issues out?"

"Bet," she said with a sardonic smile as her boss saw her nostrils flare with disappointment, "I've had more counseling than that pilot on the Newhart show. I'm all for counseling, and I've been in therapy on and off most of my adult life. I know what my issues are, and I know why I keep going back. I'm on a crash course, and there's no way to get off of it. I love Pat," Carol continued, with the words showing even more in her eyes than in what she said. "The more I get involved, the more I get smacked, the more I want to leave. But the more I want to leave, the more I think no one else would want me. I mean, I'm no spring chick. I'm an old, fat redheaded lady living month to month on one income. I don't have a lot of people knocking down my door ya know. Anyway, I just went home for lunch today," she said, staring at the blue Kleenex in her hand as she spoke. "And I saw this strange shade of lipstick on a napkin in Pat's jacket. I asked about it, and all of a sudden I'm accused of snooping.

"As I was driving back to work, I remembered what Dr. Toni would say about women being attracted to abusive people. She said I was trying to change Pat because I could never change my dad. Said that's why I couldn't leave, and those words played over and over in my mind because I remember my mom once found a number in my father's pants pocket and he did the same thing. He accused her of snooping; he just never put his hands. . . ."

Betty closed her eyes as she heard her own personal horrors as a child being rekindled. In her mind, her mother and various men were still fighting, although she'd died in an automobile accident while Betty was in elementary school. Although the physical fights had ended, in her mind they continued to rage.

"Why is it so hard for me to leave? I mean, I'm heavy, but I'm okay to look at. Right? But I just can't break free." Carol took another tissue from her boss's floral tissue box and dabbed the corners of her eyes. "Was it tough for you to leave Evander?" she asked after a gentle blow.

Poker-faced, Betty swallowed and said, "No. I haven't seen him since the night I left his house."

"And see, that's what I want. I see how happy you are with Drew, and that's what I need in my life. I keep saying, If you can do it, I can, but I know in my heart, as soon as the dust settles, we'll be back together again."

As she spoke, Betty thought of the night she planned a surprise evening for the love of her life. How she thought she and Evander were close to making a lifelong commitment when she walked into his house, filled the tub with warm water, bubbles, oils, bath fizz, and peach Mexican long-stemmed rose petals. How she cued up their favorite CD and looked forward to whispering the words "That's the way love goes" into his ear as they danced alone. But as she fell asleep awaiting him, she was awakened by the syrupy voice, which had told her so many times that he loved her, telling a friend just how he'd taken advantage of her financially.

"So what do you think?"

"Well, the oldest saying in the world, Carol, is you get what you got, and if you think you deserve to be treated better," Betty said, as the words burned inside her chest, "I think you need to find what makes you happy."

And then both ladies sat quietly absorbing all that had been said until the phone rang.

Reaching over the mound of files, Carol took the receiver, gathered herself, and said in a high-pitched, melodic voice, "Thank you for calling Robinson-Staley, attorney at law. How may we help you? Yes. Yes. Sure, one second, please, sir." Betty pressed the hold button as Carol placed her hand over the receiver and whispered, "It's that guy calling back again. You want to talk to him, or would you like me to take a message?"

Betty smiled, took the receiver, and replied, "No. I'll talk to him," and then paused for Carol to leave the room.

"Okay," she said as she grunted like a pregnant woman and stood. "Well, thanks for everything, and I'll get on that deposition you need."

Betty smiled and remained silent until Carol left and the door closed.

"This is Betty Staley. May I help you?"

After a pause he said, "Hello, Beep."

Betty removed her glasses and placed them on a sepia law book as she gazed at her closed office door. Then, in a lower tone, she said, "I've asked you not to call me at the office."

"Where can I call you? You've changed the cell again, and when I call after hours, you don't answer anymore."

"Shouldn't that tell you something?"

"Ew, well, I was just calling to see how you've been. It's been a couple of weeks since the last time we spoke, and—"

"Evander, why are you doing this? I've got a business I'm trying to keep afloat, I'm married; I'm getting on with my life. Why do you insist on calling me?"

"Because."

"Because what!" Betty said, and then lowered her voice. "What do you mean, because? What kinda answer is that for a grown person."

"I know we had something special, Beeper, and no matter how much you try to tell me you don't care, I think you still have feelings for me. I could be wrong, but all I can say is it's been damn near a year now, and I still can't get you out of my mind."

"Fuck you, Evander! I don't even talk like this, but fuck you. How dare you even say something like that after what you did? Fuck you and everything that looks like you."

"I deserve that, Beep, so get it all out. I know you will never forget, nor should you, what I did, and you may never even forgive me. But no matter what you say, I can't help what I feel for you. You having me arrested won't change that. You cursing me out won't change that. Even you marrying ole dude won't change that. What I feel is just that. What I feel, and I can't help it. I made a mistake. A bad mistake. I fucked up, and maybe it's an unforgivable mistake. But Beep, I'd rather hear your voice cursing me out than to never hear your voice again." Betty held the phone with her eyes closed, wanting to hang up on him in mid-sentence but unable to will herself to do so. "Do you love him?"

"That's none of your business."

"Yes. The answer is yes, Betty. Yes, I love him with everything in my heart and soul. Yes, I love him more than life itself. Yes, I love him, Evander, more than I could *ever* have begun to love you. That's the answer, Betty. The answer is yes." The tears began to roll as Betty felt engulfed by the emotion and feared it would show in her voice. "Say it, Beep. Just tell me you love this man."

"Fuck you," she replied between clenched teeth.

"No. Not fuck you. Say yes." Betty's heart pounded as silence pierced the air, and then he said, "I know you better than you want me to, and I know what we had was real. No matter what happened. I know what I did was wrong. But how can true love be here today and gone tomorrow? How can you love something with all of your heart one year and not love it at all the next? Maybe it's just me, but sometimes I wonder if—"

Betty hung up the phone and balled her hand into a trembling fist as she brought it to her mouth.

Every time he called, she felt as if she were spread naked on the floor again. No matter how many self-help books she ingested or how much she prayed for relief from the pain, she could still hear his voice echoing words she could never forget. "Oh, I know she's making good money," he said that night, "because I checked out her bank statement. I don't play!"

Although she shared a sisterly love for Jacqui, talking to her only made it worse. Betty had such a different perspective on men. While Jacqui had been hurt before, Betty never thought she or anyone else could relate to being emotionally raped the way she was.

Marrying Drew was far from a solution. He was kind in so many ways and on paper would appear to be any woman's dream. He would never allow her to open a door, enjoyed giving her massages, and would often do small things like read to her as they sat in front of his fireplace and cuddled. But so did Evander when they met.

Her worst fear had fulfilled itself. No matter how much she denied the feeling, Betty knew that a part of her soul was still in the arms of the first man to whom she had ever uttered the words I love you.

Five minutes after hanging up the phone, Betty sat immobilized in her chair, with her face buried in the bend of her elbow. She had no idea what time a reporter from the university newspaper, who wanted to do an article on "Successful Female Attorneys," would arrive at her office. She didn't care if the little makeup she wore ended up on her blouse or if the pain from her heart could be heard through the thin walls of unit C.

Looking up as she heard her secretary's voice, Betty said, "I'm sorry, Carol, you say something?"

"Yeah. I was asking if you were all right?"

"Hello Mrs. Rob'son-Staley? Ah, how are you?"

"Just Staley is fine," Betty said, extending her hand for the collegiate reporter to be seated. "I trust you did not have a hard time finding us."

"No, not at all." As the large, bald student, who seemed to beat up rather than chew his gum, sat, he asked, "How long have you been in this location? I've passed this place a thousand times and never noticed you here before."

"I'm sorry," Betty said, returning to her seat behind the refurbished oak desk. "Your name is?"

"Oh, my bad—" he said, removing the wad of gum from his mouth and putting it in a piece of paper torn from his steno pad. Then, leaning to one side to retrieve a wrinkled, perspiration-stained business card from his back pocket, he replied, "Rodney Jerome. My name is Rodney Jerome Wright."

"Well, nice to meet you, Mr. Wright. Can we get you something to drink? Coffee, a soft drink possibly?"

"Actually, I got here about thirty minutes ago because this is on the bus route and I didn't know I would get here so fast. So I stopped at the Chinese-food place and had the buffet. You ever had it?"

Betty smiled at his youthful indulgence. "In answer to your initial question, we've been here a little over half a year. But before we go any further, I would like to clarify something. When the secretary called, he never indicated why I was selected for the interview. There must be a number of female alumnae in this town more deserving."

"I'm sorry. I thought you knew. We're doing a piece on female alumnae nationwide. Apparently, you won a large lawsuit against—I have it in my notes here somewhere," he said, searching the yellow Post-it notes attached to the lined green pages in his pad.

"Midway Railroad."

"Yeah, that's the one. They said they had wanted to do a story on you for a while and decided this would be as good a time as any."

"I see."

"But," Rodney said, crossing his legs and relaxing himself in the tight-fitting chair, "can I ask you a question, on a personal note? You know, brother to sister like?" Betty debated if she should allow him to proceed and decided to go along by shaking her head. "As a sister working for Murphy, Renfro and Collins did you ever think they brought you in because of your race or whatever?"

Betty leaned back in her chair and looked once again at the water spot on the ceiling tile above her, and all she said was, "No." No matter what she achieved in the past or what she would gain in the future, it always seemed to come down to her complexion.

"Oh, well," Rodney said as he uncrossed his legs and planted his elbows on his thighs, "you were working at Murphy, Renfro and whatever, and I'm sure you must have had, like, a mad, crazy expense account and budget and all, but you left to do your own thing. I'd imagine you don't have, like, all the frills or whatever at your disposal, but you're more than likely happier to be in control of your life. True?"

Betty smiled slightly and then looked at the back of the closed door as she pondered his words on such an uneventful day. Thinking about the financial situation in her business, the friction in her marriage, and the conversation with her ex, she looked at Rodney and said, "Yeah. Without a doubt, Mr. Wright, I'm happier now then I have ever been in my life."

Taking the scenic route home, Betty turned off the CD player and rolled down the windows of her vehicle. The chill was brisk in the air as the sun set in her rearview mirror, and she combed her fingers through what was left of her hairdo. And then she reached into her purse for her cellular phone and hit the number ONE on the keypad.

"Jacquetta's Restaurant, where Fridays it's the all-you-can-eat seafood buffet. May I help you?"

"So, they got you working phones, huh?"

"Please. I was just headed—Why the hell didn't you stop me before I said all that?"

" 'Cause I need to know what the specials are. Besides, I thought you were going to hire somebody last week? You still looking for a hostess, or are you too cheap to pay one? Minimum wage is a trip, huh, girl."

"Stop laughing. I interviewed one alright, but don't make me start talking about Mrs. Woman. I'm getting a headache as it is."

"What was wrong with her?"

"I had Monica interview her first, and she really liked her a lot. Told me she was a dancer. She used to work at Looking Kewl. You know; that store where if you need a pair of black or brown shoes they can order them, but if you want lime green or purple, they stock them in eight sizes?"

After laughing, Betty said, "You know I don't shop anywhere they have a 'buy a suit and get a free can of soup' sale. But back to your girl. You're not looking for a cook or a manager. You just need someone who knows how to carry themselves. If she was a dancer, seems she would be perfect."

"Betty? Dorothy Dandridge could dance. Gregory Hines, Savion . . . dancers. That bitch was a ho. How can you call what she does and what Lena Horne did dancing. Dancers dance on more than just tables. Are you with me?"

"You're cold."

"Not cold, just honest."

"Well, the reason I called is because I got a serious SOS today."

"Oh, shit. Who's stuck on stupid now?"

"A friend of mine referred this lady to me who would like to sue a research-and-development corporation. So the lady comes in, and she's in her late fifties, maybe. Very upper crust lady with a slight Australian accent. So we make a little small talk about antiques, because she is a collector also, and then she starts telling me about the case.

"She was with this company for twenty-four years, and she was coming up on her twenty-fifth anniversary. Well, in the past she would handle all the retirement and anniversary parties, but since it was for her, she made sure she spread the word verbally to everyone in the firm."

"Okayyy."

"So, the day of her anniversary comes, and nothing."

"Nothing?"

"Not one thing. No card, no letter, not even a 'how does it feel.' Her boss called her in the office and sat her down and told her he was going to have to increase the office size and needed her to train a new employee."

"Damn, that's cold? But is that why she's suing?"

"Wait a minute. Now she is major-league p.o.'d. She comes back from lunch and nothing. No one is even talking to her. Well, fifteen minutes before closing, she walks out of her office and notices that everyone is gone. So she is wondering if they're planning to surprise her or something, but they left no note.

"So now she has to close up by herself, which makes her late getting out of the office."

Laughing, Jacqui said, "Now see, that's jacked up, but she can't sue for—"

"Wait. So she's driving home, still burning hot about the entire day. What she had not realized is that one of the reps the previous week had made a copy of her house key, and they had called her kids and a lot of her friends and were planning to surprise her in her house. She had this dog she called Rudolph, and they had him dressed in a special little clown suit, even bought her a three-thousand-dollar gold watch and necklace.

"She gets home, and instead of coming in the front door, as they were expecting, she used the kitchen entrance. So they debate whether to surprise her in there and decide to just wait until she walked out of the kitchen.

"Well, girlfriend is in the kitchen going off on *everyone.*"

"I know she was." Jacqui laughed. "How many did she call a mother?"

"They are listening, and she was basically talking to Rudolph and cussing out the entire office. She told me, in her quiet little accented voice, that she called 'each and every one of them an asshole one by one!' So they wonder what is taking her so long, and they hear her slamming cabinets and all.

"So then she walks through the swinging living-room door, cuts on the light, they yell 'SUR-' "

"And she had a heart attack right on the spot?" Jacqui said.

"No, she wasn't that lucky. In retrospect, she may have wished she had a heart attack. She turned the light on, and the dog ran to her full speed, while she was standing there butt-naked, with peanut butter all over her crotch!"

"You made that up!" Jacqui said, howling on the other end of the phone.

"Girl, I wish. The dog buried his face in her, licking, and the office staff, who were waiting to say surprise, just stood there with their mouths open. I damn near wet myself. I told her she had a case but that I could not represent her. I gave her a few names of attorneys at Murphy, Renfro and Collins. When I walked her to the door, I was biting my cheek to stop laughing. Carol heard most of it and was just as red as she could be. As soon as the door closed, I walked straight to the bathroom."

"You know you wrong," Jacqui said. "So what are you guys up to tonight? Wanna come over and play some spades or bid whist?"

"You know Drew can't play no cards," Betty said as she dried her eyes. "What about domino—wait, I just remembered, he wanted to do something tonight, and he sent me—" And then she thought about the card, reached into the glove compartment, and saw a cream colored box wrapped with a crimson bow. "Ahh, he left me a present in the car. He must have gotten up early this morning."

"I know you not driving and talking on that cell phone again."

"Don't worry, Mom. I have it on hands-free mode," Betty said, and then put the earplug attached to her cell phone in her ear.

"So what is it?"

"Hold on, hold on," she said with an appreciative smile as she came to a red light. And then she retrieved the gift and released the tape on the side with her forefinger, which revealed pink-scented tissue paper.

"Come on, girl, what did he give you?"

"Okay, be patient. He gave me . . ." she replied as she opened the wrapping paper to reveal a pair of white cotton French-cuff panties. "He ah, oh, how sweet. He gave me a strand of pearls." And then she glanced at a note in the box that read:

> *No matter what I say . . .*
> *No matter what I do . . .*
> *Do not take . . .*
> *Me off of you!*
>
> > *Love,*
> > *Drew*

"Dag, that should earn him at least three suave points. Long or short?"

Betty's smile eclipsed as she looked at the string on the waist of the panties, and as the light turned green, she answered, "Short. So did Evan—I mean, Stefan get the job?"

"The Burdines campaign? No, they were looking for a guy about his age, but he thinks they gave it to an Hispanic model with a little more layout exposure."

"I'm sorry to hear that. He told Drew he had his heart set on that one."

"He did, and I don't know how he does it. He reads the trades daily, is always on a diet, and he's been turned down more than a hooker's bedspread, yet he still bounces back for more. But that business goes in cycles. Now all of the Hispanic and Greek guys are getting the good jobs, and then it'll swing back to the blond-haired blue eyes, then the chocolate brothers. When light-skinned brothers come back in style, he'll be set. So, do you think this little tryst is Drew's way of making up for the honeymoon, or is it just a late, late, late Valentine's gift?"

"I don't know. But like I told you before, there's no need for him to apologize for either. He had business that couldn't wait, and then, when we rescheduled, I was working on that Double Tree Hotel case, so it's no biggy. He feels bad about it, but we're both adults."

"Well, that was mighty Angela Davis of you, my strong sis-tah."

"I just got other priorities in life now. I guess a part of being married is looking at things in a different way."

"Well, excuse the hell out of me."

"I'm not talking about it like that. If we were dating or something, small things would set me off. But they don't now. I know he'll be there, so if he has to spend time with his mom or a few more hours at work, I don't go off."

"How is his mom, anyway?"

"Tripping. She used to call, or I would call her, and we would talk for hours, it seemed. But now if Drew's not home, she just says, 'Okay, 'bye'—click, end of conversation."

"Why do you think things are changing? Is it because you all are married now?"

"I don't think so. Drew said she wanted him to give me her wedding band at one time. I mean, she didn't make it to the wedding and all, but since then she's been nice. But all of a sudden she's become very distant. Some nights she's fine, but other nights she's scared to stay in the facility alone. I don't think they're mistreating her or anything. I think it's just her mind going bad. Anyway, you all got anything planned for the weekend?"

"We may go up to the cabin for a couple of days. Just to get away for a while. Why, you want to use it?"

"You know I work every Saturday. Some of us are not like you, Miss Jordan."

"Well, I just take time for me. The closer I get to forty, the more I pamper myself. I didn't tell you, but a few weeks ago, after the wedding, I just got in the car and went up there by myself."

"That's nice. I'm glad you got to get away for a while."

"Yup. I went up there and took the book we're reading this month, lit the fireplace, did an Iyanla. Child, I had to work on healing my-self."

"Good," Betty replied with a smile. "Maybe one weekend I'll go up there with you, and you can get me back into reading."

"I really wish you would so you can stop asking me, 'And then what happened? And then what happened?' " Jacqui said, mocking her friend's voice.

"You know I'm not that bad."

"Anywho. The book this month is very badly written, but it's a good story. It's by this brother out of Mississippi, and the book is set in Starkville. It's about—"

"Who's cheating on who?"

"No one yet, but—"

"Okay, who's scandalous? Who's gay? Who's a hoochie? Who's the girlfriend who always puts her hand on her hip, hates men, twists her neck, and tells it how it t-i-s-tis!"

"You're crazy," Jacqui said, laughing. "You know I read books other than those, anyway. Who started reading *Beloved* three times and couldn't finish it, and who finished it in a weekend? So hush. As I was saying before I was so rudely interrupted, this sister, who is a surgeon, meets this brother, who's a wealthy software designer."

"Yeah, all of my black friends who are surgeons meet millionaire software designers."

"*They* are getting married," Jacqui said, her voice rising, "and they plan this huge wedding, like somebody else I know who—"

"Okay, okay, just tell the story, please?"

"Well, he has this cough that will not clear up, and when he goes to get it checked, he finds out he has—"

"HIV?"

"No. AIDS. Well, initially, girl trips, but she gets checked out, and she doesn't have it. I'm at the point in the book where he's still invit-ing people to come to their wedding. But now she's having second, third, fourth, and fifth thoughts about going through with it."

"Why?"

Jacqui remained silent and then said, "I know you didn't just ask me why? Did you not hear anything I just told you?"

"He could have gotten the virus years ago. Before they even met."

"That's not the point. Girl in the book is successful, has worked

hard to be where she is, and she going to stick her neck in the guillo-
tine with her eyes wide open?"

"No, I'm not saying that, but if she loves him, if he is the one she
was ready to say forever and a day to and all that, how can she leave
him when he needs her the most?"

"How can she stay? I mean, in the book she worked two jobs to get
through Meharry. Had to deal with all the racism, sexism, and some
other isms I ain't even heard of when she graduated, and she's where
she always wanted to be in life. Now, can you imagine being with a
man you can never be intimate without protection? Can you imagine
always having that thought in your mind that he just might not have
gotten it from heterosexual sex? That he could possibly have an invisible life? Imagine what her life would be like when coughing is the
least of his problems healthwise. When he needs around-the-clock attention? What happens when he needs—"

"Somebody to love him?"

"Yeah, right. I'm not being cold. Just honest. But anyway, the title of
the book is *Emotions,* and it's good. Like I said, not well written but a
great story. I just hope he doesn't have some punk ending where
there is a cure for AIDS or it was misdiagnosed and everyone walks
into the sunset laughing happily ever after."

"I'm sure it'll be good. Well, sweetie," Betty said, cutting off the engine and allowing her SUV to coast into their driveway, "I'm home.
He wants to cook for me tonight, girl, so I have no idea what to expect."

"Other than food poisoning, what do you think he has in store for
you? If pearls are the appetizer," she said as Betty noticed a beam of
moonlight shining through the passenger-side window onto the
panties, "I can only imagine what the main course would be."

"I know," she replied, taking her present out of the box and sticking them in her purse and then tapping her nails on her aluminum
briefcase. "But we'll see."

After saying good-bye to her friend, Betty continued to sit in the
car and looked at the darkened house. Drew had never given her
such a gift in all the months they were a couple, and she wondered
what had prompted him to do so now.

Although they were both new homeowners, Betty rented her house
out until she could find a buyer for it. She moved into Drew's split-
level home with the oval, bevel-cut stained glass in the center of the

chestnut-red front door. In the mornings, the sunlight would cascade through the glass and leave a prism of sapphire blue, yellow, purple, and pinkish white in the foyer of their home as they ate together in the breakfast nook. An S-shaped path of blue stones, lined on both sides by perennials, led from the two-car driveway to the steps of the front door of the house at the end of seventy-first terrace.

While most of the homeowners in the area had landscapers who would visit their home bimonthly, Drew took the time on weekends to trim, resod, and pamper his lawn. In the center of the front yard was a one-hundred-year-old oak tree, and at its base was a circular flower bed, which was Betty's contribution to the landscape.

Betty opened the door of the vehicle and decided that she would leave her briefcase, since she doubted she'd get any work done. As soon as the 4-Runner's door closed, the front door to their home opened.

Drew looked up at the stars in the reddening skies like a ship's navigator and then smiled at his wife. "Welcome home, Mrs. Staley," he said, and rotated a glass of champagne in one hand as he leaned against the doorway in a white shirt and black tuxedo. "I've been expecting you."

"Oh, really?" she asked seductively. "And why might that be?"

"Well, I see you carrying the box, so you must be wearing its contents, and that's a good thing," he replied as she sauntered toward him.

"You think?"

As she walked into his arms, he said, "Yes, I think. And that's not just talk, talk, talk. So how was the rest of your day?"

"My day—" Then he kissed her on the neck. "Ahh, my day was—" Then he slid his tongue around to the front of her neck and caressed its softness.

"I can't hear you, honey," Drew's deep voice rumbled between tender touches. "How was your day?"

Breaking her trance and looking around, she said, "Honey, do we really want to let the neighbors see us like this?"

"So you want to get me behind closed doors, huh."

Pulling away from his embrace, she looked him in the eyes and said sensuously, "No. I just want to get you any way I can."

Once inside their home, Betty smelled the scent of Oceania scented potpourri, mixed with a soft, buttery aroma from the kitchen.

"So you really are cooking, huh? No fast-food containers out back or anything?"

"What did I tell you? I even left the office early to start on it."

"How sweet. What's the special occasion?" she asked as he handed her the champagne glass and she took a sip.

"You insult me, honey. Why do I need a special occasion to do something for my wife?"

Betty's smile flattened as for a moment the conversation with Evander crossed her mind.

"But if you must know, this is the ten-month anniversary of the day we met. I know I missed the other nine, but I thought, traditions must start somewhere. Why not here."

"That was . . . that . . . Wait a minute," Betty said, and glanced upward. "We met on the first. I remember because I was just opening the firm and was wondering . . . You sneak."

"Okay, I'm busted. I guess the special occasion is because"—he held her close enough so that she could smell the musk he was wearing—"the earth passes the sun once a year, the calendar changes every month, a new movie is out each week, and every day I love you just a little more. I thought that was reason enough to celebrate."

"How poetic. So tell me," she said, and caressed his shoulders. "Do you really mean what you said?" she asked, looking into one of his eyes and then the other.

"Of course I do. And one of these days you're going to believe me." After Betty smiled, Drew took her hands and led her into the dining room of their home.

The table was covered with a white laced linen tablecloth, and besides the dimly lit lights above them, there were two white-orange candles flickering in an otherwise darkened room. Each napkin was folded with precision over a single pink rose, and on one of the plates was a large gold-tone envelope.

"For me?" she asked with excitement in her voice.

"Of course," he answered, and pulled her chair back for her to be seated.

As he moved around to the other side of the intimate circular table that was void of the extensions, he said, "Open the envelope?"

"Not yet. I just want—" She held his large hands and squeezed his index fingers. "I just want to look at you."

"Thank you. I wanted to make tonight the most special night you have ever had. I just want everything to be—"

"Perfect," they said together.

"And it already is," Betty said as the voices in her head dissolved. "Believe me, it already is.'"

After small talk, Drew went into the kitchen and brought out the first silver-domed dish. As she tried to guess its contents, he disappeared and returned with another and another and yet a fourth. "My goodness, Drew, you really went all out."

"I don't play," he said as he opened his napkin with a snap of his wrist, which sounded like a whip, and then spread it on his lap as he sat down. "But first, open the card."

Betty took a moment to breathe in the sterling-silver silverware, the silver candelabra, and the crystal glassware she had no idea he owned. She looked at the small gray line of steam floating from the hole in the top of the food covers and the way her husband slowly laced his fingers into a fist and rested his chin on them as he watched her. Then she broke her trance, opened the envelope, and read it to herself. After she finished reading, she smiled, and then she looked down at her reflection in the square onyx plate because for a moment she could not look at him.

"I wanted to write you something special and . . . Well, I hope you understand the way I feel."

Running her fingers over the front of the card, Betty said, "You're extraordinary."

In a childlike tone Drew asked, "Read it to me?"

With a smile in her tone, she whispered, "Okay," and reopened the envelope.

> *If ever you should doubt my love,*
> *Just think of my eyes when I look at you.*
> *Hear my voice when I welcome you.*
> *See my smile when I feel you.*
> *If ever you should doubt my love,*
> *just think on these things*
> *and hold to these things,*
> *cling to these things.*

Because there are certain things we encounter,
like the scent of sunlight on a cold winter morning,
or the warmth of a newborn's very first breath
which cannot be put into words.
There are some things I will forever feel,
one being speechless, when I think of you.
That's if ever you should doubt my love.

As her eyes turned red, she ran her fingertips over it once again and then slowly returned it to the gold envelope. All she could say with a cracking voice was, "You wrote this?"

"Of course I did."

"I love you back."

Before eating, Betty excused herself and went to the guest bathroom, where she put on the panties he'd left in her truck. While they were snug, they felt comfortable, but she noticed the cotton in the seat felt different and was a little more dense than in most cotton underwear she had worn. "Oh, well," she said, and returned to the dinning room for part two of the enchanting evening.

Bitches Brew by Miles Davis softly played in the background as Drew peeled and hand-fed his wife an appetizer of steamed artichokes dipped in drawn butter. Then, after pouring another glass of their favorite champagne, he served her a gourmet salad of baby greens with crumbled Gorgonzola cheese, red grapes, and walnuts covered in a raspberry vinaigrette. For the main course Drew uncovered a large, steaming lobster tail broiled in herbed Dijon butter sauce, surrounded by wild rice, baby carrots, and sautéed spinach, with nuts and dried cranberries.

Although prepared and awaiting in the kitchen, the dessert never made it into the dining room. After her last bite of the lobster, Drew reached out for Betty's hand. And then, with a click of the remote, the sensual baritone voice of Teddy Pendergrass replaced the jazz.

As they danced, she slid her arms around his waist and could feel the deep, strong muscles of his lower back through his coat. Betty could feel the bulge of his biceps on her upper arm, and as she slowly rotated her hips on his thigh, he kissed her softly on her forehead. Feeling protected from the world, she laid her head on his chest and squeezed her body closer to his as if she never wanted to allow the moment to pass.

"I wanna love you all over, and over again,"

Teddy sang as Drew whispered sweet nothings in her ear and cupped his hands behind her shoulders. Then he asked, "Betty?"

"Yes?"

"I know you love me. I know it's hard for you to show it. But—"

"It's not so much that, because I—"

"Let me finish, sweetie. I'm just saying I know you've been hurt, but I will do whatever I can to earn your trust. I told you that on our wedding day, and I still mean it. I know you don't really believe I love you as much as I do. And I'm willing to be here for you until you understand that no matter what happens, I'm not leaving you. We are in this until death do us part, okay?"

"I know."

"Okay?"

"What I was going to say is—"

"Betty?"

"Yes?"

"Until death do us part. Okay?" With a soft kiss on her cheek, he continued, "For us to have the type of unconditional love we both want . . . both need, that's the only way to look at it. We're in this together . . . forever."

After a pause she said, "I love you so much, Drew. I really do."

Drew brought his lips close to Betty's, and then she started to kiss him, but he pulled back. The smell of his aftershave on his freshly shaved face released a sigh within her as she repeated the gesture, and again he moved his lips. With her eyes, she asked him, What are you doing? Then, with the tip of his tongue, he methodically licked the shape of her lips. Betty closed her eyes, and she could feel the love stirring in her pelvis. As she felt his desire to love her on her stomach, his tongue touched the flesh beneath her lips. And then, bringing his hands up to cradle her come-hither face, his lips met hers, at first softly, barely teasing the surface. Then he kissed her more passionately, grasping her shoulders and holding her firmly, but tenderly close.

"Tonight I'm in . . . a romantic mood."

Drew's kiss lingered, and he pulled free the bow of his red tie and allowed it to fall to the floor. Then he released his collar button, and as he did, Betty took the lead and brought her hands up to unbutton her blouse.

"Baby. I got you tonight. Okay? Let me"—he kissed her on the cheek—"have you?" Betty brought her hands down as Drew allowed his silk-lined jacket to slide off him and onto the floor. And then, as he kissed her again, he finished unbuttoning his shirt, removed his cuff links, tossed them in the corner, and took off his slacks and shoes. With her eyes closed, Betty could feel the heat generated from his large, completely nude frame next to her.

"Damn, baby," she whispered into his chest as her fingers slowly ran up and down the hairy trail of his abdomen. "Baby . . . I love you so much. I really do."

"Turn 'um off!"

Drew leaned over and blew out both candles, and the couple danced in the darkness of their oval-shaped dining room. "Tonight, baby," he said into her hair, "don't tell me you love me," and then he backed her slowly against the wall. Spreading his feet so that he could look at her eye to eye, he said, "Tonight, I just don't want to hear the words." Drew then kissed her on the side of the neck, and the kiss turned into a bite that made her flesh melt, her knees shake, and her teeth clench from pleasure. And then he whispered, "Tonight, Betty Anne Staley, I want to feel your love."

Drew's kiss returned to her neck as he unbuttoned her blouse and her bra. Her nipples, which craved attention, stood upward, and her fingers spread flat against the wall as her husband unloosened the snap in the back of her skirt and allowed her clothing to melt to the floor piece by piece.

And then Drew's kisses slid from her neck, past the fleshy valley of her collarbone, and down to her awaiting breast. Betty's heart-shaped lips owwww'd as he took his time to passionately love her all but nude body with his whole being.

Betty placed her hands on his shoulders as his tongue slid down her stomach, and he kissed her repeatedly on and around her navel.

"You like it like that?" Drew asked in response to her moans.

"Yesssss," she purred as her cat, Tickey, walked into the room and then scampered away. "I like it just like that."

Then Drew's kisses fell to her mound, and as his lips explored the front of his gift to her, Betty's hips stiffly gyrated toward him. As he pleasured himself, she felt her breath pull from her body, and for a moment it seemed as if gravity were only a concern for others in the world. He kissed her harder, and she swiveled more passionately. And then she put her thigh over his shoulder as Drew's kisses became more and more intense. As he moved his head from side to side, Betty slid her thumb under the string of the panties to free them, but without seeing her, Drew reached up and grabbed her wrist. The seat where she noticed the extra cotton was heating up as Drew stopped long enough to say, "Don't take them off," and continued on his mission to satisfy.

The libidinous love they shared was erotic as Drew carried his wife upstairs and through the French doors that led to their bedroom. As he stood with her in his arms, candles accented every area of their room. They were on the dresser, on the television, their reflection bouncing off the mirror of their master bathroom and surrounding their bed.

Betty ran her hands up and down the fine black hair of his thick forearms as she imagined his weight on her body. As she came to rest on the black satin sheets, he slowly straddled her body and asked, "You ready for me?"

"Yesssss."

Drew brought his lips closer to her body and slowly tasted her nipple. "Are you sure?"

"Positive," she answered as her thumb once again slid between her flesh and the string of the panties.

"No," he said with a smile, "do not take them off."

The wet seat of her panties was audible as she moaned and arched her back with pleasure. Her fists grabbed handfuls of the satin; her lower body ached with anticipation; she could feel her heart pounding, and her feet slid back and forth, pulling the fitted sheet away from the bare mattress. Drew reached back without breaking eye contact with his wife and massaged the soft, warm inside of her thigh as his hands became a megaphone through which her body screamed.

Repeatedly, he maneuvered his palming until the earth seemed to move and the sound of her sighs grew louder. And then, as her body yielded to his demands of it, he cupped her love with his hand to relieve the pressure and said, "That's right, baby. Don't tell me you love me tonight. Just keep showing me."

Chapter 5

O death, where is thy sting?
O grave, where is thy victory?

—New Testament
1 Cor. 15:54

Lightning flashed its echo through the curtains, and Drew lay awake, his mouth dry, eyes closed, feet cold, palms wet. The train-like fierceness of the rain sounded as if the heavens had ripped open and poured its contents on their home on the windy morning. Outside, the skies were broken by a circular pink-orange halogen streetlight and a small oak tree growing in their neighbor's yard. The earth was cleansing itself, but inside their room, tension swelled within his body.

The coals that burned inside of him subsided. Drew laid in the spoon position alone as he blindly felt for the warmth of her body. Opening his eyes, he noticed her once again nestled at the edge of the mattress and thought of the countless nights they had fallen asleep together, only to awaken apart.

When they made love, Drew felt as if he at times broke the boundaries of earth itself and all that mattered was in his arms. There bodies moved like a pleasant conversation, each movement rewarded with a reply, each sigh with a touch. The words I love you were never uttered when emotion blossomed into motion because it was in every kiss, every scratch, every breath, every beat of their hearts.

That night, Betty's lips brushed across his cheek and then under his chin. His fist tightened, he grabbed handfuls of sheet, and his eyes rolled upward. But now, as the thunder rumbled, their bodies had parted, and they both lay alone, in a king-sized bed, together.

Wearing his white silk pajama top, Drew sat up, slid off the sheets, and sat in his wife's antique rocker. He noticed how at peace she appeared as he sipped another glass of the flat champagne from the night before. He knew she had feelings for him, but the unknown is what kept him awake that morning.

As she slept, he watched the tranquil expression on her face, the curvature of her flaccid body, the way her exposed feet blissfully nestled each other, and the soft ebb of her occasional snore. As she slept, if there was a care in her heart, it was not expressed in the way she sought comfort by digging her head deeper into the coolness of her pillow.

No matter how physically close they were when they fell asleep, Drew noticed that when dawn broke, she'd be on the edge of the mattress. As he contemplated his—their—situation, his fingertip traveled the smooth lip of his emerald-tinted champagne glass, as what ifs rolled through his mind.

"Sleeping Bodies Don't Tell Tales." It was an article Drew read while riding the MARTA train when he was on business in Atlanta. As he thumbed through the tattered edition of *Psychology This Week,* the article beckoned his attention.

> Other than "Night Terror," where an individual will let out bloodcurdling screams or "Sleepwalk," one of the most misunderstood and underreported sleep disorders couples face is what we call "Edging."
>
> If a couple start out in the spooning or cuddling phase and one of them ends up clutching the far end of the bed, he or she is indicating through their subconscious that they are looking for separation. While not necessarily in the marital sense but possibly for some personal reasons.
>
> . . . Thus, the goal of the "NEP," or "Non-Edging Partner," must be to determine the rationale behind the gulf and seek resolutions immediately.

Drew remembered the article because he read it on the jostling, overcrowded subway. For him the separation was distinct, but he had no solution to the enigma. He tried to talk it out. He sat down with her to discuss the problem, but she felt everything was fine. He tried to resolve it with romance by scheduling a standing date night, but it was thwarted by her late hours at work or his obligations to his mother.

Before giving her the ring, she was his friend. His best friend. They would drive to Disney on the spur of the moment and enjoy Space Mountain or buy a couple of disposable cameras and enjoy the sights of Sea World. She would leave him gag gifts in his car she'd bought from Spencers, and he would brush her hair past midnight as she sat between his legs and read erotic poetry. When they were "dating," in the middle of the night, before drifting off to sleep, she would talk of how she wished she could one day take a sculpting class and how she wanted to learn to speak French as well as he could.

But then the friendship tag became fiancé, dating plans evolved into matrimonial arrangements, and in his mind, would you like to*s*? turned into future I *do*s.

While Drew asked her several times afterward if she wanted to delay the nuptials, Betty's pat answer was "No." A week after they announced it to their friends, Betty scheduled a gown fitting. Before he knew it, she had ordered the flowers, reserved the church, drawn up a list of possible musicians, and was discussing menus with Jacqui. There was never a point at which he thought of backing out, but he wanted to make sure she was as interested in the marriage as she was in the wedding.

When Drew told his mother of their plans, she wept and then held his face close to hers. Although she was affected by Parkinson's disease, she ran her frail hands rigidly over his face and shoulders and told him how proud his father would be of him at that moment.

After the pressure of the wedding passed, Drew assumed things would change, but the divide increased. The afternoon calls to his office to find out how he was doing had come to an abrupt end. The Sunday morning "Let's just go for a walk" or "What about a picnic after church?" discussions were replaced with "Not today, I have a deadline" or, simply, "I can't," with no other excuse attached.

As she slept, Drew wondered if this was as good as it could be in their relationship. Was he expecting a Huxtable marriage in a Bundy world? As Betty stretched her body and inched closer to the edge of the bed, he eased out of the rocker, picked up the champagne bottle, half-filled his glass with its contents, and then, still half-awake, walked toward the door. When he crossed the threshold of the room, Betty, her voice masked by sleep, asked, "Drew? . . . Drew, is that you?"

He did not answer and continued down the hallway toward his personal domain.

"Drew, honey?" She yawned. "Where are you?"

"G'morning," Betty said, stretching her arms crucifix-like, her fist balled as she approached him. Then she smiled at him from across the room and opened her hand, which contained the panties he'd given her, looped around her finger.

"So where did you get these magic panties?"

"French Attraction," he droned.

Getting closer to him, she said, "Nice touch. I never knew just how warm things could get. So," she said as she dropped the gift from him in his lap and then readied herself to sit on his thigh, "why're you up so early?"

"Couldn't sleep."

"After last night? You couldn't sleep?" she asked as she sat on his lap and buried her head in his chest. As she did, Drew did not break eye contact with the ESPN reporter on television, nor did he move his hand from the arm rest. "If you are not still asleep, I must be slipping, huh?" Drew remained silent. Then she looked at him and asked as she rubbed her nose against his, "How are you this morning, Monsieur Sta-lee?"

"Fine. Did you sleep well?"

"I slept." Then she noticed the empty champagne bottle on the end table. "I slept fine. How long have you been up?"

"Since about five."

"What time did we go to sleep?"

"It was late," he mumbled. "Just didn't feel sleepy."

"*Umm.* So what's on the agenda for today besides the yard work?"

"Not a lot, I guess," he said, refocusing on the television. "Just going to watch the Knicks game this afternoon and then go work out with Stefan."

Betty looked at the television set as she moved her head from side to side on his hairy chest. Then the blond reporter with a gleam in her eye said, "And from the Who-would-ov-thunk-it files, after only six months together, one of today's hottest couples, Laker point guard

Cameron Carson and supermodel T'shay Tsi are calling it quits! According to their publicist, the separation is said to be amicable, and there was no prenuptial agreement in place."

"Man," Betty said, snuggling closer to the warmth of her husband, "are people getting married today just to register for gifts?"

"It seems," he muttered.

After a reflective pause, she stood and said, "Let me see if I can remember the word. What would you like for . . . *déjeuner?* Is that right?"

"If you mean breakfast, it's *petit déjeuner.*"

"That reminds me," she said, standing in front of him still nude as he watched the NBA scores. "You used to speak to me in French when we made love. What was that phrase? Something like, *ramoner cheminée?* Is that close?"

Putting his hands on her thigh as he guided her back to his lap, he looked up at her and said softly, "Yeah, that's it."

"Honey, I wish I could, but I can't," she said as she stood up. "It's about twenty 'til, and I wanted to be in the office at seven." Then she ran her fingers through her hair and said, "I know my hair is too through. Sweetie, don't ever let me sleep without putting anything on my head. Not unless you want to wake up next to a werewolf." Betty bent over, pulled his lips closer to hers, and kissed him softly; he returned the kiss without closing his eyes.

"Do you think we will be married forever?" he bluntly asked as he looked her in the eyes for the first time that morning.

Softly allowing her knee-jerk response to come out as only a puff of air and not a word, Betty replied, "Honey, not now. Okay?"

"What do you mean, not now?"

She leaned away from him.

"It's a simple question, Betty. I mean, when I hear about the divorce rates being what? Seventy-five percent or whatever, I get concerned."

Betty placed her hands on her hips and then allowed her arms to cross as she pondered her answer. Then she turned to leave the room.

"Betty, that's not the answer," he shouted, and then took a last sip from his glass. "Walking away will not make it better."

Betty slowed, then stopped, and turned toward her husband. "Drew, I'm not ready to have this discussion. Respect that, okay? I just wanted to come in here and say thank you for—"

"Respect what? Why does it have to be done when you want it done?"

"What are you talking about?" she asked, her hands once again on her hips.

"Why do we—" And then he caught himself, lowered his voice, and said, "Why do we avoid having this conversation? Why is it never resolved?"

Betty turned to leave once again and then held her head down and sat on the couch on the opposite side of the room. Seeing a T-shirt he'd left on the floor, she put it on. "Drew, whenever you drink, you want to question the relationship. And to be honest, I just don't want to talk to you in this condition. And that's what I mean by you ought to respect that."

"I've been in a lot of relationships in my life," he replied as he held the empty glass in his hand and slouched in the chair, "but never one like this."

"And what is that suppose to mean?"

"Never one where one person loved the other and she did not believe it and I loved her and she didn't—Well, you know what I mean."

Betty looked at the television set to avoid his eyes and then said, "What that means to me, Drew, is we need more time. Just like you said the night before you proposed. I mean we've both been hurt, we are both vulnerable and, I guess, sensitive about certain things. But we just need to let it happen naturally."

As she looked away, Drew fixed his eyes on her, cleared his voice, and said, "So it has nothing to do with Evander?"

Betty gazed at him and said, "Drew, why would you go there? Why would you bring his name up to—"

"Maybe because when I passed your office today I saw him in the parking lot."

"You what?"

"Yeah. And I was hoping you would tell me about it, but obviously it wasn't important enough to—"

"I didn't tell you about it because I didn't know—Wait a minute. Why am I explaining myself to you? And how do you know what he looks like, anyway?"

"Pictures, Betty. You still have his pictures in those boxes in the garage. But that's not the point," he said as she stood and walked away. "The point is, you didn't tell me!"

"No, Drew. The point is you spied on me! That you accused me, and the point is that I'm not your child, I'm your wife, and if you want to know something, you ask me!"

As she left the room, he said, "So that's how it is now, huh? Huh?" he screamed louder. "So we keeping secrets now, huh?"

Betty came out of the room with underwear on, still wearing his T-shirt. And then she walked rapidly down the hallway toward the stairs, putting one leg in her pants and then the other, her earth-toned poncho draped over her shoulder. "I know you hear me!" he shouted as her footsteps diminished down the carpeted stairway.

"Were you or were you not going to tell me? Or was I going to have to find out on my own!" Drew heard the half-jingle of her keys being ripped from the hook on the wall. "All you had to say was Drew, I saw Evander to—" And then the door slammed and apart from its echo and the SportCenter reporter, the house was silent.

Drew picked up the remote, dropped his glass, which landed on top of her panties on the carpet, and closed his eyes to erase the pain. Then in earshot of no one else, his face fell into his hands, and he mumbled the word, "Damn."

Dressed in a navy T-shirt, faded jeans, and tweed sport coat, Drew placed a full cup of hot black coffee in the cup holder of his car. As he drove, he would occasionally bring the stiff, aromatic brew up to his nose as if the pungent smell of caffeinated vanilla beans would pull him back to his center.

There was stubble on his chin, since he had not shaved, but that was the least of his concerns.

Then he returned the cup to the holder, put his cellular ear plug in his ear and called Stefan.

"What's up, man?"

"Yo, wussup, player? I'm just handling things. We still gonna do this at four, right?"

"No," Drew replied as he brought the coffee cup back to his lips for another sip. "That's why I'm calling. I need to go out to the nursing home, so I can't work out today."

"Everything ah'ight?"

"Everything's fine. I was supposed to talk to the administrator yesterday, but a few things came up, and I just remembered I rescheduled for today."

"Okay, well, that's cool. I need to head over there, anyway. My agent may be able to get me some runway work in South Beach, so I need all the gym time I can get."

"Well, that's good. Sounds like things are moving since the Burdines job fell through?"

"It's going. I know at this stage in the game I'll only get so much work, but I have an advantage over females. Once they hit twenty-five, man, if they haven't hit it, they can just forget it."

"So I've heard."

"It's a rough game, but it's the only game I know. Speaking of games," he said as his voice brightened, "did you hear about ole boy?"

"Who?"

"Bear."

"Yeah. I was watching that this morning on ESPN. They found his wife and a sister in a car, right?"

"Yeah. You know he doesn't live too far from you all. He was up in Vegas and called the cops when he couldn't find his wife. But then after that they found the bodies in his car. The kid who shot them put the gun under the seat and was riding around with them in the trunk. Can you believe that shit?"

"I heard about the last part. The news said it was something like a carjacking that went bad."

"I know, and the kid was only fourteen years old. They'll probably plead out and then get him in a juvy home for a few years and he'll be out in four."

"Yeah, that's justice, I guess."

"Yo, before you hang up, man. Dig this. Wussup with you and Betty?"

"Nothing. Why?" Drew asked, his hand over the top of the still-hot half-cup of coffee.

"Well, you know how they talk, man, and she came in the restaurant first thing this morning while we were having breakfast. As soon as I saw her, I knew I should give them some space, and then she just lost it."

"Lost it how?"

"She wasn't crying, but she was pissed. Like I said, I don't know what was said, but I knew something went down this morning or last night."

"We had a few words," Drew said, pulling into the nursing-home parking lot. "But it wasn't that big a deal."

"Well, you know me, man, and I ain't the one to be giving nobody no advice on no women. But let me say this and I'm through with it. She's a good girl, man. I mean that. I'm a few years older than you, and I can tell you, you got yourself a good woman."

"I know. We have issues like any other couple, but I'm not letting her go. You can believe that."

"Drew?"

"What?"

"Listen to me, man. The woman loves you. I haven't known you that long, but I can tell she loves you by the way she talks about you when you're not around. She always defends you no matter what, and that's important. I know her ole boy done her wrong, and I've known that nigga for years, and he ain't never been shit. But that's just how he is. I couldn't believe it when Jac told me they were even together."

"Well, like I said," Drew replied after emptying his coffee cup and coming to a stop in the parking space. "We have our problems, but we'll work them out."

"Cool. I hate to butt in, but you know we ain't got nothing but love for you and Betty."

"We as in you?" he said, and cut off his car's engine. "Or we as in you and Jacqui?"

"Jac's cool. Don't believe the hype with her. But that's just the way she is. Those two are tighter than a frog's ass in a cold pond, and I respect that. I know I'm number one in her heart, and I know one day we'll be together. No matter how many times we break up, there is no doubt in my mind about that. But I also know I'll never be her number-one friend."

"Well, player, I'll try to get to the gym later. I'm at the home now."

"Okay, cool. But dig this. Like I said, man, I hope you don't mind me all up in your business."

"No," and before saying good-bye, Drew added, "Actually I appreciate it. Thanks."

Drew removed the ear plug, folded his flip phone, put them in the inside pocket of his sport coat, and looked at the kelly-green building on the hill.

* * *

The architects designed Parkside Nursing and Rehabilitation to look smaller on the outside than it appeared when one walked through the doors. The exterior featured lush grass surrounding a rippling pond where ducks and an occasional bullfrog would appear. Inside, the state-of-the-art building was described in the newspaper as the most contemporary nursing facility in the Southeast, housing over three hundred "citizens." The walls were painted in a sedated shade of green, and the whitewashed wooden floors were immaculately swept.

Apart from the astringent scent of ammonia in the air, the atrium, with its open fireplace, big-screen TV, and pool table, looked like a country club for retirees.

Several citizens of different ethnicity stood around two men playing chess. "You don't know nufin' 'bout tat, boy!" said one of the men to the other, who was pondering his next move. "This ain't checkers. This is the sport of kings!"

As Drew stepped to the reception desk and asked for Dr. McBride, he noticed a couple sitting under an artificial plant in the corner. She was dressed in shades of blue: powder-blue eye shadow, a shiny navy strapless purse on her lap, and a sky-blue tattered bow on the buckle of her shoe. Her alabaster complexion showed deep grooves of age, and as she continuously smiled, crow's-feet appeared around her eyes. Then Drew noticed that she would from time to time whisper in his ear, which would cause him to burst out in laughter that rumbled like a hurricane. He would hold his ebony face back and put his thick hands on his jostling belly, which allowed the joy to push beyond his convulsing shoulders and then leap from his body.

As the gentleman laughed, she would pat him on the thigh as if she were chastising him, but it was evident from her eyes that she loved every moment of it.

"Hello? Mr. Staley."

"Hi," he said, diverting his attention just as the older lady caught him looking at them. "Dr. McBride?"

"Nice to meet you, sir," the young blond administrator, her shoulder-length hair pulled behind one ear, said. "Right this way," she replied, and walked toward her glass-enclosed office as he followed.

"So, Mr. Staley, thank you for coming in. Sorry to bother you like this, but I thought you should be aware of a few things regarding your mother."

"No problem. Thanks for calling me."

"You're welcome." Then she put on the reading glasses she looked much too young to wear and picked up the two-inch-thick file.

"Mrs. Staley has been with us a little over a year, and don't get me wrong, we really enjoy her being here. Up until recently she's been very active in all—"

"Up until recently?"

"She's been active in all of our activities," the administrator finished. "I don't think there is a nurse on her floor she has not knitted something for. And yes, sir, that's why I called you in. For the last couple of weeks we have really started noticing a change. I know she has a lot on her mind at this time, but she has become a little, well, a little belligerent at night. Which I might add is understandable considering—"

"What do you mean?"

"Well, I know that's a harsh word, but she's been a little difficult to work with. There is a record of her hitting one of the candy stripers, and last night, after about ten-thirty, we had to have the guys physically bring her back into the facility."

After a pause he said, "I noticed that she doesn't want me to leave most nights."

"Yes, that was notated in her charts. We can appreciate your doing whatever you have to do to make her happy, but we are also cognizant of the fact that you can't be here at all times, and in this facility, if patients are too hard to handle, then we are forced to look at alternatives."

"No, I understand."

"You have spent quite a few nights out here," she continued, tilting her head up to look through the bifocal portion of her glasses. "Apparently you were here at least twelve nights last month alone. Aren't you a newlywed?"

"It was rough, but—"

"I know you don't have any siblings, but does she have any other relatives that could maybe assist you a little?"

"I'm all she has," he said, looking at his clasped hands in his lap and then crossing his legs. "My—I mean, her sister and brother died a while back, and my father died ten years ago in November."

"Wasn't she married to one of the residents here at one time?"

"Mr. Douglass, and yes. He lived in our neighborhood, and they got married before she moved here."

"And he died," she said, looking again at the records, "in February?"

"Yes."

"Did you have any siblings?"

"A sister. Her name was Nikki, and she was killed on her bike by a drunk driver."

"I see," she murmured reflectively. "Do you remember what month she died?"

"No, why?" And then he said, "Yes, I do. She died two weeks before Thanksgiving. I remember because we didn't have Thanksgiving that year."

"And your natural father died in November, you said?" Drew just shook his head. "Have you ever noticed that most older people die in the winter? And that people tend to slip away early in the morning? If you couple that with the fact that you got married in January, it sounds like she may be experiencing heightened Seasonal Depressive Disorder. It's almost like a tree that starts to shed itself each winter and a part of her is sorta shedding as well and it affects her more and more each year."

"So what do we do besides medicating her, which I am totally against."

Leaning forward in the chair large enough for another person her size to sit on, the administrator said, "We could possibly do some counseling. But at her age therapy could be rough, and trust me, I understand your dilemma." Then she removed her glasses and pushed her hair from her face with her spread thumb and forefinger. "My dad was ninety-seven when he passed last year. Had six kids. Five boys, whom he referred to as his five all-Americans, since they were good in sports. And me.

"But when he got sick, who was there for him?" she asked rhetorically as Drew looked at the photograph of the elderly man, who was as thin as six o'clock, holding a fish with pride.

"So I quit my practice in New Hampshire and moved down here to help him the last three years of his life. In the last few years, he was very incoherent, and it got to the point where nothing he said made sense. But I was always there for him. The day he died, within hours all of his sons were in the house, and I swear it seemed as if they were pillageing, they were taking things out so fast. So I left, never looked back, and they settled his affairs. My husband at the time wanted me to attend the funeral, but I didn't. At that point he belonged to them. I let them take care of all of his personal affairs, sell the property, you name it." And then she composed herself and pushed her hair behind her ear again. "But you know something, I never felt bad about walking away once he died because I had the memories inside of me from when he was alive. And that is something no one could ever take away from me."

Looking at Drew across her desk, she said, "I've said all of that to say this. One of the nurses told me you were late to your wedding the day it was raining and we could not find your mother."

"I know, but everything worked out."

"But you didn't go on a honeymoon, right?"

"Yeah, I know." In a diminished tone he said, "I told my wife I had business, but Mom was really acting strange then, so I knew I couldn't leave."

"It's tough on relationships when you have a situation like this. It's hard for people to understand unless they have been through it. Watching, in my case, a man who was the CEO of a corporation fall so deep into dementia that he starts calling you Mom and speaks only in Russian again like he did when he was five years old," she said, shaking her head. "But all I can say is, you will never regret what you do for your"—her phone buzzed—"mother when she is gone. One second, please."

As she spoke on the phone, Drew looked behind her desk. The only photos on the credenza beside the one of her father were photos of her and her pit-bull with a blue bandanna around its neck.

"I need to step into the conference room for a hot second," Dr. McBride said. "I would like to talk to you about one other pressing matter before I let you go, okay?"

"No problem," he said, and as soon as the door closed, he pressed ONE and SEND on his cellular phone.

"Robinson-Staley, attorney at law, may I help you?"

"Hey," he said as if the words were attached to a string and yanked from his chest. "What are you up to?"

After a pause, Betty replied softly, "Nothing much."

"Did I catch you at a bad time?"

In a voice void of interest, she replied, "Just doing some research."

"I just called," he said as he gazed at the interracial couple feeding each other popcorn and laughing, as they were moments earlier. And as the older man placed his four-fingered hand on his wife's thigh, Drew said, "I just called to say . . ." Then his words faded as he closed his eyes.

"To say what?"

"Don't know."

"You don't know why you called."

Silence.

"No," he said as the apology was swallowed by his stubborn throat. "What time will you be home?"

"I don't know."

Drew looked at the couple again and said, "I just called to say I'm sorry. But it hurt me to see him sitting in the car, and I can't lie and say I didn't care."

"Drew, you've got to trust me, and I've got to trust you. No, I did not see Evander yesterday. No, I have not seen Evander in almost a year. Yes, if I had seen him, I more than likely would have told you."

"So there's nothing at all for Evander? Nothing at all?"

"I said, 'I do,' to you!" Lowering her voice, she asked, "Why would you ask me that?"

"Because I want to know!" Then Drew inhaled breath he could not exhale and said, "Im sorry. Because I would like to know."

"You are the most important person in the world to me. I know you like hearing those words, but I'm trying to show you how I feel."

"I needed to hear that," he whispered as Dr. McBride reentered the office. "I'll see you later on tonight. Okay?"

"I love you."

"I love you more," he said as he smiled into the phone.

After returning his cellular to his coat pocket, Dr. McBride walked over to her filing cabinet and opened the top drawer. Unable to locate what she was looking for, she slammed it closed and looked in the next one. "Damn," she said quietly as she tossed her hair from her face. As she looked in the bottom drawer, she asked, "Have you all made a date with Dr. Rendell?"

"Rendell?"

"So," she asked as she walked over to her desk and sat on the corner, "you guys still considering not doing it?" Drew could feel his heart beat hot and heavy in his throat. "I'm talking about the chem—"

His breath paused momentarily, and then he asked, "What were you going to say? Chemotherapy?"

Dead air.

"She never told you about it. I'm so sorry, Mr. Staley. I just assumed—" she said as Drew leaned back in his chair. "I spoke to her last week and told her she should share this with you."

"You saying my mom has . . ."

Dr. McBride's mouth opened as her head fell and her golden locks covered her face. "Yes. It was diagnosed a few days before your wedding, which is why she reacted the way she—Mr. Staley, once again, sir, I'm sorry you had to find out this way."

The colors of the nursing facility faded to blue and gray as he asked, "Is Mom in her room?"

"Well, well, well," the medium-height lady, dressed from head to toe, said as she lay on top of her freshly made bed. The rolling hum of the humidifier in the corner cleansed the menthol from the air in the floral wallpapered room.

Mrs. Staley's room displayed miniature antique pieces she treasured and would not allow to be sold at the estate sale. She had two full-sized dressers filled with neatly pressed and folded clothing. She had one dresser for her tops, scarfs, and other accessories and another for her slacks, jeans, socks, and stockings.

Her bed was covered with a colorful patchwork quilt that had been a part of the Williams family for four generations, and the goose-down pillow Drew's father used to sleep on each night was beneath her head.

She wore a yellow cotton track suit with red piping, an emerald-green Florida A&M sun visor, and her wine-colored nails were freshly manicured. Her initial expression of surprise evolved into a full smile; the effects of Parkinson's disease showed more in her left side than her right and was clearly evident in her outstretched hand.

Holding her son's hand, she said, "I wasn't expecting you here this early."

Drew managed a stifled smile and then found a chair. "So, *umm*, how are you feeling this morning?"

"I'm fine. Some good days, and sometimes I'm just dazed." Then she looked at her son, and her smile withered. "They told you, didn't they."

"Told me what?"

"Boy, you could never play cards." Then she put the sports section of the paper down and said, "McBride told you, didn't she?" Drew lowered his shoulders as he shook his head no. "I told that heifer that I would tell you!"

"I . . . I," he stammered, not knowing what to say.

"Yeah, I know. But don't worry about me. That's why I didn't tell you, and actually," she said, turning the channel with the remote, "I didn't want anyone else to know yet. I can't deal with a lot of confusion, and I know you got a life to live as well."

"I can't believe you didn't tell me about it," he whispered.

Propping her upper body on her elbows as her foot started to shake, she replied, "Honey, your sister was taken from me as a baby. Your father and Mr. Douglass were taken from me. And now I can't even control my own body. I know not telling you was selfish, and I'm sorry about that, but I gotta control something. I decided that I would leave the way I wanted to leave." Looking down at his pants as she tried to rub the shakes out of her quivering hand, she said, "How long you had them jeans, boy?"

"What about chemo?"

"What about it? Like I just said. The doctors won't decide how I deal with this. Only me. And to be honest, I don't know if I want to go through that mess. I remember taking your old girlfriend—What's her name?"

"Felicia."

"Yeah, Lecia. I used to take her down there, and I don't know if I'm ready to go through all of that treatment mess."

"But Momma. You got cancer?"

"Actually they thought I just had something in my breast. I found out about that a little after Christmas, and then—"

"And you didn't tell me?"

"Why? You were planning your marriage. You were starting your life. What good would that have done. After the holidays I decided I would have a mastectomy." Looking out the window, she said, "And that was tough. Even at my age that was tough. But I thought if it could save my life, what the hell. Well, around about the time of your wedding they say to me, 'Mrs. Staley? We will not have to do the surgery.' Then they said, 'Because this thing is galloping in your system, and we found two lesions.'" She clenched the sheet in her fist as if she were trying to will the words beyond her flesh. " 'Mrs. Staley, you have two lesions in your brain.' " And then her chest fell.

Drew's chin lay flat against his chest. "So this is why I didn't want you to know. I wanted to give you more time. Or maybe I wanted to give me more time. I don't know anymore. When they told me I had that thing, I laughed at them. I told him he was out of his gad-damn mind. But then it got to the point where it was literally all I thought about. All day long, death. All night long, death. That's why I wanted you to stay out here, because when I talk to you, sometimes I would forget about dying. But as soon as you left, the first thought in my head, every breath I took . . .

"Anyway. I thought about your girlfriend. I mean, your old girl-friend, Lecia. I remember her telling me one night that everything changed after she told people she had, she had, it. She thought that she would feel relieved, but she didn't. She felt worse.

"People looked at her like she had the plague or something. Her dad came to visit her once and was washing her plate and spoons with bleach because he was afraid that some forms of 'it' were contagious.

"When her friends would say good-bye, she said, they didn't know how to end the conversation. Have a nice day? Take care? See ya," Mrs. Staley said as she looked into nothingness.

"So I guess that's why I'm on the fence about the chemo. I'm think-ing it may be better to live like I am now for a few months than to live a few years fighting uphill."

Raising his head, Drew said, "Momma?"

"Yes, Drew, I have cancer. And you know something," she said as her hand shook faster against her thigh. "That's the first time that sentence has crossed my lips. But now that I've said it and now that we know I'm gonna die, what do we do?" And then she looked down at her hand, still shivering by her side. "Now that you know, what can you do?"

Chapter 6

We boil at different degrees
—Ralph Waldo Emerson
Society and Solitude: Eloquence

"Miss Jordan," the young lady said with only her head in the door, "there's a man on line three named Stefan to talk to you?"

Jacqui, who was still on the phone speaking to a wholesaler, said, "Tell him I will be with him in a minute," and then returned her attention to the business call.

Jacquetta's, in a span of less than ten years, had become the premier place to dine in north-central Florida. A pianist played a white baby grand in the center of the main dining area, and the air was scented with raspberry vinegar and baked goods.

Jacqui's private office had a postmodern motif, and in the corner was a black-and-red alligator golf bag from when she was serious about the game.

"B. Smith Meets Spago" was the title of the five-star review posted behind her desk and duplicated throughout the restaurant. In her office, the walls were adorned by plaques and photographs. There was one with her and U.S. senator Graham and another taken at a book signing she hosted in her establishment for her favorite author, E. Lynn Harris.

On the credenza behind the desk was a small vase filled with scented oils that slow-burned throughout the day. Although she was not a traditional believer in aroma therapy, Jacqui would often fill her chest with the ananya fragrance to reduce the tension of running what was referred to in *Black Enterprise* magazine as one of the top-ten African-American success stories in the country.

Speaking on the phone as she blindly doodled, Jacqui also listened to the white palm-sized monitor on her desk. Her restaurant was built on simple principles, so she wanted to hear how each and every patron was greeted when they walked through the door. While she had not done so in years, she had been known to tear up time cards if a customer was forced to wait for service or treated harshly. Her rules were tough and unyielding. Some former employees even said they were unfair. But word of mouth had made the restaurant the dream she'd worked her entire life to realize, and nothing was going to take it away.

"Hey, sweetie," she said after hitting the blinking light on her phone.

"Wussup? How long were you gonna keep me on hold?"

"Don't start," she said with a smile. "That was Katrice."

"So you hired the white girl, after all?"

"Yeah, I know. But she's cool."

"Is that the one who was a dancer or something?"

"One and the same. And," she said, lowering her voice and placing her elbows on her desk, "she wears these thong underwear, too. You know how you Negroes are about seeing a woman in a sundress with a thong on."

"Oh, so that's why you hired her? So she could have the guys following her to their tables with their tongues hanging?"

"No, that would be wrong. Even if business is up five percent over last year this time, but who's counting. So, what's going on with you?"

"I was listening to the news, and apparently the Police Department has released that kid for murdering Bear's wife."

"No, really? Who they think did it not—"

"Yup, Bear."

"Damn. Here we go. It's going to be O.J. all over again? Well, anything else going on?"

"Nothing much. Well, yeah, there is something."

"What? Spill it."

"I got a call from Artie this morning."

"Was it a 'you better sit down,' call?"

"Well, the guy who got the Burdines campaign can't do it. He has to go to—"

"They giving it to you?"

"Well, not exactly."

"What do you mean? Are you up for consideration?"

"No. See, I'm not up for consideration, and they are not giving it to me because they gave it to me an hour ago. I got the shoot."

"You got the shoot?"

"I got the shoot!"

"I'm so happy for you! This is going to look great in your portfolio!" Jacqui said as she turned the volume down on the restaurant monitor.

"And my checking account. To be honest, I was actually almost ready to give up."

"Not you. Not Mr. This-is-what-I-do-and-I'll-do-it-till-I-die DeCoursey."

"I did not say ready, just almost. It's just getting to the point where it's harder and harder to keep the weight off, and I need some dividends coming in. So I considered, for a New York minute, giving it all up and finding a career-type job."

"Doing what?"

"Opening a restaurant slash Internet hangout across the street from Jacquetta's. See, I don't know nothing about that Web stuff, but my thing is this. If you take any two things people like and combine—"

"Seriously," Jacqui said, her lips straight. "If modeling did not work out, what would you be doing?"

"Doing whatever."

"What did you want to do when you were twelve years old?"

"Honestly? I wanted to be an actor or a model. I wanted to be Richard Roundtree or Ron O'Neal. I wanted to—"

"Other than that?"

"There never was an other than that. I started practicing my autograph when I was six. Started taking acting classes after I saw *The Wiz* on Broadway. I would practice my Golden Globe acceptance speech in the bathroom holding a shampoo bottle, and I would go to the bookstore for hours looking at the models in fashion magazines. Since I was a kid I've wanted to do this, and this is the only life for me."

"But what if," Jacqui said with the tip of her Mont Blanc just under her chin. "What if everything you wanted to be never happens. Then what's plan B?"

"To lay down and die."

"You're being melodramatic, but I'm serious."

"Like I said. To lay down and die right on the spot. For me it's this or nothing."

Laying her pen down on the pad on which she was doodling, Jacqui reflected on the words and said, "Will this ad campaign be shot in Florida?"

"No. They're setting up the Christmas catalog shots for next year, so we will be shooting in New York in June or July. I'll finally get back to see some of my old friends in the business."

"That's wonderful," she said, reflecting on his earlier sentiment. "I'm proud of you."

After a pause, he replied, "Jacqui, I just want to be the man you think you see when you look at me."

"You already are." There was a hesitation and then a stiff knock at the door. "Wait a minute, this heifer done lost her—Why she knocking on my door so damn—Yes?" she said aloud. "May I help you?"

Opening the door was a prodigious lady with a face the color and shape of a ripe peach. Her hair was closely coiffed and accented by curls that looked like white snowflakes on a black rooftop. Her lips were full, the bottom one pinkish in color.

"Aunt Daisy?"

"Aunt who?" Stefan asked.

"So how are you, Miss Jordan?" the lady asked, her voice dipped in sarcasm. "Lawd, it would have been easier breaking into Fort Knox than getting in this place."

"I'm sorry, Stefan. My aunt just walked in from Seattle. Are you somewhere I can call you back?"

"Yeah, hit me home. I know I got a few months before the shoot, but I need to start doing a few more sit-ups to make sure everything is tight."

"Okay, honey," she said as she stood and gestured for her aunt to enter the office. "What are you doing in town?" Jacqui asked, walking around to the other side of her desk.

"So, I don't get no hug?" the matronly lady replied before they embraced each other. "How long has it been?"

Stepping away from her aunt's arms, Jacqui said, "I don't know. When was the last funeral? So what are you doing in town? Why didn't you call to tell me you were coming? I would have met you at the airport."

"Please. I don't want to be a pain in nobody's ass. I'm here on business and for pleasure. I spoke to your momma, and she told me you spend all your time here at the restaurant, so I thought I would see how you were doing." Then, looking around, she said, "But from the looks of things, you doing pretty good here. This is a cute little place you have."

"I'm not here as much as she thinks, actually," Jacqui said, motioning for her to sit as she took a chair facing her. "But we do okay here. We've increased our margins each year over the past few years, so I can't complain."

"Freda told me you used to just hire family. I know li'l Miss Woman out there ain't family with her drawers all stuck up her—"

"No," Jacqui said, laughing. "Actually, I just hired her this week. I used to hire just family, but last year I brought in a few outsiders, and honestly, things have never run smoother. Now I don't have to worry about them telling their momma if I hurt their feelings. But enough of talking about that. What business are you working on here in town?"

"Investment club. I'm a part of a group of investors, and we've met for the past twenty years or so every Wednesday night. Now, instead of buying just stocks, we're venturing into small cap businesses. Plus it's a way to write off a trip home."

"Always thinking."

"Child, you have to," she said, running her fingers over the desk, subconsciously checking for dust, and then wiping them on her dress. "When me and your momma grew up, we shared everything. We even shared a toothbrush at one time. Kids used to call me Shoes 'cause I always wore your aunt Abigail's raggedy hand-me-downs, and they called your momma Laces, well, because she was my sister. So I knew, even as a child, I had to live better than that."

"Yeah, Momma told me some of those stories. About how you all used to get pecans and oranges for Christmas. She also told me how you used to sell Italian ice cups when you were old enough to make extra money."

"Italian what? Please. We used to call 'um squeeze cup, and all you needed was some sugar, Kool-Aid, a place to sit them for a while, and you were in business. I could always make a dollar as far back as I can remember. Is that a picture of you and Bill Clinton?" she said squinting, at the photograph on the wall.

Without turning to look, Jacqui said, "Yeah, he came through one night when he was campaigning. They took about an hour to secure the restaurant, but it was cool."

"Nice. Very nice."

"So, where are you staying while in town?"

"At the Hilton."

"No. I have room at the house. Please. Come stay with me."

"No, it's okay, honey. I've already checked in, and besides, like I said, it's a write-off."

"Are you sure, Auntie? I mean, I have plenty of room."

"I know you do, sweetie, and I'm positive. But tell me something. What's going on with you and this Stevie fella Freda tells me about?"

"Stefan? He's a nice guy. Nothing serious. He used to work for this wholesaler I did business with a while back, and that's how we met. So far we're still in the how-much-will-he-or-she-get-on-my-nerves stage."

"*Umph.* I don't want to get all in your business, dear heart, but with your little business here doing so well and having everything where you want it, shouldn't you be a little more, I don't know, selective in who you date? I mean, your momma told me this guy doesn't work or—"

"Freda Mae Jordan is just being herself. Stefan's a nice guy. He has a great position with this produce company, and he's a model. Actually, he just found out today that he's going to be featured in a nationwide ad campaign for Burdines," Jacqui said with pride.

"What's a Burdine?"

"Oh, I'm sorry. It's a department-store chain."

"Never heard of it."

"Well, it's pretty big, but anyway, things for him are going fine. Like I said, Momma just wants some grandkids and I don't blame her, but I don't want to rush into anything. I want to be like you and Uncle Frank. I want to be married for thirty or forty years, and until we're both comfortable with that, we're just taking it slow."

"Oh, so you all have talked about it? About marriage?"

"Sure we have. But he's busy doing his thing, and I'm involved with not only the restaurant but a few other things. So until we can sit down and plan how we can start a family, we just want to take our time."

"How old a guy is he?"

"Forty," Jacqui mumbled while maintaining a stewardess-like smile.

"You know I love you like one of my own kids, dear heart," Aunt Daisy said, crossing her feet at the ankle and patting her foot. "You got time. You 'bout the same age as Janie, right?"

As she spoke, Jacqui's squared shoulders rounded. "No, Janie's thirty."

"You older than Janie? My goodness, I must be getting old. I thought—Well, I guess you right," she said, bringing her fingertips up to her lips and then rubbing the back of her neck. "You about the age of Tony, huh?"

"Well, Tony is forty-three, but yeah, I'm closer to his age."

"*Umph.* Well, dear heart, I think you have a wonderful little restaurant, and I will definitely be back tonight for dinner. Will you be here?"

"I should," Jacqui said, regaining her form in the chair. "I'm planning to meet Betty at the mall in a few hours, but I'll be back to close out tonight."

"Your momma tells me Betty had a big wedding. How many bridesmaids did she have again?"

Although there was an awkward pause in the conversation, Jacqui maintained eye contact. "Seven."

"That's a lot. That other little girl you grew up with. Li'l ugly bucktooth thing used to always come around at dinnertime?"

Another pause. "Helen?"

"Yeah. Bless her li'l heart. Your momma told me she got married, too? To a doctor or dentist or something. Were you in the wedding?"

"She asked me, but I couldn't."

"What about Jill? Mr. and Mrs. Smith's granddaughter."

"She got married in ninety-eight. Seems everyone is getting married now'days," Jacqui said with a fabricated smile.

"Well," Aunt Daisy said as she uncrossed her swollen ankles, "not everyone, dear heart. But I think it's best to be sure, 'cause no need in getting into it and staying married a couple of years. I told Michael that, and I thought that boy was never going to get married, but he and Eunice have been together going on ten years now. You know they looking at a summer place in the Hamptons, don't you?"

"That's nice. Auntie, I need to step out a minute to check on something. I'll be right back. Can I get you something to drink? Maybe some tea or something?"

"Lawd Jesus, no! I can't drink none of that syrup you all call tea down here," she cried, and started to laugh so loud her large breasts jiggled on top of her stomach.

Jacqui walked out the door and closed it. As she leaned against the wall outside her office, she saw her new hostess approaching.

"Miss Jordan, you all right?" Katrice asked.

"Yeah, I'm fine. Sounds like we're busy up front."

"A little, but we can handle it. Apparently there's something going on in town or something, 'cause there's a lot of TV news guys in the dining area and news trucks in the parking lot."

"So," Jacqui asked as she rubbed her temple, "how are you enjoying your first week?"

"I love it," Katrice replied, motioning her hands in the air. "I'd never done anything like this before, but it's real cool. I've met a lot of real cool people."

"Well, good. If you need any help, just ask Sabrina if she's on duty, and if not, you know you can always just come back here and ask me."

"I asked that lady," Katrice whispered, "to let me come back here and get you, but she said she wanted to surprise you."

"She's my aunt. It's fine."

"Can I ask you a question? I mean, a personal question?" Jacqui looked at her without changing expressions. "Well, maybe I shouldn't."

"Yeah, I wouldn't want them to get too backed up out front."

As Katrice walked away, Jacqui leaned over to sip water from the water fountain, dabbed her lips with the back of her wrist, and then settled against the wall with her eyes closed.

Jacqui sat in a booth at Calendars, a trendy, upscale mall restaurant, waiting for Betty to join her for a drink before they went shopping. The restaurant was decorated in earth tones, and calendars were liberally displayed in each and every corner of the establishment. As she sat dressed in a russet pantsuit with caramel alligator boots and accessories, she sipped a drink and thought about Stefan.

After Betty's wedding, their bourgeoning relationship became strained. They slept in the same bed each night, yet each day the tension increased.

Jacqui would eat at the restaurant to avoid going home; Stefan would grab a bite as he made his final deliveries. Although he made overtures to apologize, Jacqui considered dissolving the relationship altogether. Not so much because of the events of the wedding day but because the more she thought about their union, the more she saw no future.

Then, the night after a Valentine's Day she spent in the midst of a cold war, she came home, dropped her purse on the couch, and told Stefan to have his things out of her house in twenty-four hours. As he pleaded his case, she told him where he could find boxes and where to leave the house keys. She then called Betty and her mother, told them where they could find her, and she did not return home for two days.

When she returned, the home they shared looked like just a house. She walked into the bedroom, and the closets were half-empty. She looked in the top two drawers of the dresser, and they, too, were vacated.

Then Jacqui walked out onto her patio and saw the only thing left by Stefan. A crumpled white-and-green package of Newports with droplets of dew inside the cellophane wrapper. On the ground, between the sprouts of grass not killed by the winter freeze, there were butts. A folding lawn chair leaned against the wall, and below it was a bronze lighter with the initials S.W.D. engraved in the shaft.

There was a time when Jacqui would wash the dishes and watch Stefan as he sat in the chair and smoked late at night. Then he would gaze at the stars and appear to ponder about one thing or another. As she stood in her backyard, she tapped the cigarette package against her index finger, and a single filter freed itself from the others. Jacqui brought it to her lips, listened to the quiet sizzle as she lit it, and inhaled deeply.

It was the first time she had smoked in nearly six years, and then she gazed into the darkness, alone.

After Stefan moved in with a friend, for a week he refused to call to let Jacqui know where he was. And then he came to the restaurant, and as soon as he walked through the door, she started to get emotional. She turned to walk into her office, and he followed her and closed the door behind him. And then they stood face-to-face. He formed his hands and lips to say something, but nothing came out of his mouth as they gazed at each other. Since that moment, while they continued to live apart, she had never felt closer to him.

"Hey, lady, sorry I'm late," Betty said as she pulled out the chair and held her finger up for the waiter. "I love the rotisserie chicken here."

"No problem. You're always late. What's going on?"

"Slow, slow day. When I say nothing is going on, I mean just that. Nothing. Lady came to me with a parking ticket, and I thought about taking the case."

"Damn. Now that's crucial."

"I'm joking. But it has been as slow as molasses the last few days."

"I done told you how to make some money in that business. You got to get one of those 555 sue-their-ass numbers and get your picture on the back of the phone book. Run a TV ad around four A.M., when people are watching Springer reruns. One of those 'If you don't get paid, we don't get paid, because that's how much we love you' ads. I have a guy who works out at the gym with me and Stefan, and I know he must be knocking down mid-six." Jacqui opened a silver-and-gold cigarette case, pulled out a cigarette, and lit it up at the table.

"So you really going to pick up that nasty habit you had such a hard time kicking."

"For my weight," she said as she squinted. "I smoke to keep my weight down. So what's up? You gonna let me go into business with you, or are you just going to go and file as a nonprofit business, which is what you seem to be intent on running, anyway."

"Here we go again," Betty said in a singsong fashion.

"Okay, okay, no lectures today, grasshopper. But you really should consider doing it. You can do what you enjoy doing," she said, and brought the ashtray closer to her side of the table, "and make money. There's no law against that."

As the waiter came to the table, Betty asked for a whiskey sour and then said, "Robinson-Staley will either survive or die on its own. If I can't make a living doing this, then maybe I need to look at other options. Maybe getting a partner or working for a firm again."

"Please. Ain't no firm gonna let you do all of that pro bono work you doing for legal aid, and you know it."

"Well, if they don't, they don't. Let's talk about something other than shop. Let's talk about shopping. You wanna go by Galloway's and get that purse you were talking about?"

"Naw, girl, I'm going to Fields to get it. They have these slamming half-boots with a three-inch heel that will match it to a tee."

"Sorry," Betty said, crossing her arms. "I can't go in Fields."

"Why?"

"Because last time I was in there this heifer asked me could she help me. Then she started following me all over the store. Granted, when I went in that Sunday, I had been working in the yard, so I looked a little rough, but they can't treat me like that and get my dollar. Sorry."

Jacqui started to laugh.

"What? You think I'm going to patronize them for treating me like that?"

"First of all, I've seen you on the weekends, and *I* would have followed you around the store. But seriously speaking, what you wanna do? Have a sit-in or something and sing 'We Shall Overcome'? Please. I had this skinny heifer do that to me in Galloway's once. Know what I did? As soon as I walked in, she goes, 'Can I help you?' Just like a little smart-ass, right? So I said, 'As a matter of fact, you can. I need a blue scarf and a black A-line dress.' So she says, 'Well, the scarfs are over—' And before she could say another word, I said, 'Excuse me? I need you to help me.' I then told her what I needed and went and sat down. I had that skinny bitch running over the store like she was Marion Jones. Now every time I go in there you ought to see her hiding from me."

"You are so wrong," Betty said, laughing.

Shaking her head as she drew a puff and blew the smoke upward, Jacqui said, "Never do the expected, honey. When people like that come into your world, flip the script on them and you'll always be happier."

As Betty took her drink from the waiter, she said, "Well, I'm most definitely in a new-shoe mood myself."

"You feeling better about what happened Saturday?"

Betty sipped her drink and then sat it down lightly. "We're fine. He apologized over and over again, and it's over as far as I'm concerned."

"Do you think it really was Evander in the parking lot, or do you think he made it up?"

Betty looked at her friend and said, "Evander's been calling."

"He's been what?" Jacqui said, squinting from the smoke she blew out of the corner of her mouth.

"Only a handful of times, but yeah, he's called."

"And?"

"And nothing. He used to call me on the cellular, and I was so afraid that Drew would answer it. So I had the number changed; then he started calling me at the office."

"How many times have you spoken to him?"

"In the last couple of months? Maybe three times, including last week."

"Three times!" Jacqui said, waiting for details. "And?"

"Nothing to add. He calls, I tell him to stop calling, he tells me yada, yada, yada, and I hang up. It's the same thing every time he calls."

"Why didn't you tell me about this before?"

"Because there was nothing to tell."

"Have you seen him?"

"No! Jac, you know me better than that."

"Just asking. I remember when all the things went down with Yancy how I felt about him."

"Well, this is different."

"How is it different?"

" 'Cause I don't still love Evander." Betty took a short sip of her drink and then said, "I get tired of saying that, actually. I have to repeat it to Evander, to Drew, and now I have to repeat it to you."

"Hey, don't get hot with me. I'm just asking. Pull your panties out your crouch."

Pushing her drink away and then picking up both tabs, Betty said, "Come on, let's buy some shoes."

As Jacqui stood up, she put out the cigarette and said, "Don't mention shoes, because my Aunt Shoes just got into town."

"Aunt Shoes?"

"Long story," she said as they walked up to the counter and Betty handed the cashier her charge card. "She just flew in from Washington State, and she's a mess."

"Is that the one you lived with for a while when you were growing up?"

"For a while? Try five years while my mom was out doing her thing. Aunt Daisy is fine," she said as Betty signed the slip and they proceeded out of the restaurant. "She worked for a brokerage in the Northwest after she and Uncle Frank moved from here, and she's always been well off as far back as I can remember. But check this out," she said, and lowered her voice as they walked into the main corridor of the mall. "Uncle Frank is Aunt Frank."

"Bi?"

"No, straight-up gay. He used to be bi until they made a little money. Now he's just plain gay, and everybody knows it, but she doesn't seem to think anyone knows here in Florida. She always talking about how great their marriage is and whatever, and he use to be down to the Ambush every Tuesday night when they lived here."

"Dag."

"Yup. That's part of the reason she left Gainesville. I think she thought it would get out, but hell, everyone already knew."

"Well, that's some deep love."

"That's not love. She needs a twelve-step program. There's a difference."

"If push came to shove, you would not do the same thing? What if your man is gay?" Betty said as they walked into Galloway's Department Store.

"Stefan? What if Stefan is gay?"

"I know he's not, but I'm just saying, What if he was quote unquote open-minded? Would you leave him?"

"We have no kids. We have no property. And if he was gay, there would be *no* trust left, 'cause he would have lied to me, so staying would make *no* sense, so hell yeah, I would leave him and never look back. You mean to tell me if big-ass'd Andrew Patrick Staley was gay, you would stay?"

"I love Drew, okay?" she said with a smile. "Here I go saying that again. I need to get 'I Love Drew' tattooed on my forehead so I can just point instead of saying it."

"That's not the question. The question is, If his back door was open or at least unlatched, would you still be there?"

"I think we were talking about you, Ms. Thing."

As they laughed, a salesclerk crossed their path and said, "Hello, Miss Jordan. How are you doing today?"

"Hey there, how are you today?" she replied as the salesclerk rapidly walked down another aisle away from them. "See, I told you how to treat them, and then they will give you much respect."

After a smile Betty said, "You know something? If he was bi, yeah, I would more than likely leave, although I can understand why your aunt stays, since they have a history together. But outside of his being

bisexual or cheating on me, I don't think—Well, actually I know there
is no other reason I would leave him."

"No other reason?"

Betty picked up a chartreuse bracelet and said, "Until death do us
part, Jacqui. I really meant that, and I'm not going back on it."

"No matter what happens?"

Betty held the bracelet against a maroon sweater and then looked
at her friend and replied, "No matter what happens. Until *death* do us
part."

Chapter 7

And ye' shall know the truth, and
the truth shall make you free.

—New Testament
John 8:32

MAY

"Betty, how are you?"

"Consuela, my goodness," she said, and stood momentarily as the woman with the ingratiating smile entered her office. "I was so surprised when Carol told me you were scheduled to come in."

Wiping the seat with a handkerchief before sitting, Mrs. Lopez said, "It has been a long time."

Consuela Lopez was represented by Betty in a wrongful-death lawsuit. Her husband and infant son were killed when a crossing arm failed to activate, and since he was driving illegally, few attorneys wanted to devote the time and resources needed to win the case against the multimillion-dollar railroad company. But Betty took the challenge. When the final gavel sounded, Consuela walked away a millionaire, and Betty earned a newfound respect in the legal community.

"So how have you been? How are the kids? Did you start that trust fund you asked me about?" Betty asked as if they were teenagers separated by summer vacation.

"The kids are fine. My daughter took it hard for a while, but she's doing better. Our counselor says that's normal when a child loses a parent at her age. But back to that trust thing. I worked with the attorney you mentioned to me, and she took care of it."

"Well, that's wonderful. So what are you doing now'days?"

"Same thing."

"What? You still working for the Saffires?"

"Not exactly. Now I am over the house, so basically I just run things for them. I hire the help and what have you. I tried doing nothing and sat home for about six months, and it drove me out my mind, so I decided to go back to work."

"Great. As long as you're happy, I guess."

"I am, and the schedule is flexible. I'm able to spend a lot of time with the kids, and since the lawsuit, I don't need the money, so I don't mind going in half as much now."

"That's wonderful. So how can I help you?"

Looking at Betty's wedding ring, she said, "Congrats on getting married. I read about it in the paper. Even saw it in *Jet* magazine."

"You read *Jet*, Consuela? I thought you were pretty cool."

"I don't miss an issue," she said with a smile. "Frederico used to collect them in college for the centerfolds, and so I kept up the subscription. But the reason I'm here is because, as you know, I've worked for the Saffires since I came to this country. Well, he asked me to come visit with you."

Then she paused as if she expected a reaction by Betty at the sound of his name. "He's married to Nancy."

"Okay?" Betty asked, puzzled.

"Oh, I thought you may have known her. She's really big in the social circles. Nancy's maiden name is Parker. And she's the sister of Geno Parker."

"Okay?" Betty asked.

"Well, you know what happened to Toby, right."

"Yeah, he's the football player that got picked up last week for the murder of his wife and girl—"

"Don't say it, Ms. Betty. I hate to cut you off, but I use to put diapers on that child, and every time I hear someone say it, I want to cry."

"I'm sorry," Betty said softly.

"We can't even watch TV anymore. Everywhere you turn it's Bear this and Bear that. Half the stuff you hear is not even half-true. It's put out by the police department and the state's attorney's office so they can get an easy conviction."

"So what would you like me to do?"

"Represent him."

"Represent him?" Betty leaned back, and her eyebrows wrinkled. "He's got Peter Matz and the other guy who used to have a show on Court TV."

"Donald Owens. We're not satisfied with either of them. Every time you look around, they're trying to cash in on the case, and we don't want this to be a three-ring circus. I mean, everyone thinks he did it already, and they don't even know part of the facts, but you know me, Ms. Betty," she said, leaning forward. "You know the kind of person I am, and I would not come in here asking you to represent him if I thought for a second he was guilty. And I know he did not do it."

"Why me?"

"Well, I told the Parkers how good you were, and they trust my opinion. He remembers how hard you worked on my lawsuit, and so he would like to fire Owens and Matz, but he would like to talk to a few other attorneys also."

"How many others?"

"I don't know, since he doesn't want it to be leaked to the press. But I do know he would like to talk to you about it."

"I'm going to have to decline, Consuela. I've never tried a murder, and even if a portion of what I have heard about this case is—"

"But that's just it. None of it is true. These lies are just being planted to get an open-and-shut case. They want him to plea-bargain for a murder he didn't commit."

"Has he tried any of the large law firms in the area—if he's looking for local representation?"

"He knows every attorney in this town, and yes, but I would feel more at ease if he talked to you."

Betty leaned further in her chair, looked at the tattered wallpaper, and said, shaking her head, "I can't handle a case of that magnitude, Consuela. I just don't have the background or resources or the time to prepare myself. I've also heard that the state is trying to get a conviction before the November elections, which is strike two against the defense. A lot of people are trying to make political careers based on the outcome of this case." As she looked at the petite brown woman across from her, she added, "I'm really going to have to say no."

"Ms. Betty," Mrs. Lopez asked, "would you at least, then, meet with Mr. Parker and maybe give him some guidance on what attorney he should pick and which he should avoid?"

"I don't think that would be appropriate under—"

With her eyes reddening, she said, "It would really mean a lot. I don't want to talk about the case to you, but all I can say again is I would never lie to you. I know he did not do what they're saying he did. I know he's a football player and leads a crazy life. But he's no O.J., and that's what they are trying to portray him as."

Betty picked up a pen and inhaled deeply as she looked searchingly out her window at the large sign on the trash dump that read: Do Not Park Here from 7 A.M. to 7 P.M. "Consuela?"

"Please, Ms. Betty. You have got to help us on this. I beg of you."

"Consuela, I can talk to Mr. Parker," she said, they looked at her wedding portrait. "But only in the capacity of consulting on this one matter and this matter only. Like I said, I am not prepared to handle this type of case, and I don't wish to be considered."

"Thank you, ma'am. Thank you so very, very much." Then she reached into her purse and retrieved a folded piece of paper and pushed it across the desk toward Betty. "Here's all the information you'll need. He said he could meet with you in an hour."

Betty looked down at the still-folded swatch of paper on her desk. "In an hour? He can't come into the office?"

"No, ma'am. It's kinda hard for him to leave the house with all the attention, and most of the attorneys have been coming to the house to meet him."

Betty retrieved the paper and looked at the address and the gate access code. "Consuela, I tell you," she said, refolding the yellow slip of paper. "I would not do this for anyone else."

"Thank you, ma'am. Thank you very much."

As she got closer to the property on the northern side of town, Betty noticed that the small grated road was lined bumper to bumper with TV news trucks. Milling around the vehicles, she would occasionally see what appeared to be a technician adjusting a camera or on-screen talent talking with each other or adding makeup to their faces. ESPN, FOX Sports, and CNN were all represented in the gathering. Glancing at the address again, she knew she had at least a mile to drive, yet she noticed that trucks from cities as close as Jacksonville and as far away as Charlotte, North Carolina, had gathered in order to be the first to get the breaking news story.

As she got to the Parkers' driveway, Alachua County sheriffs blocked the entrance, and a portly gentleman wearing a tight-fitting evergreen shirt over a bulletproof vest came out to her truck.

"Canna' help ya, ma'am?"

Pulling out the yellow piece of paper, Betty showed it to the deputy as if it were her licence and registration and said, "I'm supposed to meet with Mr. Parker. I think he's expecting me."

"Are you the 'turny?" he asked politely as he took the piece of paper from her to inspect it.

"Well," she said, "I'm *an* attorney." As soon as she said the words, standing only feet away, a reporter's ears pricked, and he nudged his cameraman's arm. The cameraman swiftly hoisted the large camera onto his shoulder like a bazooka as the portly sheriff tipped his hat to another deputy at the call box.

The gate creaked open and the bright whiteness of the bulb of the camera shined in her face. As it did, she turned her head and saw other cameramen adjusting their equipment as well. Behind the reporters in the gray cobblestone wall surrounding the large rambling estate were the words Paradise Found. And then a reporter obstructed her view and tapped on her rear passenger side window with his microphone before being escorted away by a female deputy.

"Sorry dis thing is taking s'long, ma'am. We've asked them to oil it so it would move a li'l faster."

"No problem," she said, staring ahead and waiting for enough width to squeeze through the entrance. The more the gate would open, the closer she would inch toward it and the louder the rumble from the assemblage behind her grew.

"In the future, if ya could call us from ya cell phone if'n ya have one, we'll have the way paved for ya, okay?"

Betty remained silent, and then, as she saw the opening, she eased through and looked in her rearview mirror to find the sheriffs nudging the reporters off the Parkers' property.

Taking a deep breath, Betty slowed her vehicle to gather her composure and then noticed the enormity of the Parkers' dazzling Mediterranean-revival estate.

The area next to the privacy wall was undeveloped, but beyond it, the grass stretched without flaw up to the palatial home at its center. A horse was in the distance, and the lawn was landscaped with green

laurels and Florida palms with ripe fruit. As she drove up the driveway, lined on both sides by yellow roses, Betty felt as if she had driven
inside the pages of *Architectural Digest*.

Betty drove around to the parking area of the home and guided
her truck between two cars that cost as much as her first home. As she
sat there, she wondered to herself if she had already bitten off far
more than she desired to chew.

"Hello, Mrs. Robinson-Staley, how are you today? Sorry about the
madhouse out front," the tall, angular man said at the entrance of the
home. "They seem to grow tenfold each day."

"It's no problem, Mr. Parker. And please feel free to just call me
Betty," she said as she extended her hand without smiling. "How are
you today? Considering all?"

With a large toothy smile he said, "We're fine. Just fine, thank you."
And then he moved his body from the center of the doorway and
said, "Let me get you inside the house. The things these people can
do with a telephoto lens are next to criminal nowadays in and of itself."

Clutching her aluminum briefcase, Betty walked into the home,
her pen clamped in her fingers.

"Can I have Javier get you something to drink by chance? Maybe a
Coke?"

"Just some water, if that's not too much?"

"No problem. Zepherhills or Pellegrino?"

"Ah, either is fine," Betty replied. "Let's go with Zepherhills."

"Chilled or room temperature?" Mr. Parker asked.

Looking at Javier, Betty said, "I don't know. Surprise me."

After bobbing his head toward the Hispanic gentleman dressed in
khaki overalls, he looked at Betty and said, "Right this way, Mrs.—I
mean, Betty." And then, as he walked, he said, "And please feel free to
call me Geno."

Betty followed Mr. Parker down the red-carpeted hallway, decorated with what appeared to be seventeenth-century Italian artwork.
Mozart could be heard from the speakers in the walls. The house had
a floral scent, and fresh-cut magnolias were held in place in the clear
vases by blue marbles.

Then, as they walked, Betty saw that the double doors at the end of the hallway were open. When they entered the room, several men, who had been talking, grew silent when they saw her and Mr. Parker.

"Please. Don't stop on our account," Mr. Parker said. Which caused the other gentlemen to smile.

"Gentlemen," he said, and then looked at the lone female at the table and said, "and madam. This is Mrs. Betty Robinson-Staley. She is the attorney that if you remember lead the charge for Murphy, Renfro and Collins for Consuela." The faces went blank. "Remember my sister-in-law's maid? Well, Mrs. Robinson, I mean, Betty, handled the case when no other attorney we spoke to thought we had a snowball's chance in hell of winning the doggone thing."

"Oh, yeah, I remember now. I remember reading about it in the newspaper or something," an olive-complexioned man with dark features said. Then he said, "I'm sorry. Benyamin Stein, but everyone just calls me Benny."

"We'll have time for introductions in a moment, Benny," Mr. Parker said as he walked to the dining table, which was covered with files, faxes, and other office supplies. "You will have to excuse our mess, Betty. This has become the unofficial Free Tobias Parker headquarters," he said with a much softer smile than before.

"Not a problem," Betty replied, and as Mr. Parker sat at the head of the table, she positioned herself to his right.

As the others in the room sat, Mr. Parker said, "So, Consuela tells me you accepted the offer. Now my, or should I say our, question to you is this. Since this is the first case that you would—"

"Excuse me, Geno," Betty said. "Back up a second. Accepted what offer?"

After a pause, Benny, who wore a gray tweed jacket over a white polo shirt said, "I'm sorry, Betty. We were under the impression that you were aware of what was going on today."

"I was under the impression that—" And then Betty bit her words, laid her pen to rest on her notepad, and said, "Why don't you just tell me what is going on. Then I can see if we're on the same page."

The individuals looked at each other around the table as Mr. Parker said, "Well, we thought you were going to lead the charge. That you wanted to defend Toby."

Betty could feel the burn of the eyes peering at her as she looked at Mr. Parker. "Ah, sir, I must respectfully say that I may have misunderstood Consuela this morning. She may have told me that, but with so much going on back at the office, I assumed I would be here to—" And then she looked at the individuals around the table she was now sure were attorneys. "I assumed I was here to consult."

"Oh, our apologies, Mrs. Robinson-Staley," Benny said as he spun his small silver cellular phone in a tight circle. "First of all, I guess I should tell you who I am. I'm Bear's agent. Today we have with us a few people who have either investigated this case or assisted the family in legal matters. Now, we had a meeting a few nights ago," he said as Mr. Parker leaned back in his chair heavily. "And although it has not been leaked to the press, we decided that we took the wrong course of action previously. That bringing in all the noted attorneys was not a good idea, since we were dealing with local people on the jury. And also we did not want it to look like another case I need not remind anyone of in this room. We felt it wiser to get local representation."

"But as I mentioned to Consuela, there must be fifty attorneys in this city with better credentials who specialize in criminal law. Why me?"

"Because we thought—"

Then Mr. Parker raised his hand, and Benny's voice muted. "Because first and foremost I like you," he said in his deep, authoritative voice. In a slow, grinding cadence he said, "I watched you at work in that case against Midway Railroad, and you won the case convincingly. You took those big-city attorneys to task, and you had them running for the hills. I asked Jack Murphy for his best attorney to handle that case, and he picked you. I'll admit I was skeptical initially, but after seeing you at work, it was obvious why."

Betty sat quietly.

"And also Betty, Benny has very strong ties to the law school at the university. He asked around as well. They all still hold you in the highest regard."

"Well," Betty said, her fingers laced and her thumb stroking the inside of her palm. "I am extremely flattered but—" And then she looked around at the others in the room and asked, "Can I be candid for a moment?"

"By all means," Benny said.

"You've got a lynch mob out there." Betty sat and watched their expressions and then added, "I'm not talking about the press, either. Although I know no one will say it, one of the reasons my name has come up is because I'm an African-American attorney and Bear's girl-friend was black."

"No, no not at all," Benny said before Mr. Parker raised his hand to silence him and said, "Please continue, Betty."

"On the radio coming here I heard that the Klan may be in town to protest, since the NAACP has scheduled a march."

"Have you heard about that, Geno?" Benny asked as if he had been in the dark.

"Yeah. Reverend Robinson is organizing the NAACP because of the way the two kids who were suspects were treated by the Sheriff's Department and how they made a few illegal searches in order to find them."

"So?" Benny asked with his hands open. "What does that have to do with the Klan?"

"I guess they're just coming for GP. But my point is this. This thing is shaping up to be a powder keg. And when the pieces land, who knows what will happen in this city." As she spoke, she looked at the legal pad and picked up her pen to doodle. "It may not be such a bad idea to get outside counsel. Maybe not a nationally renowned attor-ney but someone who does not have to live in this community when it's all said and done."

"So you think if he walks the NAACP will get upset and if he is jailed the Klan will be upset," Geno said quietly.

"Well, first off, I am in no way implying that the Klan and the NAACP are analogous, and I hate even saying them in the same sen-tence. But yeah, I think you understand what I mean. In all honesty," she said as she drew the long wick attached to a cylinder with XXX on the front of it. "I would have had no problem representing your son Bear. I'm sorry I don't remember his first name."

"Tobias. But we just call him Toby."

"Well, I would have had no problem representing him in another type of case where I am well versed in the intricacies of the defense. But sir," she said, and once again laid her pen to rest. "This is a case where the state is asking for the—"

"I know, Betty. I know they want him to face lethal injection. And I also know there is also a backlash against celebrities in this country.

They, the media, the corporations, built him up, and they did a good job doing it. My wife and I were in Paris a few years back and saw kids wearing his jersey. He did one of those long-distance phone commercials, and they said the switchboard could not handle the volume of phone calls they received to sign up for service.

"I mean," he said, recalling his previous smile, "it's an amazing thing watching that and knowing you had something to do with it. They sold him as this half-man, half-animal, and the public bought it, but it's all an act. We even had the governor's office call to ask him to speak at the statehouse regarding child abuse. He has given back many times over. That's how we taught all of our children. But now that he is presumed guilty, who calls now? The governor? The telephone company? Hell, no."

Mr. Parker looked away from the others at the table momentarily and then back at Betty. "So, in answer to your question? If you were white, would you be here? I do not know. If you were a white male, would you be here? Again, I couldn't care less, because of all the people I asked about and considered, you were the one I would"—his voice dampened—"trust with Toby's life."

Betty sat speechless, and all eyes fell upon her once again. Then, in the corner of her eye, she saw Consuela at the door, and as she turned to look at her, she left.

"Geno, although I am flattered by the offer, I must—"

"Betty, we didn't bring you here to flatter you. You are good at what you do, and that is why I wanted you, as we have made clear. But just let me add one last thing. My son is not guilty. I know that is what you want to know, and he is innocent. I am not saying that as his father, either. Mrs. Washington, at the end of the table, has investigated this thing since the bodies were determined missing, and the facts will bare out what I am saying."

Betty looked across the table at Benny and then at Mr. Parker and said, "I appreciate your frankness, sir. But allow me also to avail myself of such candor and say, I could not care less as an attorney if your son did it or not. As a woman, yeah, I want someone to pay for what they did to both of those women, and if your son walks free, as a black woman I would have to answer to that twofold. But as an attorney, whether he killed them or not is not my concern." And then she looked at the others at the table and said in a lower tone, "And that's the part about this business I hate more than anything else. But it comes with the territory."

No one said a word. Mr. Parker sat quietly looking up at the ceiling fan above them as Javier brought Betty a half-frozen Zepherhills. Benny watched Javier momentarily, and then his eyes returned to Betty.

"Thank you," Betty said, and took the bottled water. "To be honest, when I came here today, I was under the impression that I would be consulting, and although it appears you don't need me in such a capacity, I don't really know, Mr. Parker, just how much good I could be to you." Betty stood and said, "So if you would excuse me—"

"Please." As he said the word, Betty could feel eyes shift toward the head of the table. "Please, Betty. Toby is my only son, and I just don't want to take this chance with another attorney. With the pressure on the state's attorney to get a quick victory, I know they are going to play hardball, and I just can't risk going in with a B-team. Would you please just reconsider?"

Betty sat behind the desk of her friend in Jacquetta's. As she made a call on the telephone, she watched the tape of the reporters outside the fence of the Parker estate on CNN.

"Hello, Robinson-Staley, attorney at law. May I help you?"

"Hey, honey, how are you?"

"How am I?" Carol asked. "We've had about four calls already asking about that Parker murder case. Are we taking it?"

"Dag, they don't mess around, huh?"

"Well, CNN just announced that the lead attorneys were fired today, and since you were headed to the house, I guess they assumed you were one of the new attorneys."

"Well, I'm glad you didn't tell them anything. You didn't, did you?"

"Of course not. But you are just consulting, right?"

"I don't know. I would have called from the car, but with the scanners out there, I decided to wait until I got to Jacqui's."

"You don't know? So are you considering helping in the defense?"

"I don't know. I mean, everyone deserves a day in court, and to be honest, if he was homeless or indigent, I would be jumping at the chance to help out."

"Help out but not defend. I mean, I've worked with lawyers who worked on murder cases before. Nothing as high profile as this, but I can tell you, they are a bird of a different feather."

"I know, I know."

"And what about resources? You would need to hire at least—"

"He's assured me he would give me a half million dollars just to bring in the people we need."

"How much?" Jacqui said, walking through the door.

"One second," Betty said to her friend.

"They are offering you that much to just assist in his defense?" Carol asked.

"Not assist. We would defend him, but I have not agreed to do it, but I didn't turn down the offer, either."

"Well, like you always ask me, what are the pros?" she asked as Jacqui placed a cup of tea in front of her friend and sat on the couch across from her, watching the coverage on CNN.

"The pros would be like I said. In spite of what he has been charged with doing, he deserves appropriate representation and someone committed to making sure his side of the story is told."

"And you think you are the best one to tell that story? No offense, Betty."

"Well, therein lies the pitfall. No, I don't. But they seem to trust me, and they want local representation, but that's still the gray area in my mind."

Jacqui mumbled, "And what if you get him off and he's guilty? Then what?"

"From what they are saying, the Klan could be in town next week to protest," Carol said.

"I know, I know. I will be on the same side of the case as the Klan," Betty replied, and curled a lock of her hair around her finger. "I have never been asked to do anything more deplorable in my life, and trust me, the thought of it literally makes me nauseous."

Betty could hear the rustle of papers in the background, and then Carol said, "Oh, yeah, I have one message for you that might not be able to wait. A realtor called by the name of Edwina Dix. Would like for you to call her today if you can ASAP?"

"She caught me on the cell phone. Everyone told me she was the best in town, but so far I'm getting the same offers I got before. I just refuse to give my house away. I don't care if I was only in it for a year."

"Betty? I sold my first house when I got married after living in it for six years and took a loss. It happens."

"Everyone tells me that, but I'm still determined to make a profit."

As Betty said good-bye to her secretary, Jacqui continued to watch the news on the television set, perched high in the corner of the office. When Betty hung up the phone and leaned back in the chair, she said, "You're going to take this case, aren't you?"

"Please, girl, I haven't hardly decided to do that yet."

"Yes, you have. I know you too well to know you will not walk away from this one?"

"So what are you saying about me, Jordan? I'm no patron saint of lost causes, you know."

"I know you're not. But I also know you like taking on a cause no one else sees as being winnable."

"Not really."

"Yes, really. You were that way in law school moot court as well as at Murphy, Renfro and Collins, and this is no different."

"What I don't understand," Betty thought aloud as she rested her elbows on the desk, "is why they want me so bad. I mean, when I asked him about it, he gave me this song and dance about talking to professors at the university about me, et cetera, et cetera. But let's face it, what would you do if your son was charged in a double homicide."

"I would get the best. And you're the best."

"That's nice and all, but you're right. You would get the best. The best criminal attorney in town or in the state. If he wanted a black female, there's about five I can name off the top of my head with experience in capital offenses. So I'm not taking their choosing me at face value."

"You're just modest, let's face it; he's white, and his son killed his white wife and his black mistress. I bet you anything they went through a list of black females, and since he knew you and had seen you work before, you got the nod."

"That's too simplistic. If Bear—I mean, Toby—was my son, I would get the best defense team money could buy. Period. Not an attorney who has never been a partner, who has tried only a handful of minor criminal cases. And not an attorney who just happens to be the same race and gender as one of the victims."

"You're going to defend him," Jacqui said, and then turned the television off with the remote.

"Why do you keep saying that? Because of the money?"

"No, because A, I know you. And B, because just now you started preparing yourself for the case. You just called him Bear and then corrected yourself to humanize him." Betty remained silent. "Let me just say this, and I know you have not asked for my advice, and I try not to offer it in things like this. But this is a white man who is accused of killing a sister and allowed a black kid to be charged with it. His father, although he has changed his tune now, was totally against integrating the university, so much so that they had protests when they wanted to name a hall after him. His grandfather was in the—"

"Jacqui, I haven't made a decision. But, well, I don't know. I guess I need to talk to Drew about this before I make a decision one way or another."

"How much time have they given you to decide? The weekend?"

"Actually, he asked if I could let him know something by five o'clock."

"Why?"

"Because stories, rumors, are starting to circulate, and he needs to have someone out there speaking for Toby."

"What about the family attorney. The guy who was just now on television?"

"He was at the meeting this morning, and to be honest, he didn't say a mumbling word. I don't think he even introduced himself. He just sat there, and Toby's agent did all the talking."

"Then do it."

"Jacqui, this case would take a year out of my life. You don't make a decision like this just like that."

"Well, yesterday you were looking for business. Now you have it at your door, so how do you make the decision?"

"When you find out," she said, looking at the television, "tell me. Can you turn it up a little?"

We are reporting from the Parker family compound just north of Gainesville, Florida. This is a story that has changed rapidly within the past twelve hours, but we will attempt to get you up to speed. First of all, the previous quote unquote Dream Team Two, as The New York Times *described them, has been disassembled. There was a news conference scheduled for six o'clock eastern time,*

but we were advised by a family spokesperson that it has been de-
layed until possibly tomorrow morning. Now in a related story . . .

"Excuse me, Mrs. Jordan," Katrice said as she peeked in the door. "I
knocked, but I don't think you all heard me."

"No problem, hon. What's up?"

"Mrs. Staley, there's a man out here who would like to speak to you."

"Did you get a name?" Jacqui asked without looking back.

"*Umm,* no, ma'am. But I can go—"

"That's okay," Betty said as she picked up her handbag. "I was
headed out, anyway."

As Katrice closed the door, Betty said to Jacqui, "If I ever need a
job, remind me not to work for you?"

"Please," she replied as she clicked off the television with the remote. "My granny used to say, Give a nigga a stick and they'll wanna
build a tree house. That's my theory with employees."

As Betty entered the dining area of the restaurant from across the
room, Katrice pointed toward a table, and Betty saw the back of her
husband's head. He was sitting with a large white man who was
dressed in what appeared to be an expensive black suit.

Betty walked up and put her hand on Drew's shoulder.

"Hey, honey, I saw your truck outside," Drew said as he stood up to
greet his wife with a kiss on the cheek. "I wanted you to meet Mr.
Ward. He's the president of Sun—"

"Federal Savings and Loan," Betty said, finishing his sentence and
extending her hand.

"Hello, Mrs. Staley," Mr. Ward said, standing. "It used to be Rob-
erts, if I am not mistaken. Correct?"

"Robinson."

"You two have met before?" Drew asked, looking from one of them
to the other.

"Well, actually I remember Mr. Ward from a banking matter I
worked on for MRC."

"Oh, yeah, that's right," he said. "So you're no longer with Murphy,
Renfro and Collins?"

"No. I have been flying solo for several months now," Betty replied
as she pulled out a business card.

"That's just splendid," he replied as he read her card, flipped it over as if he were expecting to see information on the back as well, and then put it in his shirt pocket. "I remember you from the Midway case. Maybe we can do something together in the future. Can I call you for lunch sometime?"

"I look forward to it."

"Well, let me go to the boys' room to freshen up a little," Mr. Ward said. "It was indeed a pleasure meeting you, Mrs. Staley, and I will be in contact."

As he walked away, Drew stared at his wife. "What?" she said, taking a seat.

Drew sat down and said, "I just never saw that side of you."

"You mean the businesswoman in me?"

"Yeah. You got a little bit of shark in you, too. Where did the business card come from? I never even saw you open your purse."

"Took it out before I came to the table. You like that move, huh. See, you can learn something about business from me."

"I guess so."

"Speaking of business, though, I have a situation I need your input on."

"The Parker case," Drew whispered.

"Yeah. How did you—Carol, right?"

"Who else? So what do they want you to do? Research or something?"

"Research?" Betty asked.

"Yeah, I'd imagine they wouldn't hire just a regular old paralegal for something like this." Then Drew paused as he looked at his wife's expression. "You mean, they want you to be a full assistant?"

Betty sat silent.

"Tell me, what do they want you for? To help in jury selection?"

"Actually, they want me to be the lead attorney."

Drew laughed. "Seriously. What do they want you to . . ." Then he looked into his wife's unwavering eyes. "But really, what . . . Are you serious, Betty?"

Betty remained silent.

Whispering, Drew said, "But you've never tried a—"

"Trust me, I know, and I have no idea why they really want me."

"You serious?" Drew asked. "Do they really want you to do this? Have you agreed to handle the case?"

"No. That's what I wanted to talk to you about."

"Man," Drew said as he leaned back in the chair, then looked around to see if anyone was eavesdropping. "Well, if you want my opinion, honey," he said, and took out a napkin and drew a line down the middle of it. On one side he put a slash, and on the other he put an addition sign. "Let's just look at the pros and cons. On the pros side it would be great exposure, it would be lucrative, and if he's innocent, then you would be doing what you've always wanted to do."

"Yeah, I know that, but—"

"But on the negative side—" And then he wrote rapidly on the napkin:

THE HOURS
Inexperience
The Klan
THE HOURS
The NAACP if victorious
THE HOURS

As he wrote the letters FAM, which Betty assumed would be family, Mr. Ward returned.

"This is hands down one of the best restaurants I've been to in a long time. In the men's room they have—I'm sorry, Mrs. Staley," he said to Betty as she stood up. "Are you not going to be able to join us for dinner?"

"No," Betty replied. Then she picked up the napkin and slid it into her purse. "I just wanted to stop by and say hello."

"Well, it was indeed a pleasure finally meeting you," he said, and extended his hand once again.

"The feeling is mutual, and we'll be in contact." Then Betty looked at her husband and simply mouthed the word thanks before she turned and walked away.

Betty sat in the conference room on the third floor of the Alachua County jail awaiting her client. The conference room was unique because, although it was of normal size, there was a glass-enclosed area to which the inmate would be led that was equipped with a telephone and speaker system for him to communicate with visitors.

She could hear the elevator on what sounded like a bicycle chain come up to the top floor, pause, and then rattle to a close. Still dressed in the navy blue suit she'd worn all day, she looked at her nails and then hummed to herself as she took out her fingernail file for a touch-up.

Betty was positioned at the head of a particle-board table with the words Chris Loves Fabian, Jesus Christ Saves, and Give Me Free! deeply etched in the wood.

The room itself was a perfect square, with crisscross wire running through the inside of the lone window to the rest of the world. The lights above were covered by a mesh grill; the top of the walls were painted light green, the bottom dark blue, and the tiles below were cracked, scuffed, and worn.

On the conference table was the outdated 1996–97 edition of the Florida penal code, and Betty noticed that on the other side of the thick Plexiglas was a chair bolted to the floor with large metal circles on the armrest. Through a three-by-five square of glass in the door behind the chair she could see the library and a couple of inmates studiously taking notes from the law journal. Behind them, through the bars, she saw the glimmer of the moon. Beyond them, she thought as she picked at her cuticles, was the freedom they worked so hard to achieve, and then her view was obstructed by a jailer dressed in blue.

Betty took out her notepad and tape recorder and sat them on the table, which was buttressed against the glass.

When she called Mr. Parker after speaking to Drew and accepted his offer, he thanked her and then disclosed that, unbeknownst to the press, Bear had been on suicide watch. When she asked for how long, he said, "Only one more day."

"Listen, Stew, when we were with Nike, you promised us the frigging world to switch. I brought you Bear. I brought you Gary Harrison. And I just threw in Channey because I liked you," Benny said as he spoke on the only outside line in the room, his silver cellular phone nestled in his lap. Each time Betty made eye contact with him, he would wink at her and continue his tirade. "Now Gary has made first-team NBA, and Channey lead the league in RBIs. When we could have optioned out last year, what did I say? Huh? Shit on that, Stew! The hell with a morals clause. You, your company, whatever you wanna call it, owes the Bear a half million dollars whether you run the campaign or not, and if the Bear doesn't get it, I take my other clients and walk as soon as their contracts are up. You know I will! I hear FUBU is ready to be a player in this market! They'd love to get a top white athlete like Channey to represent them!"

At the opposite end of the table, Mrs. Williams sat reading a *Life* magazine. She was a delicate woman with designer glasses she wore neatly atop of her head but rarely used. She appeared to be in her late twenties or early thirties, and her dark hair was gathered in a simple bun.

Also in the room was the Parkers' family attorney, Hereward Ivory, who simply paced back and forth and spoke to no one.

Betty glanced at the time on her watch, looked through the glass in the door for her client, and then attempted to call Jacqui on her cellular.

"That's not gonna work there, Counselor," Benny said to Betty with the phone to his ear. "You can't make calls out of this place. The walls are too thick or something." Then he looked away. "Yeah, I'm still here. Find the frigging contract and read me the clause. I'll hold."

Betty returned the phone to her purse, and then she heard footsteps coming down the hallway. As they got closer, she heard a shout echo down the hall. "Yo, when you get out the nut ward, can I get that autograph! I can sell that shit!" And another that screamed, "Gad damn, that's a big-ass'd cracker thea'!" As the reverberation of what sounded like wood against cement bounced off the walls, another voice yelled, "Whatever yaw'll feeding that big mo'fo, I want some!"

"Listen here, Stewy, my boy is headed this way right now as we speak. Hell no, you can't talk to him," Benny said, pulling the phone from his ear and looking at the receiver as he said the words. Then, bringing the phone back to his ear, he said, "What? When hell freezes over, you sorry sonova—Listen, I really gotta go, but give my best to Ginger and the girls, okay?"

And then the thick-greased steel door behind the glass slid into the wall, and two jailers stepped in and walked toward the chair bolted to the floor. Two others walked through the steel portal and stood at opposite sides of the room. As Betty looked out the doorway into the library, her view was obstructed by a man with shackles around his waist who blocked out the moon. When he came to the entrance, he dipped his head to enter and was dressed from head to toe in neon orange.

A much smaller jailer held his handcuffs as if he were leading a circus animal into the center ring. Bear, whose curly hair hung thick in his face, stood patiently with his head down, which produced a chilling impression. He had a dark olive complexion, deep-set eyes, a cleft chin, and thick lips, which he would lick as if he were thirsty.

If Betty had seen him outside the confines of the jail and not in her present capacity, due to his size and girth, she would have stared in open-mouth amazement. But she showed no reaction.

Bear was a well-proportioned seven feet plus, and unlike the basketball players she knew in college, he was not willowy in any way whatsoever. The thick muscles of his neck were planted into his shoulders like an oak tree in the ground, and he looked like the embodiment of masculinity.

Over his navel were his fingers, which were cinched close to his body and laced together to form one tanned volleyball-sized fist. His shoulders appeared to begin at the back of his head, and his arms looked like the thighs of Clydesdales.

Even at rest, Bear's muscles appeared taut, and a thick vein ran down his biceps and branched out in his forearms like the Mississippi River.

The handcuffs used to detain him looked like a cord of string around the wrist of a normal-sized man and appeared to be just as easy to break.

His neck, arms, and the portion of his chest Betty could see, were lanced by tattoos. The easiest to discern was the large number ninety-nine on his arm and a crucifix on his forearm.

"Hey. How are ya, Bear? Listen, I was just talking to Reebok, and everything is fine." Hereward glanced over at Benny scornfully, as if he thought such talk were inappropriate, then returned his eyes to Bear.

"Remember Stew? Has this cute little wife name Ginger? Drives a Ferrari Testarosa? Well, anyway, he's fighting for us there, and they're still in our corner!" Benny said as he shook his head up and down like a toy poodle in the back of a car.

Shuffling his feet, which were restrained by leg irons, Bear was led toward the bolted chair and showed no reaction to what was said.

"Yo, Betty? Is that intercom whatchamacallit on? Can he hear us back there?"

Betty shook her head yes as Bear took baby steps to the chair.

An officer behind the glass put a key in a box that allowed the sound to transmit and said, "Okay, Bear, you know the routine."

Bear sat in the chair, and as another guard came over to unshackle him, Betty said, "Excuse me?"

"Yes?" the man with sergeant stripes on his sleeves answered.

"What are you doing? I'm here to speak with my client."

"Oh, Betty," Benny said, and put his cellular phone in his inside coat pocket. "That's just the way they do things, but we never let them put them on tight. I think it's a law or something."

Bear continued to hold his head down as the jailers ran the finger-width chain through the loops of the secured chair.

"Well, ma'am, I don't know if you are aware of it or not, but Mr. Parker here assaulted an officer and this is the procedure in the facility when things like that happen."

"Do you know David Ford in Tallahassee?" Betty asked.

"Who?"

"Do you know—Never mind. What's your name?"

"My name?" he asked, then looked at the other jailers. "Bo Strong, ma'am."

"Well," she said as she wrote his name down on her legal pad, "I am here to depose my client. This is our first such meeting, and I would like for him to speak freely. Therefore, unless you would like for me to make a phone call to Tallahassee tomorrow morning, you might allow me to speak to him without the trappings of the restraints."

Officer Strong looked at the other jailers again, smiled, and then said, "What the hell. As you wish, ma'am."

As they took off the restraints, Betty could feel her heart swell in her chest. Mrs. Washington sat straight in her seat, and Hereward Ivory simply eased back unemotionally in his chair.

"So, Bear, how goes it, man? They treating you alright in this place?" Benny shouted in order to be heard in the intercom.

Bear remained silent as the last of the leg irons were noisily yanked from his ankles. As the guards walked toward the door, Bear slowly massaged his wrists and then returned his forearms to the armrest.

"If you need us, and you might," Officer Strong said, "we're right outside the door." And then she heard one of the jailers say to the other, "Don't tell me. New attorney, right?"

When the door closed, Betty looked at her client, and the air in the room was still.

"So, Bear," Benny shouted in the corner, still sitting next to the phone, "did the old man call to tell you we were changing direction in the case?"

Silence.

"Mr. Parker," Betty said. "My name is Betty Staley. Your father hired me about an hour ago to represent you, and I just wanted to visit tonight to get a grasp of the case.

"Please let me add that while I have seen your picture on the Mountain Dew ads and I've heard my husband mention you a time or two, I know little about you or what you do. And in spite of this being the biggest story to hit this town in years, I know little about what they say you have done. And actually I think that might be a plus."

With his head still down, the only sound that could be heard through the speakers was Bear's deep breaths.

"Well, Mrs. Staley, this young man led the league in sacks in each of his first five years in the league. In *Sports Illustrated* he was described as one part Jordan, two parts Stone Cold Steve Austin, and three parts rock and roll! Madison Avenue loves him, and he is the only line-man—"

"Benny?"

"Yeah."

"I'm going to need you and Mrs. Washington to step out of the room for a moment," Betty said.

Benny eased back in his chair and then smiled as he said, "Please, you can talk in front of us. We're family. We're all in this thing here together. Ain't that right, Bear?"

"Not tonight, Benny," Betty replied, and twisted the trunk of her body in her chair so she could see him. "Tonight you are going to have to sit in the visitors' lobby until I ask you to come back in. Okay?"

Bear raised his head for the first time and looked at his attorney. As he did so, Betty noticed a mouse under his eye.

"You's serious?"

"Sorry," Betty said with her back turned, and then clicked on her palm-sized recorder.

Benny folded his arms across his chest and then looked at Hereward, who was still watching Betty. "Well I'll be—Fuck it! Come on, Athena," he said, pulling out his cellular phone once again as he walked out the door.

When the steel door closed, Betty looked at her client and said, "Let's try this again." Then she noticed that he was sweating, although he was not breathing heavily.

"Is it hot in there?"

Dead air.

"Mr. Parker, I know these are not the accommodations you are used to, but how are you coping?"

Bear maintained his silence, and then he massaged his palms.

"Were the handcuffs too tight, son?" Hereward asked in a grandfatherly tone.

Bear opened his hands and looked at them as a newborn would look at its hands. As he did, Betty retrieved her recorder and clicked the OFF button with her thumb. Then, from nowhere, his deep voice rumbled through the speakers.

"First time I had them things off all day, Wood."

"Are you serious?" Betty asked as Hereward looked at her and then back at Bear.

Her client retained his silence.

"Did someone in here abuse you, Toby?"

Hearing his name, he looked up at Betty and said, "You must have been talking to my pops. He's the only one who calls me that."

Betty then said, "So, what happened? I noticed your face looks a little puffy. Did you really assault a guard?"

"I don't know. I really just rather not talk about it. There's nothing you can do about it, anyway," he said, and then turned his head and saw that the jailer was looking at him through the glass.

"So are you ready to talk about the case?"

"Not really," he mumbled. "I'd like to talk about anything but the case." Then he looked down at the intercom speaker. "I hate to sound like *I Spy* or anything, but you think these speakers could be bugged?"

"No, son, they are not," Hereward said as he walked closer to the glass and leaned against the wall. "Feel free to answer her questions."

He looked down at the speaker again and then at the glass as if he were trying to determine its thickness.

"Well, Toby," Betty said, and laid her pen to rest. "What can you tell me? What am I getting myself into?"

"What do you want to know? The truth or what you're getting your-self into?" And then he tugged on his earlobe, and Betty noticed it was pierced several times.

As she looked into his large ebony eyes, she asked, "Aren't they one and the same?"

Bear looked at Hereward, who tilted his head in affirmation. Then he stared straight ahead at the wall and said, "Well, you the attorney. Let me tell you the truth and you can decide what to do with it after that."

After being escorted through the cafeteria exit of the jail to avoid the press, Betty walked out with her briefcase in one hand, reviewing all that was said by her client. Behind her she heard Hereward saying good night to Mrs. Williams.

Betty continued to walk as not only the words Bear used but also his mannerisms replayed in her mind. She thought of how he stood on his toes in the corner of the room and methodically pounded his head against the wall. She thought of how he vividly described the sound from the gun on the cold night and how the bodies looked in the trunk and why he fled the state afterward.

"So fucking stupid," he said as he pounded his head. "So fuckin' stupid!"

"Excuse me? Mrs. Staley?" Hereward said, and jogged to catch up with her.

Although he was a tall, stately gentleman who would tell jokes with-out cracking a smile, he ran straight, without a limp, as his black wing tips smacked against the cement. Betty turned, although she did not want to discuss what they had just heard. Not even with another attor-ney.

"Mrs. Staley, I just wanted to ask—"

"Please," she offered with a fatigued smile. "Feel free to just call me Betty."

With a refined voice, he said, "If it is all the same with you, Coun-selor, I would prefer to call you by your proper name."

Betty raised one eyebrow and lowered her shoulders. "As you wish. How can I help you?"

"I know you have had a long day, and it's not my intention to detain you much longer. But I spoke to Mr. Parker and asked him in what capacity I would participate in this case, to which he advised me to touch base with you."

"Really?"

"When I say that he has full and total confidence in you and your abilities, I am not just paying homage."

"Well," Betty said, with a smile. "I may just need some homage. I was thinking about using a friend or two from my old firm, but if you are up to it, since Toby obviously trusts you, I think it would be advantageous to use you. The hours will be long, and when I say long, I mean as long as eighteen hours a day, because we have a lot of catching up to do if the state is intent on fast-tracking."

"Well, thank you, madam, and no, the hours are not of concern to me." Betty reached into her purse for her truck key, and then he said, "Having said that, let me say this. If I am going to work with you, I have got to be able to speak open and freely regarding any and every matter pertaining to the case."

"By all means," she said, placing her key into the truck's door. "I wouldn't have it any other way."

Then he backed up a half-step and slowly sat his worn leather briefcase on the pavement as Mrs. Williams passed in her car and waved good night to them both. As soon as her car drove up the ramp and out of the lot, Betty could see the reflection of the cameramen's bright lights, and then she turned to give Hereward her attention.

"You see that briefcase?" he said proudly. "It was used by Chief Justice Earl Warren."

"Really?"

"Yes. His initials are still engraved in the metal. My dad was not an attorney. He worked as an automotive mechanic by day and had a janitorial business by night. But when Justice Warren came to D.C., my father was his driver, and from the day I was born, he wanted me to be an attorney. So I went to law school for him. Not any law school," he said, gazing at the briefcase. "Yale Law School. To make a long story short, Counselor, the reason I am telling you this is to say that from the first day I stepped on that campus in New Haven until this very night, I have had that briefcase at my side. It's been good to me through forty-plus years of wills, trusts, property disputes, and what have you. It's seen a lot. Nothing of this caliber, but it has seen its share." Then, after regarding Betty's aluminum briefcase, he looked her in the eyes.

"Mrs. Staley, what you heard in there from Toby is the truth. The absolute truth. But it's going to be a hard sell. The kid is scared, but I firmly believe he will walk out of this place if you play it straight."

"Meaning what?"

"In plain English, Mrs. Staley, if you show fear, if you get flashy, if you try to sway them with your knowledge and your prose, you will lose this case? And about that I haven't any doubt."

"Why are you telling me this?"

Hereward's icy blue eyes fixed on a spot above Betty's head, and then he said, "Because a man's life is on the line."

"Well, that's a given, Hereward. My question to you is this: Do you think I'm going to walk in there rhyming, shucking, and jiving? Do you think—"

"No, I think you will walk in and show how new you are at this."

Leaning away from her truck, Betty folded her arms high on her breasts and said, "How new I am? Hereward, I'm an attorney with nine years of court experience, and I have won—"

"Eighty-seven percent of your cases while at Murphy, Renfro and Collins. Before his death you were Jack Murphy's golden girl. His protégée in many ways, and to be honest, Counselor, he fed you a few powder-puff cases to both boost your confidence and to show Franklin Renfro that he was right to bring you into the firm. I am not saying that to slight you or your accomplishments, because it's often done to new associates when a partner has stuck his neck out for them.

"But then he gave you the Lopez case, which was tailor-made for you because in all honesty, madam, the judge in the case hated Midway Railroad's attorneys and at the time Judge Travsky's father was in a nursing home. His father worked for an airline for twenty-two years, and they cut his benefits off when he needed them the most. So let's say he was not a big fan of public transportation or some of their practices.

"No one in town wanted the case, but Jack knew the judge and knew you would do well. So with no disrespect, seventy percent of the rulings in the case went your way. Also, the award that Consuela got was more than she should have received, but the railroad company was going through a major PR problem and would have more than likely settled for twice as much as they paid out. They made a token appeal but were glad to pay out the one point five million dollars, which was pocket money for a company like Midway.

"So," he continued, "why am I telling you what we have learned through our research?"

Betty said caustically under her breath, "It's good to know that I've been thoroughly investigated and approved."

"It was easy, actually. You went to the university here in town, you married a local boy, and besides that, remember the kid who came to your office to interview you last month?"

Betty showed no expression as she listened.

"We did not investigate you because we doubted your abilities in the courtroom. Although I opposed your selection, I will say that for the most part I think you are the best person for the job. You're savvy, compassionate, and above all, intelligent. And because of your intelligence I will tell you that you have gotten off to a bad start."

"In what way?"

Hereward's eyes wondered off again before affixing to hers and biting his thin bottom lip. As he did, his Nixonion jowls sagged. "The game you played in the jail earlier when you mentioned a Mr.—I think the name was Ford, in Tallahassee."

Dead air.

"There is no Mr. Ford. I know very few people in the state capital, but I could tell he did not exist due to the tone of your voice. But most importantly, the jailer saw right through you."

Betty recoiled in silence.

"If a dumb ass like that can see you are full of it, Mrs. Staley, what will the judge in this case see? What will one hundred to a hundred fifty journalists hungry for a story find? What will twelve men and women who are tired of celebrities getting away with murder and who have been sequestered see? Some attorneys are born bullshit artists. In all honesty, madam, you are not such an attorney. I was watching a Spike Lee movie with my daughter and this guy said to the other, 'Game knows game.' I think that also applies here. For some in this business, not lying may be a negative, but not for you, and not in this case. You have an honest quality about you that I don't know if you even know you possess. And that's a good thing. But don't play games, because if you don't give it to them straight, that boy we just spoke to will die. It's as simple as that."

After pondering what was said, Betty lifted her head and whispered, "So the story he gave us just now . . . which is now the third story he has told regarding this case. About how his wife drove the car and how his girlfriend was involved. You think a jury will really believe that?"

"They have no choice but to believe it, because it's the truth."

"And what does the truth have to do with justice?"

Hereward pondered what she said as he cleaned his glasses with the tail of his black tie. He was a barrel-chested man with a bulbous nose and earlobes that hung lower than most. "This type of case is out of my league. I freely admit that. But you know something? When I get on my knees tonight, I will pray to the dear patron saint Ivo for mercy and direction. And I will pray that this is one time the truth, no matter how far-fetched it may appear, will prevail." Hereward picked up his briefcase and gingerly wiped the sand from the bottom of it. "Oh, yeah, I failed to mention how I was so fortunate to get the briefcase. My father was so moved by Chief Justice Warren, he took a job doing his lawn on the weekends. Not so much for the income but because it was a way for him to expose me to such a lifestyle. Then, one day, we were working in the rose bed when we saw it. This briefcase was next to the Dumpster, beside a box which had obviously contained its replacement. I went over and retrieved it," Hereward said. "And that was the last day I did manual labor.

"So, on that note, Mrs. Staley, where would you like to meet tomorrow, and what time?"

Looking at her watch and seeing it was almost midnight, she said, "Six A.M. Do you know where my office is located?"

"Yes, I do, madam," he said with a smile and a tilt of his head. "I'll see you bright and early, and I'll bring the doughnuts."

As he walked away, Betty unlocked the door of her SUV and then turned and said aloud, "Hereward?"

"Yes?"

"Don't ever quote Spike Lee to me again. Understand?"

With a smile in his tone, he continued walking and said, "As you wish, madam."

"And another thing?"

Hereward stopped and turned around.

"You told me you never wanted to be an attorney. What did you want to be when you were eighteen years old?"

"Honestly?" he yelled. "Point guard for the Celtics like Bob Cousy." Betty smiled. "But since that job was taken, I would have settled on being an automotive mechanic, like my father. See you bright and early."

"Sleep well," she said under her breath, and then got into her truck and headed toward the bright lights at the end of the parking-lot ramp.

Chapter 8

It is a double pleasure to deceive the deceiver.
—Jean DE La Fontaine
Caracteres

In the depth of sleep, Andrew Patrick Staley was in a swing. Like a child, he would swing back and forth, going higher and higher with every pump of his legs and each thrust of his lower back.

The air was cool but dry, and occasionally honeysuckle blossoms would fall from the branches above him into his lap.

In the distance he saw a lady and could not determine who she was. When he looked down, he noticed he was swinging on the edge of a cliff. The water below crashed against the jagged rocks, occasionally splashing droplets on his feet. The sun was bright above, and the Winslow Homer-like fields behind him were lush and smelled of freshly cut grass.

But no matter how beautiful the surroundings, he could not get the image of the lady out of his mind.

Then Drew relaxed his legs and allowed his toes to touch the ground with each passing of the earth.

Getting off the swing, he stood at the edge of the cliff, and the woman gazed at him across the divide.

Her white apparel and hair were blown stiff by a breeze he could not feel. Yet she stood upright, strong and undeterred.

"Hello?" Drew shouted across the water. "Can you hear me?"

She did not answer. She only stood gazing at him.

"Sorry to bother you," he shouted, his hands cupped to his mouth, "but do I know you? Have we met?"

His voice bounced back to him without an accompanying answer from her.

Then Drew looked back at the swing, which was still in motion. Deciding that she did not want to speak, he returned to the wooden seat and started to swing again.

Higher and higher he swung. So high that he felt his feet would be scorched by the sun itself.

On the downswing, he looked, and the woman was still standing, but the wind had stopped. With hair covering her face, she walked closer to the edge of the cliff, never looking down as she came inches from her demise.

Drew continued to swing, and he wondered if she knew what was below her. Then he saw a foreboding cloud on her side of the divide, and again he slowed his pace so he could give warning. But before he could come to a stop, behind her there was a lion in the swaying cat-tails.

Instead of screaming her name, Drew leaped from the swing with his eyes on the woman and for a moment felt he was flying in the still air. He landed on the edge of the cliff with his toes over the rim.

As he tried to regain his balance, flailing his arms in the air like a windmill and with his toes clutching the corner, he looked down at the rocks that fell into the crashing waves below. And then he regained his balance and stood up. As he did, he saw the lion just inches from the lady, teeth bared, mouth wide open.

In spite of her danger the woman continued to watch him, and then he let out a scream. "Hey! Watch out! There's a lion! Behind you there's a lion!"

She still did not move.

Drew looked down at the rocks, and before he knew it, the ground beneath him shook, and he fell. A giant razor-edged rock jutted out of the water, aligned for his chest, and as he was falling, he looked up, and the lady said—

"Baby?"

"WHAT? Huh?" Drew said as he sat erect in their bed.

"What's wrong?" Betty asked, sitting on the edge of the bed and putting on her stockings.

"Ah, nothing." He could feel his heart hammer in his throat.

"You must have been having a bad dream," she said as Tickey jumped from the bed and curled up in a corner of the room. "You were kicking and mumbling something all night."

"It was nothing," he repeated, lying down with his forearm across his eyes. Still breathing hard and wet with perspiration, he asked, "What time is it?"

"A little after five."

"Why you dressed so early?" he asked, squinting at her as she stood up and walked across the room.

"Nervous energy, I guess. And also I have Carol and Here-ward— and yes, that's how you say his name—coming in at six, so I want to make sure everything is in order."

Over a yawn he asked, "But why so early?"

"Every day will be an early day from now until the trial date, which I think is going to be in September."

"Will that give you enough time?"

"I would love to push it back a few months, but my gut tells me since Meredith is the judge, I should not play that card."

"Isn't that the sister that was being considered for a Supreme Court nomination by the governor a few years ago?"

"One and the same," Betty replied as she opened a gold-toned box that was designed to look like a treasure chest and contained her accessories. "I've only had the pleasure of practicing before the Honorable Meredith Jackson a few times, and she's rigid. Actually, of the twelve cases I lost, she presided over four of them."

"*Umm.* So what time will you be in tonight?"

"I have no idea. Carol will be interviewing a few paralegals and grad students from the law school, and I need to decide on them today. Then I need to talk to the landlord about renting that vacant unit next to mine, and then—"

"Wait, wait a minute," Drew said with a clear voice. "You never mentioned how you were going to pay for this."

"He, I mean, Geno, has taken care of it all."

"So?" Drew asked.

"So what?"

"What arrangements did you all come to?"

"It was fair."

Drew sat up in the bed again.

"Okay, he gave me two hundred to set up the office and will pay me fifty per month."

"That's a lot of money. Or is it, considering what you will have to do?"

"Like I said, it's fair," Betty replied, looking into the mirror at the brooch on her conservative gray suit. "I may have been able to get more, but the time we spend negotiating would have been less time I could spend on the case." Then she cut off the light, which left only the golden tint of his night lamp in the room. Betty walked back to the bed and kissed her husband on the lips and whispered, "Sorry about last night, honey, I was a little tired. That's all."

"No problem. I'm very proud of you. You know that?"

"Thanks." And then she sat on the edge of the bed again. "I'm already tired, and we just started. I don't know how I'm going to get by on three and four hours of sleep."

With a smile that looked more like a grimace, she said, "It seems all my life I've wanted a case like this. Not a murder case per se but a high-profile case where it would be covered by Court TV and I'd be getting up to be interviewed by the morning talk shows. I would be contacted by newspapers about my thoughts on particular rulings, et cetera. And now that I have it, I feel like I have a tiger by the tail and don't know what the hell I'm supposed to do with it."

"Something tells me, Attorney Staley, that everything you need you already have." Drew took her hand and kissed her finger just below the gold band.

Betty smiled, looked at the glow of light cast on her husband, and said, "God, if only that was the case." And then she kissed him, turned out the light, and headed out the French doors.

As he heard her walk downstairs, Drew gathered his pillow under his head and pulled in a deep breath. Then he closed his eyes as tight as he could to flush out the previous illusion and wondered who was on the other side of the cliff.

With black coffee in hand and a goldenrod tie around his neck still untied, Drew rushed through the doors of Parkside Nursing and Rehabilitation. As he hurried down the hall toward his mother's room, he reviewed his appointments for the day and made a mental note to watch Betty on CNN. She called him on his cellular to tell him that she would be introduced to the national media and it would be broadcast live from the Parkers' estate at noon.

Hurrying down the corridor, he knew that the attention from the case would have an effect on their marriage. How much was still the unknown.

When Drew walked into the room, his mother, who was usually up and drinking her first cup of coffee before sunrise, was lying in bed under a sheet with the shades drawn.

"Momma?" he whispered, and put his hand on her hip.

She said nothing; she felt cold and did not move.

"Are you okay, Momma?" he asked, rubbing his hand up and down her thigh.

"No," she said as she shivered. "Can't . . . control . . . the shakes . . . today."

In the past two months, the effects of Parkinson's, which started as a twitch in her eyelid, had extended to most of the left side of her body.

She took medication, and usually it was able to reduce the involuntary quivering, but there were other times like this.

"Drew?"

"Ma'am?"

"Drew . . . you still there?"

"Yeah, Momma. What do you want me to do for you?"

"I changed my . . ." Then the words languished, and her ashen face lost expression. "Never mind. Would you just help me up?"

"Sure," he said as he walked back to the door, closed it, then returned to help her sit up.

With his hand in the midst of her back, Drew could physically feel his palm shake from her vibration, while his fingers on the right side of her body remained perfectly still.

Sitting up, Mrs. Staley gathered her composure and looked at her palm in her lap. Attempting to flex her fingers, she stared at her hand as it shook as if it was a stranger disjoined from the rest of her body. As if it were her anatomic Judas.

Drew stared at his mother, who, in the face of death, had changed her mind regarding the chemotherapy. After two months of encouragement from counselors, friends, psychologist, and himself, she felt she would try to see if the therapy would catch the disease before it claimed her body. But the months had been rough on her physically.

Previously, she would walk a mile a day on the treadmill. But after the diagnosis and onslaught of Parkinson's, her body seemed to be fighting a war and she was the enemy.

The hair she would regularly dye was graying at the roots, her nails had not been done in months, and she rarely wore makeup on her face. But the biggest change Drew noticed as he helped her get dressed was in her eyes.

Before her death sentence, she was at peace with life. But now it was a steady decline in the past several weeks into the abyss of her own demise.

"Hand me those blue pants, would'cha?" she said, pointing to the slacks crumpled in the corner.

"You wore those yesterday, Momma."

"No, I didn't!" she snapped. "I had on my green sweatpants!"

Drew picked up the pants and just out of curiosity checked in one of her dresser drawers. To his dismay, the clothing was tossed in the drawer as if it were a dirty clothes hamper.

Dirty socks were twisted around underwear, bras were mixed with jeans, and none of the previous organization was evident.

"Are you sure you would not rather wear your—"

"Boy, bring me my pants, for Christ sakes. I told you I haven't had them on!"

As he brought the pants to her, she looked at them in her hand as if the act of putting them on would be akin to lifting a heavy weight over her head.

"Give me a minute." And then Drew could see her calculating how she would navigate herself off the bed and into her apparel. Then she sipped a shallow breath into her lungs, caught the bed rail and his hand, and attempted to rise.

"Just keep on living," she mumbled. "When I was your age, I could jump around, too. Didn't know how it felt to be tired. Just keep right on living and you'll see."

Drew remained silent and held one leg of her pants as he would for a child, and then she grasped her quivering left leg and willed it into the pant leg.

When Drew bent over to assist her in putting the right leg in, she put her weight on his shoulder and said, "I done . . . I done changed my mind."

"About what, Momma?" he asked, pulling the pants over her narrow hips and fastening them around her waist. After he did so, she sat back on the edge of the bed, breathing as if she'd run a marathon. "Can you believe I used to prefer walking to riding in a car? Now you can't even tell, can you?"

"That's okay," he said as he walked over to the dresser to get her a blouse. "You want to wear anything in particular?"

"Just bring me anything." She looked at the pastel window treatment and said, "I decided I wasn't doing it."

"It what?" he asked as he retrieved her pink angora sweater, which was still folded in the bottom of the drawer, and then looked for a matching pair of clean socks.

"Not going to do it, *it*."

"What are you talking about, Ma? You mean the chemo?"

"What else," she said with dejection in her voice and her palm bouncing in her lap again. "They can't do nothing to help me at this point. No need of paying all that money to be poking and prodding on me and I ain't gonna get no better, anyway. Cutting all my hair off and looking like a fool. For what?" The more she talked, the more her hand shook. Then she lowered her voice and said, "So why go through it?"

With his shoulders rounded, Drew walked back to the bed and handed his mother the sweater and the socks, rolled into a ball. "Didn't we have this discussion a month or so ago? They still have a window of opportunity where they can correct this, but the longer we wait, the greater the chances of it spreading even more."

Then she looked up at Drew and replied, "Would you believe me if I said I don't care?" Drew stared at her without saying a word. And then he walked across the room, raised the blinds, and looked at the beginning of a new day over the hills.

"I don't care if I live or die anymore," she added, "and I mean that. So what if they find this thing," she said as her thigh shook under her hand. "So what if they dope me up with that ole mess. With me feeling sicker after taking it than I would feel with the cancer. What will I have left? 'Nother three months? 'Nother two or three years? Worrying every day about dying? That ain't living, son; that's breathing."

Drew leaned his body against the wall. "You know this is awfully selfish of you," he said, looking at a spot on the wall.

"What do you mean?" she said, looking over her shoulder.

After a pregnant pause, he said, "All my life, Momma, you have thought of no one but you, so I guess this shouldn't be any different."

"What are you talking about?"

Walking toward the bed, with a melancholy expression he answered, "Just what I said. It's been you, you, you from day one." And then he looked at the portrait of his father on the wall.

"When I was in the fifth grade," he continued, "and you helped me build that project, I won first prize, but you took all the credit. When Dad was on the road, you forgot my birthday entirely because you wanted to go gambling with your friends. Remember that? How about when I was in middle school and was at band practice and you didn't come pick me up from school because you had a hangover? I was out there until nine o'clock with a damn tuba. So now that this has come up, I wouldn't expect you to realize that after you leave I will be the last one left in the family. I thought just maybe you would want to be here for me. But I guess it's still all about you. Again."

"Can you hear yourself?" she asked as the sweater slid from her lap to the floor. "Can you hear how stupid that sounds?"

"I know it sounds stupid to you, but what can I say? Your selfishness got to me, and it still pisses me off when I think about it."

Mrs. Staley tried to reduce the shaking of her left hand by rubbing it with her right, and then she said without making eye contact. "Well, the hell with it. The hell with it, and the hell with you, too! I don't have to explain myself to you or anyone else. I'm sixty-seven damn years old. I gave you and I gave your father my life. Okay? I gave you all, everything I had," she said in a low, clear voice full of anger. "And now you want more than my life. You want me to give you my death?"

"Momma, listen, I gotta go. If you don't want to do the chemo thing," he said, walking toward the door, "fine. I'll tell Dr. McBride you changed your mind again, and she can cancel it. It's your life. Do as you please."

"Bring your behind back here!"

"No, Momma, I have an eight forty-five and a ten-thirty this morning."

"I said bring your black ass back here, Andrew. You started this," she said, and gingerly stood up from the bed. "Now I'm gonna finish it."

Drew filled his cheeks with air and blew it out to calm himself so he would not say the wrong thing and then turned around.

"This is something that I am going through. Not you. Not McBride. Not those quack psychologists, either. Me! I know me better than anyone. I say I do this the way I want to do this."

"And isn't that the definition of selfishness?" Exasperated he said, "Okay, Momma. Whatever you say. I gotta go."

"Don't you touch that door! What gives you the gumption to tell me what I should and should not do," she said, walking toward him, sliding her feet.

"Nothing, Momma."

"Speak your peace," she said, standing only a foot away from her son. "You got something to say, say it. Is it because of what I said about Betty?"

"Momma, I really don't want to go into that again."

"Well, I said what I said, and I meant it. That heifer ain't worth a quarter. I don't care what she does for a living. I didn't raise you and send you to college to marry some ole heifer like her! Ain't even got parents! I told you when you marry something like that—"

"Momma!"

"I said it! How dare you call me selfish," she said, walking back toward the bed. "After all I did raising you, working a job as a maid just so you could go to college, and then you sass me like that and talk to me like a dog?" In an angry whisper she said, "Well, the hell with you, too!"

As she got back into the bed, Drew said, "Well, maybe I said it because it was always about you. Even when you were sleeping with Mr. Douglass while Daddy was on the road!"

"What did you say?"

"Oh, I guess that wasn't selfish, huh. My mistake."

With a smile Mrs. Staley reached for her remote. Then she started laughing aloud as she turned on the television. "You are so damn gullible," she said. "That's why I didn't want you to marry that ole heifer, because she could tell you the sky was green and full of red lollipops and you'd believe it."

"Whatever, Momma. Listen, I gotta run. I will be out here tomorrow and see about getting you some maid service for the room."

"Do you really think for one second that your father was on the road for a month at a time?"

Drew, who had opened the door, stood in the doorway and could not cross the threshold.

"Do you really think a man who had a territory that was only about a thousand miles would be on the road that long without coming home?"

Drew turned. "So what are you saying."

"Boy, I assumed you knew that years ago. Everyone else knew. Hell, she even came to the funeral."

"Knew what? Who . . . who came to the funeral?" he stammered.

"Son, your father had a woman he'd been going with for fourteen, fifteen years before he died. Neither one of us believed in divorce, so he did his thing, and for years I knew about it and let it happen. Then, when things with Mr. Douglass progressed, I just let *it* happen."

"You telling me," Drew said as he walked back into the room, "that Daddy was having an affair? And that you knew all about it?"

"Honey, that's all I'm saying. I made a promise to myself that I would never even tell you what I just told you. But if your father and I could mislead you like that, what would Betty do to you? Look at what happened with Lecia? Sometimes, son, you just love too much. You were always like that. You dated that bitch for what? Two years, and after she died, you found out she didn't give a shit about you. I mean, son, think. You're a smart boy and all, but use your common sense."

Drew sat in the chair, cupped his face in his hands, and then looked at his mother over his arched fingertips. "So why are you telling me this about Daddy now?"

She paused before answering and then said "Drew, I'm dying. I still hate saying that word. But one way or the other you will be left here, and I want you to know how to manage when I am gone. That's all. I can't leave you nothing but a second mortgage and a piece of junk car. So I'm trying to leave you—" And then a tear formed in her eye. "Andrew, I'm trying to leave you a better person. I'm not trying to hurt you, son. Believe it or not I'm still the best friend you have in this world. But I want you to know how to look beyond the words when people give you—" And then her body started to shake more violently. "When people start feeding you a load of bull."

Mrs. Staley laid down on the bed, caught her breath, and pulled the sheet over her body.

"If I don't teach you anything, I want to teach you how to see truth. How to look beyond what is on the surface and see what is." Then she closed her eyes and said, exasperated, "I ain't ready to get up yet. Turn off my light, please?"

Drew rose from the chair and walked back to the door, turned to say something to his mother, and then changed his mind. Noticing he had not tied his tie, he turned toward the door, tied his goldenrod tie in a perfectly square knot, and then tugged on the end to make sure it came down to the top of his belt.

Then Drew turned off the light and said, "See you later, Momma."

"No matter what you think," she said from the darkness, "I would never hurt you. I'd rather hurt myself than to hurt you, and God knows . . ." And then the voice died. Drew opened the door a little wider to exit when he heard, "I say it out of love."

After saying good-bye without turning to look her way, he allowed the door to whisper to a close behind him.

In the health-and-fitness center, with its padded floor covered by chic exercise machines and silver weights encompassed by black padding, Drew rode the stationary bike with exuberance.

Lush green ferns tastefully decorated the corners of the building in which the sounds of Muzak looped continuously.

Women with cassette tapes, water bottles, and magazines under their arms socialized, while others on lunch break worked out quickly, without much outward concern for their appearance.

In the midst of this, Drew, with a headset plugged into the television output, pumped his thick legs so fast that the wheels of the bicycle appeared to move backward.

He wore a gray T-shirt with a butterfly-shaped sweat stain on his back and cutoff sweatpants.

As he continued his workout on the bike, the TV was tuned to the twenty-four-hour news station. Drew watched grandmotherly ladies walk the Stairmaster, a girl with red and yellow hair sweat orange, as well as a man work out on the weight bench, although he had no legs. They each had their own motivation. Drew's at this time was not to lose weight or build mass but to reduce stress.

As the bicycle quivered from the chopping motion of his body, the health club's towel was used to wipe the sweat from the seat of the bike after use fell off. As it did, an attractive young lady came over and picked it up. She had deep green eyes, blond hair, and ironically, a beauty mark over her lip in the same place as his wife.

Drew could see her saying something but could not hear the words; then he removed his headphones. "Excuse me?"

"Sorry, I was just saying you seem to be getting a great workout."

"Thanks." Drew then put his headphones back on and pedaled faster as he saw his wife's face on television.

"Thank you, Mr. Ivory. I really do not have much I can add to what has already been said. So I think I will simply field a few of your questions."

The shot stayed on Betty as a voice was heard off camera. "Counselor, what prompted you to take this case?"

Surrounded by microphones and handheld tape recorders, Betty looked toward the reporter.

"This is a horrific story," she said with the countenance of a mortician. "Two women, struck down in their prime, were found in the trunk of an automobile. No matter how the court rules, should this case go that far, there can be no happy ending." Then she scanned the room as she continued. "But a part of me has always pulled for the underdog. It's just my nature. I find myself pulling for the underdog in all aspects of life, but especially in the courtroom, which is why I've logged more pro bono hours than any other attorney in the county three of the past five years.

"Why, you may ask? Because what I have found is that the people in this country who cannot afford adequate representation are always the underdogs.

"But after talking to Mr. and Mrs. Parker and being honored by their request for my services, I would have been remiss if I had not agreed to represent Tobias, or as his family calls him, Toby.

"The more I looked at this case objectively, the more I felt in my heart that if I did not participate in whatever capacity the family would desire and if justice had not prevailed, I would in some way have been a party to the travesty.

"Tobias is the ultimate underdog. This is one time when the trappings of his accomplishment as an athlete, as a businessperson, with everything he has received from his family, are working against him.

" 'We hail you, and then we nail you,' I think one songwriter said, and it's true in a society which is in many ways tired of celebrities manipulating the judicial system. Tired of quote un quote professional sports icons who are accused of battering women and then signing autographs for the jury after the conclusion of the proceedings."

Then Betty found the CNN camera projecting her image around the globe. "But this is a man who has been wrongfully accused. While it would be inappropriate to go into details at this time, I will say that we are not interested in a plea bargain in any form and that anything short of a full acquittal is unacceptable."

Drew smiled as he continued to pump his legs on the exercise equipment. Looking down, he saw droplets of sweat on the floor, and then he felt a hand on his back. Then the person pulled the headphone pad from his ear and said in a high-pitched tone, "Wussabbee."

Recognizing Stefan's voice, Drew continued to pedal as he took the headset from his ears, still watching television. "How's it going?"

"Great man, I thought—Damn, that's Betty?" he said, raising his voice another octave. "Wussup with that?"

"She's representing Bear."

"Damn, really? I hadn't heard about that. Damn," he said, taking the headset from the bicycle next to Drew's and putting it on his head.

"Mrs. Staley, over here, please? Prior to this case, we're told that your biggest trial involved a wrongful-death lawsuit. Having never defended someone charged with a capital offense, do you think you are best qualified for such a case?"

"The best qualified is neither here nor there, because that is something that can and will be much bantered about in the press until the case is over and then thereafter. No, I do not have experience in defending a client charged with murder, but I have represented people like a particular young man who was charged with rape last year. He was even pointed out in a lineup by the victim, and the DNA matched. The case did not get as much publicity as Tobias because he worked as a telephone repairman.

"I looked in the local newspaper. There were four stories when he was charged, but when he walked out the courthouse two years ago, it was a page-three story. As a result, this man lost his wife, his kids, his home, and is still underemployed. This is the travesty of justice I am trying to prevent from occurring again.

"I believed in my client in the aforementioned case, and I believe in Mr. Parker. And let me state here that if I was not one hundred percent confident that he was innocent, I don't know if I would have wanted to devote to this case the time and resources necessary to ensure that justice is served."

Drew maintained his speed as the next question was posed to

Hereward Ivory. In the corner of his eye he saw Stefan talking to a shapely sister and then patting his chest and his hips as if he were looking for something to write with, although he was wearing work-out attire.

Then, as Drew continued with his fast-paced workout, Stefan took the pencil from a clipboard and wrote her number down on the back of a yellow workout card. As she walked away, he continued to gaze at her departure and then put on his headphones to catch the rest of the interview.

Taking his headphones off after completing his workout and trying to catch his breath, Drew panted, "She done."

"Damn. Sorry I missed that, so wussup? When did they get her on the case?"

"Last . . . last night," Drew said between breaths as he toweled off, still sitting on the bike.

"Well, tell her I said congratulations." Looking around the health center, he added, "I'm a little out of the loop now'days."

"Yeah, Betty told me . . . you guys are not together."

Looking directly at Drew, he said, "Is that how she said it?"

"Said what?"

"She said me and Jacquetta were not together or that we broke up or what? How did she say it?"

"I think she said it just like that, actually. I think she said you all were . . . not together."

"Umm. Well, no. We broke up about a week ago," he said, watching a lady wearing a purple thong leotard wave as she passed.

"So you all don't talk or anything?"

"Nah. I'm not ready to settle-damn Money," Stefan said. "Look at that freak over there!"

As a woman on a pad stretched her inner thigh muscles, both men watched, and then Drew said, "Well, I'm kinda sorry things have not worked out for you all. I know Jacqui is my sworn enemy and all, but I did think you guys were good for each other."

"There she is, there she is," Stefan said, oblivious to what Drew was saying. "That's the one I was telling you about. Up there on the top floor."

"Telling me what about? Who?"

"See? The bitch in the orange-and-black biker shorts with all her shit showing?"

"Oh, I see her."

"Remember I told you about the female who wanted to be a clown so she went to that clown college in Tallahassee? Tried to twist my nuts on top of my dick and made it look like a damn poodle when we were through?"

"Oh, yeah, I remember you telling me about her. But you said something about her not being too smart, right?"

"Yeah. If you look in her eyes, you can see the wheel spinning, but the hamster is deader than a motherfucker."

"Damn. She that slow?" Drew said with a chuckle.

"Let's just says she's a few clowns short of a full circus, but she's fine. You see that ass on her?" Drew sat straight as Stefan continued. "Man, one thing I know about is women. I might not have a college education and all, but I know females. Did you see the big head white chick on the bike in front of you?"

"Naw, I hadn't noticed."

"You had to see her. She kinda skinny? Backbone stick out like Mr. Burns on the Simpsons? Head so big she look like a walking candy apple?"

"Didn't notice."

"Oh. Well, anyway, she used to try to kick game to me years ago when I first started coming here. But that was before I met Jacquetta."

"Umm."

"I might have given her some play, too, but she was nosy as hell."

"What do you mean?"

"Always up in my business. We went out for like three or four weeks, and then she wanted to know my personal business. Like," he said in a high-pitched voice, "What's your name? What chu thinking about? Do you work? You know, personal shit." Stefan laughed.

"You are twisted, bro," Drew said with a smile.

"Man, since me and Jacquetta broke up . . ." Then his voice died.

"What?"

"Nothing. So why you up in here so early? I done told you the finest women work out around seven. This time a day all you got in here is a bunch of old wrinkled-up doctors' wives."

"Just had a stressful day. Thought I'd come in and get this over with."

"Umm. Look at that fine mother—"

"What were you going to say earlier?"

"Earlier when?"

"When you mentioned Jacqui."

"Nothing. Listen, see that chick over there with the braids? Look kinda like Debbie Allen?"

"Yeah, I see her in here a lot."

"Man, you should see her husband. He owns that 'buy-here-pay-here' car dealership on University Ave. He's a big ole fat, stank, pig-feet-eating mother, too."

"Yeah, I know him. Felton Burke. I used to handle a benefits plan for his employees."

"I know yaw'll couldn't get that fat ass of his insured."

"Actually, we couldn't, but he's cool people."

"I know you couldn't. He must be pushing four hundred pounds, and every time I go in, or rather used to go into Jacqui's, his fat ass was in there scarfing down food."

Drew looked at Wolf Blitzer on the television and said, "You miss her, don't you."

"Who, me?" Stefan asked as he looked at his friend. Then he looked up at the reporter and said softly, "Like air, man. Like mother-fucking air."

"So what happened this time?"

"Long story," Stefan said as he got on the bike beside Drew and they both began peddling at the same slow pace.

"You remember she put me out earlier this year, right? Well, I didn't call her because I moved in with my baby's momma for a while."

"Terry?"

"Yeah. So I stayed on the down low, and honestly, things started to progress with her a little faster than I wanted them to. My plan was to chill at her place until I got enough to pay the first month on an apartment.

"I sorta laid the law down with Terry and told her this was just temporary and everything was cool. I stayed in one room, she slept in the other, and I got to see Sasha every day. Even walked her to school one day."

Stefan paused momentarily, and Drew smiled as Stefan's eye glistened at the mere mention of his daughter's name.

"But D," he said, and shook his head. "One day I came home from work. I had just called Jacquetta, and she was there but would not come to the phone, and so I was thinking to myself, Fuck it. It's over between me and her. Well, I get up in the spot, and Terry had arranged for a sitter. So I walk in, and the whole apartment is dark except for this candle on the dinner table. I walk in the crib, and she walks out wearing this lingerie thing I had never seen before, and I tried to say something, but before I could get a word in edgewise, she was like on her knees on a brother, right?"

"So you and her back together again?"

"Nah, man. I was in bed with her, and she was talking family, and I was thinking Jacqui. I mean, the more I thought about Terry, the more I knew we could never have anything together. She still looking for herself, and to be honest, man, if I ever settle down, it will be with Jacqui. You know me," he said as he watched the ladies through the glass on all fours, kicking their legs in the aerobics class.

"I've been out there—out there. I don't know how many women I've been with anymore, but Jac is the only one that felt like a wife when I was with her. She is the only one that, when we made love, man, took me to another level. I don't know how to put it any better than that."

"Trust me, man, I understand."

"I mean, I have an uncle named Robert. We all call him Bobby King 'cause he looks just like B. B. King. He lives out in the projects, and sometimes I hate to even visit, 'cause as soon as you walk out the door, all you see is crack heads, dope slingers and cops.

"He once killed this man about something thirty or forty years ago and only did ten years 'cause it was self-defense. Well, he's a great guitarist, but he lives on woulda, shoulda, and couldas. He could open a fucking woulda, shoulda, and coulda store. But when those run out, then what will he live on?" Stefan said as he looked at Drew.

"So he sits in this piece of shit apartment and gets high most of the day, and to be honest, I look at everything he's done, and I try to do the exact opposite." Mocking his uncle, Stefan said, " 'I woulda took that gig with Milt Jackson, but I don't trust nobody with my money. I can play rings around Jonathan Butler. I shoulda done this or don' tat.' And that's just not me."

"That's sad."

"The more I think about it, the more I think I could never give up on being a model. I mean, he must be what? Sixty or seventy years old, and I swear the man is in the club every Friday night sitting in the same spot. Wears this fucked-up jheri-curl, loud clothes, just like people wore in the seventies, except he wears Air Jordans, and he's paying rockheads three dollars to screw.

"I mean, I look at all the men in my family, and they are not all as bad as him, but none of them I know of have a stable relationship. I just don't want to be some pathetic old-ass man sleeping with twenty-year old bassas. But it's scary, dawg, 'cause to be a black man, you gotta see a black man. And I don't even know a black man . . . except for me."

"So what are you going to do?"

"I know what I should do. I mean, after I stopped seeing Terry, Jacqui and I were doing a lot better. I didn't move in, and I didn't want to move in, but seems everything was clicking again. Then she saw a phone number in my pocket, and she—"

"Damn, Step. You were still out getting numbers?"

"I told her the number belonged to a dude I worked out with, and then she lost it. And boom. We had another argument. But the reason I lied is because she would not have been ready to deal with the truth."

"Which was?"

A Hispanic woman with an American University law sweatshirt walked over to Stefan and whispered something in his ear. He smiled back at her and said, "Really?" And then she whispered something else that made him laugh aloud and then bring his fist up to his mouth. "Cool," he said. And then he watched her departure as she walked away.

"Anyway, as I was going to say, D, I wanted to turn over a new leaf with Jacquetta. I really did, but this female I did a shoot with was in town for the weekend, and she wanted to hook up with a brother. Well, she asked me to call and gave me the digits. I honestly had no intention of going out or even calling her, but I, like a dumb ass, forgot to throw the number away.

"So I pulled out a few bills to give to Jacquetta to buy me something from the store, and what falls out on the floor *with* a condom I might add?"

"That's messed up."

"Yeah, so since then I've been in the outhouse. Again."

"Well, just give her some time, man. But honestly, you need to cool it with the ladies."

"D, trust me, man, I've tried. But they are like all over me. Especially the white bitches, for some reason. I don't know why."

"Just try saying no for once."

"I do, man, but when I was a kid, I used to be real fat, right? I mean, I was like two fifty in the eleventh grade. I was a virgin playa until I was twenty-five years old, swear to God. But I noticed that every time I lost a pound or two the females started noticing a brother.

"Remember that time Oprah lost all that weight on her show? Well, that fasting shit worked for me, and I just never gained it back."

"So now you just can't walk away from it?"

"I can, man," he said like a drug addict in denial, "but it's hard to go from being laughed at when you just walked in certain stores to find pants to having women like—Well, hello, Heather." Then the green-eyed blonde who had spoken to Drew earlier walked over to Stefan as he rode the bike. "Let me introduce you to my friend. Andrew Staley, this is Heather Coaldale. Her husband coaches the defensive backs for the Gators. And Heather, this is my friend Drew. Drew's a—" And then he broke his attention from her momentarily and asked Drew, "What is it you do again? I know it has something to do with money or something."

"I'm a financial consultant."

"Oh, a broker?" she asked as her eyes widened.

"Not exactly. I run a firm over on the northwest side of town that works with small businesses."

"Well, that's nice," she said, and then, with a quick glance, looked down at Drew's crotch and said, "Well, Danny and I may need your assistance. We just bought a nursery, and neither one of us knows a tinker's damn about bookkeeping or any of that stuff."

"Actually, that's not what we do, but if you call our office, I can give you some numbers of a few accountants who can assist you."

"Are you in the book? Well, of course you are."

"Andrew Patrick Staley and Associates."

As they spoke, Stefan volleyed his attention back and forth, watching their expressions.

"Okay, Mr. Staley. I'll call you Monday morning."

"Nice meeting you," Drew said, and then looked up at the muted television as Stefan watched her departure.

"You see the ass on her?"

"Umm," Drew replied, still looking up at the news.

"D, look at me?"

"What," Drew said, looking at Stefan.

"You mean to tell me you wouldn't hit that?"

"You have, haven't you."

"Man, she is all that. She can suck—"

"Step, you know me," Drew said, looking back at the television. "Not my style."

"So you have never cheated on—"

"Not once. Not even close."

"Wait a minute. You mean all those fine-ass'd black chicks in your office working for you? All the women I done seen you talking to in here myself, you have never once—"

"Not one time. I don't go out like that. I'm married."

"I know that, but—"

"Marriage means something to me, man." Thinking about his earlier conversation with his mother, his eyes fell to half-mast as he said, "I know a lot of people cheat nowadays, but I think if I cheated on Betty . . ." Although he was watching television, the image of Evander was all he saw. "If I ahh, *umm*—"

"You said *if* you cheated on Betty."

"Yeah. *If* I cheated on Betty, one day she would cheat on me. I just know she would, and I couldn't deal with that."

"My best friend in high school caught his woman in bed with a guy," Stefan reminisced. "He used to always brag about how fine she was and all the money he was making. Paid for her to have a full-time trainer and everything. He caught him banging her in the Jacuzzi."

As Stefan continued to tell the story, Drew imagined Evander in a Jacuzzi with his wife.

"So that's all I'm saying, man. You agree?"

"Tell me this, man. What are you going to do about Jacqui? Are you all going to get back together again or what?"

"You know what I miss the most, man? I miss being a couple. Not so much the sex, although she could sex like none other. But I miss waking up with her in the morning. I miss playing Monopoly with you and Betty and fighting about playing by the real rules or the black rules. I miss coming home and her having popcorn ready and two or three Blockbuster movies out for me to select one I wanted to watch."

"I would imagine."

"I love her. And like I said, I miss her like I would miss drawing breath itself." Stefan thoughtfully brought his hand to his jaw as if he were thinking about what used to be. And then his dark eyes fell. "The first time I made that delivery to the restaurant, I knew. I was attracted to her like Celie to Shug Avery. I tell you no lie. But Jac hurt me bad. I mean, she had me crying like a little girl, and I've never even told her that.

"Yeah, I want her back, but the more I think about it, the more I think it will never happen. And the more I think it will never happen, I just give up trying." Then he looked up, and his sad expression brightened. "Yo, yo, Gloria! Wussup! Come over here and talk to me, you fine-ass mother—"

Drew sat in the house watching David Letterman's Top Ten list when he heard Betty's truck pull into the driveway.

"Okay and the number-one sign," Letterman said, "that you may have gone to a bad chiropractor. When you walk, you make a wacky accordion sound!"

Drew walked out of the den and jogged downstairs with the enthusiasm of a puppy hearing its master's footsteps. As he got to the bottom, he could hear her close the garage door.

"Hey, love," he said as she came in with her briefcase and a thick folder under her arm. "How was your day?"

With a smile she said, "Not too good. Until now."

"I saw you again on ESPN and on Fox Sports and on NBC and on—"

"Yeah, we must have gotten fifty media calls today," she replied, and rested the briefcase on the floor and the file on the table in the breakfast nook. "It eventually got to the point where I had to stop accepting them. Oh, yeah, also, if you need me, just call on the cellular," she said, and then she walked into her husband's arms. "We had about two or three calls today from men saying they were you, and the girl answering the phone put them through. It was ridiculous, I'm telling you," she said, and rubbed her face on his bare chest.

"I'd imagine. So you said, girl. Have you hired a receptionist?"

"Yeah. In all honesty I just hired the first person who could speak and didn't have needle tracks on their arms. I also hired two paralegals, a grad student, and we will have another attorney with a little more experience trying murder cases assisting us as well."

"Congratulations. Sounds like you had a full day and then some."

"We got a lot accomplished," she said, as she took off her shoes, then bent over to pick them up.

"Don't worry about that, sweetie. I have the tub ready for you, and the covers are already pulled back."

"Aren't you sweet," Betty said, and picked up the shoes. "Don't worry about these, but I do have a box in the car you can get for me if you don't mind."

"Okay, but get upstairs before the water gets too cold."

Betty smiled and then tiptoed and kissed him on the lips. As she walked toward the stairs, she retrieved her mail and said, "So how was your day. Anything interesting happen?"

"Not a thing, but get upstairs, now," he said as he opened the door. "I'll be up there in a moment to wash your back if you like."

As he went out to her truck, Drew started whistling the theme song from the *Andy Griffith Show.*

Although it was a day that started like a slap in the face, he had left Stefan with the impression that he should try to patch things up with Jacqui, and his wife was now a nationally recognized attorney.

Looking in the backseat, he saw a file marked legal briefs. "Just like attorneys," he said as he pulled the heavy box from the SUV with a grunt. "They write a thousand words in a document and call it a brief."

After freeing the files from the truck, he saw a tie he'd left in the vehicle that was still in the backseat. As he picked it up, he noticed a magazine slide from under the passenger seat.

Drew picked both items up and placed the magazine on the backseat, but then the article caught his attention.

The black ink of the magazine was smeared as if it had been read several times. "Getting Over Him and Getting On with You" was the heading of the article. As Drew read it, he felt numb to the world and ensconced in rage.

As he scanned it, his eyes refusing to allow him to read the words, entire passages were smudged. And then he gathered himself and tried to decide if he would ignore this and wait for her to say something, ask her about it, or attempt to forget it.

Picking up the box of files, Drew slammed the door of her truck a little louder than normal and took the box in the house.

"Drew? Honey?" Betty said as he could hear her running the water to no doubt make the bath even hotter. "Next time you close my door? Close it just a *little* harder, please? I think a few hinges are still left on it," she said, laughing.

Drew remained silent; he could feel his teeth grind.

"Oh, yeah, honey? I don't know how I forgot this, but thank you so much for the roses. That was sweet."

Drew put the box down and closed the garage door. Then he walked evenly toward the stairs.

"Drew? Did you go back out for something?"

He remained silent.

"Honey, do you hear me?"

Silence.

"If you go back outside, would you bring in my—" And then Betty, who was sitting on the toilet seat stirring the water with her fingertips, jumped when Drew walked into the bathroom. "Boy, don't scare me like that. I thought you went out to your car for something."

Drew walked in without looking at her, his hands balled into a fist and in his pockets and the magazine under his arm.

"What's wrong with you?"

"Betty?"

"Yes?"

Drew paused and with his eyes red with anger said, "I didn't send you flowers today."

Chapter 9

Friends are the family we choose ourselves.
—Edna Buchanan
Suitable for Framing

JULY

"Hello."

Jacqui saw a well-dressed gentleman to the right of her in an expensive suit, but since she was not working and not dressed appropriately, she didn't turn to look. As he got closer, she recognized him but was not in the mood for conversation.

"Excuse me?"

Jacqui turned with two bags of hot food from her restaurant.

Jogging toward her in the parking lot of the strip mall where Betty's office was located, the man asked, "How are you? Sorry to bother you, but I think we've met before."

Unable to believe he still could not recognize her, although he was just a few yards away, she said, "I don't think so."

Then he got closer. "Yeah, I'm sure we have. Maybe you came to one of my services? I'm Pastor Cleon," the slightly overweight gentleman said. "Cleon Jamieson? Southside Holiness? Does that ring any—"

"Ew, I don't think so," she said, and then turned to walk into the firm.

"Well, praise the Lord, praise the Lord, I never forget a face. I know we've met." And then he ran ahead of her. "Please let me get the door for you?"

"Thanks."

Before the door closed, she saw him standing outside, smiling, and then he said, "Have a blessed day."

Unheard by him, she said, "Men are so damn stupid," and then she noticed the receptionist. "Hello, is Betty back there?"

"Betty? Oh, you mean Mrs. Staley? And who might I say is calling?" the fair-skinned receptionist with the cornrowed hair asked as she shook a bottle of lotion.

"Ahh, yeah. Just tell her Jacqui?"

"Jacqui who?"

"Listen, these bags are a little hot, honey. Can you just—"

"Jacqui!" Carol said, walking from the back office. "How are you today? Give me one of those bags."

As she took the bag, the phone rang, and the receptionist, wearing a headset as she put a dollop of lotion in her palm, answered in a professional voice.

"Sorry about that. She started this morning. We have two receptionists now. Can you believe that? She will handle the weekends, since we will be a seven-day-a-week operation for a while."

"No problem. Where is Betty?" Jacqui asked as two well-built construction workers walked out of the back office with another potbellied man sucking an unlit cigar.

"Hey there, sweet cheeks," he said as he looked at Carol. "I woke up t'day and looked in the mirror and said, 'Mirror, mirror on the wall, will this be a lucky day for us all?' "

"And what happened? The mirror spit on you?" Carol replied with a smile.

"See, Red, that's why I like you! You don't have spice. You have peppa'reka, onions, and a li'l bit of sassy'frass in you!" And then he started laughing with an infectious laugh that came from his toes and even made the receptionist laugh with him.

"Listen here, Red. We should be able to get out of this place by noon. Four o'clock at the absolute latest. But if you ask me nicely, I could hang round 'til, say, ohhhhh, nine or so. We could maybe hit the bingo game at the VFW, and after that, who knows? Maybe do something crazy like go bowling or something."

Carol smiled as he passed, the back of his pants displaying more about him than either woman cared to know.

"Think about it. I'll be around," he said as they walked out the door.

"Let's go this way, Jacqui," Carol said as they followed the three men out the door.

"What's going on?"

"Betty's next door. I thought you knew. We're leasing all four units. Two were already vacant, and we assumed the lease on the third. Betty asked Parker to pay them to relocate, so the entire building is ours."

"That's great," Jacqui said as the chubby man in the black suit passed and smiled at her again.

Then the two ladies entered the door that was still stenciled Ming-Yatsen House of Massage, Tattoos and Wings.

As they entered, there were workers painting over the large red-and-green dragon on the back wall of the room.

"She's more than likely still on the phone," Carol said, stepping over a box marked B.S. and Ass. "Ignore the smell; they said they will fumigate and it'll be better by Monday."

"Forget the smell. What the hell is B.S. and Ass?" Jacqui asked, looking at the boxes etched with bold red letters.

"Oh," Carol said, and then laughed. "Betty decided to rename the firm just Betty Staley and Associates, but I guess that looks a little funny, huh."

"Damn," Jacqui said. "Well, please, God, don't put that on a business card. Not good to get a business card from a sister who's an attorney with the words B.S. and Ass on it."

"Who's out there? Jac, that's you in there making trouble?" Betty shouted over the sound of a handheld saw cutting through plywood.

As they entered Betty's office, she sat at her old desk surrounded by boxes of files.

"Yeah," Jacqui said. "What's all this shit?" And then Jacqui saw a dark brown man with thick eight-inch dreads, a three-day beard, a lean, muscular six-foot-three body, and a tool belt shanked by a hammer that swung loosely between his legs.

"These?" Betty replied as she smiled at Jacqui's expression. "THESE," she repeated louder "are all files we brought in for research."

"Oh, you got *files* in here, too?" Jacqui replied in an impersonation of Jackee from the show *227* as the young man looked her way and blushed.

"Stop it!" Betty said, giggling. "Peter, excuse my friend Jacqui," she said, pointing toward him and then her friend. "Jacqui, this is Peter. Peter Graham, Jacquetta Jordan."

"Nice to meet you, ma'am," he said, standing and shaking her hand.

"Peter here owns the company, and he's helping us to renovate the offices," Betty said, leaning back in her chair and rotating from the ten o'clock to the two o'clock position.

"Damn, really?"

"Yes, ma'am."

"Ahh, don't say it, Miss Jordan. I can almost read your mind," Betty chimed in.

"What?" Jacqui said, her head at an angle.

"Whatever you're thinking," Betty said.

"Miss Jordan?" Peter asked with down-slanted eyebrows. Then he looked at her fingers, and his smile displayed perfectly straight teeth.

Jacqui sat the bag down on the table where Carol had placed hers and said, "She didn't studder, honey."

A crash of what sounded like falling buckets fell in the outer office. As all three ladies jumped, Peter said, "What happened? Everyone okay in there?"

"Yeah. Just knocked over something with this here ladder," the voice called back.

"Damn," he said to himself, and then said to Jacqui, "I'll be back, okay?"

"Ah, you see any skates on my feet? I'll be right here, sugar."

As he walked out, Betty and Carol looked at Jacqui, their heads tilted down.

"What? What I do?" she asked coyly.

"Girl, you ought to be ashamed of yourself," Betty said as Jacqui raised and wiggled her unadorned fingers in front of her nose. "I don't care if you're not married; you need to go to church and have some hands laid on you or something. That boy could be your son!"

After laughing, Carol said, "You two are too much. Listen, I need to go next door and check on La Shandra."

"Carol? It's La Shaunda." Looking at Jacqui, Betty said, "She's a good receptionist, but she's kinda picky about the way her name is pronounced."

As the door closed, Betty said, "Hand me my lunch, please, ma'am. I'm starving."

"Here you go." Jacqui said, passing her the white Styrofoam box from the bag. "So if they're making all these changes to the office, what happens when the trial is over? You gonna keep all these people?"

"No way. We may keep two offices, though, because hopefully, with all the exposure, we'll be able to get a little more business. But we won't need this much room."

"So how did you get so lucky to get cutie? I noticed you had him hemmed up in your office and had the fat-ass white crack man next door."

"See, I knew I should not have let you come here today. You done started already."

"What? Please. He is three-fine and has the cheeks to have dimples, too? With those sexy hazel eyes. It's a damn sin and a shame to have a man look that damn good," Jacqui said, sitting and opening up her lunch.

"Ah," Betty said softly, "yeah. I noticed."

"You noticed what? I know you ain't up in here noticing something with your married-ass self."

"Hey, you know I would never touch, but geez, I'm still breathing."

"He seems flirty, too. Did he try anything?" Jacqui asked as she settled in the chair and crossed her legs. "Wait a minute. Don't you usually work on the weekends in sweats and a baseball cap? What's up with the pantsuit? And heifer, you wearing perfume also?"

"Girl, please," Betty said as she read from the *Law Journal* and ate a forkful of greens. "The only reason I'm dressed today is because of the media attention. They have photographers all over the place taking pictures, and I don't want to look haggard when they see me. Remember. That's what happened to Marcia Clark."

"True. So, it's officially on, huh?"

"It's *officially* on. It all still seems a little surreal, to be honest, though. I mean, three days ago I'm here wondering if I would need to dip into my savings to make payroll, and now I'm wondering if we will have enough room to accommodate everyone."

Leaning forward, Jacqui asked Betty as Carol spoke to a delivery person with office supplies in the next office, "So tell me. I know you don't want to go into details. But do you believe he did it?"

Betty smiled.

"What the hell does that mean? Tell me something."

"Well, when I took the case, I wasn't really sure. I mean, the story he gave me sorta deviated from the one his father told me.

"But after thinking about it and looking at the preliminary evidence, he's guilty of something, but not first-degree murder. Now I gotta get the state attorney to take the bait, pursue first degree and nothing else, and I think we can win."

"Umm."

"But in answer to your question. No, he did not kill them. I'm positive of that."

"Now that I got that out the way, let's talk about Dick. I mean Peter!"

Shaking her head, Betty said, "You're just determined to be nasty, aren't you."

"Girl, it's been a while for a sister."

"Join the club," Betty mumbled as she put the *Law Journal* on the floor with the others and took off her glasses.

"What chu mean? You in the L.C.C.? The Lonely Coochie Club?"

"It's just our schedules and all," Betty said, laughing. "People think when you get married you say I do and start a sexfest. It ain't hardly like that."

"So is he still staying with his mom at night?"

"At least two or three nights a week. Sometimes more."

"And?"

"And what?"

"How do you feel about that?" Jacqui said with yams, stuffing, and a slitter of turkey on one fork.

"You wanna know the truth? Sometimes I really could not care less. I lived all my adult life alone, and every now and then it's nice to have the bed to yourself. To use the bathroom with the door open and not flushing every three seconds. Does that sound selfish?"

"Not at all if you ask me. Hell, I may have two beds in my room, like Lucy and Ricky, when I get married. Well, maybe three."

"Three?"

"Well we'll need one for—"

"Alrighty, then," Betty said, holding up her hand with a straw in her mouth. "So have you heard from Stefan?"

"I done told you not to bring that Negro's name up to me."

"So it's like that now?"

Jacqui put her fork down and wiped her fingertips on the napkin.

"Stefan is still searching, and the longer I'm with him, the more I think he will never know who he is."

"But he has this big shoot in a few months. Won't that lead to other things in modeling?"

"It's not even about that. Whenever I mention his searching to him or anyone else, they tell me about the shoot. It's not just about his career when I say trying to find himself. I mean, we are not what we do. It's just a part of us, and that was one of our biggest problems."

"I see."

"I mean, if everything went great in July and say he got a Karl Kani hookup, he would still be the same person deep inside. He'd just have more money."

"So you don't think he knows who he really is as a person."

"Exactly. I love, loved," she corrected, "Stefan with everything in my soul. And I wanted to be with him the rest of my life. But the more I dug into who he really was as a person, the more I saw this forty-year-old child. And that's when I started to shut down on him. And trust me, I really wanted it to work. Even when I kicked him out, I always felt, or at least hoped, we could work things out. Sometimes—I tell you no lie—I feel kinda embarrassed not to be married and have kids and all."

Betty simply shook her head.

"At this point in life you stop pointing the finger in many ways and just wonder what the hell is wrong with you and why can't you make it work and wondering if you will *ever* find anybody."

Staring at the food in her box, Jacqui reached into her purse and took out a cigarette. As she thought, she ran her fingertips up and down its shaft. "You wanna know the loneliest fifteen seconds I've ever felt?" Before Betty could react, she said, "December 31, 1999.

"If I live to be a thousand, I'll never forget it. Remember, you were in the Caribbean, and I was here, watching television. I remember Dick Clark saying, 'Fifteen seconds until the turn of a new millennium. You will never see this moment again! Grab someone you love and get ready to kiss them!' I picked up the remote and turned the television off before they got to three."

Then she looked at Betty and said with moist eyes and a smile, "I think that's why I read so much. That way I can just live through others and forget about reality for a while. Sometimes when I read a good book, it's almost like I'm dreaming, but I'm wide awake."

There was a momentary pause, and then Betty softly said, "That's why you're smoking again?"

Jacqui broke from her trance and whispered as she looked at the cigarette, "Gotta die of something."

"I always thought the two of you would be together forever."

"I used to think the same thing. Mostly because he used to always say that." The sound of a saw cutting through wood was heard in the background as she said, "I guess there's a one-year expiration date on forever now, huh," and then she returned the cigarette to her purse.

"So are you saying," Betty shouted, and then lowered her voice as the saw was replaced by several hammers, "that it's over-over for you and him?"

"I hate to say it, but yeah. I don't even want it to work anymore, and no one hates that more than me, 'cause I invested so much time in his sorry ass. I also hate getting out there again. I hate meeting some asshole and wondering if he is worth a damn in bed. I hate telling him what my favorite color is. I hate telling him how I built Jacquetta's. I just hate starting over, I guess."

"I can relate."

"And at our age—"

"At your age, skank."

"Shut up." Jacqui smiled and threw a Wet-Nap at her friend to wipe her fingers on. "At *our* age it seems you can't go out and have fun without being interviewed for a job as a wife. When you date now'days, you should just bring your résumé and a list of your four most recent boyfriends."

"Yeah, it's pretty bad."

"Pretty bad, my ass. How many job interviews have you gone on and when it was over you were naked, upside down, with your legs spread in the air and this ass saying, 'Thanks for coming in. Don't call us. We'll call you.' "

"You're cold."

"Not cold. Just honest. That's how I felt when I went out with Cleon, who, I might add, I just saw in your parking lot."

"Oh, I remember him. The preacher, right?"

"Yeah, I know. He just saw me, and since I had my hair different and was not dressed up, he had no idea who I was. I hates a stupid brother. He's cute, but his belt doesn't exactly go through *all* his loops, if you know what I'm saying. Ain't nothing sadder than a brother trying to mack who is stupid and has no memory and can't even remember the stupid-ass lies he's told.

"But on a serious note, Bet, I loved Stefan," she said, looking across the desk. "But I couldn't trust him. He was so insecure, it's a shame."

"Insecure? We're talking about the same Stefan DeCoursey?"

"He talks a good game, but he's very insecure, and all the big talk is just a cover, and I can't deal with that. I want a man to be a man and know he is a man, not by what he can give me, 'cause I can get it on my own. Not by what he drives, 'cause if he's a man, trust me, it will not matter. I just want a brother who walks into a room, and you look at him and say, 'Gad damn, now that's a man.' "

Betty looked through Jacqui and said, "That's what I used to say about Evander."

Jacqui's eye widened.

"Yeah, I know. Actually, that's the first time I've mentioned his name in I don't know when. But I saw this *Upscale* article, and it said you must first and foremost face your fears."

In a voice softer than any she'd used previously, Jacqui asked, "And what's your fears?"

"Do you really want to know?"

Jacqui shook her head.

"I fear I will be like my mom. She and Daddy never married, and as I may have mentioned, she was just in and out of one relationship after another. I had so many uncles growing up I . . . Well, anyway, that's not me, and I don't want that to ever be me.

"But my biggest fear is that—" And then Betty seemed to lose the words. "Well, I guess my biggest fear is that I may have feelings for Evander, and I know that sounds crazy," Betty added as Jacqui momentarily closed her eyes.

"I'm not saying I want to be with him. Don't get me wrong. But what I'm saying is this. You don't just click love on and off like a light switch. I mean, what he did was wrong, and I will never forget it, but I can't deny what I may feel in my heart."

"So, do you love Drew, or was he just therapy?"

There was silence. "I've asked myself that same question in a hundred different ways and a hundred different times. And each time the answer is yes. I do love him, but that doesn't change the way I feel about that asshole, and I know it's hard to make you understand. Hell, even I don't understand it."

"Do you think Drew knows how you feel?"

"Ohh, yeah," Betty said with raised eyebrows, and then looked away. "He most *definitely* knows."

"How?"

Betty pulled out the magazine from her open briefcase on the floor and placed it in front of Jacqui. "He found this in the car."

"Damn."

"Yeah, I know. Plus Evander sent flowers yesterday, and I thought Drew sent them."

"So you did exactly what Evander wanted you to do. You opened your mouth."

"We had this blowup last night, which is the last thing I need to deal with at this time. I didn't get to sleep until after three."

"Betty?"

"Yes?"

"You know how I feel about Drew. But what you did is really fucked up. You know that, don't you?" Betty sat silently. "Why did you go through with this if you were not sure? I knew you didn't want to go through with it when—"

"I couldn't say no, okay? That's all I can say, damn. I mean, yeah, I had strong feelings for Drew the night he asked me, and then I thought after he gave me the ring that things would change a little, and actually I believed they did. I do love him. I don't doubt that for a second. I'm just saying that I needed or should have taken more time before getting married."

"But Betty, *you* picked the date. *You* made the arrangements and everything like *you* were trying to marry him before he changed his mind."

"And maybe that's why I did it."

"What?" Jacqui said as she leaned back and folded her arms across her stomach.

"Jacqui," Betty said as Peter came in with the middle-aged coworker with the bulbous midsection.

"Peter, darling?" Jacqui asked. "Can you give us a minute, sweetie, to finish our lunch, and then you can knock and bang and do whatever you want to with your hammer."

Peter blushed as the white man with the cigar smiled and showed his brown tobacco-stained teeth. "Sure thing. We'll bang away out here," Peter said. "I like banging. I'll hit it hard, too," he said, and then closed the door. After he closed it, they could both hear him give a high five to the white guy and shout, "Bang! Bang! Bang!"

"See," Jacqui whispered. "I just gave him the opportunity to say something decent, and he started acting like a child. I like banging?" She laughed. "Anyway, you were saying?"

Betty's smile vanished as she said, "Maybe I rushed it a little because I thought he would be gone if I said no. This might sound terrible, but Evander is like my father in so many ways. He walks the way I remember my daddy walking. He even laughs like Daddy. And I never noticed that until I broke up with him. Drew found some of his pictures a few months ago that I eventually got rid of, but the more I thought about his aura, his demeanor—It was like he was the reincarnation of Daddy."

Rubbing her hand up and down her biceps, Jacqui said, "I hate to ask, but I know he walked out on you all. Do you think your dad's still around?"

"Yeah, he's still around, all right."

"Why you say it like that?"

Pause. "Remember I told you he called me a while back out of the blue and asked for a down payment on a house?"

"Yeah."

"Well, I didn't give it to him, but I do send him a check each month." Jacqui was silent.

"I know it's jacked up since he left us, and I had not heard from him until he found out I was an attorney. But what can I say. Having a sorry-ass daddy is better in a lot of ways than having no father at all."

"So why didn't you have him come to the wedding to give you away?"

"I thought about it. But then my foster parents, although they were tough parents, were my only parents, so I just had to tell Daddy no."

"So you have a daddy complex. That's why you love this fool?"

"Not so much that," Betty replied. "I mean, I was reading this article, and they say so often we are attracted to people who have the negative aspects of our parents because deep inside we want to change them, since we could not change our parents."

"*Umm.*"

"There's some truth to that. But I think I had—have feelings for him for more than just that."

"Damn, you actually got me feeling sorry for Drew."

"Don't get me wrong. I love Drew in spite of some of the things he said last night. Apparently, he was working out with Stefan and was telling me how Stefan talks about Sasha. And my thing is this: Until I know what's going to happen long, long run, why bring a child into the equation? I love him, but I must also love myself enough to at least be honest. I tried not to admit it to myself for months and—"

"Are you still talking to this fool on the phone?"

"Dag, Jac, you act like Evander and I talk on a regular basis."

"Just asking questions."

"Well, no. The last time he called was a few months ago."

"So what are you going to do about this?"

"What do you mean? I just told you nothing is changing."

"The next time this fool calls, you gotta break this thing off."

"What thing? There *is* no thing."

"This thing. Him calling here and stuff. The more he talks to you, I know he will ease back up in the spot."

"Please."

"Trust me. Don't give him an inch or he'll take your heart."

"That's the last thing I'm worried about."

"Yeah, that's what your mouth says, but that's not what your eyes are saying."

"New subject," Betty said, and cleared her throat. "Make my day."

"Yeah, before I make your day, tell me something?"

"What?"

"Those pictures you mentioned of Evander. They're in your desk drawer. Correct?"

"Oh, so you know me like that? You think I would take the pictures from the house and just bring them here?"

"I think that is what I just implied. Yes."

"See, that just goes to show how much you know. They're in the closet in the other office. Now, as I was going to say, make my day."

Jacqui's lips twisted as she prepared to transition out of the conversation. "Let's see. Today you and Drew make amends. Today you will see what is important in your life, and tonight you will look at your husband and no one else will matter."

"And I hope that happens," Betty said with a polite smile. "I really hope that happens."

"So, what are you two up to?" Carol asked in the doorway with her bag from Wendy's.

"Honey, I wish I'd known you were here. I would have brought you some lunch, too."

"How kind of you," Carol said to Jacqui, and then looked at Betty and asked, "Did I interrupt anything?"

"Ah, no. Come on in," Betty said in an attempt to brighten her sullen mood.

Carol walked in front of her boss's desk and placed her bag on the floor before taking a seat. "So what's up? What's the topic of conversation today?"

"What's the conversation always about whenever we get together?" Betty said, and then all three women said, "Men!" except Jacqui added, "Sorry-ass'd men!"

"I notice ole boy with the cigar was looking you up and down out there, Carol," Jacqui said as Betty smiled. "You're not married. Why don't you go out with him, or are you, and I think you said his name was Patrick, still together?"

Betty smiled even wider as Carol said, "Well, yeah, we're together. But the guy out there has one quality I just can't get with in a relationship."

"What?" Jacqui said as she wiped the lipstick from her straw and then took another sip.

"The name is Patricia, and I don't do dick."

Jacqui spat. "Oh, I'm sorry," she said as some of her tea landed on Carol. "I didn't mean to get you." And then she handed her a handful of napkins from her bag as all three ladies laughed.

"No problem. I just thought you knew," Carol said.

"Dag, so did I?" Betty said, laughing.

"Ah, no. I have been known to forget a few things about people, but that's not one of them."

Taking the napkins to dab herself dry, Carol said, "Well, actually I was married to a man before, but I think I was always bi. But since I am in a committed relationship, I just swing one way, I guess."

"Well, I'm happy for you," Jacqui said.

"Yeah, as long as you're happy, that's all that matters," Betty added. "Jacqui, remember when we were in college and we had the crush on the two twins who played baseball?"

"How can I forget that? What do I look like to you? Like I'm hard of memory or something? As fine as their asses were?"

"I know it. In those days, Carol, we both decided that we were going to marry professional athletes. We saw this article in *Ebony* on player's wives and just knew one day we would be in there with our husbands. And then we graduated."

"Right," Jacqui said, "and then we were just interested in men who had great corporate jobs with a 401k and dental package."

"Honey, I know," Carol said. "I got married the first time at thirty-three, and by that time I would have married a snaggle-tooth midget with a limp if I could have gotten his handicapped parking sticker."

All three women rolled with laughter.

"Yeah, the bar tends to lower a little the older we get," Jacqui said as she stared through Betty's window. "I just wish sometimes there was something, anything, we could marry besides men."

Carol, looking at Betty and then Jacqui, said, "Well, now that you ask, there—"

"No, honey," Jacqui replied, still staring out the window and raising her hand in front of Carol's face. "Sorry, but that one is not an option, okay? Feel free to do as you please, but I don't want that many lips in my bedroom!"

"I know, I know. But men can be so crude sometimes," Carol said as she laughed. "I think being with Pat has shown me just how much they can be like, like dogs."

"Yeah, I know. For instance, both men and dogs are scared of a vacuum cleaner," Jacqui admitted.

After a polite chuckle, Carol said, "And if a man had an extra joint in his back, he'd lick himself in public just like a dog."

"You don't want them on the furniture," Betty added with a smile.

"Ohhh, well, listen at you, Counselor," Jacqui said, looking at her friend. "Let me see. Yeah, I got one. How many cats do you see pissing in public? A dog or a man would take a dump in a burning building if they had to."

"Funny. They both like to sniff your butt before sex," Carol said loudly. And, then as the laughter died, she said, "Was that one of those TMIs you were talking about, Betty?"

"Yeah. A little too much information that time."

After the laugher subsided, Jacqui said as she put her empty box in the bag, "Well, ladies, I'm looking for another hostess. Do you have any applicants you were crazy about but could not hire?"

"Not really," Carol said.

"Well, I guess I need to place an ad," she said, taking a piece of paper from Betty's legal pad. "Let's see. I want to put in there 'Fast-Paced Training.' "

"Yeah, I know what that one means," Carol said. "I used to hear it all the time, and it would make me livid," she said as she rolled her eyes upward. "It means we're busy, and we don't have time to teach you a gosh-darn thing. Learn fast-paced or you're fired."

"Exactly. And also I will put in there 'Competitive Compensation,' " Jacqui said as she wrote the words on the pad.

Betty replied between chews, "Yeah, say competitive because you won't be paying them what the other restaurants will. But you will compete with it."

"Damn, you all are good at this. 'Duties Will Vary.' See what you can get out of that one."

"Translation," Carol said. "Every darn body tells you every darn thing to do."

"This is scary," Jacqui said. "Okay, last one. 'Apply in Person.' "

"Girl," Betty said, "you know why you want them to apply in person."

"Damn straight. This is a hostess position. If they're ugly, old, stink, or fat, the job was just filled an hour ago."

"Carol, you got that number for EEOC handy?" Betty asked with her fingers over her phone.

"You can call who you want. But it's not being cold—"

And then Carol and Betty both said as they looked at each other, "Just being honest."

Within the hour, the three ladies would end their pitfalls-of-relationships discussion.

Peter would walk back into the room with his shirt off and repeatedly make overtures to Jacqui, only to have her smile and then laugh at his attempts when he left.

Betty would receive a phone call from Hereward Ivory and Da'Ron Aaron, who was the new attorney on the case with expertise in capital murder offenses. Da'Ron wanted to meet Bear and discuss a few conflicting elements of their defense. Unlike before, Mr. Parker would join them as well.

Within the hour, Carol would repeatedly mispronounce La Shaunda's name to the point where she grabbed her bottle of lotion, said, "I quit," and caught the number-five bus home.

Carol would end the day answering phones, unpacking boxes, avoiding the construction worker with the bloated stomach, and telling Pat on the phone just how "livid" she was.

Within the hour, Jacqui would leave the office and find Cleon waiting by her car with three red carnations.

After talking for a half hour, they agreed to meet at the track later, and it was there that he gave her his phone numbers.

Later that night, Stefan would call while Jacqui had Cleon on hold. "Sorry, Stefan, but I can't talk."

"Why not?" he would ask.

"I just can't."

"You talking to another man."

Then Jacqui would bite her bottom lip to hold back the remark, but before she knew it, she said, "Not another man, Stefan. A real man. Good night."

That night Jacqui and Cleon spoke of celibacy, sacrifices in life, and why spirituality was more important than religion.

When the phone call ended, she turned the thermostat down as low as it could go, took off her clothes, lit the fireplace, unfolded her favorite comforter, and replayed the entire conversation in her mind with a glass of red wine.

As she immersed herself in the moment, she had no idea that the next phone call she would receive around midnight would be from Betty in tears. She and Drew were fighting. This time because she did not tell him how much she'd received from Geno Parker in compensation. Betty would spend the night sleeping in the bed with Jacqui, since Drew was drinking again, and would fall asleep crying.

Jacqui could never imagine that in two weeks Stefan would get a call from the Ford Agency in New York City and they would want him to move to Gotham and represent him for a possible shoot in Spain.

She also had no idea that the Saturday she spent with her best friend and Carol would be the last such day the three women would share the rest of the year.

Jacqui sat in front of the fireplace and looked at the brilliant color of the wine and eventually fell asleep thinking about Jacquetta's, Cleon, Peter's chest, Evander, Stefan's body, and her best friend.

Summer

Chapter 10

Yet each man kills
the thing he loves.
—Oscar Wilde
The Ballad of Reading Gaol

JULY

The air in the master bathroom was cool, which was in direct contrast to the record-high temperatures outside.

The word WJXT meteorologist George Winterling used to describe the weather was blistering. "The heat is due to a high-pressure ridge stemming from the Gulf Stream," he would explain enthusiastically, his hands over the map. "We can expect triple-digit temperatures until at least early Thursday morning, at which time we may get a few showers to cool things off a bit, but don't count on it."

It was a day that was so oppressive, kids marked off hopscotch grids and then canceled the games. It was a night so torrid that even the falling of the sun failed to bring relief.

The only sound in the Staleys' neighborhood that night was from the house party two doors away. The parents were on vacation, and their teenaged children maximized the opportunity.

Earlier Betty was sitting in her office when the AC unit, which normally sputtered, stopped completely.

As she formulated defense strategies with Aaron, she fanned herself with the back of the telephone book, magazines, folders, or anything else she could use to alleviate the stifling heat in the poorly ventilated office.

Da'Ron Aaron, who was a Stanford law grad originally from Kent, Ohio, stood six feet tall, wore a manicured goatee, no wedding band,

and inexpensive suits. In the sweltering heat of the office, with perspiration sticking portions of his olive dress shirt to his well-cut physique, Aaron suggested they go to the campus law library to work.

"No," Betty replied. "Do you suggest we—"

"Why not?"

"We can manage," she said, and looked at him with a deadpan expression.

Da'Ron was recruited to relocate temporarily from Atlanta, where he worked on several murder cases with similarities to what was being dubbed in the press as the "Trial of the Twenty-first Century."

Although he had never led the charge in a murder trial, the attorneys he worked for praised him as an invaluable researcher and strategist.

"So," Betty asked, "who do you suggest we depose from the NFL Players Association, if anyone at all?"

Aaron paused momentarily, took out his pocket handkerchief, which was always crisply folded, and wiped both his palms and then his top lip as he looked at the notes in his three-ring binder.

As Betty listened to his thoughts, he had no idea that although the date was in September, she was already trying the case and was not going to show any signs of mental or physical fatigue. As soon as she arrived home that night, Betty dropped her purse at the door. Before the garage door could touch the bleached white cement of the driveway, her jacket was on the back of the chair in the breakfast nook, and her blouse was on the kitchen counter.

On the back of the sofa, Betty left her skirt, and as she grabbed her mail before going up the stairs, she left her bra on the banister.

In a tub of hot water, Betty closed her eyes as the sounds of "Bach's Air on the G-String" covered the thumping reverberation of Juvenile playing up the block.

Within arm's reach was her pager, cellular phone, and the house phone. On a table next to the tub, the decorative yellow duck was replaced by a glass of wine and a handful of Triscuits on a saucer.

In the warmth of the scented jasmine oil, bath fizz, and bubbles, Betty immersed herself into the moment. As the water moved over her shoulders like a Bahamian wave, she felt as if she had reentered the womb of life and that nothing in the world could touch her, that she was floating on a cushion of air and nothing could bring her harm.

Although she tried to focus her attention on the opening Samuel Leibowitz used in a similar murder case, Betty began to slumber. Clearing her throat and sitting more erect in the tub, she scolded herself because she had a rare six hours of sleep the previous night. "I *can't* be sleepy," she said aloud to her cat, Tickey, sitting in the doorway. "I even got off early today. This is just not accept—"

Tickey walked toward Betty, sniffed the warm dampness of the air, licked his paws, and then tiptoed away. Before her cat could leave the room, Betty was snoring.

"Honey?"

Betty jumped so hard, the water splashed on her husband's suit. Breathing heavily, she panted. "My goodness. You scared me."

Drew continued to smile and then uncuffed his sleeve and placed the gold cuff link on the light blue tile of the floor as he sat on the lip of the tub.

"What time is it?"

"Night," he said as he rolled up his sleeve and reached in the water for her ankle. Rubbing his hand up her shin, he said, "Actually, it's a little after midnight. Did you get in early?"

"Yeah. About nine-thirty." As he brought her foot out of the water, Betty asked, "So how's your mom?"

"About the same as she's been the last few weeks. Since it started to spread, she's been, well, you know. . . ." And then he put her wet foot on his thigh.

"Don't do that, honey. You'll mess up your pants."

"Don't worry," he replied as he massaged the back of her calf and then slid his hand to the underside of her knee. "This water is cold, love. Don't you want to get out and get into something warm, like maybe, I don't know, a bed?"

"Actually, I kinda like it, since it was so hot today."

"Still no AC?"

"And on top of that the darn fridge broke, so I had to have Carol go out and buy another one."

"Would you like for one of our accountants to help you manage the bank accounts, honey? It'll be one less thing for you to do."

"No, that's okay. Carol is doing a good job with it so far."

As the CD replayed the first cut, Drew said, "I remember this song. You had them play it at the wedding, right?"

Betty smiled softly as she remembered how she felt for most of that day. "Yeah, it's my favorite."

"I like classical music, but it's hard for me to get into. I think Wynton is about as close to classical as I can get."

"I guess it's an acquired taste," Betty said as she wet the bar of soap and slid it across her breast and her upper arm.

"*Moi savoir,*" Drew said.

"*I know,* right? You said, *I know.*"

"Very good, you remembered."

Tapping on her forehead, Betty said, "A steel trap, you *savoir.*"

And then the progression of the music changed, and she closed her eyes and opened her mouth. "I love this part," Betty whispered.

As he poured a cupful of the water from his hand to her leg, he asked, "What do you see when you listen to this?"

Betty took her washcloth and squeezed the cold water over her breast and replied, "Water. It's like a ripple in the center of a pond. Just a tiny little ripple of water that grows and grows and never dies." She moved her head back and forth and continued: "Or like a bird that flies so high it looks like a speck in the sky. But she never uses her wings. That's what this piece reminds me of. A bird that flies high above and has absolute and total freedom."

Betty closed her eyes tighter, and for a moment her face lost all expression as she imagined that she could feel the wind in her face. "It's peaceful. This music is the beauty of things you can't see. Like a movie you watch with your soul and not your eyes."

"Deep," Drew replied as he shook his head. "But for me jazz does the same thing."

"Jazz is beautiful, but for some reason this piece—" And then she opened her eyes. "That part right there. Did you hear that?"

She continued as she stared at the navy blue tiles on the wall. "It's light, but it sounds so painful. It's almost like being in love with something or someone you cannot"—she looked into his eyes—"someone you cannot reach. You know? Someone maybe in a different city or country or maybe in another time. And you can't get to them no matter how hard you try."

Drew sat on the floor beside the tub, still fully dressed, and massaged his wife's foot. "So what made you get into classical music?"

"I have no idea." And then she said, still smiling, "Ah, yes I do. Remember how I told you I stayed in this group home after Momma died? Well, every month, they would—" She stopped talking as her lazy smile died. "Now that I think about it, this was the song they played. Mr. and Mrs. Capsella used to have us dress up in these gaudy party dresses, and we all had shoes from the Salvation Army, I think. It must have been . . ."

"What's wrong?" Drew asked as her voice trailed off. "Been what?"

"I don't want to talk about it. Did they put your mom on morphine?"

"No, not yet. You don't want to talk about the first time you heard the music?"

"I don't want to talk about it," she said, and reached for her cellular phone. Looking at the display, which read that she had missed two calls, she said, "Damn, I bet that was Hereward."

Drew was silent.

"He was supposed to call me to discuss the pretrial transcript."

Drew stared at her.

Seeing his expression, Betty said, "If you must know, I was nine when she died. It was painful, and all I can remember is all the *sweet* and *wonderful* people who were at the funeral. They went on and on about how pretty I was, but none of them wanted to take me home with them.

"My mom had three sisters and a brother. After the funeral, they had a meeting in the living room, and I was sitting in the kitchen. I guess they thought I was not only a child but I was also deaf.

"They discussed what they would do with our house—who would take the dog, who would get the carpets. I think they even drew straws for the car. But when it came to me . . .

"Well, anyway," Betty continued as she looked through the skylight at the moon above to avoid her husband's eyes, "I ended up in this group home, where I would stay until the state found a place for me to live. Salvador and Marie Capsella were nice people, and they ran the group home. They came from Sicily and owned a restaurant called Little Italy.

"But every month they would have what they called an adoption party. About twelve of us would go to a park, and we'd meet these people who wanted to adopt a child. At these parties they'd always play Bach, which is why, I guess, I started to appreciate the music.

"I was always scared. Scared, partially, that I would not get picked and also scared that I would get picked and would end up with a family like my friend Sheila?"

"What happened to her?"

Betty swallowed as if she were nine years old again and said, "She was adopted by this man. A white guy who had a black wife. To make a long story short, she ran away because he was on top of her. I think she might have been eight at the time."

Drew looked away and then back again at his wife's visibly shaken body.

"I stayed in the home for two years. I was there with mostly white kids who were much younger, so there was not much of a demand for a nine-year-old colored, as they would call me. Every month going to the park and every month coming back not knowing if I was happy or sad I was not picked. But I was fortunate. They found me a good family, and if it were not for them, I know I would have never gone to law school."

"And that's a blessing," he said softly.

"So. Now you know," she said, and flicked the water from her hand as she tried to retreat from the painful spot in her heart she hated to revisit. "Honey?"

"Yes?"

"Do me a favor? Would you get my DayTimer off the dresser? If I get out this water, I know I'll never get back in."

Drew stood slowly with a small grunt, put his hand on his lower back, and went into the bedroom.

As he left the bathroom, Betty grabbed her file as she thought aloud. "I hope they've made the travel arrangements, because Hereward has to be on that plane to Chicago by—"

"Here you are," Drew said, and gave her the black leather binder.

"Thanks. And in regard to what I just told you, I'm okay," she said with a smile, flipping the planner to the I's with her thumb and dialing the only number on the page.

Drew smiled as he turned to leave.

"Wait a minute." Then she thought momentarily as she dialed six of the seven numbers. *"Pincer pour quelqu'un?"*

"Very good. And I'm crazy about—"

"Hello? Cindy, how are you?" Betty said, holding up her finger. "First of all, thank you for the pound cake. Drew and I loved it. Is Hereward available?"

Drew leaned against the doorway and whispered, "I'm crazy about you, too."

"Hello. Jacqui, please?"

"Who might I say is calling?"

After a pause she said in a professional voice, "Betty Boop."

"Ah, *umm*, well, okay, Mrs. Boop, you said? B-O-O-P, Boop?"

"Yes. Standard spelling, Boop."

Betty smiled to herself as she reviewed the transcripts of a similar capital offense Judge Jackson presided over. In that case, Judge Jackson gave greater latitude to the defense, but unlike *State of Florida v. Tobias J. Parker*, the case wasn't the subject of TV news magazines each night.

After a pause, Jacqui came on the phone and said, "Heifer, don't be giving my people crap, okay?"

"Please. Where did you find this one?"

"She was sent here by an agency. She's a nice girl."

"And check her out." Betty laughed. "She even said *whom* might I say is calling. She talks kinda like the little white girl you had there a few months ago."

"Who, Katrice the ho?"

"Yeah. I never asked you. What happened to her? And why she gotta be a whore just because you don't like her?"

"She's not a *hoe* because I didn't like her. She's a *hoe* cause she was screwing Stefan."

"Nooo. I never knew. Get out of here!"

"Yeah. I caught him whispering something in her ear one night, and his lying ass would not admit it for all the egg rolls in China. And then she was trying to explain," Jacqui said, and sucked her teeth, "and I was like, please. Get out my face."

"Did he eventually admit to it?"

"Hello. We're talking about Stefan here, Betty. You know he would not admit to the truth if you held a gun to his head and set his nuts on fire."

"Sorry to hear that."

"That's old news, and so is he."

"He no longer even calls?"

"I haven't heard from him since he went to New York. Did I tell you he would be doing the FUBU shoot? I started to tell him if they were using him, they must have a senior citizens line of clothes. FUBU Silver, or something like that."

"Stop it! Oh, yeah, thanks for finally bringing Cleon by to meet me. Although you only stayed *two* minutes. But I was beginning to think you were ashamed of me."

"You're the one who's always busy. So do you like him?"

"Well, I don't know about that pinky-ring thing, but other than that he was fine. You all made a cute couple."

"Thanks. I'm even looking over the age thing. I talk a good game, but I really don't get into younger men. But he's mature for his age. Much more mature than Stefan."

"How old is he?"

"A little younger than you, I think. Around thirty, but when you talk to him, you can never tell, and I like that. He's not superficial at all. His word actually means something. If we're supposed to go to the movies or dinner, he is not only there on time but usually early. And also the player image I used to talk about with him is not really who he is at all."

"Good heart, huh."

"Very good heart. Hey, after going to church with him for a few weeks, I gave up smoking and cursing. The first Sunday I heard him speak, he talked about the body being a temple and how it was a divine gift from God. To be honest, after spending time with him, giving up smoking was easy. I've given that up hundreds of times, but giving up cussin' was a bitc—"

"Stop it!"

"But he really is nice," Jacqui said, her voice sprinkled with laughter. "He has never even mentioned sex, which is new to me, and he's educated. Has a master's in theology as well as a minor in Russian literature. He's really into Tolstoy and stuff like that, which I really like. It's nice to have a man you can actually play *Jeopardy* with and he gets something right besides the sports questions."

"Does he have kids?"

"Two little girls. He even carries their pictures in his wallet. I mentioned to you that his wife died of AIDS, right?"

"No, I'm sorry to hear that."

"Yeah, a drug addict who was going through withdrawal in Shands ER. Stuck a syringe in her neck one night and died within five years, he said."

"That's sad. Well, I guess the next time we see ole Stefan, he'll be sporting FUBU Silver underwear or something, huh?"

"Maybe. I won't lie. I miss him like air, but it was for the best. We had a lot of things in common, but he's happy, and I'm happy for him."

"Did you love him, Jacqui? I mean, really love him?"

"I loved him more than I loved myself, to be honest, and that's when I knew I had to cut him loose. I knew it wasn't a healthy relationship at all."

"So what do you miss most about him?" Betty asked. Then Carol laid a stack of files on her desk with colored Post-it notes sticking from them and motioned with her thumb over her shoulder that Betty's ten forty-five had arrived.

"A lot. He had a wonderful sense of humor. I loved the way he always dreamed of the future, although it looked like he should have given up years ago. And I loved the way when he focused on doing something there was nothing he could not accomplish. But in spite of all of that, he was just not the right man for me."

"It happens."

"Yeah, it definitely happens. So how are things for you at home?"

"Let's not go there. I have an appointment in the lobby."

"But wait a minute. What happened? Not another fight, I hope."

"We came close to one this morning. I want to choke him. Swear to God. I mean, cut the air off from his windpipe!"

"About?" Jacqui said, laughing.

"Just small things, but for one he took the coffee to work yesterday, so when I wake up this morning—at four, mind you—there's no coffee, no tea, or anything. Then I wanted to make myself a lunch, so I look in the fridge, and all the sandwich meat was gone, too. Sometimes, Jac, I think the man drinks meat."

"So what's going on in the bedroom?" Jacqui asked.

"Nothing. Not a thing. Right now, girl, my mind is in a hundred different places, and I'm only getting three or four hours of sleep each night, so that's the least of my concerns."

"How long has it been?"

"I don't know. Two months? Maybe longer. Honestly, I've never been under this kinda pressure. So much pressure my hair is falling out by the handful, and sometimes I even get nosebleeds from it."

"You're kidding me."

"I wish. I have this rash, and the doctor says I just need to 'reduce the stress in my life.' Yeah, right. This is like running a marathon in high heels, taking the bar exam with the phones ringing, and then having to come home and be the perfect wife. I'm sorry, but something has to go."

"Well, call me after your appointment, okay? Do you need me to have something sent over there for lunch today?"

"No, I think I'll spring for pizza for the office."

"Don't. I'll hook you guys up today, but don't get spoiled by this."

"Thanks, sweetie. I owe you one."

"One? You trying to gyp me or something? Take care, honey, and we'll talk later. Wait a minute?" Jacqui said. "Why did you call me?"

Betty paused and then looked up from her files and said, "I really don't know. Just wanted to hear your voice, I guess."

" 'Bye, heifer."

Rev. Alphonso Robinson stood five feet four inches tall in stocking feet. He was not a flashy dresser and bore none of the tenants of having a Napoleonic complex.

As he stepped inside Betty's office, his smile was polite and cordial, and his handshake was not prove-a-point masculine.

In a raspy voice he said, "It's indeed a pleasure to finally meet with you, Attorney Staley. You can just call me Reb Rob'son; everyone else does."

"The pleasure is all mine. I've followed your ministry here in town for years. I was even a part of the ribbon-cutting ceremony for the children's center you spearheaded."

Unbuttoning his jacket with his head tilted to the side, he said as he sat down, "Well, I'm honored. So how are you managing? I mean, with the press and the attention drawn to this case?"

"This is all new to us, of course, but it comes with the territory."

"Well, nice, nice," he said as he shook his head. Then he rubbed his palms on his thighs as if preparing to give a sermon, and his expression changed as he leaned back and crossed his short legs.

"Allow me, Counselor, in deference to time, to clarify why we've asked to meet with you today.

"The murder of Shavonda Ellis was bitter and inhumane, to say the least. I've known the family for going on twenty som' odd years. Shavonda and my daughter were in the pep squad at Gainesville High together. I preached the funeral, and I was allowed to see the pictures, and my soul goes out to her family for what they have had to endure.

"But the reas' I'm here is because of the way the family of Leroy Simmons was treated."

"He's the young man who was falsely arrested. I read the police report," Betty interjected.

"Correct. When they were looking for him, they knocked on, according to our estimates, about forty doors in the dark of night until he was located. Only to brutally assault this fifteen-year-old kid who had a few priors, but it was proven later that he did not commit the crimes."

"Yes, I know. The entire incident was unfortunate, to say the least."

" 'Tis true. 'Tis true," he said, and shook his head. "As you may not know, the city is refusing to settle this thing, which is going to put the family in the position of taking it to court."

Betty's brow wrinkled.

"Now, of course, we are not asking you to represent the family."

Her brow unfurled.

"But what we would like for you to do is to make a public statement against the city's actions. We have already gotten a verbal commitment to make a statement from a former state's attorney, so if you would join us in this cause, it would give us a little more leverage in justifying this gross injustice."

As she thought about what was said, Betty sat motionless.

"So, Mrs. Staley, can we count on your support?"

"No," she said without hesitation.

"No?"

"I must respectfully decline. I just can't, Reverend Robinson."

"Why not?" he asked, leaning his weight on his bony elbows.

"First of all, this case is taking one hundred percent of my resources, and I don't know if I want to go into interviews with the press, and get barraged on this issue as well."

"So you mean to tell me, Attorney Staley, that we've gotten the support of the former state's attorney, who, I might add, is a *white* man, but we cannot count on the support of a black woman who is representing a white man who happened to kill a *black* woman?"

Betty looked at her files and then back at the visitor in her office. Speaking low and evenly, she said, "No matter what I do, this case is going to come down to a racial issue, isn't it?"

"It's always about race," he said without a hint of anger in his voice. "No matter what we do or say, it will always be about race in this country. The concrete this country's foundation is based upon was mixed with racism."

"Well, sir, I have one obligation. And that is to ensure that my client is found not guilty."

"But what if he is?"

"Is what? Guilty?"

"Yeah. What if," he said in the tone of Bishop T. D. Jakes, "the sun does not rise in the east. What if Christmas is not by chance in winter, and what if *he* actually is the one who murdered both of them and left their lifeless bodies—"

"Reverend Robinson, discussing this case with you is highly improper at best and falls outside of the scope of what I *assumed* our conversation would be. What I will say is this: My client is not guilty. He has not committed a first-degree murder, and my job as his representative is to make sure the court feels the same way when the gavel lands. That's it."

"So you don't care about your community? About that youth center you came to see inaugurated? You don't care that last night the Klan burned a cross on the front lawn of our church? You don't care that you are representing a man whose grandfather was the grand dragon of the Klu Klux Klan?"

"I saw the pictures of the Klan protesting outside the courthouse. Reverend, it was about six guys. Please. A city-league football team with attitude could have chased them away. The same guys were here protesting the King holiday six months ago. How ignorant must you be to protest a *paid* vacation from work? I don't want to make light of them or what they stand for, because it deplores me, but who they are makes me laugh.

"We have kids who cannot read getting high school diplomas. We have black kids taken out of your community center and pushed through the penal system, with the only crime against them being the color of their skin. We have bigger issues than to give so much credence to a few media whores trying to get on the six o'clock news and impress their drinking buddies at the trailer park."

"So you are in favor of them marching downtown, I assume?"

"Why not? Let them march uptown, downtown, crosstown, or around town if they like. As long as they don't march in here, I have no problem with it, because we have larger items on our agenda."

"Well, Counselor, I was hoping we could come to an understanding, but you have made your position abundantly clear."

"I respect what you are doing for Leroy Simmons and his family, and I wish you well," Betty said, standing with her hand extended.

"We will meet again," he said as he shook her hand. "Our paths will definitely cross again." Then he turned to leave the room.

As he walked out the door, Betty respectfully allowed him to have the last word and then returned to her work on the case she knew would change her life forever.

Betty sat in the conference room of the county jail, awaiting her client. As she waited, she thought about Drew. She had called him several times, and uncharacteristic of him, he had not returned her calls.

As she walked over to the black rotary phone in the corner of the room, she heard the chains dragging on the floor on the other side of the wall. Then a guard with a deep southern drawl yelled, "Open six!" and closed the door to the room, which muted the sound.

Walking back to her seat, Betty saw the hulking figure she had now become accustomed to through the glass partition.

Betty looked through the glass at Bear's football-shaped face, and while she could tell by the look in his eyes that he was growing weary, he did not appear to be on edge.

He sat peacefully, and as they uncuffed him, Betty took out the files and sat them in front of her. And then she solemnly gathered her fingers together as they closed the door and looked at Bear as he massaged his wrist.

"Damn shame these handcuffs don't come in extra large," he said, and smiled. Betty remained silent. "Where is Hereward or ole Da'Ron? You burnt them out already? Them punks can't hang, huh?"

"I need to ask you a question, and I wanted to do it alone, because want—need—you to be one-hundred-percent forthcoming with me."

"Shoot."

Betty rose from her chair and walked around it. She grasped the back and looked down on her client.

"What? What chu wanna know? Hey, while I'm thinking about it, can you call whoever is in charge of this place and ask them about letting me buy some weights? I'll donate them if I have to. I haven't had a decent workout in months. And also ask them if I can get the sports page sent to—"

"Toby, I gotta know what *really* happened."

"What do you mean, what really happened?" he replied as he scratched the corner of his nose and smiled. "I've told you guys a hundred times what happened."

"Is it true you have never been arrested?"

"Never. I mean, I'm clean as a virgin. Most of the guys on the team joke about it because I have this hell-bent-for-leather image, and the worst thing on my record is a speeding ticket." Bear massaged the back of his bull-sized neck and asked, "Why are you asking me this now?"

"Because you can BS them and I don't care. My job is onefold. To make sure when I walk out of court in late October or early November that you walk out beside me. That's all. But I can't deal with surprises. I must know the truth, because they have a tight case.

"I can punch holes through steel but not if you're holding out on me."

"I told you everything. I told you how the gun fired, I told you how I ran, I told you everything. Now, what are you saying? Are you trying to tell me I should change the story again so that it's more credible?"

"This is not . . . Toby," Betty said, and then shook her head in exasperation and picked up her files.

"What? What I do? What?"

"Toby!" she said as she slammed the files in her briefcase and locked it. "This is not a goddamn game! Okay? They will kill you if we lose this thing, and you're worrying about lifting weights?" She watched as he melted to a shell of his former self. "When your father brought me on this case, he said something that literally keeps me up every night. He said he was putting his only son's life in my hands. That's an enormous responsibility. Can you imagine how I would feel if what you are telling me is true and we lose this case?"

"Ma'am? I've told you everything I know."

"Tell me this?"

"Yes?"

"Did you kill Shavonda Ellis?" Betty shouted.

"No!"

"Did you kill Karen Parker?"

"What?"

"Did you kill your wife?" Betty screamed.

"Fuck no!"

"Did you conspire to have either of them shot?"

"NO! Mrs. Staley, you mean to tell me you don't even believe me after all these meetings we've had? Day in and day out?"

"It's not about what I believe, Toby. It's about what I can prove!"

"Well, hell! If I can't get somebody I'm paying to believe me," he said, standing up and leaning against the back of the retaining room, "how can I get twelve people on the jury to believe me."

Betty sat quietly watching his every move. Then she noticed a nervous twitch of his eye she'd not seen before.

As he sat on the desk with his back to her and whispered so softly the sound could barely be heard through the speaker on her desk, he sighed heavily. "I know it was wrong to leave them in the trunk. I know my part in all of this was messed up. But that doesn't make me a murderer. I know I shouldn't have lied, but they can't kill me for lying."

Then Betty said, "Not to mention allowing the sheriff's department to run rampant through the projects and letting the kid take the fall and get beaten by the cops."

Bear was silent.

"I'm going to ask you again, Toby. And with God as my witness," she said, still staring at the V shape of his back, "if you are lying, there will be a crack in our defense. And with this thing being on the news every night and being broadcast all day all over the country, the crack will become a hole, and then our case will fall like a deck of cards.

"Toby, I'm telling—I mean, asking—you one last time. Is there anything about this case I do not know?"

Toby's muscular shoulders rose as he filled his chest with air and spoke softly. His voice cracked, and he said, "I can't stay in jail, Mrs. Staley."

"What?"

"I can't live in this place. I'm not like the rest of these guys in here."

As he spoke, Betty noticed the enormous horseshoe in back of his arm swell. "I've got a home in Vail. I got another place in Italy and the place in Florida. Now I'm living in a five-by-seven that I could fill up with my underwear from home.

"You know why I don't ask them if I can meet you face-to-face instead of from behind this glass?"

Betty sat silently.

"The first time Hereward and Benny came out here to visit me, after they left, the guards took me to this room and said it was my lucky day because they were going to check my brown eye." Bear looked up, and then without turning, he asked, "You know what that is. Right?"

Betty remained quiet.

"Well, they wanted to look up my ass, and one of them decided to yank my dick, and then that was it. I kicked his ass, and about four of them started to beat my ass with their batons.

"I never told my dad because I knew he would make a big deal out of it, and when it was all said and done, I would have to live here with these people. They said I was on suicide watch. That was just a way to keep me in a holding cell until the swelling went down. The reason I'm telling you this is because I could never fit in. There would always be a guard trying to make points with the others or some inmate too afraid to fight so he'll pull a shank or something. There would always be a governor worried about reelection and unwilling to give me a fair day in court.

"I can't live here, Mrs. Staley, and that's all there is to it. I'd rather be dead than to live a year in this place.

"The more I stay in here, the more I feel backed into a corner, and the more I feel cornered, the greater the chances of me fucking going off and damn near killing one of them just for the hell of it. If I stay here, I'm staying here for a reason!"

"Toby? You did not answer my question."

"Mrs. Staley," he said, and turned toward her. "With God the Father and His Son, Jesus Christ, as my holy witness, ma'am, I have not misled you. I have not lied to you, and I have been, ma'am, one hundred percent truthful. I know what's going on out there. They hail you, then they nail you," he said as he tapped his half-dollar-width thumb on the table. "I heard you say that, and I can't get it out of my head. Every day. Every fucking night. Everyone I meet, I talk to. I'm thinking the same thing. They hail you. Then they nail you. They hail you, then they nail you. They hail you . . ."

"Okay. Well, I will not ask you that question again. But I want to prepare you for their story, which has changed a little since the first time I heard it, but here is what the state will say in court."

Betty leaned back in her chair and said, "You had a long-term love affair with—"

"Ma'am, we have to go over this again?"

"—with Shavonda Denise Ellis," she said as she raised her voice. "That you supported Miss Ellis for over two and a half years and even paid for a total of four abortions during that time.

"Then the state will attempt to prove that you and Shavonda conspired to have your wife murdered. That you signed a mortgage on a property in upstate New York which your wife did not know about and that you were planning to start over with Shavonda there because that is where she was from originally. That you hired a hit man, who will testify that you gave him fifty-five thousand three hundred dollars, to shoot her when you were at the Super Bowl in Tampa but the murder was botched when your wife became ill and was unable to leave the hotel room.

"Then you became impatient. You wanted to end the relationship with your wife, but you did not want to pay her the estimated seven-to-twelve million dollars it would have cost to dissolve the relationship. So you decided to do it yourself. This way you could keep it quiet and keep one hundred percent of your estate intact."

"All lies," he said, looking at the cement table in front of him. "All a pack of lies!"

"Then, *Bear*, you asked your wife, Karen Marie Parker, to ride with you to discuss your marriage. So you took her to the open field of the airport where no one could hear—"

"Lies!"

"—or see what would happen next."

"Fucking lies! SHUT UP!"

"And then you had your wife, Karen Marie Parker, step outside the car. You asked Shavonda to meet you there. She had no idea that you wanted her to witness the murder so she would be an accessory to the fact.

"Not knowing much about guns, you fired and shot Shavonda, who stood in the darkness behind your wife, by accident. Your wife started to run, and like a savage animal—" Betty said as her pager vibrated but went ignored.

"Why are you doing this, Mrs. Staley?"

"Like a savage animal, you hunted her down," Betty said in a lower tone, "and shot her. Right through the heart. Bang!" she shouted at the top of her lungs and pounded her fist on the table.

"This is bullshit!" he screamed.

"Then, Bear, you decided to ditch both bodies. So you conveniently stuffed them in the trunk of the car and drove into the projects, hoping some kid would see the keys and hopefully find the pistol under the seat to get rid of the fingerprints."

Bear sat across from her, seething. She could see it in the blue veins pulsating from his forehead and the white-knuckle fist he made.

"Then, Bear, you jogged the four miles home, called a cab, and caught a plane to Las Vegas, where you partied with Mike Tyson and played golf with John Elway and your agent, Benyamin Stein. You did this while knowing that less then twenty-four hours earlier *you'd* killed two people.

"The bodies were left in the car, and the Simmons kid noticed the Mercedes with the keys dangling from the ignition. He decided to go for a joy ride and show off the car and the gun to a few of his friends. Then he left the car in the woods, which is where the sheriff's department found it three days later.

"Fortunately, the kid was with his mother, who worked about thirty miles away, at the time of the murder, so he had an iron-tight alibi. But you saw all of this happening when you returned and still you did not—"

"Gad dammit, Staley? I mean, shit!" he screamed as a jailer tapped on the glass in the door for him to lower his voice.

"You know that's not how it happened! Damn!" he said in a lower tone. "I didn't shoot anybody! I never fired the fucking gun! They did ballistics, and there was nothing on my hand?"

"They traced for the gun residue five days after the murder. We have to have more than that."

"Well, I'm sorry, but that's your fucking job!" he said between clenched teeth. His eyes bulged, and Betty could see the anger vibrating through his body. "We're paying you thousands, and I'm telling you the fucking truth. If you can't win with money and truth on your side, then we need a new gad-damn attorney, and we need one now!"

Betty paused to allow her heart to stop racing and then said, "Toby? I've represented hundreds of people. But this is my first major criminal case. My experience is limited to movies and books. But it'll also be the first murder case for the jury, and let me tell you one thing," she said, leaning toward the mike and speaking deliberately. "If the person I just saw behind this glass sits in the courtroom with me, you will be convicted of this crime. And that I can promise you."

Betty picked up her briefcase and knocked on the door to exit. As she waited for the guard to find the correct key, she could hear her broken client weeping through the speaker in the glass.

"I'll call you tomorrow, and I'll see if I can bring you a sports page," she said as she walked out of the room refusing to look back.

Betty blasted the sounds of Eric Benet's "Spend Your Life With Me" as she drove home. Although the CD was a gift from her husband, Drew was far from her mind.

All she could see was Bear's reaction to the words she said earlier, and she worried that when the pressure was on, he would make the same facial twitches he made in the enclosed room. She knew the world, and most importantly, the jurors, would be watching his every gesture and trying to evaluate if a person wrongfully charged would react in such a manner.

When she took the case, she felt she could get him to testify in his defense. Since he was college-educated, she felt she could use his being a celebrity to their advantage. But after what she had witnessed, she knew it would be the felo-de-se of any possibilities of victory.

Then she felt her pager vibrate again. Retrieving it from the waistband of her skirt, she saw it was Drew's cellular phone number.

Putting the pager in her purse, Betty picked up her phone as she drove and with her thumb dialed the digits.

"Hello, Da'Ron? Betty, are you busy?" she said as she turned off the CD.

"No," he said; she could hear the news in the background. "So what happened?"

"He did *exactly* what you said he would do."

"Really? I sorta figured he would. But do you think he got the point?"

"I'm not sure, but I hope so. He's a smart man, but sometimes he has a knack for acting very ignorant."

"I know. I've tried a lot of these cases, and you can never tell how a person is going to act when the pressure is on. Can you imagine how it must feel to look into someone's eyes and for them to look down on you and say you don't deserve to live? That you are such a threat to humanity itself that you shouldn't be allowed to even draw breath? It's a lonely feeling. I've stood behind a lot of men who had to walk that mile, and it's never easy.

"But in regard to his testifying, you never know. I've had guys like him who would walk into court and be calm as a cucumber when the money was on the line. Act fully in control of themselves and deliver all the right talking points. And then you have others who I honestly felt were innocent, but you damn near have to put restraints on them if the prosecutor said anything negative. It's not uncommon for a man to wet himself from the pressure. I've seen it happen."

"Well, he will not be one. There is no way I will let him anywhere near the stand," Betty said as she heard the click of her call waiting. Ignoring it, she said, "So what're your thoughts?"

"Regarding what? His guilt or innocence?"

"Yeah? I mean, what do you feel in your—"

"Staley, can I give you a bit of advice? I know we are about the same age, but this is all I've done since day one out of law school. Now, my gut tells me he's innocent. My gut tells me that he panicked and did some stupid shit and covered it up with lies that were even more stupid.

"But I couldn't care less what my gut tells me. Even if I defended him and found out the next day that he killed both of them, it's not my concern. And I know that sounds terrible, but that's how it is when you defend murderers or people accused of murdering. I'm a hired gun, and I do my job. And I'm damn good at it."

"Well, I do believe him. I just think that we've gotta find some way to tell him not to react so guilty."

"Be careful about coaching, Staley. You can tell him a few subtle things, but just watch your step." After a pause he said, "I'm sorry, but I'm going out in a few with a friend. Do you know of any nice places to meet people here in town?"

"This is a lot different than what you're used to in Atlanta. Not a lot of places to go out at all."

"I'm noticing that. How do you meet people in town beside church and work?"

Betty heard her phone click again. "Well, that's the eternal question. Tomorrow can you bring in that copy of the *Harvard Law Review* you mentioned to me last night? I've got a call coming through," Betty said.

"Sure, no problem. I'll see you bright and early—as usual."

Betty hit the SEND button on her phone. "Hello?"

After a momentary silence, Drew asked, "Where are you?"

"In the car. What's going on?"

"In the car where?"

"On thirty-ninth and headed home. Why?"

"I paged you about ten times. Why didn't you call me back?"

"Actually, honey, you paged three times, and I just got out of the meeting with Toby. Why? Is something wrong?"

"I need to stay out here with Momma tonight, but we'll talk tomorrow."

"About what?"

"I . . . I don't even want to talk to you, I'm so disgusted!"

Unaware of what he was talking about, Betty said, "One second," and drove to the shoulder of the road. "Drew? What are you talking about?"

"Fuck it. I'll come to the office tomorrow. 'Bye!"

Betty fell asleep on the sofa surrounded by depositions next to her pager, cellular phone, and home phone. Outside, just as predicted by George Winterling, heavy sheets of rain started to fall.

She had called Drew and left several messages on the cellular phone voice-mail box and had even called Parkside, but he would not come to the phone.

The pen she used to make notations was still perched in her fingers as she slept with her glasses on the tip of her nose. As she worked, she tried to throw herself into the case to block out her husband's voice—to no avail. And then the phone rang.

"Hello, Drew! Is that you, Drew?" Betty said into the phone.

"Hello? I'm so sorry to call so late, madam. This is Hasanati Obayana. May I ask a question of you? Am I speaking to one Betty Robinson-Staley?"

"Excuse me. What time is it?" she said, looking for her watch amongst the papers.

"It's three-thirty, madam, and you have my sincerest apologies, but I must confirm if you are one Betty Robinson-Staley of seventy-four twenty-seven—"

"Let me tell you something. If you are the press and are now harassing me at home for an interview, before we go any further, let me—"

"Are you Mrs. Staley, madam?"

"Yeah! Yes, I'm Betty Staley! What do you want?"

"Betty Robinson-Staley?"

"YES! For Christ sakes, what do you want! Damn!"

In a sympathetic yet monotone voice, the lady said, "I have the sad task of asking you to come out to the Shands Hospital, madam. A young lady bearing the name of Jacquetta Marie Jordan listed you on her driver's license as next of kin, and she and a young man were in a tragic car accident."

Chapter 11

Your old men shall dream,
Your young men shall see visions.

—Old Testament
Joel 2:28

Drew sat alone in the cafeteria of Parkside Nursing. The faces, which were all too familiar, rotated like 45s in a jukebox.

There was Norman, who wore his shock-white hair like Stalin and worked as an illustrator.

He was rarely without a pipe between his lips and a pencil in hand, and he would occasionally sketch unsuspecting diners as they ate their meals.

When Norman wore his headphones, his body language relayed to the world the music he listened to.

If it was classical, his pencil became an orchestral baton. If it was jazz, he would hold the pencil like a chopstick and tap out the staccato rhythm on the table. And if it was South Philly doo-wop, the pencil and pipe would be placed on the table, his eyes closed to slits, and the music seemed to discharge through his pores.

There was Light-skinned Florida (not to be confused with *Black Florida*, who lived in another wing), who worked for AT&T for forty-seven years as a telephone operator. But when she spoke of the time she was there, it was always "Forty-sev'm *longgg* years."

Although retired, she wore her ten-, twenty-, and forty-year pins on her collar and spoke often of how she was forced out three years before she wanted to retire.

Mercer Morse King was a chauffeur to the rich and famous. He claimed to have listened to Joe DiMaggio and Marilyn Monroe have a fight so intense, she slapped his face and asked to get out of the car in a snowstorm. He recounted how he drove King Hussein and Queen Noor from South Beach to a palatial home in Boca Raton, only to U-turn and head back to Miami. And he had birthday cards signed by Louis Malle and Candice Bergen as well as Jackie and Rachel Robinson. They were in his scrapbook, and all were signed "To Double M."

Drew sat dressed in a black Adidas T-shirt, basketball shorts, and sneakers and watched the faces he had begun to know all too well.

With his headphones on listening to a CD, he took out the *USA Today,* bypassed the financial news, and pulled out the sports scores.

Since five-thirty, in spite of all he had to get accomplished that day, the one recurring thought in his mind was Betty. Music could not soothe it away, TV only made it worse, and reading would invariably remind him of the wife he felt in his heart he could no longer trust.

The previous night, he could have gone home but chose not to. As he slept in the bed Dr. McBride had delivered to his mother's room for his use, he cut off his cell phone and ignored the messages Betty asked to be delivered to him as he watched the rain fall outside.

"Raindrops keep falling on my head," George Winterling, the television weatherman, who looked like Mr. Rogers, sang off key. "We expect a full *inch* of rain today. But the good news is, this weekend we can expect a high in the nineties with *nothing* but blue skies for the opening of Jaguar camp."

Drew knew he had to make a decision but had no idea what it would be. For the first time, he considered the "D" word. He also wondered if their breakup would have any financial repercussions. For the first time, he mentally formulated a list of attorneys and imagined a life without Betty.

Drew nursed his third cup of coffee as he looked at the big-screen television, which showed the opening credits to the *Early Show.* As Jane introduced the substitute anchor for the day, he was interrupted by the sounds from the cafeteria line.

"Aw, hell! Come on, Skeeter!" an older man said to the woman in white behind the counter making omelettes. "Why you being all stingy dis morning with the cheese!"

"Every day you say that, Mr. Carron, and every day I tell you the same damn thing. I will give you as many *eggs* as you want with your cheese!" she joked, her hand on her hip as the others in line laughed.

Drew opened his paper to its full length and folded it back into quarters so he could see the NFL training-camp news. Then he noticed a man with striking features, who looked familiar, watching him. He glanced over at the dark-skinned man and then back at his paper.

On the colorful front of section C of the paper, Drew noticed yet another report about the only story people seemed to discuss in the country.

The headline read: "DEAN CASSIDY TO LEAD PROSECUTION IN PARKER CASE."

The name sounded familiar to him, so he read the opening of the article.

> *GAINESVILLE, FL.—High-profile Dade County prosecutor Dean Cassidy has relocated to the fifth district and was immediately tabbed to lead the prosecution team in the Tobias Parker case.*
>
> *Cassidy, who achieved national notoriety in the William Kennedy Smith rape trial, immediately issued a press release which stated that in the matter of State of Florida v. Tobias J. Parker, the prosecution, due to the vast amount of evidence linking the accused to the double homicide, was prepared to only pursue two counts of first-degree murder. The state's attorney also reasserted that if Parker is convicted, the state is prepared to ask for the maximum penalty.*

As he read the article, Drew noticed in the corner of his eye a man walking toward him. It was the dark-skinned man with the rotund stomach he had noticed earlier.

Damn, he thought as the man made a beeline toward his table. He wore faded blue jeans and a brown Atlanta Black Crackers baseball cap. *I hope he's not going to want to start talking to—*

"Excuse me, sir," the man said, and then tapped Drew on the shoulder. "How are you today?"

"Sorry, I didn't hear you," Drew replied as he reluctantly took off the headphones.

"No problem. What chu listening to?" the man asked as he sat in front of him and looked at his portable CD player.

"Nothing. Just some Donald Byrd."

"Really?" he replied as he leaned back and rubbed his stomach. "I would have taken you for a Kenny G man." Then he laughed, and

Drew remembered he initially saw him and his wife the day he found out about his mother's terminal condition.

"No offense," he continued, "but most young folk now'days don't know nothing about people like him or Sonny Stitt or even Miles. But listen at me babbling on like a crazy man. I'm sorry," he said, and extended his four-fingered hand across the salt and pepper shakers. "R. L. Blue, but everyone here just calls me Blue."

"Nice to meet you, Blue," Drew said as he shook the elderly man's hand. As he did so, he noticed his hands were feathery soft, not befitting a man with such a rugged exterior.

Before Drew could introduce himself, Blue said, "Nice handshake, sonny."

" 'Scuse me?" Drew replied as he broke contact.

"Your handshake. Very important thing a handshake. It's the non-verbal hello. Do you know how many men have lost jobs and how many wars have been fought because of a simple handshake?"

"Umm," Drew replied in respectful indifference. Then he clicked the OFF button on his CD and disconnected the headphones.

"You leaving early this morning?"

"I need to—" Then he looked at Blue and asked, "How do you know what time I leave?"

"I watch everything. Sorry to sound Orwellian, but it's just something I've always done. Just like when old man Carron just walked in here and asked for more cheese? He does that at least three times a week. In about twenty minutes," Blue continued as he peered through the glass that showed the employee entrance to the facility, "li'l cute McBride will run in here looking at her watch. She always does that on Thursdays," he said, looking at Drew. "I don't know why. She's single, and maybe she watches too much TV on Wednesday nights."

Drew shook his head politely, thinking of a way to get out of the conversation.

"For instance, I know that you usually get in here around, say, six forty-five or thereabouts. You watch the *Early Show* because you like Bryant. I know you like Bryant because when he's on vacation, you don't watch at all. Am I right?"

A raised eyebrow was Drew's only reply.

"I also know you are a newlywed."

"How you know that?"

"Everyone knows that. We remember the day your momma left and no one could find her. Your wedding day, correct? That was the talk of this place for days."

"Oh?"

"You have a nice mother. My wife and I have had dinner with her on occasions."

"With who? My mom?"

"Yeah, she talks about you all the time."

"Funny. She never mentioned she knew you."

"Well," he said, and looked deeply in Drew's eyes, "maybe she's one of those women who keep secrets . . . sometimes. Maybe," he said, "and maybe not. I don't know."

Drew sat silently absorbing all that was said and unsaid.

"But you have a wonderful mother. She's"—Blue continued and then uncomfortably crossed his legs, exposing his dirty football socks—"a woman who is going through a lot right now in her life. It's tough when you walk in this place and know you will never walk out alive. Look around you. All these people are cheery and happy, and they play cards and make scarfs and talk about the children who usually never visit them, but they know in their heart that what they have done is all they will ever get done. Look at them."

Drew looked at Mr. Carron and the others at his table. He glanced over at Norman, his eyes closed, listening to music, and he looked at Light-Skinned Florida laughing with Double M and then explaining the significance of her pins.

"Within a year many of the people you look at will be dead." Blue paused as the words settled and said, "Today over two hundred thousand people will die somewhere in the world. It's a road we will all walk, some of us more ready than others." Then Mr. Blue rubbed his soft hands together, but there was no sound of friction.

"Last time I saw your mother, she wasn't exactly ready. How is she doing now?"

"She's doing better. I think the finality of what you mentioned has just sunk in and she's coming to terms with . . . Well, you know."

"Say it. Cancer. It won't bite, sonny."

"Oh, I have no fear of saying it."

"Yes, you do. Your lips just formed the word, but you would not say it. Don't fear it; embrace it. Because if you fear it, it will own you.

"I spent some time in Europe when I was a young man. A little younger than you are now. I spent about five years just traveling all over the place on this motorcycle, and it felt good," he said as he stared at his hands, "to feel like a man.

"I mean, in this country I was called shadow, smut, jig, gorilla, almost every day. Do you know how it feels to walk down the street and have people you never met say, 'Damn, look at that black mother.' But there my color was looked upon as being sexy and powerful. It was the ultimate sign of virility.

"But I digress," he said, pulling himself away from his trance and squaring his shoulders. "In France I read something I will never forget. Nicolas Boileau said, 'Often the fear of one evil leads us into inflicting one that is worse.' Think about that one."

"That's profound," Drew whispered, "but I don't fear it at all."

"It what?"

"Death," Drew shot back.

"Good," Blue replied, and looked down at his hands in an infantile manner.

As dark as his skin was, his palms were the pinkish hue of a white person's, Drew noticed. Then he asked him, "How did you know my name?"

"Like I said," he answered as he looked at Florida, "your momma talks about you all the time. I know you graduated with honors. I know you played football at Florida A&M but was too short to make it in the pros.

"I know you bought a home a couple of years ago and that you married the young lady who's on the news every night." Then he looked at Drew and asked, "How'm I doing s'far?"

"Sounds like you're a good listener."

Mr. Blue paused, and then his eyes fell. "It's interesting you would say that? I once lost a wonderful job because I didn't listen. A job I really enjoyed. So I started making a concerted effort to listen and to watch, and well, I guess that's why I seem so nosy." As he looked at his nails, which looked freshly manicured, he said, "It started with my wife. Women like that, you know?"

"Like what?"

"Like you to pay attention to them as if nothing else in the world is as important. So I just started listening to everything she said. I listened so hard, sonny, sometimes it felt like I could see the words coming from her lips. And I never cut her off. I never finish her sentences, and I never just bob my head and say, 'Honey, I understand.' "

Drew looked at his watch and then settled in his chair. "So you enjoy it out here?"

"It's a nice place, but wait a minute, I don't live here," he said with a smile that betrayed his age. His teeth were perfect in every aspect. No chips. No tarnish, but his skin looked hard as leather.

"Your wife lives out here?"

"Oh, so you seen my lady, huh?"

"I watch a little, too. How long have you been married?"

"How long have we been married?" he pondered as he stroked his chin like a wise man. "Let me think, are we married?"

"Are you?"

With a smile he said, "Yes, sonny, we're married in more ways than I can tell you with words."

"That's nice to hear."

"We're so married," he said as his jowls shook, "that we're married beyond the flesh. You see where I'm coming from?"

Drew watched him intently as he spoke.

"We're married at the marrow. We no longer have individual souls. Just one that we share; therefore, the possibility of us not being an us doesn't exist because we could not live without the other.

"I know that sounds a little strange. But that's the best way to explain it."

Drew was silent.

"We caught so much hell back in the fifties when I met her and in the sixties when we got married. We even caught hell in Finland, where she's from. Ever heard of someone catching Finnish hell? But if I had to do it over again," he said as he rubbed his stomach, "if I had to do it all over again and caught twice as much hell for half the pleasure she's given me, I would do it faster than Beelzebub was thrown out of heaven, and I mean that.

"I feel fortunate to be able to make such a statement. People toss the word soul mate around so much I hate using it, but I know in my heart that there was one person placed on this green mass we call earth for me. That she came from the very womb as the consummate fit for *only* me, and my *only* chore in life was to find her. And I did. This I know with all my heart, and few can say that."

Then Blue looked at Drew and asked, "Can you?"

"Can I what?"

Blue smiled. "Can you?"

"Sure. I mean, we have a good marriage."

"Drew?"

"What? What did my mom tell you?"

"She didn't have to tell me anything. You sleep out here most nights. I used to be your age. I know what me and my wife did most nights."

"Well, regardless of what Mom *may* have said, my wife and I have a great relationship. Mom doesn't care much for her, as I guess she has told you, but I love my wife. I really do."

"You don't have to convince me, sonny. But can I ask you something? Do *you* love your wife, or do you just *need* your wife?"

"What kinda question is that?"

"Who's dying, sonny? Your mother, your wife, or your marriage?"

Drew folded his arms across his chest, leaned back, and said, "Excuse me?"

Blue's voice lowered as he said almost to himself, "One day that question may make sense to you." Then he looked at Drew and said, "I just see people come out here all the time, and they're more dead than the people they visit. I'm not implying that that's you, but I watch and I listen, as I told you before, and if I have ever seen a young man who looked like he was dying himself, on the inside, that is, it's you. I can see it, and that's why I came over."

Drew leaned far enough back in the chair that he balanced on the two hind legs.

"Do you know what the word love means?"

Drew simply shook his head.

"What does it mean to you?"

"Love?" Then Drew returned his chair to all fours and placed his hands flat on the table. "Love is a warm feeling you have inside about something or somebody."

"Mr. Webster defines love as a deep affection or fondness. Think about that a moment," Blue said. "You called it a warm feeling. But it's also something you admire and greatly cherish. Now, after telling you that, do you really love your wife? Or just *need* your wife?"

"Of course I love her."

"You're just saying words, sonny. Think about the definition and answer that question. Let me ask you this way," Blue said as he re-thought the question. "Do you think she loves you based on that definition?"

"Yes."

"No, you don't."

"Excuse me?"

"Sonny, I can see it in your face when I asked that question. She tells you, but she doesn't say it right? She tells you the words"—and then Blue paused—"but you don't feel the warmth. Correct?"

"It's never about what a person says. It's about what a person does."

With a shrug of his shoulders and his palms open for more of an answer, Blue said, "Okay?"

"So, I look at her actions more than what she says." Then both men looked at the entrance and saw Miss McBride running by with a handful of files. "You notice everything, huh."

"I notice what's not more than I notice what is, you might say," Blue replied as his yellowed eyes asked Drew to please continue his thought.

"She has this house," Drew blurted out, holding the edge of the table like a nonswimmer would hold the edge of the pool. "A house that she couldn't rent out due to the amount of the mortgage, so we—she—decided to sell it. Well, one of the top realtors in the area is trying to sell the house, and she brought her this *incredible* offer, and she turned it down."

"How did you find out about this?"

"I saw her at a chamber function last night, and she asked me if we were serious about selling the house, because she could not continue to show it and have us back out of the deal. She's had four buyers for the house since February, and each time my wife has backed out and never even discussed one of the offers with me."

"So you see this as a life preserver of sorts. Just in case the marriage fails, she will still have her house."

"That's not it at all."

"Sonny? Don't do that, okay?"

"Do what?"

"Don't lie to yourself. That's the only reason you're upset about it. Tell the truth?"

"Well, hell, yeah. Why should she continue to have the property if she doesn't want to rent it out or sell it?"

"So what would make you happy?"

"What's happy?" Drew grunted, and lowered his shoulders. "Who knows what that is anymore?"

"You do. What could your wife come in that door over there and say to you right this moment that would make you happy? That would make you—"

"That she would at least talk to me before she makes decisions like that."

"That's not it."

"Of course it—Listen, I got to go, Mr. Blue," he said, and looked down at his watch as he stood.

"Sonny, do me a favor? Sit down."

" 'Scuse me?"

"You have at least another fifteen minutes you can sit, so finish your cold cup of coffee, save the financial news to read in your office, and talk to me, okay?"

Drew inhaled enough air to fill his chest, exhaled through his lips, and looked across the room at Florida and Double M playing Scrabble.

"Okay. She would walk through the door," Drew replied as he slowly returned to his chair, "and she would say, 'I sold the house.' And that would show me that she was in this forever. That she didn't have a plan B."

"Anything else?"

"Yeah."

"What?"

"That she wanted to start a family."

"Jeez. Well, at least you don't ask for much. And why is that important to you?"

"Same reason as I said earlier. That she was not just saying I love you. That she was showing me."

Blue looked down at the cup of coffee and then away from Drew as he asked, "Why don't you think she wants to have children, *if* that is in fact the case."

"When we were dating, we talked about it, and she wanted to do it. But as soon as she said I do, she decided that she doesn't."

"And she told you this?"

"Didn't have to. I look beyond the words."

"Isn't it funny how we can look beyond the surface to find the negative but never the good. Anyway, your mom told me she was in another relationship before you that ended a little tragic?"

"But we both had bad relationships."

"So you were kinda like two halves making a whole, huh."

"You might say so. I was thinking, with all we had gone through to find each other, that we would both value what we had."

"That rule only applies in mathematics. In relationships, two halves equate to one-half. And if she didn't have time to heal, then you were just asking for trouble."

"I asked her to marry me, but she set the date and everything. I didn't push her into doing—Wait a minute," Drew replied with a smile. "Why am I talking to you about this?"

"Because you need to get it out," Blue whispered. "Tell me what happened, son? Most men in particular, and especially black men, don't know how to get it out. So we get high blood pressure and are on medication the rest of our lives. But you want to get it out, so do me the honor by sharing it with me."

Drew remained silent.

"So?"

"She . . ." Drew said as his tongue felt heavy in his mouth. "She's still in love with her old boyfriend," and then he looked away and rubbed his hand over his head.

"And that may be the case," Blue said, void of emotion. "But she never told you that, I'm sure."

"No."

"So you're thinking to yourself, if you trap her in this relationship, which consists of two halves, with the selling of the home or pregnancy, she will stay?"

"That's not it at all! My thinking is—"

"Most women when they get out of a bad relationship will not go into another one immediately. So if she did that, it does not mean that she does not love you, only that the previous wound has not been given the time to heal.

"I would be the first to admit that times have changed. But when me and my wife met, I didn't have the pressure you guys have on you, and maybe that's why people stayed married longer. I haven't thought about that aspect of it. But in those days women were not reading trashy romance novels or looking at soap operas as much as they do now'days. They were not looking for perfection in a man. Just a kind and decent man.

"Don't get me wrong. I'm not saying all women are like that. But what I am saying is this, sonny. Some people, men and women, expect that initial chemical reaction you get when you meet someone for the first time, when you feel butterflies and your palms start to sweat. They expect that to always last, and that's not reality. And when that fake reality dies, what do you have left?"

"Your word."

"Meaning."

"When you say, 'I do,' it should mean something. In spite of previous relationships, your expectations, and everything you just mentioned. If you are not looking at doing it forever, then you should just not do it at all until you are over whatever it is you need to get over."

"Son, you don't stop loving a dog like that. How can you stop loving the person you thought you would spend the rest of your life with just like that? It just does not happen, and it has nothing to do with you.

"Tell me something? And I know you have to go in a minute, but do you ever ask her about her feelings for this guy?"

"No."

"Why not?"

"Why should I?"

"Because *you* think they exist. You just said that."

"No. I'm not going to ask my wife if she loves another man."

"Are you afraid of what she might say?"

"No!"

"Afraid of what she might *not* say?" Drew held his silence. "Then why not ask her, sonny?"

"Because that's just not me!"

"Did you ask her if she was having any problems in the relationship?"

"Yeah. All the time."

"And what does she say?"

"She says nothing."

"I have a granddaughter named Hattie," Blue said, "who was flunking out of fourth grade. Her father would ask her every day, 'How was your day?' and she said, 'fine.' 'What did you do?' 'Nothing.' And this went on day in and day out, and she continued to get bad grades.

Now, I would never compare a woman to a child, but be smarter than my son. Don't ask her what's wrong. Ask her in a different way. Find out what the problem is and you may be wrong about what *you* think the problem is."

"No." Drew smiled. "I think I'm pretty right."

"Well, you may be, but don't assume. Do you know how many people are in graveyards today from making an ass of themselves by assuming? How many great ideas we have not seen because someone assumed. How many marriages have died for the same reason," he said, looking again at his hands. "Don't assume when it comes to the love for your wife. Know."

"I think I know her pretty good."

"Then what does she want from you? Forget everything else we've discussed. Just tell me what she wants, what she needs, from you?"

"Honestly? I have no idea. My love, I guess."

"Stop using that word, son. Just cut it out of your vocabulary, because it's a catchall we use when we don't know what else to say in a relationship. What does she *need* from you as a man? As your woman, what must she have?"

"I don't know?"

Blue paused and stared at Drew as Drew looked down. "Is that why you want her to get rid of the house? So she could need you for something?"

Silence.

"That's why I said stop using that word. Find out what your wife needs. But before you do that, find out what you need." And then he stopped talking, seemingly to allow the words to marinade in the air. "After you've done that, then finding out what she has to have will come naturally. Forget trust."

"Excuse me?"

"People always say they need a partner they can trust, but it's a highly overstated emotion. The hell with understanding and commitment, too. Even sex. You kids nowadays always talking about the importance of a good sexual relationship, yet you have no idea what is making that person up under you tick. You have no idea why you want to be with them, so you don't know why they want to be with you or what would make them stay. If you understand what you want and what she needs, do you think for a minute you could be unfaithful?

That you could not be committed to each other? That the sex would not make you feel as if you were standing in the presence of the Almighty Himself?

"Sonny, fall in love with finding out what you need. This is a time when it's okay to be inconsiderate of anyone else. Once you've done that, marry yourself to finding out what your lady has to have to exist in the relationship." Blue made a fist and then tapped himself on the chest as if he were knocking on a door. "If you do that, there is nothing in the world the two of you can't overcome. Nothing."

Blue stood and rubbed his stomach. As he did so, Drew asked, "Why haven't I seen you in here before?"

"I guess I have one of those faces that blend into the scenery. Kinda," he said, looking down and with a chuckle. "Kinda like a shadow, I guess. But I'm here every morning around six-thirty if you ever want to talk. Just feel free, okay?"

"Thanks."

"I usually come early so I can catch the show." Both men looked out the window at the sunshine over the hills. "Each day it rises, it seems, from the dust of the earth. And everything it shines upon is forever changed. Everything is in a sense reborn as it travels its pre-destined course across the sky," Blue said as if it were a poetry recitation. "And when it has followed its path and meets the night, nothing is ever the same where it has touched," he continued, and then licked his thick pink lips. "Nothing can ever be the same again." Then, looking at Drew, he asked, "Can I share a story with you?"

"Sure," Drew replied, looked at his watch, which indicated he was already late, and gave Blue his full attention.

Returning to the chair, Blue said, "My daddy. He was a big man, my daddy was. But not in stature, in his . . ." There was a beat before Blue's eyes lit when he said, "Persona. That's the word I'm looking for.

"There's a little ditty he used to tell me about the fate of man. A warrior is being chased by this elephant through the deepest and darkest regions of the motherland. So the warrior sees this large tree and decides to hide inside of it. Well, when he gets in the hull of the tree, which just happens to be next to the mighty river, he looks down, and there are mice eating away at the root of the tree, and in the river there is a sea serpent.

"Knowing his condition could get no worse, the warrior looked up, and what did he see? Golden-brown, sweet molasses trickling slowly down the tree. So he began to lick it. It tasted like sugar on his tongue and made him forget what was below, behind, and beneath him. Nothing else seemed to matter but the sweetness which flowed from the tree.

"But eventually the persistence of the mice paid off, and they gnawed through the roots of the tree, and the tree fell over with the warrior inside of it.

"Then the elephant charged the warrior and knocked him into the river, where he was consumed by the sea serpent.

"So what does that mean?" Blue asked as he stood again. "Why did I tell you that particular story? Because you can have all that is sweet in life if you take care of what matters most in life. Spend your time, sonny, just looking for the sweetness of her love and in time life itself will gnaw at the roots of all you have created together. In time, all of your fears will become the serpent of reality and consume you whole. And one last thing and I promise I will let you go," he said as he looked down at Drew's head.

"You are questioning her love deep inside, and it's natural, so don't be alarmed. But rest assured that a woman like Betty would not have said, 'I do,' if deep in her heart she didn't. Do you follow me?"

Drew looked him in the eyes.

"See, it is simply against our nature not to want love. Drew, we were created by what? By love, because by definition love is God.

"Deep inside she would like to grow old with you, Drew. She would like to take her last step and her last breath with you, but there is a gap between you and her. And until one of you can figure out a way to cross it . . . Well, I think you know the rest."

Without looking up, Drew asked, "Are you a minister or something?"

"I'm something, all right. But not exactly a minister. I'm a janitor."

"I would have never guessed."

"Yeah. I kinda enjoy cleaning up the messes people make. Well, sonny, this was fun, but I gots ta get to work myself." Then he walked away with a smile.

Drew watched him step into the glass-enclosed hallway and stop to talk to another couple in the facility. As he watched Blue, Drew walked over to the pay phone to make the call he promised himself he would not make.

"Good morning, *umm,* Staley and Associates can I help you?" the seemingly uncomfortable male voice said as he answered the phone.

"Hello, Da'Ron?"

"Yeah. This Drew?"

"Yes. Good morning, is—"

"I'm glad you called. Is everything okay?"

Damn. She telling him our business? Drew thought. "Everything is fine. Is she there?"

"Cool. No, she hasn't gotten back yet. Hereward and I got in this morning and were pissed that she hadn't made it in, to be honest, but then we got the message, and we could not believe it."

"Believe what?"

"You know. About the car accident. That she was at Shands—"

Drew hung up in stunned fear as he called 411 for the hospital's phone number and prayed all was well.

Chapter 12

Nearer, my God, to Thee, nearer to Thee!
E'en though it be a cross that raiseth me.
—Sarah F. Adams
Spiritual *Nearer to Thee*

"Hello, my Lord and Savior Jesus Christ. I just want to thank you. In spite of all that has transpired, in spite of the personal losses, I just feel the need to give thanks.

"Seems since the day I met Cleon, you and I have become friends. Better friends, I should say, than I ever assumed we would ever be.

"Last Sunday, he said we should never question you. And that is not what I am trying to do, Father. But I can't help but ask why? When everything"—she paused to gather her composure—"when everything in my life, in our life, was going so wonderful." And then, in the calm of the sterile green hospital bathroom, Jacqui turned off the light, sat on the seat, bent over, and ran her hands up and down her shins as she prayed.

"It just seems, Lord, that every decision in my personal life I make I screw up. Every single one. Nothing I do at the restaurant is ever wrong. Everything I touch there turns to platinum. But in my personal life . . .

"In spite of the way it happened, Lord, in spite of the fact that I know I'm undeserving of what I, for what we, did, I ask that you look over Stefan. I ask that you ease his pain and at least allow him to rest comfortably today. I know in my heart that more things are brought by prayer than we can ever dream of. I know that we have not because—because we ask . . ."

Unable to finish the sentence, Jacqui sat with her eyes closed, chin touching her knee, listening and waiting for an answer. As she sat, she heard the door of the hospital room open and the casual conversation of two female voices.

"So I told him, if he couldn't respect me anymore, then he could just . . . Wait a minute."

"What," the other voice said.

"Is this the guy from the car accident they brought in this morning?"

"Yeah, they just brought him up from recovery. I reviewed the charts. It doesn't look good for him."

"Yeah, I heard about it on the radio coming in. Rory said the wife was drinking while driving and that's how they hit the other car."

Jacqui wanted to walk out of the bathroom and set them straight but could not will her legs to stand.

"No, I think it must have been a girlfriend or something because they had different last names, but she walked away with just a bump on the head. Ain't that how it always works out."

Jacqui's chest felt as if a bomb exploded inside of it as she listened.

"Yeah, looks like this one will either die or be a veg. I've never seen one come in this mangled and live to tell about it. It's sad, though, because he's so good-looking, for a black guy."

"Yes. So, you did the charts, or do you want me to do them?"

"No, but I need to come back in here in a few, anyway. I'll do them then," she said as Jacqui could hear the room door open. "As I was saying, I told Rita . . ." And then the voices faded, but the words remained after they were gone.

Jacqui cleared her throat and once again bowed her head.

"I now know I love him. But then again, I've always known that. I just didn't have the strength to admit it to him or to myself.

"So, Lord, I know I could never repay you for all you have done for me already, but I would like to ask that you spare him. In my heart I don't think it's his time, and I simply ask that you let him see one more day."

Running her fingers over her hair, which was freshly gathered in a single ponytail, she completed the prayer by saying, "I ask this, dear Lord, in the name of the Father, the Son . . ." And then, unable to speak, the words died in her throat, and she sobbed like a baby in the bend of her elbow.

* * *

Jacqui walked toward the fifth-floor reception room with a large orange she was given by the nurse on the night shift who put the stitches in the bridge of her nose.

Both of her eyes were swollen, and the codeine she had taken for her ribs, initially assumed broken but determined to be badly bruised, had taken effect.

The last of the police officers she had spoken to had left, and while in her heart she wondered if she would be charged with a crime, it was the least of her concerns.

As she walked into the reception area, the family she had met the previous night were still there. William Morgan's mother was ninety-six, and the doctors had informed them to pay their last respects. Jacqui walked in and smiled at him as he read a magazine, his wife's head in his lap.

"Listen there, ew, Miss Jordan? Your friend? The attorney lady? She just left. Said she had to go home and get dressed for work but would be back here after lunch."

"Thanks," Jacqui said as she took a seat and picked up the only magazine left, a worn copy of *Field and Stream*. Then the door of the room opened, and it was Cleon.

"Hey." Jacqui smiled.

"Hello, precious," he said as he came and sat beside her. "One of the sisters in the church called me this morning and told me you were here. So what happened?"

"You didn't have to come out here."

"Yes, I did," he said in a heartfelt tone, and took her hand in his. "When I got the news, I was headed to Newberry to do some witnessing, but I came right over here. So? What happened?"

"Nothing much. Did you have a hard time finding parking?" Jacqui said as she reclaimed her hand. "I know it can be a bear at this—"

"No." Cleon cut her off and leaned away. "I have a clergy sticker." Twisting his ring on his pinkie finger, as he would sometimes do when deep in thought, he said, "I know Stefan is back in town. His sister goes to my church, and I know he was involved in the accident. But why won't you tell me what happened? Is there more to it?"

"Because I just don't feel like talking about it. I've told the story to about five cops and about ten doctors, it seems, so I just don't feel like talking about it now. I just want to talk to a friend."

"Were you drinking?"

Jacqui whipped her face around and asked, "Who told you that?"

"Well, the sister who called told me alcohol was involved, so I didn't know what to think."

"I was not—" Then she paused and grabbed her ribs. "I don't want to talk about it."

"Well, at least let me take you home. I can wait on you hand and foot until you get better."

"No, that wouldn't be right."

"Why not? Doesn't he have people here in town other than Sister DeCoursey?"

"No—Well, yeah he has family but—"

"Well, let them come out here, Precious. You never take care of yourself," he said, and took her hand once again between his to rub it.

As she looked down at the carpet, the door reopened, and she once again freed her hand from his. It was Drew.

"Jacqui. Listen, what's going on? How's Stefan? How's, I mean, where's Betty?"

Jacqui covered her face with her hands and exhaled. And then she said quietly, "Listen. You all have got to give me a moment to breathe. I just can't . . ." Then she stood, picked up the softened orange, and left both men in the room, staring at her back, then each other.

Jacqui paced outside the surgical intensive care unit in an attempt to prepare herself emotionally for what she would find on the other side of the door.

Even at her age she had never felt the sting of death of anyone she was close to emotionally. Now death had surrounded her and had come to meet her face-to-face. And then she gathered her composure and opened the door.

There was a little girl who was brought in shortly after Stefan with a gunshot wound to the chest and a much older man who was dying of liver disease. Jacqui walked past both patients' partisans toward Stefan.

The only light was the bright one over his bed. The sheets were white, and he looked to be resting with the tracheotomy tube in his neck and machinery monitoring each and every breath he received and emitted.

BLEEP, BLEEP . . . BLEEP, BLEEP.

Jacqui walked over to his bed and smiled at the face that had brought her joy so many times before. But then her expression waned, and she felt his toes to see if she could detect any sign of life in them. Maybe if she squeezed them he would move, she thought, and the nightmare would cease to be. But as she held them, she noticed they were cold and lifeless, just as the rest of his body appeared to be.

BLEEP, BLEEP . . . BLEEP, BLEEP.

Jacqui rested her elbows gingerly on the silver bed rail and looked at his face again with the large bandage over his eye where his head hit the windshield, the wound still bleeding. On various locations of his torso, white tape kept spaghetti-like chords in place that ran to the monitors. As she watched him, her hands became clammy; she had no thoughts, no words or feelings. Then she felt her heart beat so heavy it seemed to move her blouse.

BLEEP, BLEEP . . . BLEEP, BLEEP.

Stefan had flown back into town on his way to his much-anticipated photo shoot in South Beach. He called Jacqui and asked her to go to dinner with him, which she politely declined because she had plans to go out with Cleon.

But after subtle pressure she went with him, and dinner became a movie, and the movie turned into a jazz club, which led them back to her house, where they enjoyed each other's company until two A.M.

Awakened by the thunder, Jacqui nudged Stefan so hard she almost knocked him out of bed.

"Wake up!"

"What?" he asked sleepily.

"You gotta go," she said, shaking her head as if she were attempting to erase a dream.

"Why?"

"Because I don't want you to spend the night."

"What do you mean? What's the difference in us making love and me spending the night?" he said, and rolled over on his side.

Sitting up in bed, she said, "Stefan, I can't do this. I just can't."

"Do what?" he asked, gathering his pillow under his head, his back turned to her.

"You can't keep me on the hook like this. I was ready to get over you, and now this, and I just can't do this anymore."

"So what are you saying? That you're in love with the preacher guy?"

"What I'm saying is that I'm not in love with you. Now get your stuff and leave. Please?"

After a pause, Stefan flung the covers back and got out of bed, mumbling to himself. And then he asked, "So can you at least drive me back to the hotel?"

As Jacqui drove, the rain fell in thick splats. She could hardly see ten feet in front of the car as she noticed other drivers pulling off to the side of the road until the worst of the storm had passed.

Jacqui regretted doing what she knew she had to do. Although her heart vehemently disagreed with her actions, her head told her she was doing the right thing.

"So this is it, huh?"

"What?" Jacqui said in a voice that masked her angst.

"This is it? This is the end of the road for us? This is how it ends?"

"Stefan, you don't want me anymore, and you know it. I could tell by the way we made—by the way we fucked. You want sex on a string with no commitment. You're not looking for a relationship. You're looking for a lay, and that's not me anymore. I deserve more than that, and I refuse to accept less."

"Aw, hell," he said as he looked out the passenger side window. "You been reading that Vanzant shit again."

"It has nothing to do with—Wait, I don't have to explain anything to you."

"Why do you do this, Jacqui?"

"Do what, Stefan?"

"What you're doing now? You know we should be together. You know that, and now you're playing games."

"You have *no* earthly idea what you want. Right now," she said with sarcasm in her voice, "you don't want me. You want me to turn around and go home and let you fuck me again. Tell the truth. That's what you really want. Right?" she said, looking over at him and then back at the road. And then her voice changed as she said, "And I am tired of getting fucked!"

"The hell with you, Jacquetta!"

"Why it gotta be like that?" Jacqui said, gazing at him.

"Here I am trying to tell you how I feel about you, and you pushing me away again, and I'm just tired of you telling me to fuck off. You know what?" Then he stared down the road. "Never mind."

"Say it!"

"I was coming back here to ask you if we could get back together."

"Whatever. So is this the point where I'm supposed to make a U-turn and go home and finish what we started last night?"

"Fuck it! You don't have to believe me if you don't want to, because it don't matter now, anyway. But that's why we went to dinner last night, and the more we talked, the more I knew it was the right decision. And then you start in with this pressure shit!"

Round-eyed, Jacqui looked at him and said, "What the fuck do you mean about pressure!"

"Just what I—Watch out! Deer!" he screamed at the top of his lungs.

The next thing Jacqui remembered was hitting what felt like a pothole and swerving the car off the road into a brick wall.

Like a bat hitting an approaching fast ball, her vehicle was knocked in the opposite direction. Jacqui's face met the steering wheel, her body restrained in her seat by the seat belt, and as she looked out of the corner of her eye, she no longer saw Stefan, and then everything went black.

Jacqui's body jumped as she felt footsteps behind her, but she continued to look at Stefan with tired eyes. "Yes?"

Cleon stepped closer and said softly, "Can I ask you a question?"

Jacqui refused to take her eyes off Stefan.

"Do you want me to leave or stay? I'm not out here to bring you any harm or make you upset. I just wanted to get you away for a while so you could get some rest."

Jacqui continued to stare in silence.

"So?" he asked in a decibel louder. "Does that mean you want me to leave? If you like, I can wait an hour or so to give you time to—"

"No need to."

"So, you're ready to go now?" Jacqui walked over to Cleon and stood squarely before him. "Where's your purse? Did they give it back to you?"

"I don't need it. Because I'm not going, and I want, no need, for you to leave now."

"Oh, well, if you like, I can bring you some dinner from the restaurant later tonight. Just call the new girl and tell—"

Like an iceberg, she replied, "No, I mean, leave as in don't come back."

"Okay," he said softer. "Well, I'll give you a little space. I need to run out to Newberry, anyway, but—"

"Don't," Jacqui said as she closed her swollen red eyes momentarily to block the tears and then reopened them. "Cleon, don't do this."

"Don't do what?" he said with a wry smile.

"You know what I'm trying to—"

"Of course!" And then he looked at the body of Stefan, lowered his voice, and relaxed the thick veins in his neck and forehead as he swallowed and twisted the pinkie ring on his finger. "Of course I know what you're doing. And I'm trying to ignore it, Sister Jordan. I mean, in the past two or three months we've had a nice time together, haven't we? I made you laugh. Made you smile, I thought." Jacqui opened her eyes and walked back over to Stefan. "I mean, I thought we had something. Everyone at the church loves you. You seemed to enjoy all of the activities we were a part of. I thought we had something special."

"Maybe that's it, Cleon. Maybe I don't know what special is anymore. Maybe I'm just tired of trying to find out what it is I want, I need, in a relationship."

"Jacqui, here is what I'm gonna do," he said, and placed his hand on her shoulder. "Whatever happened between you and him does not matter to me. The Bible says ye who has not sinned, cast the first stone, and so I am not such a man. I will not condemn you, nor will I find fault with what has transpired. But what I will ask you to do is to pray, and if you would allow me to pray here with you, not for us but for Stefan, I think—"

"Cleon, again, don't do this. I'm going through a lot, and if you had a compassionate bone in your body, you would just give me a moment to sort things through."

"I can appreciate that." Then he took his hand from her shoulder and said as he walked toward the door, "We'll miss you at prayer meeting tomorrow night."

"Thank you," she said under a stream of uninterrupted, unseen tears.

"So do you think you can maybe make it Sunday?"

Silence.

"Well, the following Sunday is the fifth Sunday meeting, and it would be nice if you could make it then."

"Cleon?"

"Yes?"

"I'll be there—"

"Praise the Lord, Sister Jordan. Would you like to ride over with—"

"I'll be there if Stefan is able to come with me."

Cleon bowed his head and walked away.

"Hello, Luther, I was just calling to find out what the final numbers looked like."

As she spoke on the phone to her restaurant manager, she watched Betty, Hereward, and Da'Ron being interviewed on ABC's *20/20*. Betty, who sported a new hairdo compliments of the owner of Carolyn's Hair and Nails, spoke like a seasoned television veteran, although she had gotten little sleep the previous night.

"Is that all we did? Man. How does that compare with last year's numbers?" Jacqui asked Luther.

After the conversation with Dr. Wallace, who was the spinal-cord specialist who returned to visit with her, she had no idea how long she would have to keep the vigil.

Betty had returned to the hospital for several hours after Drew left and sat with her until she had to rush back to her office to do the live remote with Barbara Walters.

"Okay, here is what I would like for you to do," Jacqui said, pacing across the waiting-room floor. "The key to my house is in my top-right desk drawer. Go there and look in the garage and you will see a lunch-and-breakfast sandwich board. Pick one of the busboys with Friday and Saturday off and pay them time and a half if they would come in and wear the sign for three hours during lunch and three hours in the morning, okay?"

Before she left the hospital, Betty told Jacqui that she finally had a chance to talk to Drew. That he walked into her office and asked her if she had feelings for Evander. She told Jacqui that she told him no, but as she spoke, Jacqui did not believe her.

With her back turned to the door, Jacqui sat down and heard it open. She immediately recognized the voice.

"Hey. Sorry to bother you, but have you seen Betty?"

Jacqui pointed up at the television, and then Drew looked up and said, "Damn, that's right? I forgot all about that."

As he went to turn up the volume, he heard Barbara say, "We thank all of you for taking time away from your busy schedule to visit with us." And then she looked into the camera and said with her trademark smile, "We will have more on this special edition of *20/20* from Gainesville, Florida, right after this message."

"Damn, I wanted to watch that."

"Okay, well, I tell you what," Jacqui said into the phone, "I may not be able to get in for a few—Yes, everything is fine considering. But I will not be there for a few days, it appears. If you have any questions, hit me on the cell. I always keep it with me. Okay?"

Then Jacqui pushed the antenna of the phone in and looked at the television again. "I didn't catch all she said but seems she did a good job."

"I called, and when she didn't answer, I just assumed she might have been out here," Drew replied.

"Umph."

"So," he said, and sat on the cushion next to Jacqui's on the couch. "When do you think I'll be able to get in to see him?"

"Soon, I hope. I'm not supposed to be in there as much as I am, but I ignore them and walk in, anyway."

"Have you heard from his family?"

"Family? That's a good one. His momma wanted to borrow some money, he told me, and when he told her he didn't have it, she didn't let him stay at her house when he came home this week. He had to check into a hotel. The rest of his family is just as trifling. I called his sister six o'clock this morning, and you see who's out here."

"I didn't know that."

"Yeah. But it's okay, I'll be out here with him."

"So what's the prognosis? If you don't mind saying."

"Not good. He may have a spinal separation, but they're not completely sure because of the amount of swelling. They may not know for weeks, the doctor said." And then her jaw trembled as she spoke. "Unfortunately, that's the good news."

After a stiff pause Drew asked, "That's the *good* news?"

Jacqui looked Drew in the eyes, her chest filled with emotion, and she said, "They don't expect him to live through the night."

"Oh, my God," were the only words Drew could mouth.

"So if God will give him back to me, even if he's handicapped, I would be—"

Drew put his arm around her shoulder, and her head collapsed on his chest as she cried. "I am so afraid, Drew," she said, her body shaking with fear, every beat of her heart being heard in her ear. She buried her head deeper in his chest and repeated, "I am so scared."

Fall

Chapter 13

Courage is what it takes
to stand up and speak.
Courage is also what it takes
to sit down and listen.

—Anonymous

SEPTEMBER

" . . . so ladies and gentlemen of the jury," Betty said as she looked at her half-glass of ginger ale with its melting slithers of ice. "Although we are mindful that it is dangerous to overpromise in such a case, we feel our client is innocent of the charges brought forth by the state of Florida. Therefore, it is our solemn intention to yada, yada, yada. Thank you for your time, drive home safely, good night!"

And then Betty looked down at Hereward, who read his copy of her opening dressed in chinos and a navy Yale T-shirt. As he blindly reached down and tied his water-stained chestnut Top Siders, he said, "I like it. Well, I could have lived without the *Bob Hope* close, but other than that, I like what you've done."

Looking from the small dining room of Jacqui's cabin at Da'Ron in the living room, Hereward asked, "What do you think, sport?"

As he lay on the couch and shot a purple handball toward the wood-paneled ceiling as if it were a basketball, Da'Ron answered, "I like it. You're not overselling them," he said as he caught the ball and tossed it upward again. "You're reasserting his innocence without making him appear to be as pure as the driven snow or a victim of circumstance." And then, as the ball came down inches from his nose, he caught it and said, "My only concern is about that juror. You know, the one I talked about last week?"

With his eyebrow arched, Hereward replied, "Number six."

"Yeah," Da'Ron said, and flipped the ball upward again in a straight line, barely skimming the ceiling. "This lady's mother was murdered. I know it happened—"

"Thirty-seven years ago," Betty said demurely.

"Right. And I know she's a Democrat and more than likely against capital punishment as a matter of principle. But something in my mind tells me that when they start showing the photos of the crime scene, she's going to see her mother."

Each time Da'Ron shot the ball upward, his wrist bent in the angle of a swan's neck, but it appeared that his mind was anywhere else but on the spinning purple sphere.

"In my opinion," he continued, "when they're in that room, what she's been through will be either our greatest asset or our greatest liability, and that's not a gamble I'm sure we should have taken on if we didn't have to."

Betty looked over at Hereward as she returned to her chair at the breakfast table.

"I went with number six," Hereward said, "because A, she is a black woman. Black women are less inclined to vote in favor of the death penalty. B, she's a doctor, so she's educated and will not rule in favor of her emotions, and C, she's seen, by her own admission, the way the police department can unjustly 'taint' cases. At least I think," he said, looking through his black trial notebook under the jury tab, "that is the word she used. And D, I saw the expression on Cassidy's face at jury selection. He acted like he knew something we didn't know. So, in his mind, he's thinking when he flashes those photos and looks right at her, which I know he will, he will just have to convince eleven jurors. Trust me when I say that confidence and courtrooms can make for strange bedfellows."

Then both attorneys looked over at Betty, who pulled down a lock of her frayed hair, put it in her mouth, and then looked back at them.

"So?" Da'Ron asked.

"Well, guys," she said in a weary voice, "we had this debate for three days last week and two the week before. Let's focus on the matter at hand, because as far as this is concerned, the ink is already out of the pen."

Da'Ron diverted his attention away from the other litigators and back to the ball. "Well, other than that, I think we're ready."

"Are you sure you don't want me to go out to the jail with you to talk to Bear before the trial?" Hereward asked.

"No, that's okay. I just need to touch base with him on a few minor points. You eat breakfast with Cindy. By the way," Betty questioned as she searched for her watch, "what time is it?"

"Eight," Hereward replied as Da'Ron simultaneously said, "eight-thirty."

"Oh, yeah, eight-thirty," Hereward corrected himself, and then looked at Betty as he stretched stiff and a pop was heard from his joints. "So, Counselor, I guess this is it."

"Yeah," she said wistfully. "And to be honest, after this is over, guys, I'm out. Done."

"What do you mean?" Da'Ron said as he again caught the ball inches from his nose and held it.

"I always wanted fame like this, but now that I have it, I don't know if it's me. It's been a fast trip from doing pro bono for pickpockets to having your face splashed all over the tabloids, and I don't know if this is what I want or need in my life."

"Hell, who knows what they want or need in their life," Da'Ron remarked as he resumed the tossing of the ball.

"I most certainly do," Hereward said as he picked up his briefcase and cradled it in his arms like an infant. "This case has shown me just what I want to do, and that's write. I want to write a book, not about this case per se but a book about the perils of this profession in matters dealing with celebrities.

"And I want to lecture. After doing this," Hereward added, "it would be too hard to just go back to doing wills, trusts, and divorces."

"Well, this is most definitely me," Da'Ron mumbled.

"I can see it now," Betty said as she topped off her ginger ale. "You will be one of those high-profile attorneys to the stars. Kinda guys with a house on both coasts. Correct?"

"I don't know about that, but MSNBC called, and they're developing a TV show with a courtroom theme that they would like to talk to me about."

"Really? And you're considering it?" Betty asked.

"Yeah. I've always wanted the limelight, and now that we're in it, my thing is this: You strike while the iron is hot."

"By the way, Betty, to change the subject momentarily," Hereward asked, "do you own a handgun?"

With a bemused look she answered, "No. Why?"

"There are a lot of crazies out there. I am not trying to scare you, but you might want to just get something to keep when you are in the office alone and all."

"True. You just never know what can happen nowadays," Da'Ron said. "By the way, how's Stefan doing?"

"He's doing fine. Thanks for asking. They determined last week that his injury was incomplete, thank God, so he's coming back slowly but surely. He's been in therapy about a week now, and he's trying to relearn how to walk, and it's not the easiest thing in the world, according to Jacqui."

"So," Da'Ron asked, squeezing the ball in his palm, "how's he adjusting to the therapy and all?"

"Great," Betty lied. "It's going just fine."

"Cool. Now back *to the matter at hand,*" Da'Ron said in a high-pitched, loose imitation of Betty. "Do you think Cassidy will try to plea out again?"

"Oh, I thought I told you," Betty replied. "He called Hereward at the office yesterday, and all of a sudden 'Mr. First Degree or Nothing' will accept manslaughter with a twenty-five-year stip and no possibility of parole."

"You're kidding me?" Da'Ron said.

"That's just what he said," Hereward replied. "Expect that country bom'kin to walk in tomorrow with fifteen mandatory."

"Damn. That's the way you do it in Florida?" Da'Ron asked.

"It's a distinct possibility. I did a little check on Mr. Dean Cassidy and found out he tries to bully defense attorneys with his good ole boy persona, and then they buckle under and settle for anything."

"So," Da'Ron asked as he sat up, "if they say twenty tomorrow, 'cause I don't see fifteen happening, but if they say twenty with parole in, say, fifteen, what do we do? Should we try to get them down to two counts of man two with, say, a mandatory ten?"

"We would talk to Tobias," Betty replied. "But I would also advise him not to do it. If he's innocent and we let him plea because we are afraid we cannot prove it, isn't that about as low as you can go as an attorney."

Both men sat silently.

"Hello?"

"We'll," Da'Ron said, staring down at the oak floors, "I've thought about this. Thought about it quite a bit actually, and due to the ramifications this case could hold, I think we should at least listen to a plea. Especially if they offer manslaughter."

"Are you serious?" Betty asked, and removed her reading glasses.

"I'm just saying There's a lot of incriminating evidence and the press, with the Klan protesting outside the courtroom, with the Muslims due to stage an event because they don't want Bear to get off for killing Shavonda, if we got a decent offer, we should at least listen and have Bear listen."

With a deadpan expression, she said, "You think he did it, don't you?"

"I know you are not asking me, because we've had this conversation before. I could personally give less than two shits if he did it or not. And that's how we must think about this case," he said, standing and walking toward Betty and Hereward. "This case has nothing, and I do mean *nothing*, to do with the law or guilt or innocence. Once again, this case is about how you make those twelve people *feel* in the courtroom. It's about Meredith Jackson and how much latitude she gives us to put on our song and dance. It's not about right or wrong or who committed the crimes. It's more important than that."

Betty and Hereward sat quietly as silence momentarily filled the cabin. Almost imperceptibly, Betty asked, "So, Hereward, do you think he's guilty?"

"Betty!" Da'Ron said. "It's not about—"

"Shut up!" Betty screamed. Both men's eyes bulged at the sound of her shrieking voice. "I think I've heard your speech now about ten times, Da'Ron. I know that, and I knew that when I walked into law school the very first day, damn." Then Betty collected her emotions like coins that had inadvertently fallen from a change purse.

"I've thought about what you just said a thousand times. And every damn time I think about it, the answer is yes. Does it make me a bad attorney? Maybe. But the answer is yes, Da'Ron. It matters that somebody out there put a hole in Shavonda Ellis's face. It matters that Karen Parker has a daughter that will never know her mother . . . other than a photograph." Just as Da'Ron expected of juror six, Betty spoke to the men but thought of her mother. "It matters that this child may never see her father again as a free man and she in turn may be left with two dead parents."

Da'Ron sat down with both elbows planted on his thighs and stared into the dead fireplace.

"I'm a human being first. And after that I'm a woman, a wife, a friend, a neighbor, and then maybe, just maybe, an attorney. This is something that I am not proud of, and I will not include it in my speech to the Black Lawyers Association. But yes, Da'Ron. It matters to me if Tobias blew his wife's brains out or if this is all in some way a series of terrible circumstances that may lead to the death of a man who is innocent."

And then Betty sat down at the table with Hereward and stared again at the champagne like bubbles in her glass of ginger ale.

Almost inaudibly, Hereward asked, "So, Betty. What do you believe?"

"I believe this case is going to be tougher than anything we expected. I believe it's going to test our character in ways we cannot imagine. Test our spirituality, our relationships, our humanity. But I believe that Tobias"—the room became pin-drop silent—"did not do it. Has he been one-hundred-percent forthcoming? Maybe, maybe not. But I look in his eyes, and I just don't see him killing his wife, who I assumed he loved, and Shavonda in cold blood." Then she glanced at the stately attorney and said, "What do you think?"

Taking off his glasses, cleaning them on a napkin, holding them up to the light, and then using the napkin to wipe his mouth, Hereward said, "Betty, Da'Ron," and then he paused before saying, "Oscar Wilde once said, 'The truth is rarely pure, and never simple.' I don't believe that in any case that has reached criminal court there is such a thing as the simple truth. It's almost oxymoronic when you think about it. Simple truth and criminal court. Kinda like friendly fire or painless dentistry. But having said that, I have been pondering this case longer than either of you." Then he looked at Betty and said, "The more I look at it, the more I am in the dark."

After a quick lunch Betty drove toward her home to pick up a few personal items she would need since she knew she would occasionally be spending nights at the office. Sleeping in the office kept her mind on the case and off of her marriage.

The first night she stayed at the office she heard someone outside the front door pacing back and forth. When she peeked out and saw the shadow she called the police department who sent a patrolman to check on her. Although the incident was frightful, she found it more comforting to rest in the office than in Drew's arms.

As she drove up their driveway, Betty removed the dark sunglasses she was rarely seen in public without and clicked the remote control garage door opener. As it slid upward she saw Drew's black Mercedes parked in its usual spot. Glancing down at her watch at the time she said to herself, "What the hell is he doing home?" Then she debated if she should just leave but then if he saw her come to the house and leave after seeing his car, it would be another argument waiting to happen.

Entering the house she started to call out his name, but decided not to in case he was sleeping. She could hear the television playing upstairs in his den so she would ease into the bedroom for her personal items and walk out hopefully unnoticed.

Betty tiptoed upstairs. The stairs she used to run up to try and surprise him when they were dating. The stairs he carried her up one morning when she felt sick. The stairs they made love on shortly after they pledged to be together forever.

As she got closer to the din she could hear the ladies of *The View* speaking candidly about relationships. Then she looked in the den and noticed Drew asleep.

"And that's what I want," the attractive voluptuous co-host said to the movie star. "I know that every relationship has its dark moments, but if you lose intimacy with your spouse, what do you have left? Is that what you were striving for in that role?"

Betty walked into their room and noticed the sheets tossed on the floor. There was a coat hanger under the bed, pillows tossed about and a half-eaten plate of food on the dresser. She also noticed an open jar of Vaseline on the nightstand beside a washcloth and the clothes Drew had apparently worn to work in a clump beside the door.

Betty walked toward the bathroom to retrieve her feminine products when she heard him standing behind her. *Damn*, she thought to herself.

"So how long you been here?"

"Just walked in," she said without looking toward him.

"Didn't look like you stayed home last night," he said, his speech slurred.

"No, I stayed at the cabin."

With her back turned Betty could hear him walk into the room, pick up the Vaseline jar and put it in the drawer. "I don't know why I even make mortgage payments. No one stays here anymore."

Dead air.

"So . . ." then Drew's words paused as if he did not know what to say. "How's, umm, you know. How's umm—"

"Drew, why are you not at the office?" Betty asked, still unwilling to look his way.

"Slow work day."

Then she noticed her husband as he sat on their bed. It was obvious to her that he had been drinking. He smiled back at her although lint was in his hair, and he wore his T-shirt inside out and backwards. "Drew," she asked, "why are you doing this?"

"Momma."

"You're drinking again . . . because of your mother?"

"Yeah." Betty watched him try to say something more profound as he looked upward but then he looked at her with a blank stare.

"Drew, you can't do this to yourself at a time when she needs—"

"I know that," he replied in self-pity. "But I can't be there for her." The he stood to walk away but then just sat down on the bed again. "It seems everything I've worked so hard for is falling apart. I wanted to take care of my mom financially and as soon as I am able to, she's dying. I wanted to spend my life with Felicia and as soon as I was ready to, she dies." Then looking up at his wife he said, "And then I marry you."

"What does that suppose to—never mind." Betty said, catching the words that would prompt one of them to say something they were sure to regret.

"Just what I said. I mean you and me marry. We have this expensive ass wedding. And it's just for show. I mean I love you," he said with a broad smile, "and you still in love with this—"

"Drew don't say it, okay? Not now. I have a thousand things happening all at once so please let's not go there," Betty said as she decided it would be easier to just visit the drugstore as she walked past her husband.

Walking down the stairs she heard him say, "All you going through?" Then Drew laughed loudly as he said, "My momma dying inch by fucking inch, day by day, and you talking about all *you* going through,

Betty!" he yelled as she looked in her purse and found her keys. "Remember when I first saw you? Remember what I asked you? I asked you if I fell in love with you, would you catch me. Remember that, Counselor?"

Betty reached the bottom of the stairs and headed for the door.

"You don't want me to say *it*? Is that . . . is that . . . is that what *it* is? You don't want me to say you still in love with Evander? That you caught Evander in-instead of me?"

Betty opened the garage door and slammed it behind her. As she got outside she noticed a news truck. *Please God,* she prayed to herself. *Don't let this fool walk out here and embarrass me.* She could hear Drew's voice shout, "Ain't this some shit! My momma dying and all she can tell me about is all she fucking going through?"

Then Betty leaped into her 4-Runner, clicked the remote to close the garage and drove off as quickly as she could.

Betty sat in the judge's chamber awaiting Judge Jackson and Dean Cassidy. As she waited, she took out her fingernail file and mindlessly raked it across the top of her nails. It was a warm September afternoon and although she willed them to be silent, the voices of the previous conflict were still in her head.

If she could, she would just go for a long drive and sit somewhere all alone and have a good cry. Just a cry to get out the pain of not having the old Drew beside her. The pain of not having Jacqui's shoulder to lean on. The pain of feeling conflicted about Evander. If she could, she would just allow all the tears to flow and get it over with. But she couldn't. There was no time for tears. So as she heard the footsteps coming down the hall she arched her back, cleared her throat, and put on the mask she was all too accustomed to wearing.

"Hello there, Betty, ho'yra'?"

Betty turned and saw the weather beaten face of Dean Cassidy. His hair was silver, and he wore a sport coat and a black turtleneck.

"Seems, we're a little early, huh."

"It appears," Betty responded as she shook his outstretched hand. "How are you and your family enjoying north Florida?"

"Oooo," he tooted like a train in a tunnel, "I guess you can see I'm about as happy as a pig in slop. I'm from Jackson, Mis'sipi, and this part of the state is not like Mis'sipi, but it's a far cry from that Godforsaken South Florida. I've had a burr under my saddle since the day we set foot in that place. It's good to be back in civilization."

"You like the slower lifestyle?"

"Love it!" And then he unbuttoned his jacket, relaxed his narrow shoulders, and crossed his legs as the leather chair he sat on made a creaking sound. "Now, you're from this area, correct?"

Knowing he not only knew where she was born and raised and was testing her mettle, Betty just shook her head yes as Judge Jackson walked in. Dressed comfortably with no makeup, white shirt, and jeans, the slightly overweight judge smiled and said, "Hello, hello."

Betty had seen the judge on numerous occasions, and since she had never seen her in such a setting, she was surprised and wondered what message she was sending.

"Glad to see that both of you are not only here on time but early," the fifty-something judge said as she settled behind her desk, looking at her docket.

"The reason I wanted to talk to you is obvious, but with the media attention this case will be bringing, it's very important that there be no surprises.

"As you know, I spent about twenty years as a prosecutor in this county and worked as hard as anyone in this state to get on the bench. Now, why am I telling you this? Because as you may or may not know, there are a lot of people in the upper reaches of power watching courtroom 300, and many of them are watching each and every decision I make for their own personal gain.

"I welcome this case. This is a case that will change each one of our lives, and while it may not be appropriate to say it, it's just a natural fact.

"Now that I've said that, let me tell you a little about the way we do business in my house. And I call it my house because I like things done a certain way. So to avoid embarrassment in front of the world, let's just go over a few items in general.

"Betty, you've presented before me, so this is more for Dean's benefit," she said as Cassidy reached into his inside coat pocket for a silver pen and began making notes on his legal pad, all the while smiling his cornpone smile.

"I have been known to break out and start singing if I feel you are bullshitting a little too long, and Betty knows because I've done it to her a time or two." As Cassidy looked at Betty and returned his eyes to his pad, grinning, Betty did not acknowledge the comment.

"If it happens to you, Dean, it's nothing personal, but the reason I do it is because we have twelve people in there, many of which may have never gotten any closer to a courtroom than *People's Court*. They're not used to you guys conferring for five minutes or long-drawn-out sidebars." The more she spoke, the more Cassidy took notations and shook his head up and down. "They are used to commercial breaks, and I do anything I can to keep them alert to each and every word you say.

"I honestly think we have the best judicial system in the world."

"Amen to that," Cassidy said as he tapped his fist on his legal pad.

"As you can see," Judge Jackson said, "behind my head there is a copy of the Constitution, and in my opinion no document, including the Magna Carta and the Declaration of Independence, was ever crafted so eloquently." Cassidy's smile vanished, and he looked at the lacquer-framed document as a mother would her first newborn child.

"But let me just say that if I feel things are being tainted by outside circumstances, I will step in. This bench is very proactive.

"Also, if I feel you've done your dog-and-pony act to play to the sentiments of the jurors and not to their common sense, I will take action if they come back with a bad decision. If you have not done so already, please do the research and you'll find that I am not above a nullification. I think I've done it more than any other judge in this district, and I have yet to have one reversed on appeals. Now, of course I will only do this if," and then she tilted her head up to look at Cassidy through the bifocal portion of her glasses, "the appropriate motions are filed. Do you follow me?"

"Yes'sum. This is clear as spring water in the summer, but tell me something? If the jury has a question, how much latitude will you permit? If any at all?"

"Good question, Dean," Judge Jackson said as Betty looked at both participants without showing what was going on in her mind. "I am not opposed to the jury posing questions. We have a very astute jury in this case." She looked down at her notes. "A biology professor from the junior college, an M.D., and a computer consultant, so I know they will want to be active in this case. But in my house this is how we do it. I will encourage them to send me questions through the foreman and then through the bailiff. I, in turn, will pass all questions on to both of you after they have been given to the clerk and documented. As you can see, my only objective is to see that justice is done.

"We'll have the cameras in the courtroom broadcasting this thing to only God knows where, and each day they will be begging each of you for insight into the case. This case, from the amount of evidence and witnesses, will take in excess of two months. Do not, and I repeat, do not get caught up in the celebrity aspect of this trial," she said, looking at Betty as Cassidy smiled and shook his head so hard his jowls moved from side to side.

"I direct this to you, Counselor, because Dean has been around the block more years than he would like to admit."

"You got that rit. I got more miles on me than a—"

"Now, if I turn my TV on and see, or I'm told, either of you are out trying this case in the media, I will slap a gag order on you. Understand?" she said, looking at Betty. And then her eyes shifted to Cassidy.

"Gotcha," Cassidy said as Betty simply shook her head.

"Lastly, before we get into the details, let me say this. If I feel you are abusing the court's time, I am not above telling you"—and then her voice lowered—"to sit the fuck down. So don't make me embarrass anyone else. The show will start at ten. Not ten o' one. The closing credits will roll at five and not a moment sooner. We will not come back late into the night, because I know we all have families to get home to. You have kids, right, Robinson?"

"It's Staley now, and no, we don't have children yet."

"*Umm,*" she said, smoothing a lock of her curly dyed red hair behind her ear as she looked stiffly at Betty and then said, "Well, anyway, we all would like to get home, and so does the jury. So don't play with our time. I will keep you on a long leash, but when it snaps back, trust me, it's no fun. Any questions, Robin—I mean, Staley?"

"None whatsoever."

"Any questions, Dean?"

"The state is ret' ta roll, Your Honor."

"Okay, well let's get into a few details about tomorrow and how things will run."

Betty took out her tape recorder, sat it on the desk, and laced her fingers in her lap. As the Honorable Judge Meredith Jackson discussed procedures, she wondered if she should have not given more acknowledgment to Da'Ron's warnings. That this case would be predicated not on facts or law but on the stage set by the judge.

Most mornings when she woke up, Betty would drink a glass of orange juice on her way to work, and that would serve as breakfast.

On such mornings she would mentally walk through her day and make notations of her A, B, and C priorities. But this was not such a morning.

It was the first morning she allowed herself to sleep after five A.M. Instead of meeting with Hereward and Da'Ron at the office, they would meet in their new headquarters in room 3F on the third floor of the courthouse.

Sitting in the small alcove in their home, Betty slowly ate the breakfast she prepared for herself as Drew walked downstairs, putting on his cuff links and humming. As the steps got closer, she debated if she wanted to rake the rest of her breakfast in the trash to avoid the conversation or sit and endure whatever might be said.

The butterflies were already floating in her stomach as she tried to think about anything but the obvious.

"You know, sometimes sleeping in the den is not all bad. I think the couch is actually good for my back."

Betty remained silent.

"Baby?"

"Yes?"

"I just want to apologize again about yesterday. It was totally uncalled for."

After a pause, Betty said, "I understand."

"Are you ready for the case?"

Betty just smiled and shook her head as she sipped from her cup of coffee and stared down at her half-eaten eggs.

"Good. I'd imagine you're glad to get into it, huh?" he said as he poured coffee into his "World's Greatest Husband" cup.

"Yeah," Betty droned. "Oh, yeah, before I forget, were you planning to come today?"

"Of course. Third floor, right?"

"Yeah, but you can't just walk in today. Go by the office and ask Amy for a pass. I put you and Jacqui on the list."

"Great. Well, this must be exciting."

Betty inhaled stiffly and then stood with her uneaten breakfast and said sarcastically, "Yes, it's exciting," as she walked toward the trash can to rake the food from her plate.

"Not hungry this morning?"

"Not at all," she said, feeling a hunger pain, since she had not eaten since lunch the previous day. "I've got a lot to get done before ten."

"*Umm,*" he said with a smile. "Well, you'll do well. I have confidence in you. You've worked hard on this case, and it'll pay off. I know it will."

"Thanks."

Betty retrieved her umbrella and checked the time once again before saying, "Well, I'm out. I'll see you tonight, but I have no idea what time."

Drew stood, walked toward her, and put his arms around her body. Shocked by the warmth of the embrace, Betty initially did not know what to say, and then she simply hugged him back. Drew kissed her on the cheek and said, "Once again I apologize. Good luck, baby."

"Thanks," she replied with a smile. As she picked up her briefcase, she looked back at Drew and knew something was not right. "What's wrong?"

"Nothing."

"Yes, it is," she replied as she put her briefcase down. "Everything okay at the office?"

"Everything is fine. What time should I be in the—"

"Ten o'clock. Drew, don't do this. What's going on?"

Drew held his head down and then scratched the side of his face before saying, "Momma."

Betty looked into her husband's eyes for more.

"She doesn't have long."

Walking back to her husband, Betty hugged him close to her body. "I'm so sorry to hear that. Why didn't you tell me it was this bad?"

"Because I—Well for the last two weeks I've been trying to find a way to tell you that she's moving in here tomorrow."

"Really?" Betty asked.

"She doesn't want to die there, and so I decided that I would move her in here."

"I have no problem with that, but why didn't you just talk to me about it first?"

"Because I didn't think I would need your permission to let my mother stay in my—I mean, *our* house?"

Betty slowly backed away from him, picked up her briefcase, and walked out the door.

As the door closed, she heard him say, "Betty! Betty! I'm sorry." But for her the ink was already out of the pen.

Chapter 14

Murder is a unique crime
for which we can never make reparation.
　　　　　—Series Detectives
　　　　　　　collection in Brown and Munro, eds.
　　　　　　　Writers Writing

Drew walked past his mother's room toward the cafeteria of Parkside Nursing.

He was later than usual.

After he peeped in at her, her back toward the door, still asleep, he quietly followed the yellow-and-blue line on the floor that ended at the entrance of the cafeteria.

For the previous two weeks Mrs. Staley had become more and more withdrawn. With the passing of each day, Drew could see her walking deeper into the darkness. There were times she wanted to talk to him about her condition, when she wanted to discuss in detail her final internment. But at other times she spoke with the look in her eyes akin to a man on death row or a child in a haunted house, never knowing when her moment of demise would occur.

Drew felt that his mother's not knowing seemed to be far worse than anything the tumor, which resided in her frontal lobe, or Parkinson's disease could do to her body.

Every time the code-blue alarm erupted, closely followed by scampering feet rushing down the hallway like the last day of school, her entire body would tremble out of control because she knew someone was near death in the facility.

Every day at lunch and dinner, the breath of death invariably dominated the conversation. The topics would tend to be centered on what medications were being taken to delay death, who else was near death, and who would more than likely meet death alone.

In the spring, when Drew initially discussed with Dr. McBride the possibility of moving his mother into his residence, she gave him literature detailing his options. Several months earlier she told him that she could put him in contact with an organization called Bridges because a hospice would only be used in the last six months of life. But when Drew had spoken to her the previous day, Dr. McBride advised that it was too late for Bridges.

After meeting with the nursing-home director, Drew returned to the room to ask his mother for her thoughts. She looked at him with glistening eyes and said, "I just don't want to take my last breath in here." She took a swallow and with a breathy voice said, "Too much def 'rond this here place. Just too much . . ."

Drew intended to discuss the matter with his wife the previous day. But in his heart he knew if she had said, "Let's think about it," he would have felt as if his back were against a wall. So instead, he had a few drinks and said more than he ever intended.

"Blue, how's it going!" Drew said as he walked up behind the meaty-shouldered man who was eating his breakfast in the cafeteria. "I see you're a little late this morning also."

"Yeah," he replied with a smile. "Couldn't get out of bed this morning. Wife," he said coyly, "was feeling a little amorous. So, how's Mrs. Staley?"

"Mom? She's fine. But remember I told you yesterday," Drew said as he took a seat at the small, unbalanced table that caused Mr. Blue's bowl of Cheerios to ripple, "she's moving out, so I packed up most of her stuff last night. She's moving in with me."

After a pause, Mr. Blue said as if he knew more than he could have known, "And your wife."

Drew's sincere smile turned, and his voice lowered as he said, "Yeah. With me and Betty."

"That's nice of you." And then he took his napkin and cleaned off his spoon before placing it beside the half-empty bowl of cereal. "So, what's going on in your life? I guess you're not seeing much of Betty with the case starting this week."

As he spoke, a live shot of the courtroom appeared on television, and they both looked over at the muted, big-haired female reporter.

"Yeah, the case is taking a lot out of her nowadays. Most nights she ends up sleeping at her office." And then he said as he saw the reporters interviewing Hereward Ivory, "I honestly don't know how she does it."

"Well, I don't think the boy did it. But what pisses me off is that the Klan are in town, spreading their hate. Now they got her defending a case that either way she loses in a way." Then he looked at Drew with a concerned look as he rubbed his belly. "See where I'm coming from?"

"Those are the breaks in her profession, though. She understands that."

"I know, but at what point do you draw the line? I mean, they burned a cross in Mount Carmel's front yard and then—"

"I understand. But there's not a lot she can do about it." And then Drew looked at his breakfast mate and said, "You know something? We've been meeting here almost every morning for what, two, three months, and I hardly know anything about you besides your last name."

Blue broke his attention from the television and flashed his flawless smile at Drew. "First name's Mister I guess. I stopped using my real name years ago and started using my stage name, which was simply Blue. So I threw in the R.L. to make it sound real. What else would you like to know?"

As he attempted to read behind the words, Drew folded his arms and planted his elbows on the table. "Well, for starters, you work out here, yet I never see you doing anything. How do you manage to pull that off?"

Mr. Blue started laughing so hard that heads turned in the cafeteria toward them.

"Sorry," he said apologetically. "I guess you can say I've got a good thing going here. My wife, believe it or not, was a nun for many years. She even did mission work for the Catholic Church in Calcutta. She knew Mother Teresa very well.

"But then she felt the Master call her to go into a different type of mission work, so I guess you can say she divorced the church so she could serve Him even more."

"And that work would be?" Drew asked.

"Working with people at or near death. I met her doing what she is doing today when I was a janitor back in 'fifty-eight. She had just left the monastery, and we dated on and off. Then she went her way, and I went mine. Then, in the late sixties, we met again." His voice fell. "Unfortunately, I was already married."

"Sorry to hear that. So what happened?"

"Well, I loved my ex-wife. But I was in love with Nora. So I left my wife and did something I'm not proud of."

"What did you—"

"I committed bigamy, I guess you can say. I was weak," he said as he looked across the table. "I was wrapped up in myself, and I didn't know how to deal with the feelings I had inside. So I took the easy way out. I guess that's why when I meet someone like you with so much potential, I want to, I don't know, sorta point you in a different direction than the one I traveled. A part of me used to be so much like you."

"Excuse me?"

"Well, of course I know you would not commit bigamy. I'm talking about on a deeper level. The way you work so hard at trying to build your business and handle the situation with your momma and be a good husband. I know you try hard, and I know it's tough to be all things to all people. But that's life."

"I guess," Drew said softly.

As the television reporter interviewed a man selling Free Bear and Bear Trapped T-shirts, Mr. Blue said, "Can I tell you the secret to life?"

"Yes, o wise one," Drew mocked with a smile. "What, may I ask, is the secret to life?"

Mr. Blue sat silent and stared through Drew with a deep frown line between his eyebrows that caused Drew's smile to fade. And then he leaned forward until their faces were only a half-foot apart and said, "When you close your eyes tonight, when it's quiet outside and you feel your wife's body beside you in bed, picture yourself on a hospital gurney, like your friend Stefan was." Mr. Blue swallowed as the words settled in Drew's ear. "But imagine, they are getting ready to pull that sheet over your head. Imagine if you would, that you can feel them tying something around your toe and you hear the words 'This one will not make it' and inside you are screaming at the top of your lungs, 'I'm *not dead!*'

"Then imagine as they walk away, you are counting your last breaths. One . . . two . . . three . . . four.

"With one of those breaths, Drew, what would you like to tell Betty? What would you tell your mother? What would you tell your friends or the people you work with?" he said, and leaned back. Knowing what you would tell them, and doing it. "That is the secret to life. If you master that, you are guaranteed," he said, and tapped the table with his fist, making the Cheerios slosh from side to side, "to be happy. Everything else in life, our jobs, sports, even sex, it's all bullshit. What's important is letting people know how you feel about them and not ever letting them leave without telling them that."

"I never heard it put in that context."

"Believe me, if you are open with a person, no matter what you think, your love will penetrate them. It's almost impossible for it not to eventually. But I don't mean loving them by saying the words, because that's like a Band-Aid. It just covers the wound and makes us feel protected temporarily.

"No, I'm talking about a deeper, truer love. When you love someone so hard that you can feel their fears *without* asking them. When you love them so much you help them resolve their issues about love and about life. Because as sure as I'm a black man, if you help your woman, let's say, for example, get over the loss of her father or a man who she may have loved, she will be yours forever. But you have to allow them to work through it totally without being judgmental in any way whatsoever. Because until that occurs she will always wonder what if, and nothing is worst than that."

Drew sat speechless.

Mr. Blue looked at the height of the sun in the bay window and said, "It's almost time for you to be leaving, huh."

"Yeah," Drew said, and shook his head as if he were in a trance.

"Before you go, let me just leave this with you, and if you never remember anything else I say, if you one day ever forget this ole black, shiny, ugly face of mine," he said without the hint of a smile on his spotted lips, "remember this. Whatever you are looking for in life. Is looking for you. Whatever you so desperately crave, is desperately trying to find you as well."

And then Mr. Blue stood up and said, "I hope things work out at the courthouse today. Since you're moving your mom out, I guess I'll not be seeing you round much, huh."

Drew continued to reflect on the conversation, and then he looked up and said, "This place is on my way to work. If you like, I could drop by on Friday's, and we could have a cup of coffee the same time as usual."

Mr. Blue shook his head several times before saying, "I would really like that a lot." And then he rubbed his belly and walked away.

The power washed steps of the Alachua County Courthouse were lined with the news media.

On the ground were thick black cables encircled by other cables, wrapped with duct tape, and they ran in every direction.

Brightly painted vans, which doubled as mobile studios, were in place to send the news to viewers across the country. The News Leader, Your Hometown News Team, and The Area's Most Watched News Show were splashed across the side and back of each one of the white vehicles. With the impending television sweeps, stations sent their most recognizable reporters in an effort to boost their ratings.

As Drew walked toward the entrance, flashbulbs occasionally discharged until he got to the sheriff guarding the door and showed him his credentials. And then the flashbulbs went off like Chinese firecrackers, each photographer in search of the lead photo for his or her publication.

Once he was inside the building and riding up the elevator, the enormity of the case started to set in his mind.

Inside the elevator with him were journalists from Spain, Israel, and Japan making notations to relay the story back home to their readership.

When the elevator doors opened, Drew's pulse quickened as if he would be giving the opening presentation for Tobias J. Parker himself. Then he walked down the black-and-white alternating tiles of the hallway to the courtroom door. There he saw a sign that read: Quiet, Please. Court Is Now in Session.

Drew presented his pass to one of the guards, who was dressed in a crisp green uniform. He whispered to Drew that there was limited seating, but if he did not mind the back row, he could get him in.

As he walked in, the freshly upholstered room was packed, but the first face he saw was Betty's. She looked back as soon as the door opened, and a ray of sunlight fell through the window of the room on her.

She acknowledged she saw him by tilting her head and then returned her attention to the lanky prosecuting attorney who was in the midst of his opening.

"Sir," the bailiff said, "right over here." Then he pointed Drew toward a soft spot on the bench between several reporters taking notes.

As Drew took his seat, he noticed Betty's calm demeanor, and then he sat back, unbuttoned his jacket, and listened to the tanned Dean Cassidy in action.

"The Bible tells us that in all our getting, we should get understanding," Cassidy said, and then paused for seconds, which felt like minutes. Dressed in black he paced back and forth like a panther in a circus cage. "So, what I want to make emphatically clear this morning is that our jobs, and I am referring to Mrs. Staley at this point, our jobs are vastly different," he continued as his face alternated from a smile to a grimace with each sentence.

"Mrs. Staley is without a doubt one of the top attorneys in the country. I found that out by talking to a few of the other attorneys in the area."

Drew looked at Betty, who sat expressionless.

"But as a prosecutor, I'm obligated by law to present the facts truthfully. If I were not to do so, I could be charged with a felony offense. And as you can see," he said, walking toward the jurors, "I'm a little too old and have made a few too many enemies to go to that place."

A few jurors smiled; most did not.

"As a defense attorney, Mrs. Staley does not have the same charge as I. Her mission is clear and concise. Her job is to save Mr. Parker from being found guilty. Cut-and-dry. Black and white. End of conversation. Now, I will not faunch around about the problems of the jurisprudence system in place, because believe it or not, it's the best pisher show in town."

With a grimace, he said, "It may seem like the defense has an unfair advantage given the odds in many ways are stacked in their favor and the total burden of proof rests in our hands. They don't have to," he said, and looked at Betty, "prove one dad-blamed thang." And then his smile returned.

"But this aspect is the one I enjoy the most about being a prosecutor. Because before we convict a man in this country, we will give him each and every benefit of the doubt.

"Having said that," he said, and glanced down at the index card, "we appreciate the sacrifices each and every one of you have made for the next couple of months. We have a judicial system that works best if, and only if, you can find twelve people, of mixed heritage, who are bright and intelligent, who don't read the newspaper, and know *absolutely* nothing!" Drew noticed that every person in the jury seemed to smile this time except for the older black woman who sat in the sixth seat from the door.

"There's a saying in my neck of the woods that any ole bootlegged jackass can knock down a barn, but it takes a carpenter to build one. Imagine me, if you will, as a simple carpenter," he said as he stood at the rail of the banister in front of the jurors. And then, with the motion of hammering a nail in air, he said, "Imagine that we, on the prosecution side of the aisle, have an abundance of facts and figures. Imagine," he said, nailing each item he would mention to an invisible wall, "we have fingerprints, DNA, motive, an opportunity, and a credible story.

"Now, if you would, imagine us combining these facts to fashion a case." And then he stopped the hammering motion, and his shoulders rounded as he walked back to his table and sat on the edge.

"Ladies and gentlemen of the jury, we have fashioned such a case. We constructed, deconstructed, and reconstructed this case, and the facts pointed to one person and one person only. It brings no joy to say that, but it brought no joy to see the pictures of the partially decomposed bodies that sat in the trunk of an automobile owned by the accused." Cassidy then dramatically held his breath in his chest, pursed his lips, and removed his glasses as he stared downward.

"Imagine yourself in a rush to do something very important. And let's say you had been to the grocery store and had inadvertently left two porterhouse steaks in the trunk. Can you imagine if that car was in the sun for, say, twenty-four hours? Forty-eight hours? Well, these two young women were in the back of this gentleman's car for seventy-two hours in the Florida sun. Imagine what the coroner—who you will meet in this trial—had to deal with when they removed the bodies. Imagine the smell that they must have surely encountered.

"These gals had families. Imagine how their fathers felt after getting that phone call. Sit with those mothers as they looked at their daughters' graduation portraits in the living room, knowing they would never see that smile again. I have children and would have been . . ." Then he paused and bit his lip.

"Ladies and gentlemen of the jury, I have a daughter about those ladies' age, and let me tell you something. I'd have been like a blind dog in a meat market until justice was brought to pass if it would have been me. But both of their parents," he said, and then motioned for them to stand, "are in attendance today to watch the judicial process unfold.

"No, my friends, it brings no pleasure to once again reconstruct this case, this time for your dissection. But we have facts in our corner and the weight of honesty, truthfulness, and forthrightness on our shoulders. And when the sun goes down on this case, we will prove without doubt that *only* one man could have put a hole in the front of Shavonda Ellis's face the size of a dime. A hole that left an exit wound the size of both of her fists. Only *one* man could have snuffed out the life of Karen Marie Parker with a gunshot directly through her heart.

"This was no accidental gun firing, as the defense will claim. This is a simple case where greed consumed one man who took the opportunity to maliciously kill these two young women. And that man would be Tobias Joshua Parker."

And then Cassidy bowed his head as if he were exiting a holy place, went around his desk, and as he sat down, said, "Thank you for your time and attention to what I have said."

Drew watched a few of the reporters walk hastily toward the exit of the courtroom, retrieving their cell phones as they departed. There was a slight murmur as individuals whispered among each other.

The judge leaned her weight on her elbow and spoke to the bailiff, who passed a note to the television cameraman, and then she motioned for the attorneys to approach the bench.

Betty stood and walked toward the judge with Cassidy, and as they huddled in conversation, a tall African-American gentleman walked into the room dressed in a black pinstriped suit.

As he spoke to the bailiff, Drew saw Betty on her way back to her seat. And then she made eye contact with the tall, well-dressed man, and her eyes bulged as if she had seen a ghost. Drew looked at the man again, who stood smiling. A flash of rage swept over Drew, like heat from an open furnace door, when he remembered who the man was and wondered why he was there.

Chapter 15

Injustice anywhere
is a threat to justice everywhere.
—Dr. Martin Luther King Jr.
Letter from a Birmingham Jail

"Room 405, please . . . Thank you." Jacqui held the pay phone tightly to her ear as she tried to block out the background noise. Judge Jackson had recessed the courtroom for thirty minutes while she and both attorneys attended to what she would call "housekeeping matters."

The additional telephone bank installed by BellSouth was lined with reporters who did not have cellular phones. A coven of journalists anxiously watched the people on the phone as they spoke.

As she waited for Stefan to pick up the phone, Jacqui scanned the lobby in search of Drew. When she saw the tall, immaculately dressed man walk into the courtroom, she had no idea it was Evander until she looked into her friends' eyes.

It had been well over a year since she met him, and he now wore only a thick triangular growth of hair under his lip, and his head was completely shaved.

After he walked in, Jacqui immediately looked over at Drew, who seemed to snort smoke from his nostrils like a bull.

As the judge spoke to the jury, Jacqui, who sat three rows behind her friend, wanted to do something, anything, to defuse the possible situation, but nothing came to mind.

And then the judge temporarily dismissed the courtroom, and

Jacqui stood before anyone else and headed for the exit. Her thought was that both men would meet in the lobby and do something to embarrass themselves, or more importantly Betty. But as Drew stood to leave, Evander stared at him but remained seated.

"Hello, honey, how are you doing today?"

"Out of breath," Stefan gasped. "But I'm . . . I'm doing. How . . . How are you? What's going on down there?"

"Not a lot. Is she working you hard today?"

"I hate . . . physical therapy," he replied, and then said, "She's getting ֝. . . ready to leave. One second, baby."

Jacqui heard someone scream, "Hey, that's Bear's father!" and then an onslaught of reporters left, but it still did not seem to make a dent in the crowd stuffed in the small lobby.

"Hey dere, sweetie," a white hippie who wore his hair in a ponytail and looked uncomfortable in a shirt and tie said. "Are you gonna be much longa?"

Her mouth relaxed, Jacqui stared at him so hard that she imagined his flesh must have burned in spots. Then she just broke out laughing, shook her head, and looked away.

With the phone still clamped to her ear, she saw Drew standing in front of the large plate-glass window, looking out at the city. As he peered through it, he thumped the glass with his wedding band as if he were checking to see how thick it was.

"I'm back," Stefan said. When Jacqui, who was still watching Drew, did not answer, he said in a nasal tone, "Hellooo, anybody home?"

"Oh, I'm sorry," she said, breaking from her trance.

"Myra's gone. She's going to try to get back on this floor tomorrow and give me a little . . . more leg therapy. I'm starting to feel a little tingle, so that's a good sign."

"Good. So what else is going on?"

"Besides that, I was listening to that Tony Robbins guy last night on television."

"Why were you up so late?"

"Some nights it's like that. I think it's the pain meds I'm taking or something. But as he was talking about five-year plans, I took out the tape recorder you gave me and recorded a few of my goals."

"I've never believed in that personally."

"Why?"

"Because," Jacqui said in an attempt to assist him in avoiding heartbreak, "I think you should just do your best every day and everything you want you will get, anyway."

"Maybe that works for you," Stefan said, "but for some reason, listening to my voice say the words made me feel as if I was one step closer to achieving it."

"What are your goals?" she said quietly.

"To walk again."

Jacqui closed her eyes and remained silent. She was informed by not one but three neurologists that due to the severity of his injuries, the chances of his walking were less than one percent.

"I know you don't believe it, but there is no way I'm going to let this thing beat me. Even if they have to put in two more rods. Even if I have to do therapy twice a day, I'm going to walk one day . . . unassisted."

"I know you will," Jacqui said with a smile in her voice but not on her face.

"And my other goal," Stefan continued, "is to make you my wife?"

Astonished, Jacqui put her thumb in her ear to block out the noise. "Can you say that again, honey? I'm not sure I heard what you said."

"I want to marry you. That's if you'll have me, now."

"Baby, don't go there. You know I love you. That has never been a question." And then Jacqui watched Evander coming out of the courtroom like John Shaft. As he buttoned his coat, he looked both ways as if he were looking for someone, and then he walked toward Drew, who had his back turned, staring out the window.

"So what if we did it this year? I would like something, anything, positive to come from this crazy-ass year."

Jacqui watched Evander making a beeline through the crowd toward Drew.

"You there?" Stefan asked.

"Yeah."

"You can't say nothing?"

Jacqui had no idea what was going to happen. All she could see was the headline: "SPOUSE OF ATTORNEY ARRESTED FOR ASSAULT."

"Jac, what's up?"

"Stefan . . ."

Evander walked up to Drew, and Jacqui could see him spin around.

Evander said something to him, and the next thing she saw was Drew pointing his finger into Evander's chest.

"Yeah. Wussup?" Stefan asked. "You trying to tell me you don't want to get—"

"Honey, I gotta go. 'Bye!"

Jacqui dropped the receiver and tried to get through the crowd. As she maneuvered her way sideways through the mass with her elbow extended, she heard Evander yell, "Fuck you, nigga. You can't tell me where I can come and—"

Drew grabbed Evander by the scruff of his neck and smashed his face against the plate-glass window as a lady screamed, "Oh, my God, they're fighting!"

"Say what! Huh! I can't hear you!" Drew said, squeezing his throat.

A sheriff, his jaw stuffed with tobacco, pulled out his baton and bull rushed through the crowd screaming, "BREAK IT UP! BREAK IT UP, GAD DAMMIT IT ALL!"

As Drew pulled back his fist, Jacqui yelled as she ran toward them, "Drew! Don't do it!"

Drew held Evander's face pinned against the glass as if he were trying to push it through. Then the robust officer dropped his baton, grabbed Drew's arm, and twisted it behind his back.

Evander backed away with tears in his eyes and clutching his throat. Jacqui could see a smatter of blood on the window as well as on the ridge of Evander's eyebrow. Then she went over to Drew, who was backed against a wall with the officer behind him.

"You okay?" she asked.

"Back away, lady!" the officer shouted.

Another officer ran over, saying, "What's going on over here!"

As the initial officer briefed him, Jacqui repeated, "Drew, are you all right?"

"I'm fine," Drew replied as he tried to squelch his anger. His eyes were rimmed in red, and as he inhaled, his chest vibrated with rage.

"Don't worry about anything," Jacqui said. "I saw the whole thing."

As he rubbed the beads of sweat from his forehead with his free hand, he said, "Listen, when you go back inside, if Bet—I mean, *she* finds out about this, just tell her everything is all right. I'll explain it to her tonight. Okay?"

Then the burly officer grabbed Drew's free hand, handcuffed both hands behind his back, and shouted, "Coming through! Make way! Coming through!"

Jacqui returned to her seat, and as soon as she sat down, she noticed Da'Ron nudge Betty with his elbow. When he got her attention, she turned and looked back at Jacqui and smiled.

"Okay, Defense, you have the floor," Judge Jackson said. Betty remained seated, the residue of the previous smile still on her face.

Jacqui heard the courtroom door open, and when she looked back, she saw Evander walk in with a bandage over his eyebrow and retake his seat in the last row. Betty continued to sit as a buzz of whispers grew inside the room.

Tapping her fingernail against the microphone, Judge Jackson said, "Testing one, two, three. Is this thing on?" A few people laughed sporadically around the courtroom. "I said, De-fense, you now have the floor."

Betty was silent and then picked up her index cards and said, "Well, Your Honor, after hearing that I am one of the *best* attorneys in the country, I guess I was just waiting to see what I was going to say myself."

The courtroom laughed.

Betty stood and shuffled the index cards in her hands thoughtfully, without looking down at them. Then, in one motion, she tore them down the middle.

"I guess in keeping with every good opening, I should start by saying the words ladies and gentlemen of the jury." Looking at the cards torn in half and then into quarters, Hereward whispered into Da'Ron's ear, and then Da'Ron shrugged his shoulders.

"In spite of what was said earlier, this is my first large case and my first year without the resources of a large law firm at my disposal. Am I nervous? A little."

And then Betty walked over to the wastepaper basket and dropped the cards in it. She looked into the crowd of onlookers and saw Evander. Then, without breaking eye contact with him, she said, "For weeks I and the members of this defense team planned how we would open. But the more I thought about it, the more I thought I would just like to speak to you one to one. There are times in each and every one of our lives when courage is not an option . . . but an obligation. For me this is such a time." Then she turned and faced the jury again.

"If you would, ladies and gentlemen, I would like to ask a small favor of you. When my client walked in today, I noticed a number of you refused to look at him. Instead," she said with a smile, "I caught a few of you trying to *sneak* a peak at him. So, would you be so kind as to do me a huge favor? Would you simply look at my client?"

Betty walked behind Bear, who was dressed in a charcoal suit with a monochromatic shirt and silk tie.

"Look at him. He is in so many ways an anomaly of nature itself. His birth weight was sixteen pounds, five ounces." A female jury member pinched her thighs together and winced. "Both of his parents are under six feet tall, and he was six-eight in the tenth grade. The average player in the NFL at his position is around two hundred seventy pounds. Tobias is three hundred and forty, with almost no body fat, and is one of the fastest individuals on his team.

"So I want you to look at him and see this man who many of you may have come to know due to his extraordinary abilities on the gridiron.

"You may have seen his Reebok commercial. The one where he's in the cage," Betty said, focusing on a single juror with a smile, "and the little girl pulls his hand toward her to kiss it, and he starts roaring like a bear? And he grows fangs? You guys saw that one?"

Almost every person smiled and acknowledged they had seen the commercial—except the lady sitting in the sixth seat.

"Well, good," Betty said, standing behind Bear, her hands rubbing his massive shoulders. "Because the ad is one of the most successful the company has ever had. It's seen in six countries, and he's one of the most recognizable faces in the league, according to the NFL Players Association.

"Yes," she said, looking down at her client, who continued to gaze at the jury with his eyes out of symmetry. "I want you to look at the man you know as Bear." Then she walked away from him and said, "And now I want to introduce you to Mr. Tobias J. Parker.

"For instance, did you know that the first dollar this man earned professionally went to build a home right here in Gainesville for a needy family. And that each month, through his foundation, a home is built somewhere in the country anonymously by Mr. Parker. Did you know," Betty said as she stood next to the jury box and looked at

Bear with them, "that this man is an accomplished ballet performer? How many three-hundred-pound men do you know who can fly through the air?"

The comment prompted sporadic chuckles.

"Mr. Parker also attends Mass each and every day he is not out of town during the off-season. I'm not telling you these things to say that sometimes very good people do not make very bad mistakes. But it does speak to the heart of the man."

Betty turned toward the jurors and said, "When I was a child out in the Midwest, my father could barely read. He was a singer," she said as she reminisced. "Could read sheet music like you wouldn't believe but could hardly write his name. Go figure. But one day he got a letter and asked me to read it to him. I must have been about five at the time.

"I remember opening the official-looking envelope, and on the top of the page it said, 'The People of the State of Oklahoma Versus My Daddy.' I could tell what I said made him sad, but it made me proud. Why? you may ask. I always thought my daddy was a great man, but to read that he was going to go against all the people in our state," she said with a smile, "I knew in my heart that my daddy was indeed the black Clark Kent.

"But Daddy did not share this joy, and when I look over this case, I can surely relate to how he must have felt.

"What I would like to do, if I may, is to briefly lay out what occurred on the night of February twenty-seventh.

"It's a very simple case to follow. It's a mixture of love, fear, and anger. But before I do so, let me say that my client is guilty of having an affair. You can convict him of that. My client is also guilty of bad judgment and even poor taste. But other than that, my client is as innocent of the crimes charged against him as any one of you. And this we endeavor to prove.

"On the night in question, Tobias Parker was packing to go on a previously arranged golf weekend. His wife told him he might need to pick up a few additional items from the mall before he left town. She mentioned items such as underwear, T-shirts, et cetera. Tobias asked her to do it for him, and she said no. She insisted that he ride with her, since he would be gone for so long. Tobias agreed to do so, and as they were headed to the mall, she said she wanted to make a stop first.

"By this time," Betty said, putting on her glasses and pointing her finger upward in a scholarly manner, "it was almost time for the mall to close. But she drove, to Mr. Parker's surprise, to the radio station, which employed his longtime girlfriend, Shavonda Ellis.

"Now, so that I will not cloud the issue, Karen had known Shavonda as a friend of the family for years. Her mother at one time worked for the Parkers, and she had known Tobias most of his life. But Karen had only found out through a third party recently that Tobias and Shavonda had been romantic since she started high school.

"Unbeknownst to Tobias, Karen called Shavonda and asked her if she could ride with them to have a late-night drink before Tobias went on his trip. Asked her not to tell Tobias, since it was going to be a surprise.

"Karen Parker knew of Tobias's affairs in the past. He had fathered a child in Vermont while in college and another in Toronto the year he and Karen were married. A month before this tragic incident, Karen had a miscarriage and was diagnosed as going through depression as a result. So she picked up Miss Ellis, and then she drove past the mall without saying a word to either of them.

"She parked the car and then got out of it. She then pointed a gun at Tobias and ordered him to get out of the vehicle.

"When he did, she forced him to lie on his stomach in the mud in spite of the fact that it had been raining.

"Mrs. Parker, in her anger, pointed the weapon at Shavonda Ellis," Betty said, her arm extended stiff, as if she held a gun. "This young lady, who was only nineteen years old, was at this point hysterical with tears.

"Shavonda got out of the car as ordered, and then she held up both of her hands and started walking backward as she begged for her life.

"This enraged Mrs. Parker, who screamed for her to stand still. But Shavonda persisted in walking backward. Karen Parker screamed, 'Make one more step, nigger, and I'll blow your f'ing brains out!'

"Shavonda at this point was hysterical. She continued to walk backwards, and then the gun shot was fired. BANG!" Betty shouted at the top of her lungs and slammed her fist on the rail of the banister so hard her glasses fell to the carpet.

"One bullet! In the face! It exploded, killing that poor child before she hit the ground!" Then Betty calmly picked up her glasses, walked over to her table, and retrieved a Kleenex from her briefcase and cleaned them off.

As she returned them to her face, she said, "Before the echo could leave the air, Bear leaped up to try to grab Karen, but fell short. She fired again, nearly missing him, and then she started running.

"She ran through a wooded area at the far end of the airport, with him in pursuit of her. Then she spun around to fire again, and he charged her and knocked the gun out of her hand. Mrs. Parker fell to the ground but gathered herself enough to try to grab the gun. With him on top of her, she did so, and he pulled her hand downward, which disengaged the firing pin. This time shooting her in the chest and exploding her heart with the hollow-point shell records will show that she purchased that day to kill him with."

Betty stood silent before the jurors. Jacqui could see her friend reading their faces, and then she said, "My client, Mr. Tobias Joshua Parker, did a very foolish thing." She paused and walked halfway between the jurors and the prosecutors' table.

"He was all alone in a field with not one, but two, dead bodies. He had no alibi. There was not one witness who could collaborate his story. He had more opportunity than they give you in the U.S. Navy. So what did he do? What would you do if you were him?" she said, looking at a young black man on the jury. "If you had a reputation as a man who had several well-publicized affairs. If your nickname was Animal or Beast or Bear. If you knew anything you said or did would end up on ESPN or the CBS Evening News. What would you do if your hand was close enough to the gun to have the residue from the gunpowder on it? Would you call 911 and report the double homicide of your wife *and* your girlfriend? Maybe you would. Maybe you would have made the correct decision. The responsible thing. But I trust you can understand *why* my client did not.

"One thing the prosecution will have a problem convincing you of," she said, folding her arms, "is motive."

Betty walked back toward the jurors to make sure they did not miss a word she was saying. "Why kill your wife *and* your girlfriend? In this state, he stood to lose no more than twenty million dollars. This is a young man at the peak of his career. His earning potential was easily in the nine-figure range, according to *Forbes* magazine. His family is very affluent. Why would he murder her in cold blood, leave her in his trunk just to avoid paying alimony?

"And also, why kill Shavonda? He had taken care of her and her family, we have found out, since he received his first check from the NFL. How did it benefit him to kill her?

"The prosecution will give you opportunity, and this we will concede. They will show you the weapon, and this, too, we will not challenge. But they can never give you a plausible motive for this man, with the world at his footstool, to make such a cowardly mistake as to maliciously commit such a crime."

Betty stood tight-lipped, as if restraining her emotions, and then looked back at the jury. Spacing each word separately, she said, "Ladies and gentlemen, they're asking for first-degree murder. To be convicted of such a charge, they must prove beyond a reasonable doubt that Tobias willfully, deliberately, and with premeditation killed Karen Marie Parker, his wife of five years.

"They must prove that he willfully, deliberately, *and* with premeditation snuffed out the life of Shavonda Ellis. A young woman he freely gave, documented by canceled checks, over twenty-five thousand dollars a year.

"As funny as the Reebok ad was, I must tell you it is as far away from the truth as the north is from the south. As right . . . is from wrong. The man who sits before you is not an animal. That's simply clever marketing. When this occurred, he acted like a scared child and ran away," Betty said, walking toward, and resuming her position behind, her client.

"Tobias is not a perfect man. You can convict him of that. He has made his share of silly mistakes, and he made one big one on the night in question which he will never forget or forgive himself for, I am sure. One day he will have to look into his daughter's face and explain why he walked away. But your charge as jurors is to see through the smokescreens. To see through the celebrity. To see through what people have said out there on the streets. Your charge is to listen to the whispers of your heart. And I know," she said slightly above a whisper and squinting her eyes, "that it takes courage to do so. It takes courage to seek truth in spite of cries of racism, sexism, classism, and even elitism. But when these cries die down, the voice of reason sinks in, and it's then and only then that we can find that which we seek. It's only then that we can find justice.

"Tobias has had a wonderful life. A life filled with many of the trinkets many of us can only dare dream about. But to charge him with such a crime would indeed be the deepest and darkest injustice.

"My best friend gave me the biography of the man I consider to be the greatest individual of the twentieth century," Betty said as she looked at Jacqui. "And a quote from one of his letters has always stayed in my heart. He said, and I quote, 'Injustice anywhere is a threat to justice everywhere.'

"In closing, I, too, thank you for making the sacrifices you have made to ensure that justice is served. You will learn more about DNA than you will ever want to know. They will try to explain to you why no one tested Karen's hand for gunpowder residue. You will meet officers and coroners and doctors and friends and athletes and you name it over the next few weeks. And there will be nights when you go back to the hotel as a group and wonder to yourself why you are a part of this. When you have watched *The Klumps* for the fifth time on cable, you will no doubt think, *Why didn't I throw away that jury notice?*

"But with everything you will read, hear, and think about in the next few weeks, let me assure you that this system will only be as sound as you are. You, ladies and gentlemen of the jury, are the linchpin on which justice itself is hinged. The system works only because of you."

Betty smiled and then walked back to her chair and sat down as she said, "The defense thanks you for your time."

The courtroom exhaled, and the only noise was the tap-dancing sound of the stenographer. Then Judge Jackson arched her back and adjusted her microphone.

"Now that you have had the opportunity to listen to both the prosecution and the defense, please allow me to make one final statement. Since we are taking the unusual precaution of having three alternates, I would like to reassert that our only mission is to see that justice is served." Then she paused and rested her weight comfortably on her elbows.

"I also want to make sure one last time that each one of you understands that the state has chosen to pursue a conviction on two counts of first-degree murder. If you come back with a guilty charge on both counts, in this state you must decide if the defendant must live or die."

As she said the words, Jacqui watched Bear's shoulders for a reaction. They remained squared as Betty put her arm around his back and whispered in his ear.

"Now, I know you were asked this not once but several times during jury selection," Judge Jackson said, looking at the black woman in the sixth chair. "And I am aware that each and every one of you answered no. But I want to ensure that after thinking about it, if you have any reservations, this is your opportunity to walk away. So I ask you again, and please indicate yes by raising your hand. Will you have *any* objection to returning a guilty verdict that may result in the defendant being put to death?"

Judge Jackson leaned back as Jacqui watched attorneys on both sides gaze at the jury box for verbal and nonverbal reactions.

"Okay," she said, leaning toward the microphone and again running her fingertips up and down the shaft of the gavel. "Having said that, the law requires that you have an open mind. The law requires that anything you may have seen, read, or heard which even remotely pertains to this case be blocked out. Now, I am not stupid. I know that each and every one of you have heard about this case to a certain degree. Let's face it. We live in a real world. I am aware that the intent of the law and the reality of what is are often vastly different." And then Judge Jackson lowered her head and spoke slowly. "But this is one time that I will insist that you attend to the letter of the law.

"Thank you very much, and the court is dismissed until tomorrow morning at ten."

Jacqui walked from the private entrance of her office in the back of Jacquetta's and out to her car. It was past midnight, which brought to a close another day in which she had been able to survive on only four hours of sleep.

Her days started at six A.M., when she would arrive at the restaurant before heading over to the hospital to be with Stefan. Then it was off to court, back to the restaurant, back to court, back to the hospital, and then back to the restaurant to close out the receipts.

Jacqui's aunt Daisy had finally decided that she had had enough of Seattle, and she and her homosexual husband had moved to Florida. While she was of assistance in regard to sitting with Stefan, the bulk of the responsibility still rested on Jacqui's shoulders.

As she drove home, she thought again about his proposal and why he would ask her at this point in their lives.

The guilt of what she had done to him accounted for many sleepless nights, but she did not want to marry him out of pity or obligation, nor did she want to marry him knowing he would more than likely never walk or have children. It was not his physical limitations that bothered her, but knowing him, she wondered what would happen when he had worked hard at therapy for a year, or two years, with little or no results. She feared that would be the time when he would settle into acceptance, and she was not sure if she could go through the daily look in his eyes that screamed, You did this to me.

Then Jacqui turned up the stereo to block out the thoughts and heard the radio announcer say with laughter in his tone:

"That's right, sir. It's not a rumor, although I know a lot of rumors have swirled regarding this case, but this one we are told is true. Both men had to be separated. Apparently, the husband accosted the boyfriend of Mrs. Staley. I guess Betty Staley's getting her freak on, on the side, huh.

"Now isn't this interesting that she is defending a man who is accused of killing his wife and his girl—"

Click.

Jacqui turned the radio program off and ran her hand stiffly up and down her arm. "Damn!"

After Drew released Evander's neck, Jacqui tried to explain to the officers what happened, but they would not listen. Evander was told he was free to go, and Drew was taken down to the basement of the courthouse for questioning. By the time court was over for the day, he was allowed to go home. But he was told in no uncertain terms that he was not to return to the courthouse during the proceedings.

And then Jacqui's car phone rang.

"Hello?"

"Hey, baby cakes," Stefan's voice croaked. "Where are you?"

"On my way home. Receipts didn't balance again. How are you feeling?"

"Not bad. I ended up having two therapy sessions today, so I'm a little sore, but we do what we have to do, right?"

"True."

"So is everything all right with Drew?"

"It's fine. I take it you saw it on the news?"

"Yeah, and I was just listening to this call-in radio show discussing it."

"Considering all, he's all right, I guess. I spoke to Betty, and she's fine."

"Good." Stefan grunted in pain, which he would do from time to time when he was having trouble breathing, and then said, "So you never answered my question?"

"What question?" she stalled.

"Jac, you know full well what question. Do you want to get married this year?"

"Baby, shouldn't you be doing this with a ring?" Stefan was silent. "You still there?" Jacqui asked.

"Why're you doing this?"

"What do you mean?"

"Since the day we met almost, we talked about getting married. Now that I'm . . . anyway." Jacqui could hear his voice grow weaker.

"Stefan, do we really have to talk about this now? I've been up since—"

"Do you still love me? Just answer me that one question."

"Honey, that has never been a question at all. I will—"

"Even though I can't—I can't fuck!" She could hear him swallow hard. "You mean to sit there and tell me you still love me as much as you did before?"

"Stefan, I never wanted to marry you for the sex, if that's what you were thinking. How could you stand there—I mean, how could you say that?" Stefan remained silent as Jacqui came to a red light and mentally kicked herself for the slip of the tongue.

"I never thought your love for me was conditional."

"Stefan, stop doing this to yourself. You know full well that I still love you. I damn near got down on my knees and asked you to marry me about this time last year. Remember? I even bought the frigging ring, which I had to return, so don't question my love for you. And another thing. Hello? Hello, Stefan?"

Then Jacqui hit the END button with her thumb and returned the phone to its cradle as a mixture of love, and anger flowed through her body.

Chapter 16

In the end, every flower loses its perfume.
—Italian saying

NOVEMBER

"Ieyyy, love to love ya bayyybee."

Betty tossed her body for comfort as the Donna Summer song played on the FM radio station.

She pounded the couch cushion with her fist to loosen the foam stuffing, and it resisted. So she lay half-asleep, half-alert, her face on the scratchy, rough, and lumpy pillow, knowing that this could be the day she would never forget.

"Ieyyy, love to love ya bayyybee."

As she attempted to rest on the cot she bought for the office, she curled her body into a ball, and her stomach felt as if it were tied in a Windsor knot of emotions.

She had hardly eaten a bite since the jury went into deliberation on Tuesday.

Of all the decisions made regarding the case, she felt the best was to give Tobias a tennis ball to squeeze under the table when he became upset. Before she thought of the idea, she could hear a low, growling sound whenever the prosecution would present incriminating evidence. On the last day of the defense's presentation, Hereward made an argument in support of putting him on the stand. But the more Betty watched him squeeze the palm-sized ball, the more she realized that such a move would be tantamount to judicial suicide.

Seconds passed like hours. She was supposed to be the rock of support for her staff, but as it came down to the moment of decision, she felt she was slowly losing her will.

And then she felt lips on her cheek.

Still half-asleep, she wondered why Drew would be kissing her; then she realized that she was in the office and that he did not have a key, so who could it—

"Good morning, sleepy head," Da'Ron said with a slight smile on his thick lips. Even though he barely smiled, his dime-size dimples were visible.

Betty sat up from the cot wearing a T-shirt with Andrew Staley and Associates on the front of it and sweatpants with no bra or panties. As she regained her composure in the overly air-conditioned room, her nipples stood erect.

With her eyes and body still in a transitory state, Betty folded her arms. In a raspy voice she replied, "Good morning. You're here early, huh?"

"Yeah, I know," he said, dressed head to toe in a white sweat suit. "For some reason I think today will be the day." Then he sat behind Betty's desk as she tried to comb her hair out of her face with her free hand.

"Today is Thursday," he continued, "and with tomorrow being Friday, trust me, they don't want to take a chance at being here over the weekend. They'll come through for us today."

Betty eased off the cot and without a reply walked unsteadily toward the private restroom in her office where she kept her clothes.

"Since the case is over," he said over the sound of running water, "I watched a few of the news magazines last night?"

"Why?" Betty asked, and closed the door.

"Because I wanted to know what they thought of us and the job we did."

"Well, after looking at, reading about, and researching this case for all these months, the last thing I would do when I went home would be to watch it on television. But oh," Betty said as she squeezed the aqua toothpaste onto her toothbrush, "I forgot that you want to be a Star Jones–Jack Ford TV star."

"And your point would be?"

Betty started to say something but decided not to do so as she brushed her teeth.

"I mean, for me it's just a medium to explain the law to the masses." Betty made a "yeah, right" expression in the mirror. "Betty," he said louder as Betty could hear him making a cup of coffee. "Do you take one sugar or two?"

Looking upward and to the right, Betty tried to talk without spilling the white foam of the toothpaste on herself. With her tongue curled, she said, "No, thank you."

"Okay. Check it out. I was talking to Hereward last night, and he didn't sound too good." Betty listened closely without trying to speak. "I don't know if you know it or not, but ole boy has a bad ticker."

Betty spat out the toothpaste and rinsed her mouth.

"Yeah, I know," she said, and looked at her face in the mirror from each angle and then at the top of her head to see if there were any bald spots. "So, is he doing okay?"

"Considering all, I guess so. The day before he had to address the jury, I thought he would have to use one of those nitroglycerin tablets he has in his briefcase."

Betty put on her underwear and bra as she said, "I noticed he was looking a little flush on Monday in court also."

"I saw that, too, so I called him yesterday to ask him about it, and he said he was doing fine. But anyway, he now thinks number six is the one we had to convince. He feels good about everyone else. But personally I'm now thinking she's in the bag. I would worry about that foreman more than her. What do you think?"

Betty put on a pair of black jeans and a black D'Angelo T-shirt as she replied, "Go figure. I don't get into trying to gauge them one way or another anymore. I think when you start doing that, you start playing to one jurist and run the risk of losing the other eleven."

"But if you ask me, if that old heifer walks out smiling, it's in the bag. I've seen her type before, and she's trying to keep her cards close to her vest. Even when I made a few jokes during my presentation, she sat there like an oil painting or something." Then Betty came out of the bathroom buttoning the last button of her maroon sweater and walked in front of Da'Ron.

"Can you hand me my shoes?"

"*Umm,*" he said with a dazed look in his eyes.

"My shoes, Da'Ron. They're under my desk. Can you hand them to me?"

"Oh! I'm sorry," he said, snapping back to reality. "Shoes. Coming right up! Shoes," he continued as he disappeared under the desk like an ostrich sticking its head in the ground. "Wait a minute. You must have, like, fifty-eleven shoes under here, girl. Which ones do you want?"

Betty laughed and said, "The black ones with the silver buckle. You see them?"

"Got 'um," he said, and handed the shoes to Betty. Then, as she walked to the cot and sat down, she could feel his eyes on her backside.

"Can I ask you a question?" she asked softly.

"Anything," he replied.

"Why did you kiss me this morning?" Then her eyes met his.

"I was hoping you would ask that. In a way I did it to say thank you. Hey, I know I sorta dropped the ball in my summation. I know you could have lectured me about grandstanding. But you didn't. I was thinking about the article written in the *L.A. Times* last night where the reporter thought my mistakes were a part of our overall strategy. So when I walked in this morning thinking about that, I called your name twice, and you didn't move. So I decided to just kiss you. I hope I wasn't out of line."

Betty maintained the somber expression of a death-row chaplain and then said. "Da'Ron, you are right. I could have let you have it after your 'performance.' But I didn't because I knew Hereward and I could patch it up. At least I hoped we could. I like you, Da'Ron."

Da'Ron's eyebrows raised. "I also respect and admire you. But although this case is coming to a close, if you ever do something like that again. I will fire you. So help me God."

"But Betty. It wasn't even like that. I mean—"

"You can leave. And you can leave now!"

Betty tapped on the glass of Jacquetta's to get the attention of her friend, who was on the phone.

As she saw Betty, she was surprised and trotted over to the door as she continued her conversation.

"Listen, Betty just walked in," Jacqui said as Betty asked who was on the phone with her facial expression.

"Okay, honey," she said, which told Betty who it was. "If Betty doesn't think the verdict will be in today, I'll be out there to have lunch with you, okay?"

As she ended her conversation, Betty followed her to her office. Soon as she was in the refurbished office, Betty looked for the couch she would always park herself on, but it was missing. In its place was a taupe leather sofa, which made the office smell like rawhide.

"I love you too, baby. Talk at you later? . . . Yes I'm excited, too . . . I'm so proud of you. . . . Okay, good-bye." As she clicked off the portable receiver, Jacqui said, "So, Mrs. Lady, you slumming on this side of town, huh? Will today be the day or what?"

"Ah, excuse me, but where's my couch?"

"Girl, I told you I was going to put some money into this place."

"I know you said that, but as cheap as you are, I was thinking that meant you were going to buy a doily or something. I walk in here, and it's the Taj Mahal."

"Please. All I got was the couch."

"And the wallpaper."

"Okay."

"And the carpeting."

"Well, now I had to—"

"And the end tables."

"Now, I had those in storage alrea—"

"And the track lighting."

"Okay, okay, damn," Jacqui said, laughing. "I went down there, and you know how that is. One thing led to a whole new office."

"Well, can I sit on this thing?"

"Please. Just like you used to."

Betty pulled off her shoes and sat on the sofa. As she did, she bounced her bottom gently on the cushions to loosen them, laid down, and nestled her toes under a large decorative pillow.

"Umm," Betty purred, and she looked at Jacqui, who was working at her desk, "this one might just work out, after all. I have to break it in, of course, but I might just forgive you for not *asking* me before buying it."

"Heifer, you're sick. So, I won't ask you about the case, because I know you're sick of talking about it, and I refuse to ask you about Drew because I know you are tired of thinking about it."

Betty smiled weirdly and closed her eyes.

"So are you guys going to do something to celebrate at the office after this is over? I know you're going to miss working with them. They must feel like family by now."

"Let me tell you. Sometimes you even get sick of family."

"Are you going to do any more interviews after this thing is over?"

"I'll do the bare minimum, but then I just want to disappear for a while."

"And do what?"

"I don't know. I've spent so much time on this case, I haven't even given it much thought, but I know I don't want to run the firm anymore."

"You're kidding me."

"No, I wish I was. I decided I'm closing the doors in December, when the lease is up. This case has set me up right financially, so I could take care of Carol, and then after that . . . I really don't know. Maybe I'll lecture. Maybe I'll call one of those literary agents up who have been badgering me to write a book about the case, like Hereward is doing.

"Or who knows," Betty continued, and she looked at her friend. "Maybe I'll buy me a restaurant. Call it the Side Bar or something tacky like that."

"Sweetie, you don't even want to compete against Jacquetta's," Jacqui said, looking over her bank statement. "I can't believe how well we're doing. Maybe if we can have a triple homicide this time next—" And then she saw Betty's face and said, "My bad. Sorry I went there. I got a little caught up."

"No problem. I'm sure all the businesses are making a killing—excuse the pun—on this thing. To me," she said as she searched for a comfortable spot, "it's blood money." Then she looked at Jacqui and said, "Don't tell me, I'm laying on a blood couch, right?"

Jacqui's lower lip fell as she said, "Sheasshh."

Betty smiled and asked, "Did you see the news last night?"

"You watching again?"

"Yeah, I watched last night. I couldn't believe them crackers in the Klan were in front of the courthouse again."

"Girl, when I was there on Monday, they had bomb-sniffing dogs, were physically searching people and everything."

"Yeah, one of the sheriffs told me. This thing has become an event. They had a request to fly a blimp over the courthouse, for Christ sakes. It's just sick."

"But what I can't understand," Jacqui said as she retightened her ponytail, "is they, the Klan, are protesting that Bear is being charged. But he killed a white girl, too. And he has had Shavonda on the side for years. Yet they're still protesting?"

"They consider him a legacy. Even though he's gone *astray*, he is, and will always be, one of theirs, they say."

"Sick, sick people."

"But see, you are trying to rationalize what they are doing with common sense."

"I guess," Jacqui said.

"Racism is like that. For instance, I was riding here this morning thinking about the morning the verdict came in in the O.J. case."

"Man," Jacqui said, laying the document she was reviewing on her desk. "I won't forget that one. We were struggling around that time, and I was trying to cook, clean, and do everything else to keep this place afloat, and then white folks just stopped coming by.

"People who would drop by every day when we served breakfast on their way to work just never came back again. That's the damndist thing."

"Yeah," Betty added, "I remember very well. I was at Murphy, Renfro and Collins, and they were all in front of this TV they had put in so we could watch the trial.

"I was working on a case, and in my gut I really didn't want to go down and watch the verdict.

"Leading up to the day, there was nowhere a black attorney could go in this country and not be asked about the case. I was so proud to have esquire printed on my checks, but that's—"

"That's why you took that off your checks?" Jacqui asked. "I always wondered about that."

"Exactly. I was in Publix waiting in the checkout line, and while I was writing the check, this little blonde asks me if I thought he was guilty, and I swear you would have thought she said E. F. Hutton or something. Seemed everyone in earshot stood still to listen.

"So I decided to take it off my checks and never discussed what I thought about the case.

"Well, on the day of the verdict, I remember it was right after lunch, and I was walking past the conference room with my salad. I think it was Carol who grabbed me by my arm and yanked me into the room.

"As Johnny and O.J. stood, I looked around the room, which must have had at least a hundred people in it. There was Ronald the janitor, who had been with the firm for over twenty years, and Charlene, this girl who Murphy would hire occasionally as a paralegal. And that was it.

"And then I saw the bailiff hand Ito the decision, and my heart was racing. As they were reading the counts, I was thinking, *Why in the hell am I so nervous about this?* Then they said not guilty," Betty said, shaking her head and looking up at the ceiling tiles.

"I looked at them, and you would have thought I had walked in the room with my Jesus Was a Black Man, T-shirt and Farrakhan sweatbands.

"They looked at us. No one said a word. They just stared as if we had three sixes in our forehead.

"I looked at Ronald, who was openly smiling and saying, 'Thank you, Jesus, thank you, Jesus.' Renfro fired Ronald before the verdict came on the six o'clock news that night, I think.

"And poor little Charlene just bowed her head and walked out before they finished reading the decision.

"And me, well, I refused to let them run me out. Jac, I put my lunch down, folded my arms, and I was determined to be the last face to walk out of the room. I just knew they were going to talk when I left, so I was thinking, *If you talk about me, you will do it someplace else.*

"For weeks I tried to understand that case and why people, including Carol—who kinda showed her butt, too, and wouldn't talk to me—reacted as viscerally as they did."

Jacqui asked stoically, "What did you just tell me?"

"Yeah, I guess that's right. I was trying to reason with racism."

"So," she asked Betty, "do you expect them to come in with Bear's verdict today?"

"Yeah. I'm kinda hoping so, so I can finally get over this."

Jacqui said, cutting on the television, "I just wonder how many Ronalds will lose their jobs after this one?"

As she lay there, unable to answer the question, Betty's pager went off. She reached without looking in her purse for it and prayed it was not Drew, Evander, Da'ron, or another reporter.

And then she read the orange-lit numbers. "Jacqui? Who's number is 335-7—Oh, never mind."

"What? Who is it?"

Betty sat up and turned off the pager. Then she stood and said, "The verdict." Looking at Jacqui, she said, "It's showtime."

Hereward walked into Betty's office dressed in a new suit and shoes.

"Well, check you out," Betty said with an open smile.

"Yeah, I know. I went through the entire trial with five suits, and the wife went out and bought this one for me. I wish she wouldn't have done it," he said, going to his work area. "But the kids have flown into town, the house is stuffed with grandkids, and she wanted me to look good on television for a change."

"Well, you look great."

"Thanks. Where's Da'Ron?"

"I haven't seen him. Did you call him?"

"Yeah, I called him on his cellular. When I called him, believe it or not, he was having lunch with Pierre Cossett and signing autographs."

"Well, I'm sure he'll be here shortly. Did you speak to Tobias this morning?"

"Yes, ma'am. He's in great spirits for the most part."

"Good."

"Yeah. But—" And then Hereward straightened his tie and said, "I tell you something. He mentioned one thing that made me a tad uneasy."

"What?"

"He looked at me and said he would rather be dead then to go to jail for doing something he did not do." Betty listened and then, thoughtful, rubbed her hands together. "I've thought about this case every which way, and I really don't see any weak areas in our case. Well, excluding the time line, which Da'Ron sorta flubbed a little, but I thought you mended that aspect rather nicely in your closing."

"I remember Bear saying something like that to me too, but he's going through a lot right now. How many decent nights of sleep have you gotten?"

"Sleep? I seem to be vaguely familiar with the concept. I mean, my wife and I have had more arguments about nothing than we had in the previous thirty years combined," Hereward said, looking at the ring.

"Yeah, it can be draining."

"Very much so," he said, and loosened his collar with his forefinger. "Do we have any Snapple in the fridge?"

"Sure, Carol bought some a couple of days ago," she said. As he walked into the kitchenette, Da'Ron walked in the front door.

"Sorry I'm late, guys. I had a meeting with ABC News at Lilian's. Did I miss anything?"

"Not a thing, Sport-o. Just getting ready for the show," Hereward said as he cleaned the top of the small glass container with his hand-kerchief. "I guess you've had your share of these things, huh."

"Yeah I've been through one or two," Da'Ron said. "But this one re-minds me of O.J. because—"

"Listen, Da'Ron," Betty said, still looking down, "I forgot to file those documents on Carol's desk, and she's not in yet. Would you take care of it for me?"

"Sure. No problem. But like I was going to say—"

"Now," Betty said, and looked him in the eye as Hereward gazed at Betty and then back at Da'Ron and at Betty again.

"Oh, well. *Umm.* Okay, I'll do it now."

As he walked out, Hereward appeared to know something and said, "I think he was getting ready to start pontificating for us."

Betty remained silent. And then she said as she looked at the "Living Well" section of the newspaper, "Well, I don't think Bear should be concerned at all."

"He's giving it his best, Betty."

"I know. But his presentation was initially our strong suit, and I'm upset with myself for not doing it, I guess. Plus I think I should have grilled the coroner a little more about Exhibit 74A. And also I know we will win, but what if?"

"What if keeps me tossing and turning also," said Hereward. "What if we lose, you mean?"

"No. I mean, what if he's guilty."

The courtroom was stuffed shoulder to shoulder to shoulder with onlookers.

Betty sat watching the large black-and-white schoolroom clock above the even larger state seal of Florida.

It was three minutes until the jury would be seated.

It was four minutes until the Honorable Judge Meredith Jackson would walk out and sit on her throne.

It was five minutes until she would begin her banter and about six minutes when the words would be read by the jury foreman.

Just six minutes, she thought. *Just six more minutes and it'll all be over.*

As she sat dressed in a new suit, compliments of her best friend, with everyone around her talking about the case, with Da'Ron talking to Benyamin most likely about representation and Hereward breathing laboriously, Betty's mind was on Drew.

The camera above the heads of the jury would occasionally pan and stop on her, and she could hear the motor move the lenses to zoom in on her image. She knew her family back in Oklahoma was more than likely watching, as well as relatives in New York State.

She wondered if her father was somewhere watching and telling a disbelieving party, "That's my little girl." She could feel her mother's presence, saying the same.

She could only imagine the course of conversation at her previous law firm. But of all the thoughts that traversed her mind, the one that hurt the most was watching the essence of her marriage slip through her fingers, like sand through an hourglass.

Every day there was a little less to go home to. A little less to say I love you about. Every night there were fewer reasons to stay, more to leave, and fewer reasons to try to make it work.

Betty looked back up at the clock. Four minutes and counting as Hereward leaned over and whispered something in her ear, and although she had no idea what he said, she shook her head and returned to her thoughts.

Betty thought about the time Drew took her to Manhattan on the spur of the moment. They rode in a carriage through Central Park as snow drifted from the sky.

As he took off his overcoat to cover her exposed legs, she felt like Ali McGraw in *Love Story.* That night, she fell asleep on the couch, and when she awoke, the room was totally redecorated.

Drew had quietly had the bed removed and in its place, in the darkened room, was a quilt surrounded by numerous scented candles of various shapes and sizes.

When she awoke, Betty initially thought she was dreaming until she saw her husband-to-be dressed head to toe in black silk pajamas.

Sitting in the courtroom, Betty brought her hand up to the spot on her neck where Drew left a five-day passion mark before running his tongue in her ear and whispering erotic words to her.

She thought about that night and how, after they had made love on the floor, on the couch, and against the wall, they made love on the balcony of the suite. The next morning, they watched the sun kiss the Big Apple good morning, together.

The previous November, when she was planning the wedding, she could never fathom that a year later she would be planning their divorce.

As the clock continued to click toward the moment of judgment, Betty noticed a sheriff look at Bear.

The first thought she had was that he was another officer who wanted an autograph, until she looked at Bear and noticed the glazed look in his eyes.

Leaning over, she said, "It's almost over, Toby. Are you okay?" Bear sat silently as his smile widened and eyes narrowed. "Tobias? You okay?"

Bear looked at Betty and then at the empty jury box furiously squeezing the tennis ball.

Perplexed, Betty tried to ignore the oddity, and then the bailiff approached the door and opened it for the jurors to enter. As they did, Betty watched their faces. One by one they walked in as if they had rehearsed, not showing any emotion one way or the other. Then she noticed number six walk in with the first smile she had displayed during the trial.

Da'Ron nudged Hereward, who elbowed Betty to make sure she saw the obvious, but none of them looked at each other or Bear.

Bear continued to gaze at the jurors as if they were on the line of scrimmage in a game and his mission was to conquer them by the sheer will of his spirit.

Again Betty leaned toward Bear as she noticed that the judge would be entering in exactly forty-five seconds.

"Tobias? Are you—"

In a bearlike growl, he said, "I'm not going to jail, Mrs. Staley."

"I know." She smiled. "You've spent your last night in jail. We're going to—"

"Fuck that." And then his smile grew sinister, and his eyebrows pointed downward like an arrow. Bear's thigh shook rapidly, as if he were consumed by fear, and then Betty noticed his free hand under the tail of his coat.

"Bear, what are you talking about?"

"I am not going back to fucking jail!" he said between clenched teeth as he continued to smile.

Betty looked at the clock. Thirty seconds and counting.

Leaning closer to her client as Hereward nudged her, since the judge was behind the door, Betty said in a calm voice, "Tobias, what do you have under your coat?"

"Don't worry about it," he said as the tennis ball dropped from his hand and rolled under his chair. Betty looked at the sheriff again, who noticed the tennis ball then looked away.

"Tobias. Don't do anything crazy. We'll win today, and even if we don't, we still have grounds to appeal. But don't—"

"All rise!" the bailiff exclaimed as the seven-foot defendant tucked whatever was under his coat under his waistband and buttoned his jacket.

As Betty—who remained seated momentarily—rose, out of the corner of her eye she noticed the bulge.

Judge Jackson took her time getting to her chair as Betty looked back for Jacqui, as if just seeing her face would give her direction. Jacqui stood there smiling at her and then gave her a thumbs-up sign.

When the rest of the attendees in the room sat, Betty felt momentarily confused and then saw Evander in the back of the room. She swallowed nothing, returned her attention to the front of the room, and sat down.

As she did, Hereward prodded her again and motioned for her to look at the jury.

Number six was not only smiling; she was now looking at Cassidy, who returned the smile.

"What in the hell . . ." Betty said quietly.

Judge Jackson made a short statement regarding her appreciation, which Betty thought was just her last opportunity to get worldwide face time on television, and then a man stood up and screamed at the top of his lungs, *"Birds fall from grace and others fall from the sky, but when they hit the ground, they both bleed!"*

Ready for anything that might happen, a sheriff immediately grabbed the man by his wrist and, when he resisted, put him in a choke hold and dragged him screaming obscenities from the courtroom.

"They're doing it, anyway," Hereward said.

"Klan?" Betty asked.

"Of course," Da'Ron said as Judge Jackson pounded her gavel to return the court to order.

Betty leaned toward Bear again and whispered, "What in God's name are you planning to do?"

"I'm shooting someone. I don't give a fuck who. It might be that bitch judge. It might be that old bitch grinning at the prosecutors. I don't know, and I don't care."

"Tobias, you don't want to—"

"You don't know what the fuck I want to do." Betty could see his large nostrils flare as he spoke. "Do you think I'm going to jail for some shit I didn't do and let them kill me? Fuck that! Let 'um kill me right here and now like a man, but I'm taking somebody with me!"

"Okay," Judge Jackson said, her voice rising, "let's try this again. Will the defense stand?"

Betty could feel her chest tighten with fear. Her knees shook. Her tongue felt as if it weighed a pound as she, Hereward, Da'Ron, and Bear stood as one.

Another man stood up on the other side of the room and screamed, *"Birds fall from the sky and—"*

Before he could finish the first sentence, a large black sheriff, who was nicknamed Headache, snatched him from his seat. He was lifted as if he were litter and escorted out of the room so quickly his feet did not touch the floor.

"Okay. Anyone else want a ride today?" Judge Jackson shouted, and she pounded the gavel on her desk. "It can be arranged for you. Just speak up! One-way ticket out with an escort. We'll *not* have ANY demonstrations today, and I mean it! When the verdict is read, I want silence, and if we don't have it, I will fill up the van going to the county jail!"

The chatter increased as she yelled, "EVERYBODY, SIT THE HELL DOWN! NOW! Before I clear this courtroom!"

When calm eventually returned to room 300, she said, "Now, that's better. Okay, Mr. Foreman. Have you arrived at a decision?"

"Aha, yes, we have, Your Honor?"

"You can stand, son," she said to the nervous foreman, which made a couple of people laugh in the audience. "Okay, how say you?"

Betty swallowed, she could feel everything around her getting black, and she felt faint.

"On the charge of first-degree murder of Shavonda Patricia Ellis." Bear reached inside his coat. "We the jury"—Betty grabbed his arm— "find the defendant—" Hereward fell to the floor, grasping his chest. "Not guilty."

The room exploded like a nuclear warhead.

Men and women ran full speed toward the door. Bear fell back into his chair from Betty's shove, and with relief and his hand over his weapon. Betty looked over at Hereward, who was covered by Da'Ron. She looked back at Jacqui, who looked at her with a blank expression. And then Betty sat down to attend to Hereward as Da'Ron put the nitroglycerin under his tongue.

"Move out the way! I'm a doctor!" a voice screamed as Betty looked up to see a man stepping over people to get to the front of the room.

In the midst of the hysteria, Betty moved out of the way to give the doctor room.

The jury was ordered to leave immediately by Judge Jackson, who broke the head off her gavel and hammered the handle on her desk.

Then Betty Ann Robinson-Staley leaned against the wall and watched as all hell broke loose in the courtroom.

Betty sat in the processing room with her client as they completed the paperwork for his release. The air was dank and filled with the musky, expensive smell of cologne Bear was prohibited to wear before.

"Come on, Mrs. Staley," Bear whined. "Can't you get them to move a little faster?"

Betty just stared at him.

"What? What I say?" he asked with his palms opened.

"Nothing, Tobias."

Then the officer said, "All right Mr. Parker. Just let me get this one last form signed by Judge Jackson and you're free to leave. Now, Mrs. Staley," he added, "someone from your office mentioned that he would be leaving through the private exit for security reasons. Is that correct?"

Befuddled, Betty looked up at the pale-faced officer, since she had not heard of such arrangements.

"Yo, my agent, Benny, did that. He told me this morning, but you know something?" Bear said, walking toward the window and looking down at the demonstrators amassed below. "The more I think about it, the more I think I want to walk out the front door. I mean, after all, I'm wearing a six-thousand-dollar suit. Why not get some play."

"Sure thing. Oh, yeah, one other thing—"

"No problem, Fats. You've been nice to me, man, since day one. I'll take care of the autographs for you before I leave, yo."

The officer looked at Betty with an I'm sorry expression and then thanked Bear before leaving the room and locking the door behind him.

As soon as the door closed and she heard him walk away, Betty said, "So where did you get it?"

"What? Huh? What are you talking about? Did I miss sumptin'?" he said with a smile, softly tapping his fist in his hand.

Betty sat awaiting more of an answer.

"Yo. Mrs. Staley, on the strength, how's Hereward doing?"

Without looking at him, she replied, "It was erythema. He'll stay in the hospital overnight, but he'll be fine. What the hell were you thinking, Tobias?"

"What was I thinking? What are you talking about? Yo, you bugging."

Betty stood up and said, "You're going to tell me where you got that damn gun from, or I'll—"

"Okay, okay!" he shouted. "I had connects!"

"But why? Why would you do something so stupid?"

"Did you see how confused the jury looked when Da'Ron screwed up? I couldn't take a chance on spending one more night in jail, Mrs. Staley, and that's on the strength. But also because"—then Bear's eyebrows fell—"cause for the first time in my life, I was not in control of anything. Everything, including if I would live or die, was being decided by others, yo. And I couldn't deal with that." Looking toward the door, the deputy exited as Bear spoke as soft as a baby's touch and said, "I didn't kill them, Mrs. Staley. I know you are not sure if you want to believe me or not, but I never pulled the trigger. See this ring?" he said, emptying his jewelry from the manila envelope. "Seeing it again was all that got me through a lot of days." Holding it between himself and Betty, he said, "I loved Shavonda. I tell no lie. It wasn't just a slang bang thang, either. She was my girl, 'cause I could talk to her about anything, and we always had it like that. But Karen? God knows I was in love with her. I loved her more than anything on this earth besides my daughter, and now that I'm free, I got no reason to lie to you or anyone else. Tomorrow this will be a part of your history, yo. But I have to look at my daughter and live this every day the rest of my life."

Then the steel door opened, and the officer who tried to get his keys out while holding three footballs, said, "Mr. Parker, can you sign these here, too?"

After most of the news media had left and quiet returned, Betty sat in the courthouse.

Jacqui, as well as several other friends and associates, had paged her more times than she could remember. Every other page seemed to have a 212 or 310 prefix as the news shows wanted to line her up the next day for her thoughts regarding the case.

Tired of checking the pages, she sat in the outer office of Judge Jackson long after the judge had left her the key. She did not want to return to her office because Da'Ron was giving a press conference there. There were news media outside of the hospital, so she could not visit Hereward or Stefan. A neighbor left a message that several news trucks were parked at her home, so as she watched an episode of *Sanford and Son* on TV, she felt a hostage to all that had happened.

Then she picked up the phone, and as she dialed the digits, she could not block out the faces of Shavonda Ellis and Karen Parker. She could still hear Shavonda's father stand up and scream, "God has seen all that has happened here! Somebody will pay!" Then he was pulled from the courtroom by a member of the sheriff's department.

Betty could not forget the uncomfortable moment when she washed her hands after the verdict in the basin next to Karen's sister, who said she held no animosity for what had happened.

"Hello."

"Yeah, it's me."

"I know," Drew said. "I was hoping you would call."

"Well, it was . . ." And then she smiled. "I guess you can say it was a long day." Betty noticed for the first time that her skirt was ripped at the seam from the struggle with Bear.

"So I heard. I just heard that Hereward is doing fine."

"Yeah, I heard that, too." The first awkward silence crept into the conversation. They had hardly spoken in weeks, and now that they were conversing, neither seemed to know what to say.

As she searched for the words, Betty took the white envelope from her purse with the name "Andrew Patrick Staley" typed above two words: "Divorce Documentation."

"So what else is going on," he asked.

Betty tightened her lips and then said, "Nothing." She dropped the envelope in the trash pail and asked, "How's your mom doing?"

The silence swelled.

"About the same. Actually, worse, I guess. She rarely sleeps at night, so I end up staying up with her, because if I don't, she'll walk around the house in the dark and hurt herself. And sometimes," he continued, "she sits in the bathroom and says she's waiting for the bus, or she'll start yelling for no reason at all that she has to get home or her grand me'mow will spank her."

"Yeah," Betty said softly, "I remember her doing that one night I was there."

"It seems to get worse every day, and she won't even let hospice come in to help, but anyway, I don't want to talk about that right now. I'm living that every day. I just think we need to talk, but I understand you need a little time to unwind after everything you have—"

Betty reached down and retrieved the envelope. With a tear on the lower rim of her eyelid, she said, "I'll be there in about an hour," and before he could say anything else or could hear the tears in her voice, she hung up.

Then she walked over to the judge's couch and pounded the cushion with her fist to loosen its foam stuffing.

"Ieyyy, love to love ya bayyybee."

Betty hummed the tune that was trapped in her heart. Then she curled up in a ball and closed her eyes, for she knew this was one day she would never forget.

Chapter 17

Be not forgetful to entertain strangers:
for thereby some have entertained angels unawares.
                                    —New Testament
                                    Hebrews 13:2

After Betty gave Drew the envelope, he stood without speaking. He had so many thoughts regarding what he wanted to say, but they were short-circuited as he attempted to maintain his equilibrium.

"Are you saying you don't want to try counseling? That you don't want to even talk about this? That you're just ready to end it all right here and now?"

Betty's puffy eyes looked away from his face as if she knew in her heart that it was something that she should not have faced on such a day. But when she looked back at him, he could tell she wanted, needed, closure. "Drew, I need air, because I can't breathe. And I just don't know if I can get it in this relationship. In fact, I'm sure I can't."

Drew backed up two paces as if he had received a body punch, yet defiantly folded his arms across his chest. "So what are you saying? That I was smothering you?"

"I don't want to talk about it."

"You don't want to talk about asking me for a divorce? Betty, do you see what you're doing?"

"I can't stay in this relationship, Drew. I, I just can't." And then a tear fell down her cheek, although her voice remained strong. "I'm not doing this on the spur of the moment. I've known I wanted to do it for a while."

Drew walked toward the wall and then turned. "But why?"

"Drew, can't you see it?"

"No!" he shouted as he walked toward the television. " 'Scuse the fuck out of me, but I can't. I mean, we've had problems, but I thought we had something that we could work toward."

"Drew. We never talk anymore. We don't make love. You want kids, and I don't! Drew, you had a fight with Evander at the courthouse. The place I work. This fool is on Tom Joyner doing interviews now and why? Because you had some juvenile fight with him."

"I told you I was—"

"Don't say I'm sorry! I swear to God, if I hear those two words again—"

"What?"

"Nothing." Betty steeled her composure and said, "Drew, you are not the man I married. You may think it's a small thing, but when we were dating, you wanted to take me to the Bahamas. You would come by the office and just bring me *Boston Market,* and since the day we said I do, I can count on my fingers the times you've had lunch with me.

"We always—" She swallowed, clenched her teeth, and said, "We always said that would not be us. And as soon as we got married, you became that person."

"Anything else?"

"Drew, don't make me—"

"Anything else, Betty! I think you owe me that fucking much."

"Okay, you really want to know?" she said, and put her fist on her waist. "Support. I went through this trial alone. Not one time did you give me moral or any other support."

"I asked you if I could come down and help you with the paperwork, with the media duties, with the finances. What else do you want!" And then Drew, with one swing, knocked a vase off the television that landed against the wall and smashed to pieces. "Damn!" he screamed.

Betty looked at the shards of blue glass and said, "I guess I just wanted you to be my husband. That's all, not my business partner. I just wanted you to be there for me."

Drew approached his wife, and she refused to leave her spot on the floor. "Is that all?" his voice rumbled.

"Drew, that's enough. Besides," she said with him standing inches away from her, "I think this all went too fast. I just came out of a bad relationship, and you did, too, and we were just looking for love. Maybe we needed to spend more time falling in like before falling in love."

"So, you don't love me? Is that what you're saying?"

Shaking her head, Betty said, "Don't you *ever* ask me that again. You've doubted my love since day one, and I am tired of answering the question."

He smiled and looked away as he said, "I guess you answered that one. So you want to end it all. Right here? Right now?"

Mrs. Staley staggered into the den with her hands barely touching the walls, as if she were reading Braille, as Betty and Drew looked toward her.

"Hey, suh," she said, looking at Drew, "I'm looking for my husband. You seen't um?"

Drew's eyes fell to half-mast as he continued looking at Betty. "Momma, I'm Drew. Your son, Andrew?"

"Oh," she said with a smile, which was devoid of her false teeth. "How you doin', boy? When you get here? I thought you were still at Flam'bleu."

"No, Momma, I graduated from FAMU years ago. This is my—our," he said as he closed his eyes momentarily before reopening them. "This is me and Betty's home."

"Betty? Who that?"

Drew looked at his wife and held up his chin.

"Hello, Momma Staley," Betty said pleasantly as the tears continued to stream down her face.

"Oh. This pretty brown-skinned girl name Betty? What happened to Lec—"

"Momma," Drew interrupted, "Felicia died almost two years ago. Remember, we went to the funeral together."

"*Umm.* Well," she said, looking back at Drew, "where your daddy? He 'pose to take me to the hos race tonight."

"Daddy's been dead seven years."

"Aw, boy, hush yo mouf!"

Betty turned around and walked toward the exit of the den. Before she left, Drew said, "One second, Momma. Betty, you never answered my question."

"Drew, the answer is yes." And then the deep pain in her heart manifested itself in every aspect of her face. "Right here. Right now. If you—" She turned away from him. "If you need me, I'll be at Jacqui's, and I'll be moving my stuff out of here next weekend."

"Come back to see us again, and if you see my husband out there, tell 'um I'm ret' ta go?" Mrs. Staley said with a sock-puppet smile.

Betty smiled back at her and said to Drew, "I will always, always, love you." Then she quietly descended the twenty-one carpeted steps of their home.

"How you, old man," Mr. Blue said as he walked up behind Drew and Vulcan-pinched the meaty portion of his shoulder.

"So did you all kiss and make up? I bet you all were celebrating all night."

Drew smiled as he cradled the nondescript mug in his large hands. "No, it was actually a pretty quiet night."

"I would imagine she's on cloud nine. I saw her picture on *People* magazine on the way in this morning. You know she's going to be on the *Today Show* next half-hour, don't you?"

"Yeah, I heard."

"You don't seem excited. The entire town, the nation, I guess, are talking about that case. By the way," Mr. Blue said as he sat down at the table in front of Drew, "my wife asked me to ask you this question. When the verdict was read and Ivory had the heart thing and fell to the floor, did Betty push Bear, or did he black out for a moment? I said he was feeling faint and she was trying to grab him by his arm. My wife thinks she pushed him down. So what happened?"

"Actually, Blue, I never asked her. I guess with everything going down, he was just overcome with it all."

After a soft clap of the hands, he pointed his stubby finger at Drew and said, "Just like I suspected! There was no way she could push that big ole man down like that. So, how are things? Are yawl still not talking?"

"Well, I guess that's an understatement."

"What do you mean?"

As he pulled out the envelope, Drew said, "She's ready for a change. Says she can't breathe."

"Breathe? What do you—" And then he flipped it over and read the writing. "Ohhh."

"Last night was tough. I won't lie. With the situation with mom and then this, it felt like the world was on my shoulders, but then, I don't know. This morning I woke up"—Drew took a deep breath that filled his large chest—"and it didn't feel as bad. I think the not knowing is what hurt more than anything. Now that I know she wants to end it, I'm okay."

Mr. Blue leaned his round body away from Drew as Matt Lauer said with his trademark smile, ". . . and after this commercial, we'll have one of the attorneys in the Parker case. The lead defense attorney, Betty Robinson-Staley, could not make it in, so filling in for her will be Da'Ron Aaron. And with Mr. Aaron will be none other than Tobias 'Bear' Parker, who will be doing his *first* live interview." Neither Drew nor Mr. Blue looked at the television.

"You can't be okay with this, son."

"Honestly, I am. If she had just left and not given me this, I would have been wondering where her head was. Now I know." Mr. Blue stared at Drew without saying a word as Drew gazed at the unopened envelope on the table between them. "I'm sorry," he said, and then looked at the television, squinting his dark brown eyes, "but I refuse to let this woman destroy me. I refuse to let *any* woman destroy me again. I have a business to run, my mom to take care of, and I gotta maintain my sanity."

"You also have one other responsibility. You have a marriage to save." Then Mr. Blue rubbed his fingers down the corner of his mouth as if he were in search of the right words. Speaking deliberately, he said, "Let me tell you a little story, son, and I swear I'll try not to bore you to death.

"When I was in my late twenties—early thirties—I had it all. I had a little home on about three acres. I had this beautiful baby-blue Lincoln Continental. I'll never forget that car. I had a daughter." Then he lamented, "Like I said, I had everything.

"My wife," he continued with a tilt of his bushy gray eyebrows, "is the love of my life now. But she was not my first love.

"My first love was named Irene. Irene Belém." He sang the name and looked away.

"We used to fight like cats and coons, but man, oh, man, the love I got from her made it all worthwhile.

"She was so beautiful, Drew," he said, looking upward. "I could not even call her by her name. I called her Doll because that is what she looked like. A walking, talking, breathing, flesh-bearing doll baby.

"Well, one Saturday morning, I went out for milk, saw another opportunity, and literally never came back home again. I left the Lincoln, my little girl, and my doll baby, looking for something.

"I left love and acceptance looking for what?" And then he paused before answering his own question. "Love and acceptance. And I swore I would never do that again."

After a pause, Drew asked, "What happened to your ex-wife?"

Mr. Blue remained silent, as if the reverberation from the words he had just spoken were louder in his ear than the words Drew had said. Then he looked at Drew and said, "No, I never married Doll. At least not in the traditional sense, but she died a few years ago in that very same Lincoln, and until the day I leave this earth, I'll think that was God's way of punishing me.

"Like I said, I love my wife, but there is not an hour that passes that I don't think of my Doll. And my daughter," he said, and then cleared his voice. "She looks as beautiful as her mother, and I see her once or twice a week.

"But the reason I am saying this is because I learned so much from that relationship. When I look back on what we shared, Drew, it was not perfect, and I think in my heart she was glad I never came back. Why? Because I never complimented her. She would cook breakfast for me every morning, clean out my car, and when we made love, believe it or not, she used to kiss my feet," he said, and blushed.

"Not once," he said, counting off on his fingers, "did I say thank you. Not once did I say I appreciated it or even that I was sorry if I did her wrong. Not once did I call this captivating and engaging woman 'beautiful.'

"I called a month after I left and talked to her. She said I was welcome to come back home, but in my heart I knew she didn't mean it. And that's when it occurred to me that there is one simple truth when it comes to women. You can get anything you want from a woman *if* you give them everything they need. Naturally, I don't mean in a material sense, but telling her she's smart, beautiful, that she is wanted. If you tell her that you love her and can *not* live without . . ." Then his voice faded.

"I also learned that we search so hard for satisfaction. And sometimes our soul knows exactly what it looks like. Our soul seems to have a picture of it. It knows these things as vividly as you remember how that funny gapped-tooth picture you took in the second grade looks. But your eyes can't see it. Why? Because it's in there," he said, pointing toward Drew's chest.

"So when the thing your soul has searched for comes into your world, your eyes may not recognize just how special it is. Your soul will be begging you not to walk away, but you will. And you will walk past it again and again, until you learn.

"Learn from my mistakes, son. When this happens . . . I beg of you . . . listen to your soul."

"I did, Blue," Drew said sadly. "My doll was my heart and soul, or so I thought, and she told me she didn't want to be with me. And I am okay with that."

Da'Ron's face appeared on the television screen next to Bear's. Both men sat shoulder to shoulder in the tight shot and looked as if they had been up all night long partying.

Drew sipped his coffee and said, "I just never knew that leaving me would be so much easier than loving me."

Mr. Blue stood up with a grunt. As he walked toward the television, he looked around to see if anyone was watching. Seeing that no one else was paying attention, he cut off the TV with Da'Ron in mid-sentence.

Then he returned to the table, and without sitting, he said, "Drew, listen carefully to me for a moment? I know things are looking bleak, but hold on to what I am about to say to you.

"There is no such thing as darkness." Then he sat slowly, as if his lower back were in pain, and said, "Darkness is just a concept, not a reality. No matter how dark things may appear, it's never totally dark, and there's always a way out. There is *always* a light which will lead you to the truth. You only have to find it, so don't give up, son, on finding the light in your relationship. Okay? Darkness is a concept . . . not a reality."

Drew held his head down and then closed his eyes. As he closed them, he tried to cleanse himself of the memory of Betty.

With his eyes shut, he could see her face the morning after they made love the first time.

He could see the way she hugged her pillow and would occasionally smile to herself when she was asleep.

He could see her expression after receiving the ring from him.

Drew could feel the way she would walk up behind him and wrap her arms around his shoulders and lay her head on his when he was working at his home computer.

Drew could smell the airy scent of her perfume and feel her breast on his back.

Then Drew opened his eyes to say something to Mr. Blue, and he was gone.

He looked around the cafeteria and saw no signs of his Friday-morning-black-coffee companion. As he stood to leave, he noticed the envelope Betty had given him. Drew picked it up and on the back of it, scrawled in red writing were the words *"It's just a concept."*

Chapter 18

A great marriage is not so much finding the right person
as being the right person.

—Marabel Morgan
The Total Woman

"... and my heavenly Father, I would also like to thank you for so many of the other things, but mostly I would like to thank you for the small miracle you have brought to pass in Stefan's life.

"I thank you for bringing him from the brink of death's door and giving him back to me. He's a very special man, Lord, and I simply ask that you give him direction for the rest of his life.

"While I know it's not for me to say I do, I also know I love him, and I pray for your guidance over his life.

"I also thank you, Lord, for blessing Betty to win the case, and I pray you touch her heart in regards to Drew. If they are to be together, Lord, give her a sign. Let her find her very own burning bush in the midst of nothingness to cling to.

"Well, Lord, I need to go in and see Stefan now, but thank you once again for blessing him, and I pray these things in the name of the Father, Son, and the Holy Spirit. Amen."

Jacqui, who sat in her car with the heater on, looked at the entrance to the hospital, the place that had become her home away from home. Every day she would visit and meet new friends who were in deepest despair. Most of them would eventually leave with smiles; many would not.

Jacqui turned off her ignition and got out of her car, knowing this would be the last day she would make such a trip. Stefan would be discharged at the end of the day and would move in with her until he was able to stay alone.

Walking toward the hospital's entrance, she thought about the day she pushed him in his wheelchair through the hospital's Japanese rock garden. As he looked at the water flowing softly over the smooth stones, he asked her without looking into her eyes if she would ever consider marrying him.

It was on that day when she told him she never wanted to get married to anyone. That she had resolved to spend the rest of her life alone.

As soon as she spoke the words, she could feel his heart tear, and they never spoke to each other the same again.

Jacqui saw her aunt Daisy walk through the exit of the hospital. "Hey, what are you doing out here?" she asked.

"Child," she said to Jacqui, smiling, "I plumb forgot today was Saturday. I was thinking it was my day to sit with him."

"I know. The days do seem to run together after a while. So what's he doing up there."

Aunt Daisy stood in front of Jacqui, her large purse dropping from her shoulder. "He's like a kid at Christmas."

"Really? Well, good."

"Yeah. But I tell you something, I just hope he's not too despondent if he's not able to walk again like he wants to."

"I know," Jacqui replied. "But he's a strong brother, and he's come this far. Maybe the doctors are wrong."

"I know you love him," Aunt Daisy said out of the blue, "but are you in love with him?"

"Why you ask?"

"Just curious," Aunt Daisy said as an elderly white couple walked out of the hospital, crying and carrying a Get Well Soon balloon.

"I remember you said things were shaky before this all happened, but are you doing all of this because you love him, or are you just feeling guilty?"

"I love him," Jacqui said. "I'll admit that I felt guilty at one time, but I understand that we are on a predetermined course in life and—"

"Will you ever consider marrying the boy?"

"No."

"No?"

"No." Jacqui's eyes widened to drive home the point. "I love Stefan, and I always have. But when he was what he considered to be on top, he didn't want me. He was saying he didn't want to marry at one time because of the money issue, but when his big break came, what did he do? He broke. He just up and moved to New York, and I can't forget that. He never told me he was going or anything. One day he was looking at apartments here, and then next thing I find brochures of apartments in New York in his coat pocket.

"Call it petty or whatever," she continued, "but I'm not sure if the shoe was on the other foot that he would be here for me, and if I am not sure of that, then I can't—then I won't say I do. But not saying I do has nothing to do with the level of my love for him."

"*Umm*. You've obviously given this much thought," her aunt replied.

Jacqui simply shook her head yes.

"He really does love you."

"I believe you, and I love him, too."

"Well, all I can say is do what you think is right. Listen," she said, and pulled her purse up higher on her shoulder, "if you need any help next week getting him settled in the house, call me, okay?"

"Thanks."

As her aunt walked away, Jacqui felt bad for having spoken so bluntly to her, but she knew if she could not say the words, she would weaken, and that was not something she wanted to do.

When Jacqui walked into Stefan's room, he was getting dressed as a nurse checked his blood pressure.

"Hey, Ms. Jordan," the nurse said, "so you taking my boyfriend home today?"

"Yesssss," she said with a smile. "I guess to give him baths from now on you'll just have to come to the house and do it."

"I gotz no problem with that," Stefan chimed in with a smile.

After laughing, the nurse said, "Well, I might just have to take you up on that one." Then she pulled the thick Velcro of the blood-pressure cuff, which made a loud ripping sound. "Okay, cutie pie, I am all done with you." She rubbed her hand on his freshly shaved head. "We're gonna miss you. You know that?"

"I'm gonna miss you all, too." Then he looked at Jacqui. "But I need to spend some time with my lady."

"Well, 'scuse the hell out of me," the nurse said with a smile as she picked up her charts and winked at Jacqui. "Well, Ms. Jordan, you better take care of this one, you hear me?"

"I'll do the best I can."

After she left the room, the lovers gazed at each other. As she looked into his eyes, Jacqui wondered what he could be thinking, and then he said, "Damn, I feel good about getting out of this place."

Jacqui walked across the room and kissed him on his lips.

With a look of shock on his face, he said, "Where did that come from?"

"I just miss your lips." And then Jacqui kissed him again with more passion.

As she kissed him and their tongues intertwined, someone passed the open door and said, "You kids wait until you get home for that."

Jacqui slowly brought her hands up to his face as he sat in his wheelchair, and then she got on her knees.

She pressed her lips against his harder and then bit his lip as he sighed with excitement. Then her hands slid down to his chest.

It was not as big as it was before he lost weight, but he was still hard and all man. As she rubbed his chest hair, something nudged her elbow. She immediately opened her eyes and saw Stefan smiling back at her.

"You like?" he asked.

Jacqui looked down at what looked like a pitched tent and then said, "Where the hell did that come from? I thought—"

"I wanted to surprise you. I woke up one morning after a dream, and lo and behold, Stefan Jr. was wide awake."

Jacqui leaned down and kissed him on the spot, and then she smiled at him. "You know you are incredible, don't you?"

"You think so?"

"I know so. I mean, you were not supposed to be here, and you are. I was told you would never be able to use your hands or get this, and look at you," she said. "You sitting here with pure wood in your pants."

After laughing, he said, "Baby I'm not incredible."

"Yes, you are."

"I wish I could take the credit, but I can't. We all need something to hold on to. And you were that something for me. If it were not for you, I would have died on the operating table, but I could never do that to you."

"Meaning?"

"Baby, I know you better than you know you. You'll never admit that because you don't want to feel vulnerable, but I know you beat yourself up with this accident. It's all over your face. And I know the reason you will not marry me. It's because you don't know if it's because you love or feel sorry for me."

"That's not it," she said. As she laid her head on his lap, she could feel his excitement on her face.

"Then what is it?" He ran his still partially curled fingers over her face as she closed her eyes. "Is it because I wouldn't marry you when you wanted to get married?"

"Yes," she replied softly. "I know it's small of me, but that's how I feel."

"And I understand. Actually, I can't say if I were in your position that I would not feel the same. But all I can say is, we all mature at a different time and in a different way.

"After I lost weight, my body became my whole world. I would go into restaurants and have strange women pay for my meal. I would . . . Well, anyway.

"But when I lost my body, honestly, it made me a man, if that makes any sense."

Jacqui held her head up and looked into his eyes. "Stefan, you were always a man. I knew you had some child left in you, but I wanted to marry you because I saw that you could become more than what you were. I always knew the man you are today was in there somewhere."

Stefan closed his eyes as he slowly put his hand on the back of Jacqui's head. As she lay there filled with emotion, he said, "Thank you for seeing that. I never thought anyone would or could know me as well as you can." Then, as she closed her eyes, he whispered, "Jacqui, would you do me just one favor?"

"Anything," and then she ran her hand up and down his withered thigh.

"Would you take this off my finger, please?" She opened her eyes and saw a heart-shaped diamond.

"I'm not asking you to marry me today, so don't get scared."

With her mouth open, she said, "But honey . . . what . . . who . . . how did you buy this?"

Stefan smiled and said, "Can I see how it looks on you first?"

Jacqui slid the ring off his finger and put it on hers.

"Whenever I was in therapy with that sadistic bitch downstairs"—he laughed—"I thought about this moment. I thought about this look on your face. I thought about how I would give it to you."

"But Stefan? Who went out and bought this for you? Aunt Shoes?"

Looking away from her, he said, "Well, she knew I had it, but believe it or not, Jacqui"—and then he put his curled fingers on her face again—"the week before I saw you, I bought it while I was in New York.

"I could have flown from New York to Miami without a Gainesville layover, but I wanted to propose to you."

Stefan closed his eyes and said, "Then we made love that night, and I was going to make you breakfast in bed and give it to you. But you told me I had to leave, which pissed me off. So I kept it in my coat pocket."

"Oh, my God," Jacqui said as her eyes started to tear.

"So when you are ready, just let me know and I'll get down on my knees, my belly, or whatever," he said with his male-model smile, "and ask you to be—"

"I do, I will, I want—I love you, Stefan, and yes, I will marry you!"

"Are you serious, baby?"

"I love you so much." And then she put her arms around his shoulders and kissed him again.

"*Awww*" came the collective sigh of two nurses passing in the hallway. "Ain't that sweet!"

"I love you, too, baby," he said as her warm tears fell on the tip of his nose. "I love you, Jacquetta . . . Marie . . . Jordan . . . DeCoursey."

Winter

Chapter 19

Now that we have shown our power,
Let us seem humbler after it is done.
—William Shakespeare
—*Coriolanus, act 4, scene 6, 1.103*

DECEMBER

In college towns, certain things were everlasting. The sun would roll over the trees planted by the city that lined University Avenue and cast unique and interesting shapes on the streets. When the football team would lose, the entire town would seem to be depressed as if they had collectively asked the prettiest girl for a dance and she had rejected them one by one. And there would be small clusters of white kids wearing black clothing and accessories, with piercings in places many people did not have spaces.

But other than that, everything else seemed to have changed for Betty in the small college town.

The once-warm fall had become a full-fledged winter by Florida standards. Children, unused to such a climate, waited for their school bus and pretended to smoke cigarettes as they blew between their pinched fingers into the frigid air and watched their breath float upward.

Women wore mink shawls to work and boasted, "I've had this thing fifteen years. I never get to wear it since we moved down south."

Outside her office window, Betty could see bald spots in the grass from the news trucks that were camped around her office for the trial. There was a large hole left unfilled that at one time contained a satellite dish. The laborers who were supposed to fill it had to leave town abruptly to cover a drug raid in Deerfield Beach and never returned.

She could see violent orange neon spray paint, which remained on the grass, and concrete sidewalks with the initials NBC, CBS, ABC, and most of the other major news organizations.

On her desk, Betty had initially circled December 7 in red as the last day she would be in the office. Under the date she wrote and underlined the word *Emancipation*.

Then it was crossed off and under it the word *Freedom* was written. In blue ink that word was crossed off for the words *"I'm out!"* Then that phrase was simply replaced by the words *"What's next?"*

Since the reading of the not-guilty verdict, she watched a rally on CNN at which Rev. Robinson prayed and asked God to touch her heart. The minister, who mentioned her by name, added that there was power in innocent blood and that the women were not slain in vain.

Two separate foundations were established in the victims' names. Betty asked her paralegal to drop off an anonymous contribution to the funds that raised money for women's organizations. The amount of her donation equaled one-third of the funds she had received from the Parker family.

Since the not-guilty verdict, Betty was invited by Bear's agent, Benny, to an all-expense-paid trip to the Bahamas. The intent of the trip, he said, was to thank the jurors for their time. He also added that along for the trip would be noted individuals from the world of sports and entertainment. Betty declined the offer without giving him a reason.

Since the verdict, Betty had told Carol that she was closing the firm and wrote her a check that would allow her to retire from work. While Carol asked her to take a few months to decide if it was what she really wanted to do, Betty knew the once-hot fire would never return.

Lastly, since the day of the verdict, she had not spoken to her husband. Her engagement ring, which she had not removed since the night he proposed, was in her jewelry box with her Bar Association pin, her Run Jesse Run, button, and her high school graduation ring. She often found herself feeling the base of the finger with her thumb, and although she had only worn it for a short period of time, the loss of it ran deep.

* * *

In her office, Tickey tiptoed toward her milk as Betty listened to jazz musician David Sanborn. There was no reason to be at her desk before eight in the morning, but each morning she was there.

Going into the office took her mind away from her personal life. When she walked through the doors, she felt in control. But she knew that would soon be coming to an end, and after redecorating her home and catching up on her reading, she had no idea what she would do with the rest of her life.

"Well, Mrs. Staley," Peter, who had previously helped Betty in the remodeling of her office, said, "I think we got all the big stuff packed up, including all them books of yours. All I need to do is get the truck here Friday morning," he said, clapping his large hands, "and we'll have all of your stuff out by the end of the day."

Betty gave him a tight-lipped smile and continued to read the news-paper.

As he wiped his hands off on an old T-shirt, he sat in the chair in front of Betty's desk. "Are you serious about Jacqui?"

Betty removed her glasses and gave him an open-mouth smile. "Yeah, she's getting married on the island of Nevis on the last day of the year."

"Man, o', man," he said, and rubbed his hand over his muscular forearm. "She's doing it up right, huh. I guess she's excited."

"Yeah, a little. So much to do in so little time. That's one of the reasons I wanted to close this place down, 'cause I want to help her arrange it."

"Well, that's nice of you. She's your older sister, right? I didn't want to ask while she was here that day."

"Jacqui?" Betty said with a smile. Before she could say no, the word "Yes" flowed from her lips.

"It's nice you all so close. Reminds me of me and my sister."

"Yeah, we're pretty tight," Betty replied, and relaxed her body in her well-worn chair. "I can count the times we've had arguments on one hand, believe it or not. We've just always clicked."

"I was really digging her that day she was here. Could you tell?"

"Yeah, Peter, *we* noticed."

"Was it that obvious?"

"Well, showing your nipples kinda gave it away. So, you don't have a girlfriend? Or were you just going to try and add *my sister* to your stable?"

"Actually," he said as his eyes glistened, "I've had a few, but I've been celibate for a few years now. February will make the fifth year. And I know you don't believe me," he said as Betty tilted her head downward. "I'm no saint. Don't get me wrong. I've had well over two hundred different women, but the older I get, the more I know that's not the life for me. So now I'm waiting until . . ." And then he paused in thought.

"Until?" Betty said as the word with which Drew would end his love letters flowed in her memory.

"Yeah. Until I meet Miss Right. I guess it's because I was in love once before and things didn't work out."

"Sorry to hear that. It happens."

"Yeah. A psychiatrist I met on the Internet."

"You met her on the 'net?" Betty asked, remembering that was how she originally met the man with the screen name "DLastRomeo," who she later found out was Drew.

"Yeah, in one of them chat-room thingamajigs. You heard about them, right?"

Betty shook her head vaguely.

"My cousin," he said, motioning his hands from side to side, "who handles payroll for our company, is deep into that stuff and showed me how one night. I don't usually tell people that because they think you're a pervert or something, but I enjoyed it because sometimes when women see me they want me, but after we talk, I know they only want to get, well, you know. Sex'd.

"So, anyway," he continued with Betty's full attention, "I met her down in Orlando at Universal Studios, and to be honest, she completely turned me off.

"Her smile—I can never forget her smile. When Maisie smiled, Mrs. Staley, it showed more gum than teeth. She had this weave in her head, and I was afraid to touch it because I didn't want it to come out. But that's not the worst thing. I mean, I'm an ass man, and she had none. And when I say none, I mean ironing board stand next to the wall and block out the sunlight and the moon—none a'tall.

"So, after the date was over, I didn't even want to kiss her good-bye, she was so jacked-up looking. The first time we had sex, I wanted to do it on the floor because I didn't want her in my bed. And then—"

"Wait a minute. Back up. She was, as you said, jacked up," Betty asked. "But you still had sex with the girl?"

"Yeah. I mean, I wanted to like her, so I thought if we did that— Well anyway, to make a long story short, we kept talking, and I fell head over heels in love with her mind."

Looking at Betty's calendar and then back into her eyes, he said, "I've never in my life met someone so perfect for me in so many ways. The things I didn't care for about her just seemed to fade."

His voice weakened, and Betty could feel Peter's sincerity as he continued. "We met in May, and by November we were talking marriage!"

"Are you serious?"

"My hand before God with my heart wide open," he said, closing his eyes and making a slow X over his chest. "At that time I was working in the plumbing business with my dad, and I was doing okay. So dig," he said as he subconsciously grabbed his crotch and crossed his legs. "I bought the ring, and the wedding dress was all paid for. She had planned to sell her practice and move here to Gainesville with me, and we even bought a house."

"Geez, you guys moved a little fast, don't you think."

"Yeah, I know. But honestly, she was my very first love." His eyes glazed over as he said, "When me and her made love, it was almost spiritual. Know what I mean?"

Betty shook her head in agreement.

"I went from being totally repulsed by the woman to almost melting whenever she touched me. I tell you no lie. As a matter of fact, before her, honest to God, I didn't believe there was a God."

"Man." Betty laughed. "You mean to tell me you fell so deep in love, you became a believer?"

"Something like that, and my grandfather is a pastor! It was like for the first time in my life I could feel God when I made love to this woman, and I knew I could never live without her in my world." Then Peter sat silently looking at Betty but appearing not to see her at all.

"So," Betty asked with hesitation, "may I ask what happened?"

He broke his gaze, and his fingertips slid under his sad eyes. "I can't believe it's been five years. Five long years." Then he arched his back in the chair and said with a stronger voice, "She left me in February. About four months before the wedding."

"No!"

"Yeah."

"Are you serious?"

"On my birthday!"

Deep-grooved wrinkles appeared in his forehead as he said, "The night before my birthday Mrs. Staley, we made love and..." He closed his eyes and swallowed. "I can still feel her body beneath me, it was so good. It seemed every movement she made, I made, was perfect. Then, the next morning, we had an argument about a shirt I left on the floor, of all things. I got pissed off and called her a bitch, and she left and never returned."

"Get out!"

"Yup. I found out later that she was fucking, excuse my French, this teacher for about three months before she left. Go figure.

"But that doesn't change the way I felt or feel about her. She drove this green Camry, and to this day, I know she has traded it, but don't you know my head turns whenever I see one.

"If her cheating on me changed everything, I guess I would have to question my love for her. Don't you think?"

Ignoring the question, Betty said, "Geez, I'm sorry to hear you all didn't make it."

"Well, most of the pain is gone now. But yeah, I still think about her every day, and I know I will until the day I die."

Looking around her office at the bare walls, he said, "I remember when I came here the first time and saw your husband's pictures up, and I was digging that. You had one in that corner"—he pointed as both of them looked at the blank space—"and you all looked so happy in it. Both of you were barefoot, and he was carrying your shoes, on the beach or something." Then Peter shook his head as Betty restrained her emotions.

"There's a line in *Mo' Betta Blues*, where Wesley says, *'Ain't nothing mo' beautiful than black folks in love,'* and I really believe that," Peter said.

"So, to answer your question, that's why I'm celibate. I mean, after you've driven a Lex, you don't want to ride the city bus. You just sorta wait." And then he smiled. "You wait until you find another Lexus."

"Very well put."

"But I won't make her out to be the villain or nufin'. I was working eighty to one hundred hours a week, and I really didn't give her the love she deserved. I guess I deserve what I got, but it taught me an important lesson."

"And that would be?"

"To never take love for granted. That if you're *blessed* to find some-one who you love, who just happens to love you just as much, to value that love and treat it with caution, because there are no guarantees you will ever have it again.

"Sometimes it could feel like an old blanket, my dad likes to say. She might irritate you and feel itchy and even get on your nerves sometimes, but when she's gone, man, is it cold."

Betty looked out the window at an icicle on a tree branch and said, "Yeah. It can get cold."

In her car driving down the avenue toward *Francesca's Party, Wedding Planning and More,* Betty pulled out her cellular to call Jacqui. As she held the phone to her ear, she drove past Drew's office and saw him through the window at his desk, talking on the phone.

"Jacquetta's, where Tuesdays you can get—"

"Jacqui, Jacqui!" Betty cut in. "What are you doing answering the phone?"

"Girl, I had this skinny-legged heifer working here last week, and then this morning she calls in and—"

"Can I call you right back?" Betty said as she did a U-turn in the road.

"Yeah. What's up?"

"I just saw someone I used to know and thought I'd say hello."

"Okay. Hey, before you hang up, did you call the hotel?"

"Yup, they had a cancellation, after all, so I booked a suite and a room for me at the Old Manor Estate Hotel, and I have Drew in the Racquetball Club."

"You didn't get him a crappy hotel, did you?"

"No, I wouldn't do that. Besides, Stefan's going to stay with him the night before, so that wouldn't be right, now, would it? And the rooms are wheelchair accessible. I asked," she said as she parked in Drew's parking lot.

"*Umm.* Well, call me back when you get a chance? I want to make sure we're not forgetting anything."

"Listen at you sounding all nervous."

"I am, aren't I? Can you believe me? Damn near forty and getting nervous about something like this?"

"Yeah, trust me, I can."

"Okay, 'bye," Jacqui said as the other line started to ring. "Talk at you later."

Betty sat in the parking lot of Drew's office for over fifteen minutes.

While she wanted to walk in and say hello, she didn't know what type of reception to expect. Then she thought she would call him but decided not to, since she could see he was busy working the phones. So she sat in her SUV and watched him and wondered how things went so wrong so fast for them.

Then she saw him stand from his desk with the phone still to his ear, and as he spoke, he put on his coat.

He must have an interview, she thought to herself. Then he said something to his office administrator, put on his black overcoat, and jogged out the door toward his car.

As he ran, she wanted to flash her lights, but she remembered how upset he was the night she said good-bye and decided not to.

Then he looked her way as if he could feel her gaze and blew warm air into his fist. The first thing she noticed was his smile. Then Drew jogged toward her truck.

He came up to the driver's side window and tapped on it with his knuckle. Betty did not want to roll it down initially because she wanted him to get into the truck, but then she allowed it to slide down halfway.

"It's nice to see you here. I wasn't expecting this at all."

"Nice to see you, too," Betty replied. "I was just headed over to the wedding planner's office and thought I would drop by."

Drew just stared at her face as if he were looking at her for the very first time.

"What?" she said with a smile. "Come on, boy, get in?" Then she cleared the seat next to her. "It's cold out there!"

"That's okay. I kinda like the cold." Then he said, "You look amazing. You know that?"

"Thank you," she said quietly. "You're looking okay yourself, Andrew Patrick."

"Thanks. Listen," he said, jogging in place for warmth, "is that roof still leaking in your house?"

"Roof leaking?"

"Yeah, remember Edwina Dix asked you about getting it fixed before you could sell it? I have a friend who owes me a huge favor, and he said he'd fix it. You just need to pay for the materials."

"Oh . . . Well, thank you."

"No problem. And he's a nice guy, so he won't try to jack up the price of the materials or anything."

"Good," Betty replied.

"Well?" he said as if he were ready to end the conversation.

"Well," Betty replied. "So, *umm,* how's business?"

"Slow," he said, blowing into his fist again. "But that's only because it's December and no one wants to save any money until after the first of the year. But other than that, everything is fine. Are things back to normal at the—But wait. Stefan told me you were selling the firm. Is that true?"

"Not a lot of assets to sell, so I'm just closing the doors."

"Will you miss it?"

"No. I'll miss practicing law, but all of the other stuff you put up with will not make it worth the while. The last few days of that case got crazy, so I just need some time to get away from it, I guess."

"I would imagine. I didn't want to tell you, but someone left a package against our door one night, and we thought it was a bomb. They had the bomb squad out here and everything."

"I heard about it through one of the police officers. It got so crazy, Hereward used to leave his gun in the office so I wouldn't be without protection. He started carrying one with him everywhere he went."

"That's sad. Have you ever picked up a gun?"

"Yeah, I took a course in college, but I never owned one."

"Well, I'm glad it's over."

"So how's Momma—Mrs. Staley—doing?"

"Worse," he said without changing expression. "She's really slipping fast."

"Sorry, Drew," she said as he rubbed his hands together. "Would you please come and get in the car?"

Drew looked toward his office and then ran around to the passenger side. As he closed the door, he said, "It seems every day you look at her and cannot imagine it getting worse, but then it does."

"I have a little unexpected free time," Betty said, and aimed the heat vents toward him. "I could come by and—"

"That's all right," Drew said stiffly as he looked into her eyes. "I have a couple of nurses, and at night I can handle it by myself."

"Oh."

"No offense."

"None taken."

"She decided that she would like to be buried in Baton Rouge, so I've contacted the funeral home there, and when the time comes, I'll fly her back home." Then he reached into his inside coat pocket and pulled out the dirty envelope with the divorce papers inside it.

Betty looked straight ahead as he laid it on the seat between them.

"I've read this thing, I don't know how many times," he said, staring at a lady who got out of a VW Beatle and meticulously wrapped her baby up. "I don't know if I want to sign it." Then he looked at Betty and said, "But I can't swear that I don't, either." Betty shook her head in agreement.

"I mean, this has been one hell of a year. And I guess I hear all the things that you said about us getting married too fast and had we not done that then maybe we would have more of a foundation when the times got tough." Betty gripped her leather-wrapped steering wheel as she thought of the words he was saying. "I like to think that losing my mother and . . . and well losing you has changed me a little." Drew looked at Betty and said, "I've not had a drink in over two months, and I'm going to the gym an hour a day every day now."

"Congrats."

"Thank you. I can't even say it's been hard. Losing my mom and losing . . . Well, that was hard. The other stuff is cake."

"Drew, it wasn't easy for me, either. I haven't—I haven't had a decent night sleep in months."

Drew sat quietly.

Then Betty reached into her purse and said, "That's why I got this, and I thought it might be something we could consider." Then she handed Drew a marriage counselor's business card.

"I don't know if I want to be married, either, but I guess this is a start."

Drew stared at the card as if it were a contract, and then he rubbed his thumb over the textured paper. Handing it back to his wife, he said, "I don't know if that would be a good idea at this point."

"What do you mean?"

"If you don't know if you want to be married and I don't know if I want to be married, why go to a counselor? Shouldn't you use them if you want to be married but you don't know how to make it work?"

Betty took the card and put it back in her purse. "I guess you're right," she whispered. "I just thought—"

"Listen," Drew said, looking down at his watch, "I have an eleven o'clock I need to prepare for. I'll call and leave the roofing guy's number on your voice mail, okay?"

"Thanks." There was a beat of silence, and then she looked at the people trying to shelter themselves from the cold as they ran across the intersection and said, "Listen. Regardless of what happens to us, Drew, from the first time I saw you in Jacquetta's, I knew I loved you, and I knew I wanted to spend the rest of my life with you." Then Betty peered over her steering wheel as she continued.

"I don't know what happened between that day and this one. I don't know what will happen to me—us—tomorrow. I don't even know what I want to happen," she whispered, "but I do know I loved you before I even knew you." Then she looked into his eyes and momentarily held her breath.

Drew replied quietly, "You know in your heart I've always loved you as well. But sometimes I think back to what happened and how you said I was not there for you." Drew looked at his office as his secretary walked out, apparently looking for him, then went back inside, rubbing her triceps. "I wish I knew what to say or do for you when you were in the eye of the storm, but when I think back, Betty, I went through a lot this year with my mother as well. I know it will never be written about in *USA Today*, or what have you, but it was important to me. And yes, I would have liked for you to have been there as my wife."

Betty sat quietly thinking what he had said. Then Drew leaned toward her, and for a split second she thought she could feel his lips graze her cheek. She could imagine him kissing her as he would each time they parted in the past and saying, "I love you," in her hair. But this time he leaned toward her only to get his feet out of the truck.

As he prepared to get out, his hand covered hers, and both of them looked down at the same time. He seemed to notice that she was no longer wearing his band; she noticed that he still wore hers.

And then he smiled, retrieved the envelope, shook his head, said good-bye, and ran toward the building.

Betty lay on the couch in her office, waiting for Jacqui to bring her dinner. As she watched television, there was a knock on the outer door.

"Who? Jacqui? It's open," she said, and then sat up from the couch and returned to her desk as she continued to watch Martin Lawrence pretending to be SheNayNay.

"I thought you would never get here. I haven't eaten a mouthful since yester—" Betty's shoulders drooped, and she sat speechless as Evander walked into her office.

"Since yesterday? That's a long time. But sorry," he said, wearing the sweater and slacks she had bought him for his birthday two years earlier. "Were you expecting someone else?"

She refused to answer.

Then he closed the door to her office and settled into a love seat against the wall. "Dag," he said, looking at the portable TV. "I haven't seen Marty-Mar in years."

With the remote Betty turned off the television.

"Man. Well, Beeper, listen. I just wanted to come by and say hello. That's all. I don't expect anything of you at all."

Squinting her eyes, she asked, "Why . . . are you here?"

"Like I just said, I wanted to see you and to say hello. I mean . . ." he said, and then bit his bottom lip. "So much has happened in the past year and a half, and I don't think I was ever given a chance to fully explain how I felt and what happened the night you were at my house."

"Honestly, Evander, there's no need to explain."

"Of course there is," he said with a smile. "I've had a little time to reflect on this, and the more I think about it, the more I can understand how you must have felt that night. But honestly, Beeper, what you *thought* you heard was really taken out of context.

"I was talking to my boy in Orlando, and we always kick it like that. Like we the man and stuff when in our hearts we both know we're full of it.

"He was going to get married years ago, and a month before he was supposed to say I do, he was saying this and that about his lady. I know it's hard to accept, but it was just a stupid man thing. A game. Nothing I said I really meant from the—"

"Was applying for that Visa card in my name a part of the *game*, too?" Betty asked as she heard the chirp of an activated car alarm outside her office.

"No!" And then Evander gathered his composure. "I mean, no, that was a mistake. A big, fat, messed-up mistake, and like I even told him that night, I had every intention of paying you back when all was said and done. I got busted, and I went to jail, and I have a record as a result of it, but—"

"You also have a restraining order as a result of it as well."

"Beep, listen to me. If I didn't care for you, would I have sent you flowers once a week during the trial? Would I have been in court almost every day as well to show support? If I didn't care for you, I could have fucked up your boy right there in the courthouse, but I didn't. Because—"

"Hey, girl, why you leaving the door open in this place," Jacqui said as she brought in two large white bags marked To Go. "I just—" And then she looked at Evander. "What in the hell is he doing here?"

Betty remained silent.

"Hello, Ms. Jacquetta. Long time no see."

"What the hell's going on, Betty?"

Betty refused to answer as she continued to stare at Evander.

"Me and your friend are just talking. Just kicking it," he said, staring back at Betty. "I was just about to tell her how I was going to mess up her *husband* that day if you and the police had not stepped in, and the reason I didn't was because I didn't want to make a scene. Unfortunately, we made one, anyway, as fate would have it. I couldn't believe he would go off like that knowing what position it would put you in, Beep."

"Well, *umm,*" Jacqui said, "if memory serves me, you cried like a li'l—"

"I was not crying! Actually, I don't know why I'm even talking to you in the first place!"

Both of them looked at Betty, who calmly said, "Jacqui, don't worry about it. What were you saying before she came in, Evander?"

Jacqui's eyes bulged.

Evander's smile returned as he crossed his legs, grabbed his ankle, and leaned comfortably in the chair.

"As I was *going* to say, Beep, I know you're closing this place down. I know that you and Drew have broken up. Seems since the day I almost kicked his ass," he said, and rolled his eyes at Jacqui, "everything that happens to you—"

"Betty!" Jacqui shouted. "What the hell is your malfunction! Get this nigga out of your office!"

"Jacqui, don't do that! I want to hear what he has to say."

Evander looked at Betty with mouth-open amazement and then said, "Thank you. Where was I? Oh, yeah, everything that happens seems to get back to me, and I just wanted to say that—"

"Forget this, girl," Jacqui said, shaking her head with frustration and placing the two white bags on the couch. "I don't know where the hell you get off doing this, but if you want me, you know where I'll be."

As Jacqui left and slammed the door behind her, Evander said, "Damn. Some people. But anywho," he continued in a softer tone, "after all this time, I can't get you out of my mind. Every day I realize how much I screwed up, and I admit it because I should not have been playing that childish game with my boy. But all I am asking for is one more chance."

Betty smiled at him and shook her head. Then she said, "You know something, Evander? Since the day I left you, I've had questions in my mind."

"Like what?" he asked sweetly.

"I wondered how I could be so wrong about someone. How much I thought you were one person and you turned out to be another. Since the day I left you, I've been unable to love because," she said, still smiling, "I was afraid of getting hurt. Since the day I left you, I wanted to fall in love. I wanted to fall in love with Drew so bad, but I couldn't. I couldn't give him one hundred percent of myself."

Evander's eyes narrowed, and his smile widened.

"I couldn't do it because of you. Because of what you did to me. And it was not until today," she said, still smiling, "until this very moment that I realized just how much I love him and how much I hate you for what you did to me."

Evander swallowed his smile and said, "Listen, Beeper, if—"

"I swear to God almighty, Evander, if you *ever* call me that name again"—she snatched open her desk drawer—"I'll . . . I'll—"

"What you got?" he said, smiling. "You got a gun in there?"

Then Betty swung the chrome revolver Hereward had left and aimed it at his face.

"Oh, shit! Beep—" he said as she pulled back the hammer. "Okay, okay, Betty, Betty. What's wrong with you, girl? How you gonna point a gun at me? After all we shared. Betty?"

Jacqui ran back in with her mouth open. "Betty," she said sedately, "what the hell are you doing? Just make this punk leave. Okay?"

"No, Jacqui," she said with both hands on the grip of the pistol, "it's bigger than that now.

"This is the man who took my womanhood. This is the man who took me financially for more money than I even told you about. This is also the man who broke up my marriage. This is beyond just letting him walk out of here now."

"Come on, Beep—Betty. Now, stop playing around, girl," Evander pleaded. "If you gonna go off like this, I'll just—"

"BANG! BANG!"

Betty fired two shots into the wall above Evander's head, which caused dust and debris from the Sheetrock to explode and cover his clothing.

"Look up. Does that look like I'm playing to you? Huh?"

Evander stopped breathing. Both of his hands went into the air as if he were looking for the Holy Ghost.

"Okay. Okay Beep—Betty—I'll leave! I'll never come back again!"

"Are you serious? You think I'll let you just walk out of here? Don't you know I could kill you right here—"

"Betty!" Jacqui said, trying to get her friend's attention.

"I could kill you now and walk away with manslaughter tops and no jail time? You think I won't? I have a restraining order against you. You had a fight with my husband," she said, still smiling as tears leaked from her eyes and flowed to the bottom of her jaw. "You came here tonight and threatened violence, and I have a—"

"Betty, please, put down the—"

"Shut up, Jacqui!" Betty yelled. "And I have a witness who saw the whole thing. Don't you know I could kill you right now and walk away scot-free?"

Evander eased off the couch onto his knees and said, "Please, God, Betty. I'm sorry for everything I did to you. I'll never come back. Honest to goodness. If you let me leave, I'll never bother you or Drew again. I swear to God and three or four mo' white folks!"

With the smile still remaining on her face, Betty laid down the gun slowly and said softly, shaking her head, "I swear, Evander, if you come near me again, I will plant your ass so deep in the ground—"

"I won't! I swear, Beep—I mean, Betty! Betty, I won't!"

"You got three seconds to leave. One—"

Evander was out the door before Betty's lips could form the word two, and Jacqui collapsed on the sofa.

* * *

As darkness fell in the small college town and the heat of the excitement diminished, Betty and Jacqui sat in the office amid the boxes in silence, neither knowing what to say.

There was no background noise from the television or radio. They just sat, and occasionally their eyes would follow Tickey as she walked stealthily across the floor, or they would look up at the holes left in the wall.

"Betty," Jacqui eventually said, "I know how much you—"

"Not now," Betty whispered. "You my girl, but not now. Okay?"

"Okay."

And then Betty stood up; she walked around her desk and out of the former home of Betty Staley and Associates.

When she got outside, wearing only a thin blouse in the blistery cold weather, Betty leaned against the wall. Prickly bumps immediately rose on her arms as the wind cut through her flesh. She never noticed that someone had spray-painted in bold red letters K.K.Koon as she thought about Drew. Then she hugged her body tightly, tucked her chin to her chest, and cried like a baby.

Chapter 20

As long as we don't forgive,
who and whatever it is
will occupy rent-free space in your mind.
                                        —Isabelle Holland
                                        The Long Search

"So as you can see, this plan will give you the tax benefits you need for the business, with an element of liquidity for emergencies as well," Drew said to the woman sitting across from him in his office. Her facial features were delicate, and she sat as if she were taught how to sit "like a lady" in finishing school.

"I think I follow where you are coming from," she said. "I will present this to Dad and see what he thinks, but from what I see, I think it's simply a matter of dotting the I's and crossing the T's."

"Well, great," Drew replied. But instead of standing as an indication that the meeting had come to an end, he continued to sit and look at the lady who was the daughter of "Joe Neal. Rib King of Florida."

Her name was Virginia, and she appeared in all of the statewide ads for the chain. She was known from Pensacola to Key West for her trademark delivery of the line "Now that's gooooood eating, at a price I can afford!"

When Drew met her, she was nothing like what he expected. Virginia was Spelman educated, an honors student, well-read, and unlike Betty, she seemed to notice the small things about him, such as what cologne he was wearing or how well his tie matched his suit.

"Well," he stammered. "Ah, when can we pencil you in for another appointment to close the deal?"

"I don't know?" Then she looked at his lips, and her eyes slid up to his. "But I will present it and see what happens. My question to you is Can we have lunch sometime?"

"Excuse me?"

"Well, *Mr.* Staley, I noticed that you stopped wearing the ring, and last time I came here, if memory serves me correctly, your wedding picture was up. Now I see it conspicuously missing. So?"

"So?"

"So," she repeated, "can a sister at least get a drink from you before everyone else jumps on the bandwagon? I know you got them lined up around the block."

Drew smiled and said softly, "Well, first of all, thank you for the offer. But honestly, I think it might be a little early for that."

"Was it because of the pressure from the trial? I know that couldn't help the marriage at all."

"You can say that, but I can't say that's the only reason."

Methodically, she crossed her legs and pulled down her mid-thigh skirt. "Is it a separation or a full-blown you know what?" Drew simply gave her a smile as she said, "No, I am not subtle about anything I want, *Mr.* Staley. I know you're a few years older, but that just makes things a little more exciting. What do you think?"

"Well, I think—"

"Excuse me, Mr. Staley," the voice on the intercom said. "I know you are in an interview, sir, but there is a Mr. Blue on line six who says he needs to talk to you and could not call back. Should I try to—"

"No. I'll take it, Grace. One second please. Okay?"

Then Drew stood up, looked at Miss Neale, and said, "I really need to take this call."

"Okay," she said, still sitting.

He smiled. "So?"

"So?" she countered with a smile as she remained seated.

"Okay. Can I call you tonight and we can take it from there?"

"That's all I wanted to know, *Andrew.*" Then she smiled brightly, stood, and said, "I'll talk to you tonight, okay? Don't stand me up."

Drew returned her smile as she walked out of the office.

"Hello."

"Well, I'll be, sonny, how are you—"

"How are you doing!" Drew said excitedly.

"Fine and you?"

"Can't complain. You know I still go to Parkside every Friday morning looking for you. Including this morning, I might add."

"Sorry, son. I needed to get away for a while to collect my thoughts."

"Everything all right, I trust."

"My wife died."

Drew's head dropped. "I'm . . . I'm sorry to hear that."

"Don't be. She's in a better place, and I know that with all my heart. She's been dying for a while, but I just never liked to talk about it. The more I spoke of it, the more power it had over me, so I would always just put it in the back of my mind until I had to deal with it. And that was what I've been doing the last month or so."

"Is there anything I can do for you?"

"Yeah, actually there is."

"Anything?"

"Tell me something? Are you and Betty back together?"

Drew paused as he received the unexpected question. "Mr. Blue, my goodness, your wife died, and you're worried about that? Please, I want to be there for you. I mean, you've been there for me since day one."

"Sonny, you will never get it, will you?" he said in a voice weaker than Drew had noticed before. "My helping you is my way of giving back. I help you, I help myself."

Drew listened closely to his words.

"I don't know what or how I can get through to you. I met you last spring, and I've wanted to help you through this phase, but every step you take forward, you take three backward because you don't listen."

Drew watched Virginia Neale walk across the parking lot and knowingly wave back at him.

"Don't ever . . ." Then Mr. Blue paused mid-sentence as if he were trying to hold back his emotions. "Stop the self-pity, son. Unless you learn to get over some things, Drew, you'll never be happy, and remember, son, happiness is not what you do in your business. You may build a billion-dollar business, but what happens when you go home?"

"Blue, I respect where you're coming from, but one thing you keep forgetting. Betty left me. Betty asked me for a divorce when I was at my lowest as a man. When my mom was dying and everything else in my world was—"

"Do you *really* think she wants a divorce, Drew?"

"Well, having the papers drawn up is a funny way of showing how much you care. What do you think?"

"She's a lawyer, son. She can draw up papers like that in three minutes or less, and you know that. It's not like she had six meetings with an attorney and then decided to do this. So answer my question. In your heart, do you believe she really wants a divorce? Do you think she loves you? Honestly."

"Honestly?"

"Yes. What do you feel in your heart?"

Drew leaned back in his chair and swallowed his immediate response. "I feel—I think she . . . I don't know; I just can't—"

"Drew, you need a good strong sip of humility, son. I don't know any other way to say it. Your feelings are hurt, but you have to look at the big picture.

"Do you know what the true test of humility in a relationship is? It's sometimes *knowing* you're right . . . but having the *guts* to say I'm sorry. It's knowing that every other person has it just as hard as you do. That your cross is no heavier than hers and hers is no lighter than yours. Humility . . . true humility is one of God's greatest gifts to us, but it only works if we learn to use it."

"Blue . . ." Drew closed his eyes and a little more of his heart to what was being said. "Why do you care, man? Your wife died, and all you care about is me and Betty, who you have never even met."

"Call me crazy, but I don't want you to be me. I lost it all and was blessed, fortunately, to find love again. Do you know how rare it is to find love once in your life? I mean, true love?"

Drew opened his desk drawer, took out the divorce papers as his eyebrows curved downward, and rubbed his hand over his mouth. Then he took out a pen, and with his hand shaking, he signed all three places highlighted in yellow, refolded the document, and returned it to its envelope.

"You still there?" Mr. Blue said in a voice so weak it came out as a murmur.

"If what Betty and I had, Blue, was true love, then maybe true love is not for me."

After concluding the conversation, Drew wrote Virginia Neale's phone number down on a piece of paper, put it in his inside coat pocket, and picked up the envelope.

Walking down the hallway, he dropped the envelope in the outgoing mail tray and told Grace to make sure it went out in that day's mail.

Chapter 21

No doing, without ruing.
—Sigrid Undset and Kristin Lavransdatter
The Bridal Wreath

Betty and Jacqui sat in the café of Books for Thought with a four-inch stack of bridal magazines between them. As they sorted through the pages, Betty said, "You're really going to wear white?"

"No, you didn't," Jacqui replied. "I can wear white. I'm . . . I'm . . . I can wear white, and let's just leave it at that."

"All righty, then. What about being walked down the aisle? Maybe we should ask one of the deacons of the church to go with us to give you away."

"No biggy," Jacqui said as she tore off a small piece of her bagel and put it delicately into her mouth. "I was talking to Francesca about that, and she said the way she has it planned, it won't be necessary. She's just going to have me coming down the aisle and—"

"The aisle? We'll be outside."

"I forgot. Well, it's kinda like an aisle, I guess, 'cause there will be this long roped-off area," Jacqui said, illustrating with her hands, "leading up the cliff."

"Oh, yeah, the cliff, where we can watch the sun setting. I remember she showed us the slides of that."

"Exactly. When I saw that, I was done. And then Drew and Stefan will be at the top, and you will go out before me," Jacqui said, smiling to herself and picturing every word she said. "And the waves will be crashing, and the minister will be—I can't wait, girl. This is going to be too romantic, and you know I'm not into all that mushy stuff, either."

"I can't believe you're stealing my idea," Betty said with a fake pout as she reached in her purse for her fingernail file. "You know that's how I wanted to get married."

"Trust me, it wasn't my idea. Stefan is the one who wanted this, and I knew how you felt about it, so I backed down. But if it were me, I'd go down to my uncle's church in a heartbeat."

"Sure you would."

"I'm serious. But I'll admit, the more I get into it, the more exciting it becomes. But I still refuse to go barefoot, like Francesca suggested. That's out!"

"Right. All Stefan has to do is say, 'Gul, take off dem dere shoes' and you'll be barefoot jumping a broom like Kizzy."

Jacqui smiled. "You can't *even* make Stefan believe no mess like that. So, this is the first day you have not had a job to go to since—"

"Since I was in the tenth grade. I've always had a job, and now I'm looking for work. Speaking of which, I was thinking last night of an idea I wanted to hit you with. What if you and I open a restaurant and—"

"You kidding me? Don't you know why I haven't expanded Jacquetta's? I don't need the headaches. Hell, I can't find enough quality people to fill that place, never mind another one, and when you add to it," she said as Betty simply looked at her, "payroll, tax complications, and then building the customer base. I just don't see how in the world I could ever commit to doing something like that again."

"And you did all of that in one breath. If you had used two, you would have really shot down the idea."

"I know, but it's a lot of hard work."

"Jacqui, I could run it."

"Betty, only thing I trust you running is a track. Please. No offense, but Carol ran your office. How you gonna run a restaurant where more receipts come through on a bad Wednesday night than you all dealt with in six months?"

"Because it can't be too hard," Betty said as she shaped her unpolished nails. "You've been able to do it for a while."

"Oh, so it's like that, now?" Jacqui replied, folding her arms and leaning back.

"What I'm saying is this. I'll dump in two-thirds of the start-up capital, and I'll run it day to day. You give me your expertise, and we split the profits fifty-fifty."

"Profits?" Jacqui smirked. "You're a novice. You can just forget that word for the first three years. Listen, I don't know. I mean, in this town you gotta have a hook. An angle."

"Check it out. Bee-Jay's Cyber Café."

Jacqui unfolded her arms and said softly, "I like Jay-Bee's better, but it sounds nice. It could look good on the billboards. But other than the Internet stuff, why would I eat there? You can get good food anywhere, and plus—"

"The board."

"The board?"

"The board. We could call it the hookup board or something more imaginative. I don't know yet. But you know how many lonely women and men are looking for someone special? We have this board with profiles on them. Every meal over a certain amount they can pick a name from the board if they see someone there that they like. If not, we can stamp their card for their next visit. But to play you gotta eat, and we can have pictures and everything in a file!"

Shaking her head, Jacqui said, "Expensive. How do you maintain it?"

"What does it cost you? A Polaroid and the time for them to fill out a form. Done. Every time they eat, Jacqui, they can meet a person. And it doesn't even have to be for romance. If a person is new to town and would like to meet a person who likes bowling or if a dude wants to find three more guys to play basketball with, they can do it at Bee-Jay's Cyber Café. Looking for a roommate who smokes? Bee-Jay's Cyber Café. See, this way it's not like we're just running a dating service."

"Well, it is different," Jacqui admitted.

"And," Betty continued, pointing her fingernails upward to get a better view of them, "it'll be fun, and at this point in my life, I need fun. I think the cyber part will really work. We can lease the computers and charge by the minute for that, but the board is where we'll get the repeat business and publicity. Plus, you know I have a few media contacts, so I am sure I could get my friends at *Essence* or *People* to do a story on us, and who knows, maybe we could franchise!"

"Fran-what? Give a sister a rope and now she wants to be a cowgirl," Jacqui said as if she were thinking aloud. "Listen, we'll talk about it *after* the wedding, okay? I think it's worth at least revisiting."

"It's a good idea. Come on, admit it. You said Stefan will be doing some work modeling head shots, so we can use him in the ad campaign. We can even use items from your existing menu to cut down on replication."

"Okay, okay, it has teeth. I don't know about the expenses and if it would be in violation of city ordinances, with that meeting people aspect, but it could be something to explore. So," Jacqui said, and changed her tone, "will you be looking for someone on the big board?"

Betty's smile faded as she returned her fingernail file to her purse. "Naw. I'm off the board for a while this time."

Looking deep into her friend's eyes, Jacqui asked, "Has Drew signed the papers?"

"The envelope I gave him was addressed to the clerk of court," Betty replied as she thumbed through a magazine, "and I called and as of Friday it was not received."

"Do you love Drew?"

"I refuse to ever answer that question again."

"Why does that question always get on your nerves?"

"Because!" Then Betty calmed herself and opened a bridal magazine. "Because people, you included, Drew included, have been asking me that since the day we married, and so I kept looking at myself and saying maybe I was doing something wrong. And that's not fair. But it doesn't matter now," she said, and looked out the window and across the street.

"And why is that?"

"Because I'm enjoying my freedom."

"So that's why you're wearing your wedding ring again?"

"No," she said, looking squarely at her friend. "That's to ward off evil spirits and jerks. It works on most of the evil spirits."

"It has nothing to do with Drew still wearing his?"

"I wish I had not told you about that. No, it has nothing at all to do with that. I've just come to the realization that I'm not the marrying type, and I'm okay with that. I might—"

"Betty, get the hell out of here with that." Jacqui closed Betty's magazine and returned the periodicals to a neat stack between them. "This is Jacqui, okay?"

"And what is that supposed to mean?"

"What you are trying to tell me is that you want to live the rest of your life single?"

"I don't need a man to make me whole, Jacqui. I've learned how to heal myself, and I'm okay with that."

"And I understand that. I know a lot of women who don't *want* or *need* a man in their life and others who have chosen to be that way, and I respect that. You are not such a woman."

"How do you know?"

"Betty, I've known you half your frigging life. I think I know you pretty well. I noticed the way you walk when you're in love. The way you enjoy going into Victoria Secrets and buying lacy panties and bras. I notice the way you look in Bath and Body Works when you know there's no one home to smell like apricots for.

"I notice these things, and yes, some women don't need a man to make them whole. But you need a man. Not to make you whole but to make you happy." Betty stared at her friend, and then Jacqui said, "Okay. Happier. And more than that, you need Drew. So tell me. Do you love him?"

"I can't believe you," Betty said, and then looked at the calendar on the wall. "I remember a year ago on this very date, when we were going over the menu for my wedding, you were trying to talk me out of it. It was you who called him a 'freak,' if memory serves me correctly."

"I didn't call him a freak."

Betty's mouth formed a circle. "Yes, you did! You called him a cyber freak, a pervert. You called him weak; you called him—"

"Well, things changed."

"Changed?"

"I guess . . . I changed." Then Jacqui leaned back in her chair and rubbed her hands on her thighs. "This time last year I was bitter about a lot of things. But the more I found out about Drew and the more I listened to you talk about him, the more I knew I was out of place, and I think . . ." Jacqui said, and looked away. "Damn, this is hard to admit to myself, never mind say to you."

"What?"

"Okay. I was a little . . ." Her lips crinkled as her large hands slid along her slicked-back hair. "A little jealous. Betty, look at you. You're beautiful, smart, slim, younger than me, and I was just seeing you getting married, and then I would lose my best friend. What did I have left? A pretty nigga who I asked to marry me and he said no.

"I don't really have any family, no other true friends. Just the restaurant and you. And it took me getting more and more into the Bible to see how wrong I was.

"I've tried to be the best friend I could to you, but I guess when you needed me I was selfish, and that's why I want you to be with Drew. I want to see that smile again that you showed me the day you were married when you came up and hugged me. I've never seen that look in your eyes since that day, and I know it's in there somewhere."

Betty looked down at the bridal magazines, unable to look at Jacqui. "You, *umm*, mentioned Stefan. What has changed?"

"For me and Stefan? Truth be told, I stopped loving him for a while. It took a lot of prayer for me to get over the guilt, and I did that. But when it was all said and done, I forgot who he was and fell in love with who he had become, and that's the best way I can explain it.

"And I know people will talk. They will look at me like I settled and—"

"No, they will not."

"Of course they will. I know I would have. But I honestly have not. It's something different when I look in his eyes that tells me he's stronger then he's ever been. Maybe because his soul's been tested. I don't know, but I know it's there. And that's what I've always looked for when I looked at him. But," Jacqui whispered intently, "what are you going to do?"

"There's nothing I can do now."

"Why?"

" 'Cause I went a little too far," she droned. "The night I gave him the papers, did I want a divorce? Kinda I guess. I really just wanted the pain to go away. But then so much happened that day. I guess I wanted him to just tear them up in my face and say—well say he wasn't letting me go.

"But when I went out to see him last week, the way he looked at me was different. Like he, like he was looking at a stranger. Not the way he'd ever looked at me before."

"So basically what you're saying," Jacqui replied as she took another bite of her bagel, "is you overplayed your hand."

"I think what I wanted to do was drive home how frustrated I was. But then when he told me he wasn't sure if he didn't want to sign the papers, well, all of a sudden things changed."

An icy pause froze the conversation, and then Jacqui asked, "So what are we going to do now? Do you think getting together in Nevis might spark something?"

"Nevis is not about us. It's about you and Stefan, and so I'm not even thinking like that."

"Do you think he's seeing anyone else?"

"I don't know. In my heart, knowing him, I would say yes, only because I know how much he enjoys the couple thing. But then again, well, I don't know."

"So what do we do?"

"At this point we do nothing. We let the dust settle, and if he mails the divorce papers, then I'll know. If he doesn't, then I'll know he still cares." As she spoke, Betty looked again across the street at people going into a club called *A Love Supreme*. Then she looked back at her friend and continued.

"Yeah, I still love Drew, and I told him that I would always love him. Yeah, I wish there was a way I could make it right, but if this past year has taught me anything, it's taught me how to fall in love with me again."

Jacqui sat up in her chair and said, "Well, it'll be okay."

"I know it will. I even think I'll adopt a baby. I don't even care if it's male or female. There are so many little black babies out there needing someone to care for them, and since I sorta need someone to fill that void in my life . . . well, I was thinking . . . What?" she said to Jacqui, who was shaking her head.

"What you say sounds good, and you are right about the black babies and all, but you're not just going to quit and give up on your husband, are you?"

"If he mails the papers, he doesn't want me, Jacqui."

"Betty, I know this is a bad analogy, but you gave him the gun, put the bullet in the chamber, and told him you wanted the relationship to die? Now you gonna get mad if he pulls the trigger?"

Betty rose from the chair and said, "If he loved the relationship, if he loves me, nothing could make him pull the trigger."

"So, where you going?"

"You got change? I need to make a quick phone call."

Reaching into her purse, Jacqui said, "Where's your cell, and be-sides, who you got to call with your no-job-having self?"

"It's in the car, and I know that *Ms Black Enterprise*," Betty said as she took the change. Then she turned to walk away and said, "But I still have a husband. At least I think I do."

Chapter 22

Nothing is impossible.
We just don't know how to do it yet.
—L. L. Larison Cudmore
The Center of Life

THE FINALE

Betty left her friends' table and went to the pay phone to call Drew's office.

As she listened to the phone ring, she wondered what she would say to him. What if he had already mailed the envelope? Would it be too bold of her to say, "Drew don't mail it, because I love you and I— Oh, hello?"

"Yes? May I help you?"

"Hey, *umm, umm,* Gloria, how are you today?"

After a pause the lady answering the phone said in a dry tone, "Hello, Mrs. Staley. This is *Grace.* How are you?"

"I'm sorry. I always seem to mess up your name. I don't know why I can't seem to—"

"That's okay. May I help you?"

"Oh, well, is Drew there? If he's busy, then I can—"

"He's not busy, he . . . well, he had to fly to Louisiana."

Betty could feel her heart stop as the owner of the bookstore passed her and waved by wiggling her fingers.

"Baton Rouge?"

"Yes, ma'am. He drove to Jacksonville this morning to catch his flight."

Betty looked down at her watch. "What time is his flight supposed to leave?"

"Well, I don't know if I—" And then Betty heard someone in the background say, "Give me the damn phone!"

"Betty? How are you," she said curtly.

"Fine, Peg—"

"This is Peggy. Listen, Drew left here around eleven, and he's not expected back until next Monday."

"Yes, I know. Grace just told me. I was wondering if one of you could give me the flight num—"

"I don't think we should, Betty."

As she put her finger in her ear to make sure she heard correctly, Betty said, "Excuse me?"

"I don't think we should give you the flight information, if that's what you were going to ask."

Betty leaned against the wall with the phone cradled to her ear as Jacqui came around the corner to see if she was okay. "And why is that?"

"Because he left and distinctly said *not* to give it to you. I'm sorry to be so blunt—just following orders."

Betty's eyes transfixed. She quieted her tears, refused to show emotion in front of her friend, thanked Peggy, and said good-bye.

"So?" Jacqui asked as she motioned with her hands. "That was quick. What did he say?"

"He, *umm,* was not in. Had to step out a moment."

"Oh. Well, listen, I need to run that deposit by the bank before they close the window," Jacqui said, and pulled her oversized purse up higher on her shoulder. "You want to ride with me and maybe see a movie or something tonight? You know that new Nia Long movie is supposed to be good."

"No," Betty said as she attempted to snap out of her daze. "Go ahead and spend the time with Stefan tonight. So what do you all have left to do now?"

"Well, I need to make an appointment with Carolyn to get my nails done the day before we leave, and guess what?" she said as Betty feigned interest. "She has something called a paraffin-wax treatment. Have you heard of that?"

"I used to get one when I had my nails done."

"They paint wax on your hands, and when it dries, it takes off the dead skin?" Jacqui picked at the dried skin on her hand. "Is that all there is to it?"

"Basically, and your hands feel soft afterward."

"Well, I may do it. I have these calluses from working, and I know he likes soft hands," she said, looking down at her vibrating pager. "Listen, this is the restaurant paging me again," she said, and walked backward. "Are you sure you want to get in this business? I'm going to call them from the car, but if you change your mind about the movies, let me know, okay? 'Bye!"

Betty simply shook her head as Jacqui disappeared out the door.

Betty looked back at the phone again and wondered what she should do. But she thought if he left specific instructions for them not to tell her his flight information, then the papers were undoubtedly mailed. And if he had mailed the papers, regardless of what she wanted, he was ready for a change.

Felicia the youthful dread-wearing owner of the bookstore said, "Betty, how're you doing nowadays? Congratulations on the case!"

"I'm doing fine, and thanks," Betty replied, looking across the street once again at the crowd going into *A Love Supreme.* "Oh, yeah, thanks for that novel you recommended. I really enjoyed it."

"Have you read the new Dickey novel?" Felicia asked as she pointed toward the artistic cover. "I can't keep the darn thing in stock."

"Jacqui bought it," Betty said, still looking across the street at the club and trying to read the marquee. "She was telling me something about one of the love scenes in it."

"Oh, yeah, that's right. Jacqui bought it the day it hit the shelves. I bet she can quote that brother word for word. So," Felicia asked, looking across the street with Betty, "are you headed over there?"

"What's going on? I've never seen that place this busy."

"That blues group is there. You know, with the big white dude who plays the harmonica?"

Betty's mouth slightly opened, and then she said, *"The Blues Travelers?"*

"Yeah. You heard of them? They're supposed to be there tonight and tomorrow night."

As she headed for the door, Betty said, "I'll be back, okay?"

"Okay, 'cause we have a funny new book by Van Whitfield I just know you will—" And then the door closed.

Betty went to her 4-Runner, retrieved her cellular, and then stood in line for fifteen minutes to get into the club.

Night was about to fall as Betty looked up, saw a plane flying above, and wondered if it was headed to Baton Rouge.

Although Drew was on his way to Louisiana, she knew she would feel a certain closeness listening to his friend's group.

As she waited in line, Betty called her contact at the clerk's office, who said she may have seen the divorce papers but was not certain.

"Well," Betty replied, "if you get them, just hold them, because we both have to sign in front of a notary, anyway. I don't know what I was thinking."

Once inside the blue-lit club, the sounds of John Coltrane's, "A Love Supreme" oozed from the speakers like honey. There were portraits of jazz gods and goddesses in the foyer, such as Monk, Miles, and of course, Trane, as well as Ella, Duke, and Dizzy.

Young black, white, and Hispanic professionals ordered Sex on the Beach and Cosmopolitans as they mingled, and occasionally someone would ask Betty for her autograph.

Finding a vacant table in the corner, Betty pulled out her cell phone. Then she tapped her front tooth with her fingernail in thought. *Who else do I call?*

She didn't know Mrs. Staley's maiden name, and Drew never mentioned in detail any of her relatives in Louisiana, so there was no way to get the information by dialing 411.

And then Betty saw him.

She sprang to her feet, and as soon as she did, a couple grabbed her table, but she didn't care.

Betty wove through the crowd toward him. *He must have missed his flight or changed his mind,* she thought. It didn't matter, because he was there.

Betty walked up behind him in the dimly lit restaurant, and then the man turned around with a brunette on his shoulder. He looked down at Betty and cried, "Hey, I know you. You that—"

"Yes. Thank you," Betty said, and then turned and walked back toward her table, which was occupied.

Betty rubbed her hands stiffly over her mouth to gain her composure, and then she took out her phone again with no idea whom she should call.

It occurred to her that she could contact the newspaper in the city and they in turn could give her the obituary department.

Her hope was that they would be able to provide the date and time of the funeral so she could fly up to be with him.

As she waited on hold, a seat became available next to a large gentleman wearing a black short-haired mink coat.

"Yo, yo, 'scuse me? Mizz Sta'lee," he said, looking over his purple-tinted shades. Betty turned toward him with the phone still pressed against her ear. "I have a seat here if you like?"

She shook her head no and then turned away.

As the operator put her call through, the gentleman stood up and walked toward her. "Listen. My name is Johnny Harbert. You might have heard of me?"

"Hi." Betty smiled and turned her back to him again.

"Yo," he said a little louder, "I'm a friend of Bear's. He my boy. We ball together in Oak-Town. He supposed to be here in a minute."

Still oblivious to what he was saying, Betty backed up, bumping into a man and spilling his drink all over his suit.

"Gad damn bitch! Watch where the hell you going!"

Betty mouthed the words *I'm sorry* as she waited on hold and then turned and jogged toward the exit with her head down. She then bumped into a lady, almost knocking her to the ground.

"Oh, hell, no she den-nd't!" a lady with a thick Hispanic accent said, and Betty turned, walking backward, and said, "I'm sorry." Then she bumped into someone else in the doorway.

Betty spun around. "I'm, I'm, . . . Oh, my God," she said as she looked into his eyes. "What—what are you doing here?"

"I guess I could ask you the same thing."

"I *umm*, I *arrah*," she said, looking at Drew as the lady on the line said, "Obits, classifieds, can I help you?"

Betty hit the END button with her thumb, and the cell phone dropped to the ground.

People continued to walk around them as Drew picked it up and handed it to her, and she said, "So? How have you been?"

Betty could tell by his red eyes that he had had a long day. "Can we go outside to talk? This entrance is getting kinda packed," she said, and grabbed his hand. For the first time, he pulled it away from her. "What's wrong?"

"Nothing," he said, and then looked around the club as if he were looking for someone. Then he made eye contact with a woman who excitedly waved for him to come over and gestured toward a seat she had saved.

Betty's eyes ricocheted from the woman to Drew and back to the woman again.

"Listen," he replied, "I don't know how . . ." Betty looked at him and then again at the woman, who continued to smile his way. "I don't know . . . Damn, this is awkward," he babbled as he scratched his head and then rubbed it.

"You don't know how to say what?"

Drew took a breath and held it, then said, "Listen, over at the bar is a lady who I asked to meet me here." Betty felt weak in the knees, as if she wanted to faint, but refused to grant him the satisfaction. "She's a client, and we went to the movies Saturday night."

As the people continued to pass them like water around rocks in a stream, Betty asked, "Why are you telling me this?"

" 'Cause I think you should know."

"Why should I know? I should know what? What should I know, Drew?" Betty folded her arms and set her jaw for anything he might say.

"Well, I don't know. Mom passed away Sunday morning and—"

"I gathered as much," Betty replied as her voice lost its defensive tone. "I called the office and they told me you were flying out. I know you told me she wasn't doing very well but it still shocked me. How did she go?"

"In her sleep. I went in her room to take her breakfast and as soon as I opened the door . . . I knew that day would be the day."

"I'm so sorry to hear that. I know it's tough. How have you been doing?" Betty asked.

"I've had a year almost to prepare myself for this but it still feels like I am walking across broken glass. That's the best way I can explain it. She tried her best to prepare me but . . . well anyway," he said as he attempted to regain his train of thought, "I was supposed to fly back with the body to Baton Rouge, but the flight was canceled, and I couldn't fly out until tomorrow. So as I was driving back to Gainesville, I was thinking about Virginia. That's her name. She's a nice lady, and the more I thought about her and the good times we had, the more I knew I had to be honest with her," he said, and then reached into his inside coat pocket and pulled out the divorce papers.

"I told her I mailed this. I put it in the outgoing mail tray four times, and every time I pulled it back out. On Friday I had to run down the mailman to get it. So I know if I can't let this damn letter go, I'm not sure if I'm ready to let go of what we had, either."

Betty stood off balance, looking at the dirty, wrinkled envelope between his fingertips.

"Actually, I'm kinda glad you didn't mail them," Betty replied, and took the envelope from his grasp.

"Are you really?"

"Yeah, because they were not notarized, and so it would have just held things up, anyway."

Drew's lips flattened.

"I think it's best to get these notarized as soon as possible." Then, in one motion, Betty tore the envelope in half. "I mean"—she ripped it into quarters—"as soon as possible. What do you think?" Then she dropped the pieces to the floor.

"Betty, honestly I, I don't—" Then Betty yanked him toward her and kissed him passionately on the lips. As she kissed him, she could tell his eyes were still open, but it didn't matter to her. Then she pulled her lips back and looked at Drew.

"Betty, we still have a lot to—"

Betty pulled him toward her again and pressed her body against his.

Then she pushed him step by step against the wall of the foyer, underneath the portrait of Ella Fitzgerald. As the Blues Travelers started to play in the background, she refused to let go of him or the moment.

She felt his hand tentatively grasp the back of her arm. Without breaking the kiss, Betty grabbed his forearm and locked it around her waist and then held his lips closer to hers. Someone passed by and said, "Why don't you get a room for that shit?" But it didn't matter to Betty. Just feeling the width and girth of Drew's body next to hers made her body sing.

She released the kiss and looked at his eyes, which were closed to slits. Drew opened them slowly and swallowed softly. The band broke into its rendition of "Love and Greed" as he bent over closer to her ear so she could hear him.

"No matter what happens..." He closed his eyes to finish the thought. "No matter what happens to us, whenever you touch me, it feels like home."

Then Drew cupped her face in his hands and wiped away her tear with his knuckle. With her eyes closed, she could hear a smile in his voice as he said, "Well, I'll be damned." Then she opened her eyes and saw Virginia sitting with Johnny Harbert and Tobias "Bear" Parker.

Drew brought Betty's face back toward his and said, as he looked at her heart-shaped lips, "This morning, when I woke up, I knew I would see you today. I didn't know if you would call the office or not, but I told them *not* to tell you where I was just in case because I just knew we would meet today somehow, someway. And to be honest, Betty, I really didn't want to see you.

"When I was in Jacksonville at the airport, I was looking for your face. I know if I were in Baton Rouge I would be doing the same thing. I've never felt anything so strongly in my life. And look what happens. I guess if something is really meant to be—"

Unable to let him finish the sentence, Betty pressed her lips against his one more time as he held her in his arms. Then, backing away from his kiss, she said as she shook her head, "I will never let you go. Do you understand me? No matter what happens from here on, I love you, Andrew, and I will say it as much as you need to hear it, and I will never, ever, let you go again."

With a little more than twenty-four hours before Jacqui's nuptials, Betty waited for her friend as she lounged and enjoyed a drink on the shore of the ocean.

She and Drew, who snorkeled on the other side of the island, flew to the Caribbean from his mother's funeral in Baton Rouge, Louisiana. They spent two days in Freeport, a weekend in Negril, Jamaica, and Christmas in Martinique, rekindling the love they assumed had burned out.

Without the pressure from her role as an attorney and Evander being not only a distant but a faded memory, Betty could focus on Drew. The touch of his hand on the flight to the islands reminded her why she fell in love with him. The scent of his cologne called up nights he held her so tight she never wanted him to let go. And when he would kiss her on the cheek for no reason at all, she knew that no matter what she accomplished, without Drew her life would never be more than just ordinary.

On the sun-soaked island of Nevis, Betty and Drew had breakfast under forest-green philodendron leaves in the mornings, which were the size of elephant ears. After lunch they would go for walks and take pictures of little girls dressed in brightly colored clothes jumping rope. The children's iridescent faces were in every hue of mahogany, and their soft brown eyes were filled with promise.

Instead of following the tourist path while on the volcanic island, they decided to take public transportation, which was a bus that stopped at a spot in the road designated by a stick with two cans nailed to it.

As they waited, a man approached on a bicycle with a face cut from granite and stopped in front of them to adjust his front brake.

"Hello," Drew said.

With his head cocked to the side, he said, "You visiting, no?"

"Ah, yes," Drew replied. "From America. How are you?"

The man smiled as if such a statement were a given and then said, "Well, the best way to visit diz 'ear place is to be a part of the fine art of '*limin*'."

"Limin'?" Drew asked. "What's a limin'?"

The man looked at his brake and said, "That oughta do ya teal I git home." Then he looked at Betty and then at Drew. "Ye'mon. The fine art of limin', which means to enjoy the art," he said, getting back on his black-and-white cowhide seat, "and to enjoy the pleasures of doing nut'ten. Not a tang." Then he smiled and rode off. "You all be good, now."

The man rode and swayed from side to side as a kid would after receiving a new bicycle. And then, eventually, he disappeared into the horizon, where red and gold coalesced as one.

As Betty and Drew stepped on the bus, they were immediately taken aback when the people riding said as one, "Good day!"

"Ahh, hello," Drew replied. Then he reached into his pocket for the money to drop in what amounted to a cut-off Pepsi bottle, which contained the fare.

"Daz all right, mon," the elderly gentleman with the Rastafarian appearance said. "You pay when you depart."

"Oh," Drew said, "Thanks." Then he and Betty walked through the smiling brown faces toward the back of the bus.

"Can you believe you pay when you get off instead of when you get on?" she whispered, and took her seat.

"Ah, yeah. I think that's how they do it on the subways in New York also," Drew joked.

The bus rambled, sputtered, and backfired through lush rolling hills and mansions that rivaled any Betty and Drew had seen in America.

The lanky palm trees seemed to stand taller than any they had seen in Florida and appeared to grow out of the sky and simply grace the earth below by touching it.

But the biggest difference noticed by Betty were the people. As they rode the bus, the driver played the tune "No Woman, No Cry," and it seemed as if the entire bus sang and swayed like the tall palms to the sounds of Marley.

Two girls sat in front of Betty and Drew, wearing their plaid green skirts and white school-uniform blouses. While they rode the bus, they would look at boys, whisper something to each other, and laugh aloud.

Then the smaller of the two girls grabbed the back of the seat in front of her and yelled, "Cutler, right 'ear!" And then the bus came to a stop in front of what appeared to be their house.

The house was painted red and had orange shutters and a lime-green door.

As the bus pulled off, Betty saw a man come out and wave to the driver and then let the girls in the gate.

Also on the bus was an elderly lady with skin that looked like re-laxed leather in appearance; a little girl sat beside her with her head on the lady's lap. Although the older lady appeared to be blind, she braided the child's hair in perfectly woven rows.

She would sing with the others on the bus in French with a Haitian accent, and her eyes, which were yellowed, looked upward as if she saw something no one else was able to enjoy.

Betty held Drew's arm close to her breast like a teddy bear and would occasionally kiss his sleeveless biceps. Then she noticed a man sitting across from them who would not stop staring at her. He wore a burgundy KANGOL hat and a four-fingered ring that read: "Or-mondo." When he made eye contact with Betty, he immediately looked down at her breasts, licked his thick lips, and slowly lowered his sights before returning his eyes to her face.

Unable to believe how forward he was, Betty smiled and then rested her head on her husband's arm and discovered for herself the pleasures in the fine art of limin'. As they rode the bus Drew took out his cellular phone and called Blue. He listened to his friend's laugh as he told him of the changes in his life. Then he put his wife on the phone to speak to Mr. Blue. After thanking him for his role in bringing them back together she consoled him with regards to his loss and insisted that he have dinner with her and her husband.

That night, Drew built a fire, and Betty taught him how to play "Make My Day." She explained to him how the game originated. How she and Jacqui often survived on one meal a day while in college. It was on one such night when they were both feeling hunger pains and were concerned about where their meal would come from when Jacqui asked Betty to "make her day."

Drew read to her from a book of love poems written by Nikki Giovanni, and as the moon reached its zenith, he asked Betty to turn over. Then he pulled out the massage oils and rubbed it deeply into the muscles of her neck, shoulders, and back.

His long, strong fingers seemed to play chords, and with every note she lost her will to say no to anything he asked of her body.

Then he gave her the look.

Betty and Drew made love in the sand, at the edge of the ocean, which could make even the stars above envious.

Initially, Betty was reserved, afraid someone would appear as they made love among giant boulders. But when he touched her in just the right spot, with the ocean providing the background music, she lost her inhibitions and allowed her body to merge as one with his.

Walking through the lobby of the hotel after speaking to someone who asked her for an autograph, Betty reached into her pocket for the key to the bridal suite she had shared with Jacqui for the past four nights.

As she opened the door and set down the bag she retrieved from Drew and Stefan's room, Betty removed her shades and looked at the suite, which was in total disarray.

The blanket was on the floor, the dishes from lunch were placed on the dresser, and paper from the bags, which contained Jacqui's accessories, were around but not in the wastepaper basket.

Betty closed the door and said, "Now, you know we're going to have to leave that girl a nice tip to clean up all this mess. I can't believe you spilled the tea and just left it on the carpet," Betty said as she picked up the pitcher.

Jacqui didn't reply.

"Jacqui? You in there?"

There was no answer.

Betty went to the bathroom and knocked on the door. "Don't tell me you in there *praying* like you were on my wedding day," she said with sarcasm.

"Girl," Jacqui uttered softly from behind the door, "I don't know how you went through this."

"Went through what?" Betty replied as she faced the bathroom door with her hands on her hips.

"This day. I'm more nervous than a dead-beat dad on Oprah. If Stefan were an hour late, I wouldn't be looking for him. I'd be looking for bullets and an attorney. Wait a minute. You're an attorney, right? I might really need you before the day is out."

"Stop being silly," Betty said as she leaned against the wall.

Jacqui opened the door and said, "Well, how do I look?"

Betty turned to look at her and was taken aback momentarily. Although she helped her pick out the dress, she could never imagine she would look so beautiful. Jacqui's hair was layered and accented with baby's breath. Her eyebrows were arched, and subtle earth tones had been applied to her radiant dark skin.

Her white form-fitting wedding gown was covered by a slim sheath of reembroidered lace, and her silk shrug fell loosely over her ebony shoulders.

"Jacqui?" Betty breathed her name.

"What?" Jacqui turned and looked in the mirror again. "That heifer put too much makeup on me, didn't she? I told that little— And I gave her a twenty-five-dollar tip just to—"

"Jacqui?"

"What? It's my dress, right? Is it too tight in the hips?" she said, and tugged at the seams.

"Jacqui? Honey? You look . . ." Then Betty walked up behind her, and she turned around. "You look amazing, girl." Jacqui smiled with relief. "I wish I could find a better way to say it, but you really shocked me when you opened the door?"

She lost her smile. "Shocked you? What was that supposed to mean? That sounds like I look scary or something. What you mean by shocked you!" Jacqui turned around and looked in the mirror, attempting to touch up her face with the makeup brush.

Betty softly grabbed her wrist and removed the brush. Then she turned her back toward her. "Jacqui, I have never seen a more beautiful bride in all my life. And I mean that."

"Really? You're not just saying that 'cause I paid for you all to come down here and you need a ride home?"

"No, girl." Betty hugged her but was careful not to smear their clothes with makeup. Then she closed her eyes and stepped back from her. "So, are you ready for this?"

"Are you kidding me? There is no way I am letting Stefan get away from me. I swear, I am *never* going through this again. Now I understand the rationale behind until death do us part. Who in their right mind would want to do this twice?" Betty smiled and went to the couch and sat down beside the bags she had just returned with.

"So what you got in there. And this room," Jacqui said, looking around, "don't look all that bad."

"Please, Jac, let's not even discuss this room. And how did noodles get on the wall?" Betty looked at her and leaned back on the cushion. "You know, you really should wear your hair like that more often and get rid of that ole ponytail."

"Girl," Jacqui said as she sat on the chair in front of her friend, "I can't deal with going to the beauty parlor like you every week. Besides, my man likes my ponytail, so there!" she said as she twirled her neck and folded her arms across her midsection.

Betty smiled and asked as she crossed her legs, "Do you think you're going to miss being single?"

"I doubt it. I know you did for a while, but I enjoyed having Stefan live with me before, so I don't think nothing will change now. We'll just be official."

"Well, I, as you may or may not know—" Betty began, sitting forward.

Jacqui interrupted her by saying, "Whatcha got in the bag?"

Betty replied, "If you will let me get to it, Miss Thing. Geez." Then she smiled and said, "As you may remember, Drew and I had a rough year. Well, at least a rough ten months."

"No, you said it right the first time."

"Shut up. Who asked you anything," Betty said over a laugh. "But seriously, after we got back together, I really and truly did a lot of soul searching 'cause I didn't want you and Stefan to fall into the same traps and problems we did. And to be honest, Jacqui, I'm glad we had a few problems, because it really made us stronger. There is no doubt that we will make it now."

"You say that with a lot of confidence."

"I know," Betty said, looking down and then back at her friend. "I've never felt it so strongly before, I guess."

After a pause, Jacqui said, "I'm happy for you. For Drew, too, but you know you my heart."

"Well, anyway," Betty said, and cleared her throat. "In this bag there are a few things I'm giving you so that you'll never lose the love in your relationship."

"I thought you forgot," Jacqui said as Betty brought the bag closer to her. "Something old, something new, something—"

"Forget those old wives' tales. That's *so* twenty-first century. We're starting new traditions, so I thought I would give you something else."

"Oooo kayyy. Well, you know I'm always down for something new and different."

"Great. Well, first and foremost," Betty said, "I am giving you four gifts.

"Four little reminders to hold on to, because trust me, there will be nights that you will wonder why in the hell you married that fool over there," Betty said with a smirk as Jacqui smiled. "But you know something? That's okay. Don't panic like I did when that happens.

"So, for starters . . ." And then Betty pulled out a white parchment scroll the length of her hand.

"What's that?"

"This," Betty replied, "is the most important of all the gifts I will give you, in my opinion. Besides my friendship, of course." Then she handed the scroll to Jacqui. "Of all the things I didn't have a clue about when I got married, this is the one that would have saved me the most grief in my marriage."

Jacqui removed the royal blue ribbon and unrolled the paper. On it, written in Old English script, were the words "I WAS WRONG."

Then Betty said, "I know this may look silly, but trust me, it was easier for me to say I love you than I was wrong.

"It was easier to say that I made a mistake or even I'm sorry than to just say I was wrong. Don't make that mistake.

"No three words in my opinion, including I love you, are more important than the words I was wrong."

Jacqui nodded her head in agreement as Betty pulled out ten Archie comic books and videotapes of the movies *Friday* and *There's Something About Mary*, wrapped with a lavender ribbon and bow.

"Okay, now this one I'm going to need a little help with," Jacqui said, her eyebrows knitted with curiosity.

"This one you can never overlook. Take time to simply laugh with the brother. Of all the things I missed when Drew and I were going through our hard times was the sound he would make when he laughed. I think I missed that more—" Then she thought before continuing. "I missed it more than making love to him. The way he would—" she began, and then caught herself.

"Well, anyway, don't forget how important it is to simply laugh with your husband."

"That was sweet. Thanks."

"Okay, number three is one I want you to use liberally. Although I suggest once a week, if you use them up this week, I ain't mad at cha," Betty laughed. Then she pulled out a stack of index cards she had made up with the words "Love Coupons" on the top of them.

"Aw, hell, now you talking!"

"Calm down," Betty said as Jacqui leafed through the cards. "One night a week, make sure you make love in a special way. I'm not talking about when-you-rub-his-ankle-in-the-middle-of-the-night-with-your-big-toe sex. You get some, and both fall asleep afterwards.

"No, I'm talking about roses on the sheets. I'm talking about blindfolds and melted chocolate and kissing his—"

"Okay, okay! I think I got the picture," Jacqui said, looking at the cards.

"His fingers, nasty woman. You know something? You should be a superhero. Wonder Woman and Nasty Woman! I was going to say his fin-gers!"

"Yeah, that's what you were going to say," Jacqui said with her eyebrows arched. "But that's not what this card says!"

"Give me that!" Betty said as she snatched the card from her friend. Then she read it, and her face relaxed. "Ooo, that card? Well, you don't *have* to have a car battery. You can use a flashlight and even duct tape if you—"

"Betty, you're a freak! And I'm not even talking closet freak. Just a big ole truck-stop Ho!" Jacqui said, laughing aloud but holding on to the cards securely.

"Well, what can I say," Betty replied. "Remember me and Drew went for a couple of months without touching each other and slept in the same bed. And there were some nights he would walk out the shower, Jac, and it would be just flopping and . . . just . . . well, suffice it to say," Betty said, and rubbed the back of her neck, "I became adept at holding on to mental pictures and squeezing my legs together, if you follow me."

Both women laughed aloud as a knock came at the door.

"Yes?" Betty replied.

"I'm Felix, from the limo service? I just wanted to let you know I was here."

"Thanks, Felix," Betty said. "Give us about three minutes and we'll be out, okay?"

"As you wish, madam."

Then Betty looked back at Jacqui, and her smile waned. "Well, the last gift is the most personal to me."

"What is it?" Jacqui cried with juvenile excitement in her voice.

"Calm down." Then Betty reached into the bag and pulled out a small palm-sized stone.

"So? What do I use that with? Massage oils, motor oil, or—"

"Heifer, where is your Nasty mobile and Nasty cave? Stop it!" Betty said, holding the rock in front of her friend. "This is my *last* gift to you."

"Betty, it's a rock."

Then Betty closed her hands and covered the stone. "As you know, when I was nine, Momma died in the car accident. When I was on the road that day, it was raining and all I could think of was what would happen to me. I've never been more afraid in my life," Betty said as if she were afraid to close her eyes for fear of reliving the moment.

"It felt as if I were in the storm for hours, although I'm sure it was only five or ten minutes before this officer asked me to sit in his car and gave me a sip of hot cocoa.

"After I drank the cocoa, I was watching them load my momma into the ambulance. And before I knew it, I was out of the car, under the yellow Do Not Cross ribbon, and running toward her.

"I remember skinning my elbow as I slipped and fell, on a piece of gravel. Then, when I stood up, I saw my momma. She opened her eyes, smiled at me, and then her eyes closed. I knew she would never open them again. And she never did.

"But as I was walking back to the patrol car, somehow I had this rock in my hand," she said, and opened her hand again.

"This rock was with me when I passed the bar exam. It was with me the day you and I met. And it was with me the first time I saw Drew.

"I never told you about this rock because for some reason I thought," she said, looking at the stone, "if it was able to stay in my hand that night without my knowing it, it must have possessed magical powers. So if I told anyone about it, even you, it would just be a rock.

"My father had left us. My mother was dead, and so I held on to this rock. It was my strength when Evander and I had problems. I held it in my hand at night and sometimes cried as I took my bath when I thought about losing my husband. There were times, Jacqui, when I could depend on nothing, it seemed but you and this rock.

"As you know, I don't enjoy flying, so I brought my rock here and held it on the flight.

"This little rock saw me through the roughest year of my life," she said, and handed the stone to Jacqui. "But I survived. The first year will be tough. But just remember, you'll always have a part of me in the palm of your hand, and when times get tough, remember the rock."

Jacqui closed her eyes, put the rock in her lap, and reached for Betty's hands. Then she sighed, said a silent prayer, and then looked at her friend and said, "Thank you."

Betty stood beside Drew on the edge of a cliff with the waves crashing beneath them.

The wind would occasionally blow the tail of her bridesmaid dress, brightly colored sailboats sailed in the background, and birds flew close to the surface of the troubled turquoise water below.

While they enjoyed the last few hours of daylight, the moon sat in the southern skies, beckoning the night as Betty glanced at her husband.

Drew stood tall and proud in front of the female judge and behind his friend's wheelchair as they awaited Jacqui. From time to time Betty noticed that he would rub Stefan's shoulder for support as the groom stared unblinkingly toward the crest of the white sandy hill.

Drew was dressed in a cream tuxedo and black slacks that matched Betty's conservative V-cut dress. Stefan, who changed his mind several times before deciding on his attire, wore a black tuxedo and a black shirt with a mandarin collar and red boutonniere. His chair was special-ordered and was equipped with white piping on the metal portions and a white leather seat and backing. White lilies were woven between the spokes of the wheels, and as he waited, he removed his white leather gloves.

Occasionally, Drew would reach down and grab his shaking hand to reassure him that everything would be okay as the musician played a round-bodied acoustical guitar. The gentleman had a fair complexion, a bald head, and dark shades and played like an angel on furlough from heaven.

His hand moved sensuously up and down the neck of the instrument as his thumb and fingers strummed the body. Every note he played reverberated through his being like a racquetball and echoed in his face as his bare foot tapped out the rhythms in the sand.

Then Betty and Drew looked at Stefan as he said, "Oh, my God."

"What's wrong?" Drew asked as if he thought Stefan might be in physical pain; then he looked in the direction Stefan was staring as Jacqui came over the slope of the hill. She walked with such grace that bikini-clad lovers took a moment to simply admire her beauty.

Jacqui winked at Betty as she walked confidently through the lush subtropical foliage.

Betty then mouthed the word beau-ti-ful, as Jacqui walked toward them. To which Jacqui simply smiled, stuck out her tongue, and crossed her eyes just as the photographer snapped the picture.

Knowing the moment was captured on film, Jacqui laughed out loud and looked at Stefan, who was laughing as well. Then as other onlookers approached to take in the event, Jacqui stepped up to her fiancé, exhaled slowly, and took his hand.

* * *

As the judge delivered the words, Betty watched her husband and fell more deeply in love with him with every sentence uttered by the magistrate.

And then the judge looked at Stefan and said, "Do you, Stefan Dwayne DeCoursey, take Jacquetta Marie Jordan as your lawfully wedded wife?"

Stefan, who looked unblinkingly at Jacqui throughout the ceremony, held his head down in silence and then motioned with his two fingers for Drew to lean closer to him.

After he whispered into his best man's ear, Drew asked him, "Are you sure?" and Stefan shook his head yes. Then he checked to make sure his wheels were locked on the chair, put his curled fingers on the armrest, and with Drew's assistance, lifted himself to a standing position.

As Betty looked at Jacqui, she could tell she was both scared that he would fall and proud that he would even try to honor her with such a feat.

Stefan rose to his angular six-four frame and looked down at his bride. Jacqui reached out for his hand as Drew placed his hand on his back for support. As he stood wobbly, he looked at Jacqui and then at the hot white sand below.

"My Jacqui," he said somberly, and cleared his throat. "Through everything, you were there for me. When I was not a man, you stood beside me. When I was afraid I would be alone, you were there to guide me. So I ask that you honor me by taking this ring, for it's you I would wish to wed and to hold in my heart forever."

Then he gazed into her eyes and said, "Through sickness and in health. Through our pain and our sorrows. Through our joys, and may there be many, and our fears and hopes and dreams.

"Through the tears which will make us stronger. Through the wind and the rain. I ask that you be my wife from this day forward, until our souls become one at rest in heaven. With this ring, Jacquetta Marie Jordan, I thee wed."

The judge looked at Stefan as if she had no idea he had made up his own vows and said with raised eyebrows, "Okay, then."

Then she looked at Jacqui's tear-streaked face, not knowing what to expect.

Breathing heavily, all Jacqui could say was, "I love you, Stefan. And I do," she panted as she shook her head. "I do."

* * *

Drew sat on the ground with his wife between his legs and her head on his chest. Stefan and Jacqui sat on the edge of the cliff, their toes dangling over the edge.

Although they enjoyed the reception earlier and had shared laughs, this was a moment to sit and reflect.

Betty looked at her friends sitting in front of her and thought about her husband. Occasionally, he would softly kiss her on the top of her head for no reason at all as she lay nestled in his chest, and she thought about how much she missed such moments.

Then Betty, breaking away from the emotions inside her, said, "Okay, guys, it's almost a new year and—"

"Yo, yo. We ain't making no resolutions. I don't believe in them, anyway," Stefan said.

"Well, if a certain *bigmouth* person would let me finish," Betty said with a smile, "I was going to say . . ." She paused to think of something else to say besides her original suggestion.

"Baby," Drew whispered, "you are *so* busted," and then the others laughed.

"I have an idea," Jacqui said, and poured her husband a glass of champagne. "Why not just make a toast. Any toast you would like to make," she said.

"Well, we better do it fast if we want to do it this year," Drew replied, looking at his watch and reaching for the bottle of champagne. As he poured a glass for himself and his wife, he said, "We got about four minutes. Who wants to go first?"

Stefan, with his champagne in hand, looked over the dark gray ocean with only the stroke of the moon shining across it and said, "Me. I'll set it off first."

"Okay," Betty replied, and wrapped herself deeper inside the warmth of Drew's body. "Gon' withcha bad self, Mr. Stefan."

Stefan continued to look at the white foam waves below and then at his legs, which no longer felt like a part of his body. With the champagne glass perched on his knee, he looked at his wife and said, "To the ones I love. Man," he said, and looking at Betty and Drew, "that's a mouthful already. But never has it felt more appropriate.

"My toast is that we never take each other's friendship for granted, that our kids will play video games together until we make them go home, and that every day we remember what we shared today and just how special it was. Times like this pass like a shooting star, so you have to hold them in your hearts."

Then he looked at his wife.

Stefan leaned over and kissed her in the spot a tear resided previously and said, "I took you for granted, but thank you for never giving up on me, because you showed me the true meaning of love. It would have been easy for you to leave me, and I am not even talking about after the accident.

"You have redefined love for me. Because now, for me, love is taking a simple friendship and setting it on fire with passion and feeling the burn, together. That's love, and I love you, Mrs. DeCoursey."

As Jacqui leaned on his shoulder, Drew said to Betty, "I hope you don't expect me to compete with that."

The others laughed as Betty said, "Ah, you better, Mr. Romeo."

"Okay," Drew said with a smile. Then he looked at his watch, held his glass before him, and said, "To us," and sipped his drink.

"To us?" Betty said, her chin touching her chest, "That's all? Stefan talking about kids playing together and all you can say is 'To us'? You better come better than—"

"I got you, baby. Just calm down." And then Drew's face became serious as he said, "Jacqui, Stefan, all I can say is that no one wants rain. But we all want rainbows. Now that you're finally married, remember that it's necessary to have one to enjoy the other and appreciate it for what it brings.

"And to the love of my life. First of all, Betty, I know I told you before, but I am so proud of you and what you accomplished with the case. Although we had rough times, I followed every single aspect of the trial and shared in every objection and 'overruled' that occurred.

"But much more than that, I can honestly say that sometimes I shudder to think that God could have given someone like you to me.

"I wonder what I could have ever done to have been so lucky, so fortunate, so blessed, to find you. But then at night I pray that whatever I did to deserve you, I continue doing it each and every day.

"So my love, here's to you and me and the us I pray we will always be."

Betty sighed as Jacqui said under her breath, "Damn, I'm glad you didn't have anything planned." Then she looked at Betty as Betty continued to look at Drew in awe.

"*Umm,* okay," Jacqui said to Betty, "close your mouth. It's my turn." Then she looked at Stefan and said to the group, "When God, in His infinite wisdom, designed and created this thing called a soul, I know that he decided to put the four of ours in the same space and the same time.

"And I know that we were predestined to meet each other and always, in some way, be together.

"To you, Mr. Stefan Dwayne DeCoursey. Thank you for making me Mrs. Jacquetta Marie DeCoursey. But more than that, I want to tell you that as we walk through life, there will always be bumps and curves in the road. But in spite of what may happen to us when the sun rises, know that my hand is always within your reach. I love you. I honor you. And God knows, I respect and cherish you. You take my breath . . ." And then she buried her face in his chest.

Betty and Drew smiled as Drew looked at his watch. "Well, love, that leaves you all of forty-five seconds to do it."

"That's more than enough time," Betty replied as she turned toward Drew and said, "For the life of me I will never understand why we took our love for granted. It's something we both wanted, yet I guess we ignored it until it almost died.

"As you know, honey, when we met, I was hurt. When we married, I was scared, and every day thereafter I tried to separate fear from pain from love. Unfortunately, it was only after you took your love away that I was able to feel just how much I loved you.

"So," she said, and held her glass up in her quivering hand, "if you are ever afraid. If you, Andrew, ever feel alone in this world, close your eyes," she said, and softly placed her free hand over his eyes. "Feel the sand between your toes. Listen to the sigh of the waves, smell the salt in the air, and remember just how much I love you."

The moment shared by the lovers lasted for hours. Long after the burst of colors came to an end, they sat and replayed the events of the day as if they were watching a movie together. As the moon traveled its course across the sky, Drew took his wife's hand and turned it over. As she opened it, he whispered softly as he traced the "M" in her palm, "Remember, the day we met I did this?"

Betty watched the movement of his index finger.

"The reason I did it is because I knew I would never let you get away. I knew that tracing the 'M' in your hand would always make you mine."

Laying her head on his chest, Betty closed her eyes, inhaled deeply, and replied, "Until death do us part, Drew. Our love will last until death do us part."

Epilogue

We love because it's the only true adventure.
—Nikki Giovanni
Reader's Digest

It's a new year, but most importantly, a new day, and so I have decided to do something I have not done since I had a crush on Morris Day. I'm starting a diary. One day I may want to look back to see where I've been, and this will be my guide.

My husband, Andrew, asked me a question, and I had no idea what he was talking about. When he posed the question, I was thinking of it in the literal form. That's one of the drawbacks to being in my former profession, I guess. You listen so closely to words, you miss what's being said.

It has been an interesting year. A phenomenal ride, one might say.

If someone would have told me the things that would happen to me, my husband, and my best friend this year, I would have attempted to have them committed.

This year saw me humbled. It saw me degraded and made to feel small. It also saw me triumph and become the woman I am now. Not because of what I accomplished but for what I allowed to happen. And simply put, I allowed myself to forgive.

Andrew once wrote a poem for me, and I told him I enjoyed it, but he never knew that I put it under our mattress on my side of the bed. He never knew that when I moved out after the case, the first thing I packed was the poem. Andrew also never knew that I memorized it and would say it whenever I needed to feel his touch. It was almost a ritual for me. Each night I would say the Lord's Prayer, repeat Philippians 4:13, and then I would say these words:

If ever you should doubt my love,
just think of my eyes when I look at you.
Hear my voice when I welcome you.
See my smile when I feel you.
If ever you should doubt my love,
just think on these things
and hold to these things,
cling to these things.
Because there are certain things we encounter,
like the scent of sunlight on a cold winter morn,
like the glow we share after making love or the warmth of a
*   newborn's very first breath*
which cannot be put into words.
There are some things I will forever feel,
one being speechless, when I think of you.
That's if ever you should doubt my love.

Of all the things that have changed for me, I think the greatest is the fact that I now believe.

My momma, bless her soul, had a wild side, but she used to tell me that faith was holding on to a handful of absolutely nothing and squeezing it until it became something.

As a child, those words sounded like gibberish. It was not until I was able to step back from the words that the meaning filled my heart. And when that occurred, indeed my world changed.

To be honest, Drew blew me away. This is a brother who was successful, handsome, intelligent, and I'm sure could have had any woman he wanted. Yet with all the baggage I brought to the table, he wanted me. I never understood or accepted why he wanted me. Even when I gave him indications that I was not sure I wanted him, he still wanted me.

There were many days I pondered this question. Many nights when we lay in bed together and I refused to hold his hand because I was waiting for the other shoe to drop. Would I catch him cheating? Did I need to continue to check my credit-card accounts and bank balances on a weekly basis? Would I wake up and he would one day be gone?

Would he be taken out of my life like previous men? Like my father? Like my stepfather? Would I look and not find him? Like my ethics and belief in my former profession? Like my mom?

But then I decided to forgive the pain inside. To me that was the epiphanous moment, when my entire life changed. Forgiving my father was easy. Forgiving the men who had walked in and out of my life was simple. But forgiving myself for the mistakes I had made took everything within my being. But I did that, and I became a new person almost overnight.

I forgave myself for not being there for my husband when he needed me the most. Was he perfect during this time? That's not for me to say. But when I could have held his hand, I didn't, and that I promised myself would never happen again.

I also think the whole "until death do us part" thing was a little much for me to fathom.

I love Drew more than I have ever loved any man in my life. But being with him every single day?

Until the day one of us stop breathing?

Forever?

Then it occurred to me that forever was simply too much for us to worry about. So I decided to fall in love with him a little more every day and let forever take care of itself.

My husband asked me in an e-mail if he fell, would I catch him? Now, after all we have been through together, I know what the answer is. No. Why? Because we've fallen together . . .

Forever

FOREVER

TIMMOTHY B. McCANN

ABOUT THIS GUIDE

The suggested questions are intended to enhance your
group's reading of Timmothy B. McCann's FOREVER.
We hope you have enjoyed this story of love,
marriage, faith and renewed friendship.

DISCUSSION QUESTIONS

1. In the novel, Drew is influenced heavily by the two major women in his life. But how does his love for Betty affect his relationship with his mother and how does his love for his mother affect his relationship with Betty?

2. Betty's father left her and her mother when she was in elementary school. Do you believe it influenced her marriage? Her professional life?

3. Do you think Drew forced Betty to get married or did she force herself?

4. Betty struggles throughout the novel to retain her independence i.e. not accepting assistance from Drew or Jacqui financially or selling her home. Why is it important to her?

5. The night Drew proposed he made sure to do several things to make the night memorable. Discuss each act and beyond the fact it was romantic, why do you think he did it?

6. In the novel Drew develops a drinking problem. Why does he become dependent on alcohol?

7. One of the major themes of *Forever* is holding on to love in spite of the cost. There is a parallel between how Betty and Stefan do this and how Drew and Jacqui hold on. Discuss how they contrast and compare.

8. Jacqui goes through a vast change throughout the book. Besides Stefan's accident and her spiritual growth, why is she such a different person?

9. Initially when we meet Drew, he is strong but in the middle of the novel he appears weak in some aspects and then emerges at the end strengthened. Explain his metamorphosis throughout the year.

10. The night of the crash, do you think Stefan really had an engagement ring? Do you think his proposal to Jacqui was based on need or on love?

11. In her heart, do you think Jacqui believes Stefan loves her or is she willing to settle in order to create the love she always wanted?

12. Do you think Bear is innocent?

13. What's the symbolism of Drew's dream in chapter 8?

14. Why is it so hard for Betty to say, "I'm sorry," to Drew?
15. Like the biblical figure Saul, Stefan is changed dramatically by a singular event. But he begins to change before his accident. Discuss how?
16. Mr. Blue tries to mentor Drew through the last half of the novel. Ultimately how successful was he?
17. All three attorneys defending Tobias Parker have the goal of seeing him walk free but that notwithstanding, how did their goals differ?
18. At the beginning of each chapter there is a quote which summarizes the chapter. Discuss the various ways each quote does this.
19. In court Betty tears up the cards she made notes on. She also tears up the divorce papers toward the end of the novel. How do these two events compare?
20. What are the distinguishing characteristics of the authors writing style?